Una Horne has lived in the Bishop Auckland area of Co. Durham for most of her life. Trained as a nurse, she gave up her career to raise a family but began writing some years ago when her two children were grown up. She developed her writing skills on short stories and also published a couple of romantic novels under a pseudonym.

Her regional novels, *Lorinda Leigh, Bright is the Dawn, Come the Day, Under the Rowan Tree* and *A Time to Heal* have led to Una being hailed as the new Catherine Cookson. *The Jewel Streets* is her sixth novel for Piatkus, and her latest book, *When Morning Comes* is available in hardback.

GW00372437

Also by Una Horne

A Time to Heal
Under the Rowan Tree
Come the Day
Bright is the Dawn
Lorinda Leigh
When Morning Comes

The Jewel Streets

Una Horne

PIATKUS

For Valerie and Peter

My thanks are due to Mrs Armstrong of Boulby Grange, also the staff of Saltburn Library for all their help. The work is a product of my imagination and I have combined fact with fiction in describing Saltburn-by-the-Sea and the surrounding area for the sake of the story.

PART I

Chapter 1

Hetty Pearson stood by the wrought-iron gates and looked up at the strips of iron tortured into curlicues and bows and dangerous-looking spikes. She changed the straw box containing her few possessions from her left hand to her right and moved from one foot to the other, easing the place where her new shoes had rubbed in the long walk from the station to Hope Hall.

Sighing, she looked up at the ironwork again, noting the fancy 'H' intertwined with leaves, looking so much like the letters on the lectern cover in the chapel at home and therefore slightly sacrilegious. She missed Morton Main suddenly, acutely; it was a pain so sharp it sliced through her and she would have turned round and gone straight back to the station except that she knew she didn't have enough money for a ticket.

'You're fourteen now, pet,' Mam had said as they stood on the station at Bishop Auckland, only that same morning it had been but it felt like aeons ago. 'Howay now, be a good lass, don't get upset. You know you're lucky to get a place so near, only the North Riding after all. You might have had to go south, think of that. Lots of girls do.'

'I'm all right, Mam,' Hetty had said.

Maggie Pearson gazed at her daughter who'd looked anything but all right, her face so white beneath her mop of dark hair, and body as thin as a skinned rabbit. There was a hunted look in her eyes too, like a rabbit's. Maggie pushed the thought from her for though she felt like gathering Hetty to her and running out of the station and along the path to the bus stop where the bus would be turning round to go back to the village, she knew she had to try to send Hetty on her way cheerfully.

'Look now, it's farming country, you'll have meat every day. You'll come home with roses in your cheeks and fat as butter,' she said.

'I don't want to get fat,' said Hetty. She didn't want to talk about where she was going, she wanted to remind her mother that Cissy wouldn't go to sleep if she wasn't told a story first. Cissy was just a baby, not yet three, and she liked the story about the fairy who lived in the shed in the garden best. But the train was coming in, there was no time for anything else but a hug and then she was on the train and waving to her mother whose face was suspiciously red as she dabbed her eyes under the brim of her shabby black straw hat.

'Write every week now, won't you, pet?' Mam called.

'I will,' promised Hetty, and it was all she could say for she was too full of panic now that the time had come and she was actually leaving.

'An' do what you're told, be a good lass now.'

The train was pulling out and Mam was a forlorn figure in a shabby straw hat and down-at-heel shoes, getting smaller and smaller, and then she disappeared altogether. Hetty settled back into her seat and stared fixedly out of the window, willing herself not to cry. She took out the letter which had come with the postal order for her fare to Yorkshire and instructions for the walk from the station to Hope Hall.

She read the letter again as she stood outside the locked gates on the lonely moor. Maybe she had made a mistake, maybe this wasn't the place at all. Wasn't it supposed to be a working farm? Here there was just a drive curving round a small copse, not a house in sight. And anyway, there was a heavy chain on the gate fastened with a padlock and no sign of anyone to unlock it.

'You'll have to ring the bell if you want to get in that way.' The voice came from behind her, unnerving her, making her jump. She turned to find her eyes in line with the finest pair of boots she had ever seen and she stepped back, bumping

4

into the gates. There was a boy on a horse, a great horse, bigger than the cart horse old Mr Gibson had to draw his butcher's cart at home. It pranced a little and snorted and she watched it warily, not taking her eyes from it to give its rider more than a quick glance. He was young, not much older than she was, thin and tall with a freckled face and light brown hair sticking to his forehead under his riding hat.

'Walk around the wall, you'll come to the main entrance,' he advised her. He wheeled his horse away without more ado and cantered over the moor. He might have showed her where, she thought tiredly, picking up her box and beginning the trudge round the eight-foot-high wall. It went on and on. Surely the whole farm wasn't walled in? She had to dodge overhanging branches, sycamore and elm mostly, and further on a stand of ash. She was just beginning to think the wall encircled the whole moor never mind the farm when all unexpectedly she came to a gate, not half so imposing as the first one but open and with a gatehouse to one side. A small man in old-fashioned breeches and braces over his collarless shirt, stopped raking the gravel path in front of the cottage and leaned on his rake, surveying her up and down.

'I reckon you must be the new lass for t'house,' he said. 'Not afore time neither. You're late.'

'I had to walk from the station,' said Hetty. 'Then I went to the wrong gate.' She stood waiting. Though it was already September and there was a cold wind blowing across the moor, she felt hot and tired.

The man propped his rake by the wall and pushed his cap back on his head. 'Well then,' he said, 'I reckon you'll be ready for a nice glass of my Joan's lemonade. Come on in and rest a minute before you face that lot up at the Hall. It won't hurt Mrs Peel to wait a mite longer.' His face creased into a smile and his blue eyes twinkled from the wrinkles and Hetty felt better immediately. She had been on the way since early morning and here it was two o'clock already and if she could just sit down a minute or two and have a cold drink, well then, she could face the world. She followed him inside, noting the date above the lintel of the door: 1798 it

5

said. Oh, it was an old house and when she got inside it looked even older. There were tiny latticed windows with flowered cretonne curtains and an old brick fireplace with a round oven and bright brass handle.

The old man spoke to a diminutive elderly woman who was standing at the table kneading dough – teacake dough, Hetty realised. It had nutmeg and spices in it, and the smell, together with that of baking bread, made her mouth water and she had to swallow hard. It was ages since Mam had been able to afford to put spices as well as currants in the teacakes, even when she could afford to make teacakes.

'I don't know Bill, where's thee manners?' scolded the old woman to her husband and then she turned to Hetty. 'I'm Joan Oliver, love, and this is my man, Bill Oliver. Bill is gate-keeper for the Hopes and general handyman too and that means he's at everyone's beck and call. Come away and sit down, love, take the weight off your feet. You're but a slip of a lass – are you sure you're old enough to leave school?'

'I'm fourteen, Mrs Oliver,' said Hetty as she sat down on an apple-backed chair with a horse-hair cover which immediately began to prickle against her legs, reminding her of her grandma's chairs at home in Morton. Her spirits lifted slightly. They lifted more when Mrs Oliver put a glass of lemonade in front of her, cool and cloudy and with a slice of real lemon floating on the top.

'Now I've got some new bramble jam, first of the year,' said the old woman. 'I'm sure you could eat a bit of bread and butter with a spoonful of jam?'

Hetty nodded, unable to speak.

'There then, get that down you, and then Bill will take you up to the big house.'

'Thank you, Mrs Oliver.'

Half an hour later she was trudging behind Bill Oliver up the road and there, round a bend, was Hope Hall. It was a big house, all right, she thought, and she was going to be housemaid in it. Fervently she hoped she wasn't going to be the only one. It wasn't a grand house like the bishop's palace in Auckland, no, nor yet so big, and there were stables and cow byres and barns to one side of it and never in a million years could she imagine a cow byre on the side of the bishop's palace. But the house was imposing for all that; solid stone set square against the moorland wind, two storeys with high mullioned windows and tall chimneys with fancy pots.

'Watch your shoes, lass,' advised Mr Oliver. 'Keep them out of the muck, I see that stable lad's fell behind in his work as usual.' There was horse muck on the cobbles, and hens rooting about in the yard, and in the corner a dog set about barking, warning them away.

'Shut thee mouth, Jess,' said Mr Oliver, not unkindly, 'this here's Hetty and she's coming to work here so you'd best get used to her.' The dog wagged its tail and retreated to its kennel where it sat down, watching Hetty with bright intelligent eyes.

'You found your way then?' The young rider she had met earlier was crossing the yard from the stables, and smiled amiably at Hetty. With his hat in his hand, he had a red ring around his forehead where it had rested and his hair had been pushed back over his head so that it stuck up untidily. Hetty smiled shyly at him.

'Aye, Master Richard. I brought her in,' said Mr Oliver. 'Now seeing as you're here, you'll mebbe take her into the house?'

'Right enough.'

Mr Oliver gave Hetty her straw box which he had been carrying on his shoulder and with a word of thanks she followed the boy into the house through the door which led directly into a sort of rear kitchen. Hetty's heart was beginning to beat uncomfortably. She stared at the stone-flagged floor, only recently scrubbed by the look of it. Master Richard's boots left a trail of what looked suspiciously like horse muck as he led the way through to a large inner kitchen, a room with a black-leaded range not much different from Hetty's mother's in Morton. But there was a newer range beside it, the latest thing with a red-tiled oven door and surround and a cheerful fire burning in the grate. 'Vaughan's Model Oven 1925' it read in raised lettering on the oven door.

'This is the new maid, Mrs Peel,' said the boy, and winked

at Hetty. He picked up a fairy cake from the tray on the scrubbed kitchen table and went off munching it, through a door at the other end of the kitchen.

'Don't go through there with those boots on, Master Richard!' the woman in the large white apron and old-fashioned cap called after him, and sighed as the door banged to and he was gone. 'He's been told time and time again to come in the small door and leave his boots in the lobby,' she grumbled. 'Now there's more work to be done and Ethel's afternoon off.' She turned back to Hetty, who was standing with her box before her like a shield.

'So you're the new housemaid. Hetty Pearson, isn't it? There's not much of you, is there? Such a skinny bit of a thing, you are.'

'I may be skinny but I can work,' said Hetty, drawing herself up to her full height and lifting her chin. If anyone else said she was skinny she would scream, she thought.

'Hmm, I'm sure. Well, you should call me Mrs Peel, I'm the housekeeper here at the Hall. Come on then, I'll show you where you're to sleep. Bring that box you're guarding with your life and you can leave it upstairs. It'll be quite safe there.'

They climbed narrow flights of stairs, six in all, two to each floor so that Hetty was thinking that if they went any higher they'd burst out through the roof. Mrs Peel stopped on a tiny landing and pushed open a brown-painted door.

'That's it then,' she said, puffing. 'Trust Ethel to have a day off when there's a new starter to bring up here. Put down your box and hang up your coat. I'll give you an apron when you get back down and then you can clean up after the young master. Let's see what sort of a job you make of that.'

Wondering how she would find her way back to the kitchen, Hetty watched the housekeeper disappear down the staircase. She stood a moment in the silence, or rather listening to the muffled noises of the old house. Somewhere a door banged; a pigeon cooed close by. There was a squeaking sound. Oh God, don't let it be rats, she prayed. Hetty had had an irrational fear of rats ever since she'd found one climbing into her young sister's pram and it hadn't run away when she flung her arms at it and shouted, just turned and stared at her with red-rimmed eyes.

She shook her head. After all, she was not a bairn anymore, she was practically grown up, working for a living, she wasn't frightened because she was on her own in the attic of an old house. She picked up her box yet again and took it into the room. Mind, an attic it is, she thought despairingly. The roof came right down to within six inches of the floor and the floor itself was of rough wooden planks. Whoever had built the house hadn't thought it necessary to use good materials up here.

But there was a tiny window and red-checked curtains, drawn so that some of the afternoon sunshine got in and lit up the two beds with their red-checked counterpanes. There were two tiny chests of drawers and a washstand with a cheap pottery basin and jug standing on it and some soap in a soapdish, all decorated with unlikely pink roses and violent green leaves.

One of the beds was obviously in use, the bedclothes had just been pulled together rather than made, so Hetty put her box on the other and started to unpack when she remembered that Mrs Peel had said she was just to leave her coat and go straight back down. There was a hook on the back of the door so she hung her coat on that, then she looked in the small mirror over the washstand and pulled her comb through her hair.

I'm not going to think of anything, she told herself in the mirror, I'm not thinking of Mam or Dad or home nor nothing. I'm just going to get on with it, do what I'm told, think about nothing, else I won't get through the rest of the day without making a baby of meself. I won't cry though, no matter what. But her feet hurt. Hurrying, she rummaged through the box and found her old school shoes. They had steel segs in the toes and heels to make them last and clattered a bit on the floor but they were well polished and, most important of all, they were comfortable. The relief she felt when she put them on was instantaneous and her spirits lifted. She even managed to grin at herself in the mirror and she snatched another minute to look out of

9

the tiny window at the moor and the track she had so recently travelled, snaking away into the distance.

Why, it wasn't that different from the fell back home, she thought. Though from this distance the heather wasn't half so bonny as that back in the Durham dale. Feeling better having come to this conclusion, she closed the attic door after herself and made her way downstairs.

Only she must have taken the wrong turning on the first landing she came to and suddenly the floor was stained and polished so that it shone and a lush red carpet ran down the middle. And when she got to the head of the next flight of stairs, the banisters were polished mahogany and the stairs themselves were broad and shallow and swept down grandly to the next floor.

Hetty hesitated. Maybe she should go back, but now she wasn't sure which way she had come and felt thoroughly disoriented. And worse, there were people talking close by. She shrank back into an alcove but it was too late, there was a man looking down at her with exactly the same expression on his face as her gran wore to inspect her shoe when she'd trodden in some dog dirt.

'Good lord!' he said. 'Just look at this, Richard.' He put a hand on Hetty's shoulder and pulled her forward into the light. 'It's a bundle of rags. I'll lay you odds on she's here to see what she can pilfer from the bedrooms and we've caught her in the act!' Roughly he grabbed her wrist. 'Don't think you can get away, girl, I'm going to hand you over to the police!'

A bundle of rags? Why, she had on her good dress, it wasn't a rag at all. Oh, it might have a darn in the elbow where she'd torn it on a fence but it was a nice cotton dress, with blue flowers on it. Mam had got the material in the market at Bishop Auckland. Hetty burned with humiliation. She tried to tug her arm away from him but his grip was firm.

'Let me go, you great bully! This is a nice dress an' all, me mam made it for me!' Hetty twisted and writhed to get away but his grip was hard on her shoulder, the fingers biting in cruelly. So she lashed out with her foot, catching him on the shin with the steel segs in the toe of her boot. He swore and jumped back but he didn't let go.

'Leave her alone, Matt, do. She's not a thief, she's the new housemaid. I suspect she's just got lost on her way downstairs.'

It was Master Richard who was with him, oh, praise the Lord for that, she hadn't noticed at first. He wouldn't let this man with his cruel face and slitty blue eyes hurt her. Richard was her friend, she knew it instinctively. He carried some clout too, for the one he called Matt let her go immediately.

'Oh God, where did they pick this one up? I suppose it was a Durham pit village judging by that execrable accent. No doubt she came cheap, that's all Father cares about.' He bent down and rubbed his shin, wincing. 'Get out of my sight,' he said to Hetty. 'And don't think I'll forget you lashing out at me. What the hell have you got on your feet? A pair of pit boots?'

Chapter 2

'What are you doing, coming in through the front of the house? The back stairs not good enough for you then?' Mrs Peel frowned as Hetty pushed open the baize-covered door to the kitchen. She didn't seem to be looking for an answer which was just as well, thought Hetty, for she could hardly speak she felt that mortified. That Matt, whatever else he was, was a nasty, superior sort of bloke and he had been so contemptuous of her that her face burned at the memory. She had fled down the grand staircase and instinctively made for the back of the house and found the kitchen. She came to a halt, breathing heavily, feeling sweat trickle down her spine.

'Come on then, fill the bucket and get that passage cleaned up, before the master sees it. He can't abide muck from the farm in the house and Richard's a good lad really, we don't want to get him into trouble. There's a sacking apron hanging there.' The housekeeper pointed to a bucket standing by the stone sink under the window and obediently Hetty picked it up and stood it in the sink. There was a hot tap. By, that was a good thing, hot water out of a tap. What would Mam give for such luxury? Even as she filled the bucket and found a bar of Sunlight soap and a rag under the sink, she pondered on where the hot water came from, how it was heated. As far as she could see there was no set pot or any sort of boiler.

'Hurry up now, get on with it, you're not going to turn out to be a day-dreamer like the last one, are you?' Mrs

Peel's tone was sharp and Hetty hastily lifted the bucket out of the sink.

'No, Mrs Peel,' she said, wondering who the last one was and why she had left. Maybe if she could make friends with the other girl – Ethel, was it, the housekeeper had called her? – maybe Ethel would tell her all she wanted to know.

'Mind you clean it up properly and then when it's dry you can polish it,' Mrs Peel said as she went out through the baize door again.

There weren't many marks on the floor and it was easily cleaned for this part of the hall leading into the kitchen was covered in a dark linoleum. It was only when Hetty was on her knees that she could discern the pattern of leaves and squares in various shades of dark brown. She scrubbed away until the linoleum was spotless and then sat back on her heels feeling satisfied. She pushed a lock of dark hair back behind her ear. Thank goodness Mam had cut it for her before she came. Mam was a dab hand at cutting hair. It was so easy to look after when it was cut in a short bob and anyroad it was all the fashion; all her friends were having their hair cut.

Hetty's thoughts always went off on a course of their own when she was doing anything so boring as scrubbing a floor. Though her movements were automatic she was thorough if she was thinking of something pleasant, such as how her mam had cut Hetty's best friend Dorothy James's hair for her, making a real good job of it and even using a razor on the ends so that the blonde hair nestled into the nape of Dorothy's neck. Hetty was that proud of her mam. By, she was clever an' all, she was. And Mam only charged tuppence and Dorothy said that if she'd had to go to the hairdresser in Bishop Auckland it would have cost one and sixpence, which of course Dorothy hadn't got, being as how her father was locked out of the pit along with most of the miners. Bar the safety men that was. Hetty's own dad was studying to be an overman and then he would go down the pit even when the men weren't working just to make sure it was safe. By, she hoped he passed his examination.

Suddenly Hetty's attention was jerked back to the present as she heard a door open somewhere at the front of the

13

house beyond the sweep of the staircase. A man laughed and she shrank back. She didn't want to meet that one again, oh no! Picking up her bucket she retreated into the comparative haven of the kitchen quarters.

'Come on then, lass, take off your pinny and wash your hands and come and have your tea,' said Mrs Peel, smiling at Hetty, who blinked in surprise, the change in the house-keeper was so marked. Mrs Peel was sitting at the head of the table which was now laid with a plain white cloth and there was fresh bread and slices of tongue and pickled beet-root and the biggest, ripest tomatoes Hetty had ever seen. There were three men sitting at the table, all of them in their shirtsleeves and corduroy trousers held up by braces and wide leather belts.

'Yes, Mrs Peel.' Hetty hurried over to the sink to do as she was bidden for as she smelled the food there suddenly seemed to be a gaping hole in her stomach, she was so hungry. It was hours since she'd had the bread and jam at the Olivers'.

'This the new maid then?' commented one of the men, the eldest of the three. He was a short man but brawny, with grizzled hair and the weathered red face of a man who worked in the open air all day. Just like the farmer on the hill above Morton Main, thought Hetty, a nice man who used to let the miners' children look at the lambs when they came in the spring and gather blackberries from the hedgerows in the autumn so long as they didn't tramp across the fields. Hetty smiled shyly as she sat down at the table and took the cup of tea Mrs Peel handed to her.

'This is Hetty,' said Mrs Peel. 'Hetty, this is Mr Jones, our herdsman.' She was looking at him in a way which Hetty could only describe as soppy. In fact she was a little embar-rassed for the older woman, but Mr Jones seemed not to notice it.

'And there's Sam and Bob, sitting there making pigs of themselves wi' the tongue,' he said. The other two men, Sam, a lad in his teens and Bob, not much older, grinned, taking no offence at all. 'You'd best dig in, lass, you look as though you could do wi' a bit o' meat on your bones. Are you sure you're old enough to leave school?'

14

'I'm fourteen,' asserted Hetty. She took a slice of bread, thickly spread with creamy farm butter, and placed a slice of tongue on it to make a sandwich. Oh, it was lovely, the meat thick and tasty and the bread fresh and crusty. For a minute or two she could think of nothing else but her sandwich.

'You like your meat then,' observed one of the farm hands, Sam it was, the younger one. 'Did your mother not tell you not to bolt your food?' Hetty put the sandwich down on her plate, her face bright red. She looked across the table at him, ready to retort. By, she'd had enough of humiliation for one day, she thought. But Mr Jones beat her to it.

'You mind your own business, young Sam,' he snapped. 'I've not noticed you be backward in coming forwards when it comes to eating. Get on with your own meal, there's plenty to do outside afore you go home tonight.'

'Aw, I didn't mean owt, I was only funning,' protested Sam. 'An' you know it's my turn to get off early. I'm going to the pictures in Hutton, they're coming to the church hall tonight. A cowboy it is.'

'Come now, Mr Jones,' Mrs Peel said sweetly, 'I'm sure the lad meant nothing. Let's not have any bad feeling at the table. If there's anything I dislike it's words said at the table.'

'You're a good woman, Mrs Peel,' said the herdsman. 'But we have to keep the young ones in order, haven't we? An' happen the lass didn't have much dinner.'

Hetty stared at her plate, her hunger gone.

'Finish that sandwich and drink up your tea, Hetty,' ordered Mrs Peel. 'Don't forget that floor will be to polish now it's dry and I'll need you later on to help with the family dinner.'

The sandwich tasted like sawdust to Hetty but she ate her way steadily through it and drank the strong sweet tea. By this time the men were finished their meal and Mr Jones had taken a pipe out of his pocket and was looking at Mrs Peel enquiringly.

'Do smoke if you wish, Mr Jones,' that lady said.

'Please may I leave the table? I've had suficient, thank you,' said Hetty, and Bob and Sam exploded into laughter.

15

Now what had she done? Wasn't she just following the lessons in manners she had been taught at school?

'Go and get on with your work,' Mrs Peel said, frowning at her while Mr Jones half rose in his chair and gave the lads a glare which quelled them in an instant.

Polishing the linoleum in the hall, rubbing at it until her arm ached and the smell of lavender polish hung heavy in the air, Hetty willed herself not to cry. By, she thought, it had been a long day and not at all as she had thought it would be. She was so confused and her head ached with tiredness. Maybe tomorrow would be better. Because if it wasn't she didn't know what she would do. Run away? But where would she run to? And anyroad, Mam needed her to send some of her pay home, things were so hard for them there.

Desperately trying to lighten her mood, Hetty began to think of Saltburn. How lovely it had looked earlier in the day when she had taken half an hour between trains and hurried along the clifftop to gaze out to sea, with the sands stretching along to Marske on one side and Huntcliffe soaring on the other. She remembered coming on the chapel trip to Saltburn-by-the-Sea when she was little. By, it was nice. The houses were all grand with bay windows and lace curtains and they swept down to the top of the cliff in terraces all named after jewels. When she had made her fortune she would go to live in the jewel streets, oh yes she would. One way or another she was going to do that.

At nine o'clock Ethel came back from her afternoon off and Hetty's heart lifted as soon as she saw her. She was older than Hetty, about nineteen, and as round as a barrel with red cheeks and mousy brown hair and the brightest pair of sparkling hazel eyes which twinkled merrily as she looked Hetty up and down.

'So you're the new lass, are you?' she said. Hetty waited for a comment on her skinniness but Ethel said nothing. Or at least she did, but it was a nice comment. 'I wouldn't mind being thin like you,' she said. 'I bet you could be a model like those on the front of *Woman's Weekly* when you get a bit older. Or even a film star with those big dark eyes and wavy hair.' She held up a strand of her own mousy locks ruefully. 'Do you think I'd look better if I bleached mine? It's neither one thing nor the other as it is.'

Hetty was shocked at the idea. Only fast girls bleached their hair, or at least that's what Mam said. Nobody in Morton Main did anyway. Luckily, she didn't have to give an answer for Mrs Peel had just come into the kitchen from the front of the house and heard the question.

'I see you two have met,' she said. 'But mind you, Ethel Weldon, if you bleach your hair you'll be out of here like a shot, make no mistake about that. And don't be putting ideas into Hetty's head, neither, she's only fourteen, you should be setting her an example. Now where have you been? You're half an hour late already. I've had to serve in the dining room for you.'

Ethel pulled a face at Hetty behind Mrs Peel's back. 'Sorry, Mrs Peel. But it's a long walk up from the village, you know.'

'I hadn't noticed it getting any longer than it always is,' retorted the housekeeper. 'Come on now, I want to get finished in time tonight.'

There was no doubt that Ethel was a good worker, thought Hetty. Once she had an apron tied round her middle she set to with a will and soon all the dishes from the family's meal were carried through from the dining room and between the two of them they were washed and dried and put away in the wall cupboards. After steaming mugs of cocoa the two girls were dispatched to bed.

The day had gone on forever, thought Hetty wearily as she trudged after Ethel up the last few stairs. There was electricity in the main part of the house but not in the attic and both the girls carried candlesticks in their hands. The flames cast eerie shadows on the walls of the dingy top landing. Hetty was glad that she had Ethel with her, her imagination had been vivid enough in the daylight. Now she stared straight ahead at Ethel's back, determined not to look into the shadows. 'For fear of something 'orrible,' her brother Frank would have said – but then, he'd always made fun of her being scared of the dark.

Inside the bedroom, with the door shut and the curtains

17.

drawn against the great black emptiness of the moor, it was cosy enough. When the girls had undressed and washed in the tepid water from the jug they jumped into bed and blew out the candles. Hetty lay on her back covered only by the sheet for it was a warm September night and the heat had risen through the house until it was trapped under the eaves.

'It's a warm room, anyroad,' she remarked, and Ethel laughed.

'Oh, aye, mebbe it is now, but wait until the winter sets in proper – you'll change your mind then all right. An' be glad of a hot water bottle, I reckon. I'm glad you've come, though, Hetty. You'll see, we'll get on like a house afire. I'm fed up having all the work to do mesel' since Jenny left.'

'Why did she leave? Was she getting married?'

'No, not her, though I daresay she wished she had been. No, she left in a hurry with a bun in the oven.'

Hetty sat up in bed, shocked to the core. 'A baby, do you mean? And she wasn't getting married?'

'She wouldn't say who the feller were, though I have me suspicions. She was no blooming good at housework anyway. Forget about Jenny, don't waste any sympathy on her. You'll have enough to think about, wi' your looks.'

Hetty lay quiet, wondering what she meant for a few minutes. Her back and limbs were aching with tiredness but her mind was buzzing so that she felt she would never drop off to sleep. Then what would she do at five-thirty in the morning when she had to get up to light the kitchen fire? Maybe if she had one or two questions answered . . .

'I met Master Richard today, he seems nice. But the other one, Matt, who is he exactly?'

'Be careful not to get in that one's way, Hetty,' answered Ethel. 'He's got a nasty tongue all right. Thank goodness he's away at the university most of the time. Master Richard's a nice enough lad, though. He goes to school at Barnard Castle during the week but comes home at weekends. It's a pity Master Matthew is the eldest, that's what I think. He treats us like dirt.'

'I know. I got lost on my way downstairs and ended up at the front of the house and he said I must be a thief. He . . . he said I was a bundle of rags.'

18

'Take no notice. Like I said, he's just got a nasty tongue. Thinks too much of himself, he does. What are they anyway? Nowt but jumped up hill farmers. Because the master made some money with the minerals on his land, they think they're gentry. But you can see for yourself, the master still farms, it's in his blood.'

'I've never met him.'

'You will soon enough. He's all right and the mistress too – though you don't see much of her. Mrs Peel runs the house as you might have noticed. A bit strange is the missus.'

'Strange?'

'Aye. Well, you'll see for yourself as I said.' Ethel yawned hugely. 'I'm tired. I've been walking out with my boyfriend. I've got a lad, you know.' She said it as though Hetty would not believe her but Hetty did. Ethel was a nice girl, anyone could see that.

'What's he like?' she asked.

'He's a lovely lad and he likes girls with a bit of flesh on them. Something to take hold of, he says. He works at the Moorcock in the village. The heavy work and that. But he's got ambition. One day he'll have his own pub, he reckons.'

Ethel fell silent and Hetty turned over on to her side and closed her eyes. It would be a full day tomorrow. Goodnight, Mam, she whispered. Goodnight, Dad. God bless all the family. Give Cissy a kiss for me. And the others an' all, but especially Cissy. For a minute her heart ached to see her little sister and then she was asleep.

19

Chapter 3

The days at Hope Hall began to settle into a routine for Hetty. She and Ethel were up while it was still dark, and while Hetty saw to the fire in the kitchen, Ethel lit the one in the dining room so that the room was nicely warmed up before the master came down to breakfast at seven-thirty, for autumn on the moor could be cold. The boys, when they were at home, didn't rise for another hour and Mrs Hope never came downstairs at all in the mornings. Instead, Mrs Peel prepared a tray of buttered toast with the crusts cut off – a scandalous waste of food Hetty thought when she first saw it, but then she supposed the bits went to the hens so it wasn't so bad. There was a dish of fine blackcurrant jelly on the tray and a silver coffee pot and dainty cup and saucer and plate. Though how anyone could drink coffee instead of tea at that time of the morning, Hetty couldn't imagine. Not that the mistress drank much, mostly the tray came down untouched, showing little regard for the careful preparation Mrs Peel had put into it.

The master sent for Hetty that very first morning, even before he had his usual interview with Mr Jones. A good job, she thought, that Mrs Peel had got her her uniform from the dressmaker in the village the night before. Somehow she hadn't felt the same about her dress with the blue flowers since Master Matthew had been nasty about it.

So she stood before the master's desk in the black dress and black cotton stockings which she hated with a fervour she had never felt for any other items of clothing in her life. The pinafore she wore was a bit on the big side and the cap

20

came over her ears but Mrs Peel said she would grow into them. Mr Hope was writing in a big book and Hetty stood quietly watching him. She soon forgot about what she was wearing for she was so interested in him and the way he wrote, with great flourishes and much underlining which her teacher had told her was a bad thing and not the right way to emphasise anything. His fingers were strong and brown with fine hairs on the back and he was tall and broad and older than her own father, maybe as old as the mine manager at Morton though he was better dressed, she could tell that. His leather riding boots, which were stretched out and crossed one over the other, were easily as fine as those of Master Richard and polished so brightly they reflected the light from the windows. She could see them plainly for they came almost all the way through the kneehole of the desk. There was a smell about the place just like that in the mine manager's house and it was a moment before Hetty identified it as bay rum, or at least that was what Dad had told her it was. She wrinkled her nose. It wasn't very nice.

The room was though, she thought, her attention wandering. It was large and high-ceilinged with the walls covered in bookcases filled with books which didn't look as though they were there to be read; they were all bound in a dark red leather with the titles picked out in gold lettering. On the top of the desk there was more red leather, this time well-used and scuffed. By, thought Hetty, I would read the books if they were mine. They made her fingers itch to get at them and open them up and see what they said.

'Now then, Miss Pearson.'

Hetty jumped. Never in her life had she been called Miss Pearson. She looked back at Mr Hope who was gazing at her from under bushy eyebrows which were startlingly dark though his hair was silver.

'Yes, sir?'

'Hetty, isn't it? How old are you, Hetty? You're very small and thin.'

'I'm fourteen, sir.'

'Hmm. Old enough, and perhaps it's a good thing you don't look older.'

21

She couldn't think why that should be. 'I can work, sir,' she volunteered.

'Yes. Well, I expect you can. For if you don't you'll be on your way home before you know it. There are plenty more where you came from,' he said, his tone impersonal, distant almost, as though his mind was on other things.

Hetty closed her mouth tight to stay the retort rising to her lips but she could feel the angry colour in her cheeks and there was nothing she could do about that. This man – and he was nowt but a man, her dad always said no one was better than anyone else no matter how much money or fancy houses they had – this man had learnt no manners when he was a bairn, that was for sure.

'Well, that's all I wanted to say. You can go and get on with your work. And mind you do what Mrs Peel tells you, then you'll be all right.' He bent his head over the book once again, appearing to forget all about Hetty.

'Thank you, sir,' she said. If he forgot his manners, she wasn't going to. She had got as far as the door when he spoke again.

'Don't bang the door,' he said. Resisting the impulse to fling it to as hard as she could, she closed it carefully without a sound.

The day went by quickly enough. She scrubbed the kitchen floor while Ethel turned out the bedrooms, and she cleaned and polished the stairs while Ethel did the hall. Hetty even got to use the vacuum cleaner and marvelled at how easy it was to clean the carpets with it. It gave her something to think about. How did it work? She puzzled over it, it was better than worrying that she would meet up with Master Matt and he would be nasty again. By, she didn't know whether she could control her tongue if *that* happened. And it stopped her thinking about home. It was nice that Ethel was there. Even when they weren't working together they would pass in the hall or elsewhere and Ethel would grin at her or pull a funny face, oh yes, it made Hetty feel good.

'Well, that's the boys away again, thank goodness,' said Mrs Peel when they sat round the kitchen table at noon and ate shepherd's pie that was like a dream, so loaded with meat it was. And the potato was creamed with butter and crisp and brown on top, and there were carrots and cabbage, and rice pudding with nutmeg on the top to follow. Hetty was busy thinking how lovely it would be to sit down to a meal like this at home with little Cissy and the boys and Mam and Dad, they hadn't done that for a long time even before the lockout. The thought almost took away her appetite.

'Master Richard's all right but I can't abide the other one, I don't mind telling you,' said Mr Jones. 'Well, he's gone now, until Christmas, I hope. That lad has no idea how to look after his own horse. Why only t'other day he came home with Marshal all lathered up—'

'Yes, well, best not talk about the family, Mr Jones,' said Mrs Peel. 'You never know who might be listening.'

Hetty came back from her dream of home and realised they were discussing Master Matt. He'd gone and until Christmas! A wave of thankfulness swept over her. Now she didn't have to be looking over her shoulder all the time in case the hated voice caught her unawares.

'Nay, I'm saying nowt more, you're right, Mrs Peel.' Mr Jones shook his head and took out his pipe with his usual enquiring glance at the housekeeper.

After Mrs Hope's tray had been brought down and the washing up was finished, Ethel washed out the cloths. 'Come on, we have time for a walk round in the fresh air,' she said to Hetty. 'No one's going to miss us for ten minutes or so.'

They walked through the orchard which was at the back of the house, behind the farm buildings. The apple trees were stunted and neglected-looking and the few apples left on them were scabby. But the wind blew hard across the moor and the orchard was unprotected. The trees were all bent before the prevailing wind. A few hens picked about under them and a litter of piglets grunted and squealed over fallen apples and Hetty laughed in delight at the sight of their snouts, all black from burrowing in the sparse soil.

'We'll walk to the ridge, shall we?' asked Ethel, and without waiting for an answer strode to the edge of the trees and on, up a narrow path between the paddock and the heather. Only five minutes later they were on top of a small ridge and there the moor was laid out before them, nothing but heather for miles save for the roofs of the village below, the little stone church, and sheep scattered about searching for fodder.

'It's lovely, Ethel,' said Hetty.

'Is it?' Ethel gave the view a dismissive look and sat down on an outcrop of stone, patting the space beside her in invitation. 'I don't know. I've lived here all my life. Now I like a bit of life – to go into Whitby. Once I went to Harrogate with the mistress – her family lives in Harrogate. At least they did, I think they're dead now. I liked Harrogate but I wouldn't like to live there, not unless I was a nob. But there's plenty to do if you have the money to do it.' Ethel sighed and looked down at the village. 'My dad worked in one of the Hope mines but it closed down and now he's out of work.'

'Mine an' all,' said Hetty. 'I mean, he works in the pit and now it's closed down.'

'Life's bloody awful, isn't it?' said Ethel, and Hetty blinked. She'd never heard it put in such strong language but when she thought of it, yes, life *was* awful.

'Will Master Matthew be gone a long time?' she asked hopefully as they made their way back to the house.

'Until Christmas with any luck.'

Hetty felt as though a load had been lifted from her shoulders. Christmas, that was weeks and weeks away. Weeks when she wouldn't have to worry about meeting up with him, just his father. Master Richard now, he was all right. Did he take after his mother? She still hadn't met Mrs Hope. Hetty reckoned she must be really poorly to have to stay in her room all the time, poor woman.

A few days later Hetty got to see Mrs Hope. It was on Ethel's half day.

'Take the mistress's tray up, Hetty,' a harassed Mrs Peel told her, 'and mind you don't trip and spill anything. The mistress can't abide a messy tray. And don't make a clatter neither. She'll have a headache, I suppose, she usually has in the mornings.'

Hetty had had to wear her best shoes until she could have the segs taken out of her comfortable ones down at the

24

cobbler's in the village. By, she thought as she crossed the hall and started to climb the stairs, she'd been that glad when she got her old shoes back, even if it did mean she would have to have them mended more often now.

There was a bowl of fresh flowers on a table outside Mrs Hope's door and on impulse Hetty put down the tray and took a rose out of the display and laid it on the tray. There. When her gran had been badly she had really appreciated it when Hetty took her roses from her dad's prize bushes. 'The scent makes me feel better already, pet,' she had said. Smiling slightly at the memory, Hetty knocked at the door and, as she had been told, opened it and took the tray inside without waiting for an answer.

'Who are you? Where's Ethel?'

The windows were shrouded with heavy curtains and it was dark in the room and stifling. The voice coming from the bed was querulous. Hetty put down the tray on the bedside table, moving a bottle and glass aside to do it.

'My name is Hetty, ma'am,' she said. 'I'm the new maid.' There was a stale, sour smell in the room which made her gag a little. The poor woman, had she been sick? Maybe a sip of tea and a piece of toast would do her good. 'I've brought your breakfast tray,' she added. Without thinking Hetty crossed to the window and pulled the cord and the heavy curtains swished back, flooding the room with light. She looked for the catch to open the window and was stretching towards it when a sharp cry stopped her.

'Leave that window alone! If I want it open, I'll say so. Who did you say you were?'

'Hetty, ma'am. I'm the new maid. I've brought up your breakfast tray.' She moved back to the bed. 'Will I help you sit up, ma'am?' She bent over the bed and took hold of the dishevelled bedclothes to pull them straight. The thick satin-covered quilt had slid to the floor and she picked it up and replaced it on the bed. Meanwhile the woman lay there watching her through narrowed eyes. Hetty had grown accustomed to the half-light and saw Mrs Hope was a woman perhaps a little older than Mrs Peel, though she had an abundance of dark hair which was spread over the pillow

25

and down her shoulders. Impatiently she pushed the hair back from her forehead.

'I don't want any breakfast, I don't feel well,' she said. 'Take it away.'

Hetty gazed at her. Poor woman, she thought. She remembered the time she'd had diphtheria when she was ten and how awful she had felt. She'd wanted to be left alone then, but when the nurses in the fever hospital had washed her and brushed her hair and changed her sheets, how much better she had felt. And surely Mrs Hope would feel better if she ate a little breakfast?

'Do you have a headache?' Hetty asked, quite forgetting to call the lady 'ma'am'. 'I can fetch some fresh water and bathe your forehead, if you like? And if you have a clean nightie . . .'

'Go away, I said!'

'Oh. Yes, ma'am.' But still Hetty hesitated. Mrs Hope opened her eyes properly and stared at her balefully but after a moment her gaze softened as she saw the genuine concern in Hetty's expression. Oh, well, she might as well let the girl do what she wanted, then perhaps she'd be left in peace. Besides, the thought of having a wash without having to make the effort herself began to seem appealing.

'Go on then. There are nightgowns in the top drawer of the dressing table. But don't chatter, I can't stand anyone chattering in the mornings.'

'No, ma'am.' Hetty fairly skipped to the adjacent bathroom where luckily there was a bowl she could use and lovely fluffy towels and fancy soap. She held the soap to her nose and it smelled lovely. She almost remarked to Mrs Hope how lovely it was but stopped herself just in time, remembering about the chattering.

Shortly she had coaxed the invalid into having what Hetty's gran called a proper wash and Mrs Hope was sitting up in bed with the pillows propped up behind her and her hair tied back with a blue ribbon, the bed freshly made up.

'Now wouldn't you like a nice cup of tea and mebbe a bit of toast?' Hetty coaxed. 'I know when you don't feel well you don't want to eat but my gran always says if you're badly you need good food to be able to fight it. An' there's a nice coddled egg and it's still hot. See, it's under this cover. Doesn't it look nice?'

Elizabeth Hope looked at the tray which Hetty had brought to her side and hesitated. Maybe she could drink a cup of coffee. 'I hope that is coffee, not tea?' she said, frowning slightly.

'Oh, yes, I forgot, it's coffee. If it's cold I can bring some fresh?'

'Just pour me half a cup, it will do.'

Somehow, when Hetty took the tray back down into the kitchen most of the egg had been eaten and two pieces of toast. In the bedroom, Elizabeth lay back on the pillow, her headache faded to insignificance. The curtains were drawn back to let in the light and she had a wrap over her shoulders to save her from the draught from the window.

'I'll just open it a little bit,' the girl had said. She had a gentle touch that one, and a way with her. There was no denying Elizabeth felt better. Perhaps she would get out of bed in an hour or two and sit by the window. She looked up as the door opened without a preliminary knock. Havelock, of course, bringing in the stink of the farmyard no doubt. She picked up the bottle of cologne which Hetty had placed conveniently on her bedside table and dabbed a little on her temples.

'Good morning, my dear,' he said, striding into the room and across to the window. 'What's this? Feeling better this morning or did that fool of a girl Ethel do this without your permission?'

'No, no, Havelock, of course she didn't. In any case, it wasn't her, it was the new girl, Hetty.'

'I'm not sure about that one, she's nobbut a child herself. She can't be much use, little and thin she is, there's nothing to her. I don't doubt she'll have to go at the end of the month.'

'No, she won't,' Elizabeth said with some heat. 'I like her and you're not going to get rid of her like you did Jenny.'

Havelock looked impatient. 'The lass should have kept her legs crossed, then she wouldn't have been in trouble,' he snapped. 'What did you want me to do, keep her on and look after the brat?'

27

'Why not? After all—' his wife began, but he was striding to the door.

'I'm not arguing with you, I have better things to do. I'll see you later on if I have time but I'm late, I have a meeting in Thirsk.'

'Good morning to you, Havelock,' said Elizabeth wearily as the door banged to behind him. She sank back on to her pillows and stared out of the window at the clouds chasing across the sky. There would be a storm, she thought dully. Slipping down the bed she turned her face into the pillow and closed her eyes. Her headache was returning.

Chapter 4

'Hetty! Hetty! Eeh, lass, I'm that glad to see you,' cried Thomas Pearson as he strode down the station platform at Bishop Auckland. Hetty gazed at him, too full to speak for a minute, her heart in her eyes. He wore no cap like most of the other men, he could always be picked out of a crowd by his bare head with its mop of dark hair. No matter what the weather, Thomas didn't wear a cap. He wore no overcoat either, though the snow was falling fast now and settling on Hetty's shoes as she stood there, her basket by her side. He did wear a white scarf, tied at the front and tucked into the vee of his waistcoat, and his pitboots with steel toecaps shining through the snow which encrusted them for his pit-boots were weatherproof – which was more than could be said for his shoes.

All this passed through his daughter's mind in the few seconds it took him to reach her and peck her on the cheek. Her arms went up and she hugged him and felt his cold cheek against hers, freshly shaved and smooth. She smelled the clean smell of him, Sunlight soap mingled with Wood-bine cigarettes. She felt the thin cloth of his suit, damp now with the snow.

Thomas put an arm around her shoulders. 'There now, pet,' he said awkwardly and glanced around in case anyone was watching this display of emotion. 'Howay now, we'll get the bus home if we hurry.' He picked up her basket box and put it on his shoulder and they walked side by side out of the station and down Newgate Street to the bus stop for Morton Main. They didn't speak again until they were sitting

29

side by side on the bus, except to answer the conductor who limped up to them and handed out tickets in exchange for tuppence.

'Thanks, Jack,' said Thomas. Jack, who had been wounded in the war and had one leg shorter than the other, leaned on the back of the seat and smiled at Hetty.

'Back for the New Year, are you?' he asked. 'What's it like in Yorkshire then?'

'All right,' she said.

'Aye. Well, I must say, you're looking well on it. Growing into a young lady she is, Thomas, you'll have to keep an eye on her in a year or two.' Jack grinned at him man to man but Thomas frowned.

'Nowt of the sort,' he growled. 'My Hetty's been brought up right, a good lass she is.'

'Oh, aye, I never meant owt, I didn't,' Jack hastened to say, and stood up straight and went off down the bus in search of more fares.

Hetty was staring out of the window, trying to see through the falling snow. There were few people about on the road, this was the day after Boxing Day and any Christmas festivities were over with, folk saving their strength for the first footing on New Year's Eve. The snow was laying thickly now. The bus began to slip and lurch from one side to the other until they came to an open stretch of road where the wind had blown up a drift against the hedgerow and spread it out whitely across the black road. The bus stopped, stuck hard.

'I don't doubt we'll have to dig her out, Jack,' shouted the driver, getting out of his seat. He had come prepared for there were a couple of shovels in the luggage rack and he took them down.

Thomas got to his feet. 'You stay where you are, Jack,' he said. 'I could do with some practice with a shovel anyroad.'

By, he was a good man was her dad, thought Hetty as she watched his back, which was all of him she could see, rising and falling as he dug away the snow. But when he got back in the bus and sat down beside her, he was panting slightly.

'I'm out of condition, pet,' he said, giving her a rueful

30

glance. 'But never mind, there's talk of the pit starting up shortly. We'll get three days only but it's better than nowt.'

Hetty smiled in delight. 'Oh, Dad, isn't that grand?'

'Aye, grand,' he said laconically. 'But I reckon I'll have to get myself into better condition than this if I want to make any money.'

The bus stopped at the garage and the driver went into the office. The passengers watched anxiously and there was a chorus of groans when he came back out.

'Sorry, folks,' he said. 'I daren't go no further. There's the bad bank over to Morton village and I don't want to get stuck there. So it's everybody out, sorry.'

'Howay then, lass, we might as well get started,' said Thomas and shouldered the basket box. Together they faced into the wind and tramped up the bank and along the road to Morton Main. But when the pit winding wheel and slag heap appeared mistily through the snow, it was all worth it for Hetty. The snow clung to the slag heap, making it look like a mountain she had seen at the pictures, in the Alps that had been. The winding wheel with the little houses clustered at the bottom could have been Switzerland too, like the overhead railway which took Mary Pickford and her lover to the top of the mountain.

'Home at last,' said Thomas, and Hetty came back to Morton Main which after all was just a pit village in Durham with its houses in long terraces. They turned into the yard of the house in Office Street and it was home and her heart filled with love for this place which was lovelier by far than any Alpine village, of course it was.

All the family was gathered in the kitchen, except for Eddie of course. He was making cars in Oxford and rarely managed to get home. But there was Mam and Cissy and Frank, and they clustered round her, and Cissy held out her arms to be held. Hetty hugged her and kissed her and the tears sprang to her eyes.

'Where've you been, Hetty?' asked Cissy, and Mam laughed and said Cissy was always asking for her, she never forgot. The fire was hot for though the coal allowance had stopped when the men were locked out, Dad and Frank had scavenged the slag heap for small bits of coal that had been thrown away and the blaze was satisfying and warm. They all sat round the old black-leaded range and talked and talked.

Mam had ham broth bubbling away on the gas ring and Hetty had a great bowl of it, with pieces of leek and carrot and turnip floating in it. The leeks and carrots had been grown in the garden but Frank had 'liberated' the swede from Farmer Buck's field, and very nice it was. Mam worried when he brought one in but Frank said the family should come before any farmer's cattle, and anyroad, surely they wouldn't miss one measly old turnip?

Hetty had to tell them all about Yorkshire though in truth all she knew was Hope Hall and the village at the bottom of the hill where most of the men worked in the drift mines, would you believe, or had done when they were working but the depression had hit them an' all. And they weren't even coal mines but something called alum and ironstone, which was needed for the steel mills when they were working.

Hetty told them about Christmas at Hope Hall and how there was a giant Christmas tree in the hall with garlands and lanterns and baubles. How there was a present for everyone under the tree, even for the staff, and she opened her basket box and showed them her Christmas gift. The family was silent for inside the bright wrapping paper were two pairs of black lisle stockings.

After a minute Mam cleared her throat and said, 'They'll be very useful, pet.' Frank and Dad looked at each other and Hetty saw they were scowling.

'We had a lovely dinner on Christmas Day,' she said, quickly wrapping the stockings back up and pushing them in her box. 'And I went to the service in the chapel at three o'clock. Then on the night the family had a party. There was dancing in the hall. They were doing the Charleston, Mam. Just like on the pictures it was.'

Hetty stood up and, humming the tune, danced a few steps, her whole body suddenly alive, hands making circles in the air.

Frank laughed. 'You look as though you're washing the

windows, our Hetty,' he scoffed, and she sat down again, deflated.

'Well, it was nice,' she said. It *had* been nice: the electric light flooding the hall as though it were day, the ladies' dresses, so short and skimpy and in the latest fashion, shimmering as they whirled about, their feet tapping on the parquet flooring which Hetty would have to polish the next day before any of the guests were out of bed. Not that she minded, oh no, she had loved to watch them. And the men in their white ties and elegant tail suits laughing and talking and drinking punch from the bowl on the side table which Hetty had the job of refilling more and more often as the evening went on. Everything glittered and sparkled and once, when she thought no one was looking, she took a few sips of the punch, and by, it was lovely, all fruity.

'Go on, Hetty, have some more,' said a voice in her ear. 'No one will see, they're all too busy.' It was Master Richard. Nervously she pushed the glass behind other abandoned ones on the table.

'I . . . I was just about to take the dirty glasses back to the kitchen,' she murmured, and pulled a tray towards her and started to fill it. Her hands were shaking so badly she knocked a glass on the floor. The record on the gramophone had just come to an end and the splintering sound on the hard floor rang loud and clear. There was a sudden hush.

'That will come out of your wages, girl,' said Havelock Hope, crossing over to her and speaking quietly. Someone put another record on and the music started again. Hetty heard it dimly, a song which always sounded slightly scandalous to her: 'The Black Bottom'.

'It was my fault, Father,' Richard said. 'I knocked her hand.'

Havelock gave him a level stare then turned to Hetty. 'Get a dustpan, girl, and clean that up.'

'Yes, sir.'

As she worked her way round the floor where the dancers were shrieking with laughter now and the dancing was becoming wilder, she lifted her head and saw Matthew Hope, his arm around a girl as he drew her into the alcove under the sweeping staircase.

33

'No, Matt,' the girl was saying weakly, but she was following his insistent lead, her silvery dress clinging to her body and shimmering even in the shadows. Matt looked up. He saw Hetty's startled gaze and threw her a dismissive glance, indicating the green baize of the kitchen door. Hetty fled, intimidated. When she returned with the dustpan and brush, she kept her head averted from the alcove under the stairs.

The evening was spoiled for her. Her feet hurt and her head throbbed dully, probably from the alcohol in the punch. She had only had a few sips, but then it was the first time she had ever tasted alcohol. She swept up the pieces of broken glass and took them out to the kitchen and she may as well have been invisible for all the notice the crowd in the hall took of her. Except for Master Richard who smiled at her as she passed.

'Don't look so worried,' he said to her. 'It's Christmas. You'll be going home in a day or two, won't you? That will be nice for you.'

Hetty's forlorn feeling fell away to be replaced by a small glow within her. Yes, she was going home for the New Year, and would see the family again. Would Cissy have forgotten her?

The snow was halfway up the back door when Frank opened it the day after Hetty arrived home, though it was a fine day, cold and crisp with a blue sky and clouds as white as the snow scudding across it in the sharp wind. Hetty dug out a path to the gate, for Frank and Thomas were off with their shovels on their shoulders to offer to dig the paths out for anyone in Old Morton who was willing to pay them a penny for the service.

Afterwards she went to see if Dorothy was home, and there she was, and the two girls ceased to be adult workers as soon as they told each other their news and then they were bairns again. They got out their old sledges and polished up the runners which Dad had made from brass stair rods and went sledging down the road until the gritting cart came along, and then they went on to the old pit heaps and sledged down them, pretending they were on an Alpine run.

By, it was grand, Hetty thought, there was nowhere like Morton, not anywhere in the world. But then she saw that some of the pitmen had cleared the snow on the far side of the latest slag heap and were grubbing for small coal, their hands red and chapped and their mufflers tied tight around their caps, and her happiness dimmed.

Why didn't they open the pits? Everybody needed coal, didn't they? She asked Dorothy what she thought but her friend pulled a face and shook her head.

'My dad says they only need the miners when there's a war nowadays,' she said. 'They use electric instead of coal.'

'Let's go home, it's dinnertime,' said Hetty sadly. But when she had filled herself up with broth and Mam's home-made bread she began to feel happy again and all ready to rush out once more with her sledge.

'Can I come, Hetty?' asked Cissy.

Hetty hesitated but her sister looked so anxious that she nodded her head. 'All right, but mind you do as I say,' she warned. So Cissy was dressed in her warm coat and hood and her legs encased in button-up leggings which Mam had got on the second-hand stall in Bishop Auckland market. One of Dad's scarves was tied round her neck and criss-crossed over her chest and she wore the mittens Hetty had knitted her for Christmas with a pair of Frank's old socks over the top to stop them wearing out.

The pit heap looked too steep when they had Cissy with them so they took the sledge into the field where the pit ponies were kept when the pits weren't working. The ponies weren't there, of course, it was too cold. No, they were in the stables up at the farm where it was warm and they had good hay and oats to eat, paid for by the mine owner.

'A good pony costs a lot of money,' Dorothy's dad had said once to Hetty's. 'Men can be replaced any time.'

'Aye, well,' said Thomas after a short silence, 'I wouldn't see the poor beasts hungry meself. It's not their fault, the state of the world.'

Hetty remembered that as she and Dorothy pulled the sledge with Cissy sitting on it up the slope of the field. It wasn't too strenuous, a hard frost had already settled on the snow and there was a deep icy crust to it. At the top they turned the sledge round and Dorothy sat in front with Cissy behind her. Hetty pushed and jumped on the back though there was hardly room and she had to put her legs around Cissy. The sledge flew down the bank, faster and faster, and Cissy shrieked. There was a fence at the bottom which separated the field from the edge of the slag heap and it was coming towards them far too fast by Hetty's reckoning.

'Watch out, Dorothy!' she shouted. 'Turn before you get to the bottom.' But whether her friend heard she couldn't tell though Dorothy was pulling as hard as she could on the rope which was supposed to steer the sledge. And the sledge did swerve slightly for it hit a hummock of grass sticking up out of the snow and suddenly Hetty was lying on her back in a deep snow drift, all the wind knocked out of her.

It took a minute or two for her to collect her wits before she realised Cissy had stopped shrieking, and she sat up and pushed the snow aside and saw the men from the heap had abandoned their sacks and were running down to the bottom where the sledge was upended in the snow. And she couldn't see Cissy, though Dorothy's red scarf she could see, it was tangled round the runner of the sledge.

'Cissy!' Hetty cried as she scrambled to her feet and plunged through the snow, her legs so wobbly that she slipped and slid and fell down and even rolled at one point, and then she slithered to a halt by the group of men.

'Bloody hell,' said one of them quietly. 'The poor bairn.' He was bending over a bundle about three yards up the slag heap and was feeling it with his hands. Turning to his companions, he said, 'Gan and alert the safety men. We need the doctor. And someone get the stretcher from the ambulance room.'

'Howay, pet, this is no place for you,' a man's voice said, and Hetty looked up into Mr Cowie's face – Mr Cowie who lived in Chapel Row and was a marra of her dad.

'But where's Cissy, Mr Cowie?' she whispered. 'Where is she?'

'They're going to take care of her now,' he answered as he put an arm around her to take her away. But he paused and looked back.

'That's not Cissy,' he muttered to himself. 'That's Dorothy James.'

Hetty wrenched herself away from his arm and rushed over to where the men had turned Dorothy over and were brushing the snow from her face. She lay still, her eyes not quite closed, her face unmarked but for the blood beginning to matt her fair hair, just above her right ear.

'Where's Cissy, Dorothy?' Hetty shouted at her. 'Where's Cissy?' She trembled from head to foot, a fierce trembling which shook her head and her teeth and even the slope of the pit heap including the stone by Dorothy's head which was a peculiar shade of red. And then she saw Cissy: a small round hump in the snow by a post in the fence. She hadn't been found before because the men didn't know she was there so they weren't looking for her, and anyway she was wearing a covering of hard snow like a blanket, only one hand sticking out. It was that which Hetty saw. Frank's sock was missing, but the mitten which Hetty had knitted was still on the hand.

Mr Cowie picked Hetty up as though she were a baby and carried her round the pit heap and up the bank to the village, and she let him for her brain had stopped working. She couldn't see anything but the small hillock of snow with the mitten sticking out of it. But when she got to the top of the street she heard Mam's voice and she was screaming for Cissy. Hetty lifted her head and saw her running up to her and held out her arms to her mam.

'I'm sorry, Mam, I'm sorry . . . it was my fault, I shouldn't have taken her,' she said. But Maggie didn't even see her; she ran straight past Hetty and Mr Cowie and on down the bank to where the men were bringing up the stretcher.

'My bairn, my bairn!' Mam was moaning and leaning over the bundle lying there, stopping the men who were struggling through the snow until Dad reached her and held her away and Hetty could see that it took all his strength to do it. And then Hetty saw Mrs James running towards them, her mouth open as she struggled for breath, her hair streaming down her back where it had escaped from its pins. She hunched over the second stretcher for a minute and then she turned to Hetty.

37

'It was your fault, you young hooligan!' she said. 'I always said you'd get my lass into trouble!' She pushed her face into Hetty's and the girl shrank back.

'Steady on, missus,' said Mr Cowie. 'It wasn't the lass's fault at all, don't light into her. She's had a shock an' all, man, can't you see that?'

'A shock? A shock did you say? I'll give her shock!' She turned back to Hetty. 'It should have been *you*, Hetty Pearson, do you hear me?'

Chapter 5

Hetty thought of that day obsessively for months, even years. Had she been too enthusiastic in pushing the sledge at the top of the bank? Should she have been more careful when Cissy was aboard?

'A freak accident, Hetty, that's all it was, pet,' her father had said. 'It wasn't your fault, no, nowt of the sort. The Lord giveth . . .' But he had bowed his head and looked away from her into the fire and the arm he had put around her in comfort had fallen away. And Mam – well, Mam didn't say anything. She simply looked at Hetty and Hetty was sure that Mam blamed her.

Eddie came home. Hetty was out doing the messages at the Co-op store and when she arrived back he was already there, sitting in the kitchen where the curtains were kept drawn against the light in these days before the funeral, according to custom. At first Hetty hadn't recognised him in his good suit and white shirt, she thought it was a new minister who had come to make arrangements for the funeral. Then he had risen to his feet and taken a step towards her.

'Hetty,' he'd said, and put his arms around her, and she had laid her head against his chest.

'Did you remember to buy bread, Hetty?' asked Mam, and Hetty lifted her head. Mam had hardly spoken to her since the accident and when she did it was always instructions to do this or that.

'I'm sorry,' she faltered. Mam always made the bread but now there wasn't enough fuel for the oven, not when Dad wasn't going scavenging on the heap. Though the neighbours were good and many a bucket of coal or kindling was left by the yard gate, it wasn't enough.

'I'll walk back with you,' said Eddie. As they walked down the street to the corner and along the wet and slushy road to the store, they were silent. But then they had to pass the field and Hetty's eyes were drawn to it. The snow was patchy now and the bank looked very steep.

'You know,' said Eddie, taking her arm, 'I've always found it hard to sledge on grass. You too, I suppose. You'd have expected it to be hard going. But the ground was fast because the ponies had eaten the grass down to the bare earth and it had frozen underneath. You weren't to know, Hetty. Don't blame yourself, lass.'

She said nothing, she was too full of misery. They got to the store and bought the bread and Hetty managed to avoid most of the eyes that were turned on her, whether in sympathy or blame. Eddie carried the basket home which was something he must have learned to do in Oxfordshire for if any of the boys had seen him with a basket in his hand in Morton Main they would have called, 'Lassie-lad!' Hetty thought. Briefly she marvelled that she could think of anything so ordinary at such a time but small, irrelevant thoughts ran through her mind on top of the misery, and maybe if they hadn't she would have gone completely mad.

Hetty was a week late in returning to Hope Hall. She was dreading going into the kitchen and having to face curious questions for the accident had been in the papers and the results of the inquest too. 'Death by misadventure' the coroner in Bishop Auckland had said. Had the whole story been in the *Whitby Gazette* as it had been in the *Northern Echo*?

'Come in and sit down, lass,' Mr Jones, who was sitting at the table, said. 'I'm sure we're all very sorry for your trouble. There, we'll say no more than that, we know how you must feel.'

Mrs Peel put a large cup of hot, sweet tea in front of Hetty and pushed the plate of buttered teacake closer to her.

'Thank you, Mrs Peel,' said Hetty, though she wasn't hungry in spite of the walk over the moor.

Sam and Bob came in, Sam full of the bicycle he'd got for Christmas and how he'd cycled over to Whitby on New Year's Eve to a big dance and the girls that were there and how he'd kissed one or two to let in the New Year. Bob laughed and said he didn't believe any of it, and Mr Jones stood up and ordered them to be quiet. Could they not see who was there? Bob and Sam had looked over at Hetty and Sam muttered an apology before sliding into his chair.

'That's all right,' she said. She hated the unnatural hush which usually greeted her since *that* day. She longed for things to be back to normal. Let them laugh and talk. Why, they hadn't even known Cissy, it had nothing to do with them.

It was different with Ethel; Ethel she could talk to. She hugged Hetty and kissed her on the cheek and after that acted as she always had. She talked about her boy in the village and how they were saving up to get married, and after a while Hetty found herself responding naturally. As week followed week and the year turned to the spring, the two girls grew closer until Hetty was dreading the day Ethel would get married and leave Hope Hall.

'Why, there'll be a new maid and then you'll be the senior and be able to boss her about like I do you,' laughed Ethel when Hetty tried to tell her how she would miss her. A lot of rubbish, of course, she was the least bossy girl Hetty had ever met.

The two sons of the house had gone back to school or college or whatever. Richard came home for weekends but he didn't mention Hetty's tragedy; perhaps he knew nothing about it. So she lived and worked in Hope Hall and it was becoming almost like home to her. Not real home, not Morton, but home nevertheless.

'Why don't you come downstairs today, Mrs Hope?' asked Hetty. 'It's a lovely day, you could sit in the garden, the fresh air would do you good.'

'Oh, Hetty, you're always trying to get me out of this room, aren't you?' Elizabeth Hope smiled at the girl;

sometimes she thought Hetty was the only friend she had in the world. How long was it since she had come to Hope Hall? Why, it must be almost two years now. 'Do you know, Hetty, you are turning into a very pretty girl,' she said, and Hetty went pink.

'You are, though,' insisted Elizabeth. Hetty had grown at least three inches in the last two years and her figure, though still slight, was a woman's figure, slim-waisted and round-hipped, her breasts swelling against the black dress of her uniform. Her hair was a little longer than it had been when she first came – the fashions of 1927, Elizabeth supposed. But it seemed to curve in naturally to the nape of her neck and soft curls peeped from under her cap and around her ears.

'You're just trying to change the subject,' said Hetty, and Elizabeth smiled; they were so easy with each other now. Suddenly she made up her mind.

'I'll come downstairs,' she said, and Hetty beamed. She had suggested it every morning for ages. Mrs Hope had always refused but now she had decided on it even before Hetty asked her. 'I'm fed up with you asking, Hetty, you never give up, so I might as well get it over with.'

'There now, I'll have you ready in no time. Oh, won't everyone be surprised when they see you?'

'Do you think I can make the stairs?' Doubt assailed Elizabeth and Hetty, rather than blithely reassuring her, put her head on one side and considered.

'You are a lot stronger now, Mrs Hope,' she said. Indeed, Elizabeth had put on a little weight and had been walking up and down the room on Hetty's arm every day for weeks now. Moreover, the mysterious bottle had disappeared from the bedside cabinet; when the last one was empty she had not asked Hetty to get her another from the chemist's in the village. The bottle had worried Hetty. After all, she never saw a doctor at Hope Hall yet the master always had a prescription for the draught ready. Once she had asked Mrs Hope what it was but the reply had been evasive. And Ethel said she didn't know either.

Mrs Hope was still pale and easily tired, Hetty's thoughts ran on, but how could she ever get properly well unless she had some fresh air? Fresh air was the best medicine, hadn't Mam said that often? And her gran too. Hetty felt the familiar ache when she thought of her mother. Letters from her had been so few since *that day*, the day when Cissy . . . she pushed the thought to the back of her mind.

'I think you can manage it,' she said to Mrs Hope. 'Though I tell you what, I could ask Master Richard to help, just to see you downstairs and into the garden.'

Elizabeth smiled. 'Richard, yes,' she said. He was a good boy, had already been in to see his mother this morning, which was more than Matthew had done. Or had Matthew gone away again? He sometimes did without bothering to say goodbye, to her at least.

'I'll see if I can find him,' said Hetty.

She ran down the stairs, her heart light. Richard, she was sure, would be in the stables. It was a beautiful autumn day, the dahlias and chrysanthemums were out in the flower garden: wine-coloured dahlias, stately and impressive, contrasting with the pale lemon buttons of the spray type. And behind, the great tawny chrysanthemums and beyond them the wall. The heather was just turning but still showing swathes of purple sweeping across the moor. A few leaves lay on the ground under the apple trees but even they were hanging on to summer as long as they could. Hetty surveyed the scene. Yes, she decided, Mrs Hope could sit just on the edge of the porch, sheltered from any breeze but able to see all the beauty for herself. She turned the corner of the house and made for the stables.

Richard was there, as she had thought he would be. He was saddling Tansy, his grey mare. He had his back to the door and Hetty watched him for a moment. He was in riding breeches and a blue shirt with wide braces over it, and the light from the open door fell on his light brown hair as he swung the saddle over the horse, murmuring to her, 'Steady now, lass.' He pattted her neck and Tansy whinnied and turned her head to him.

Hetty liked Richard. He had left school now and was at the university in York. He managed to be home quite a lot and Hetty was glad it was him and not Matthew. When Matthew was home he had taken to looking at her in a way which made her uncomfortable but Richard was always nice to her. He lifted his head now and caught sight of her and smiled.

'Morning, Hetty,' he said over his shoulder. 'What can I do for you?' He finished tightening the girth before giving her his full attention.

'It's your mother, Master Richard.' Hetty stepped forward and smiled, pleased to be giving him such good news. 'She's decided to try sitting in the garden for a while and we wondered if you would come and help her down the stairs?'

'Gosh, that's grand, Hetty,' cried Richard. He looked so pleased that she laughed in delight and suddenly he picked her up and swung her round and lifted her easily into the saddle on Tansy's back, not astride but across so that her feet dangled just below the horse's belly.

'Let me down, do, Master Richard! What will your father say if he sees me?'

'He'll say "Well done, Hetty", of course he will. We none of us know how you've managed it. We've been trying for ages, ever since she began to improve. And that was your doing too, Hetty. You're a witch, I think.' He laughed up at her and Tansy snorted and danced a few steps and Hetty hung on to the saddle nervously.

'Let me down, do, Master Richard.'

'Oh, all right.' For a moment he was irritated. Why did she have to call him Master Richard? It was silly in this day and age, for goodness' sake. He raised his arms and took hold of her by the waist and lifted her easily to the ground. 'Come on, we'll go now before she changes her mind. Hang on a minute, I'll get Sam to see to Tansy for me.' He walked further into the stable and for the first time Hetty noticed that Sam was there. He had a pitchfork in his hand but he had been so quiet she hardly thought he could have been doing much. Watching her with Richard, she thought, and blushed as though she had been doing something wrong. When Sam put down the fork and came forward he gave her a funny look, knowing somehow, and that upset her even more. But she forgot about him as she walked over to the house with Richard.

He strode through the kitchen and Mrs Peel called after

him, 'Take off your boots, Master Richard,' as she did so often. This time he heard and sat down on a hard kitchen chair to remove his boots. Hetty brought him his soft indoor shoes and they went upstairs to where his mother was waiting.

'Oh, Richard, I hope I can manage it,' Elizabeth said tremulously. Evidently she was beginning to have second thoughts.

'Of course you can,' he answered. 'Now, are we ready? Come along, let's not waste any of this lovely sunshine. Besides, I have work to do.' His brisk manner had the desired effect and, with Hetty and him on either side of her, Elizabeth made her first foray down the stairs and out of the front door to where Hetty had already placed a comfortable basket chair piled with cushions beside the mock Grecian pillars of the porch.

They settled her in the chair and Hetty went back for an extra shawl, just in case it was needed. Richard kissed his mother.

'There now,' he said. 'What do you think of the garden? Bill Oliver certainly can grow dahlias, can't he? Aren't the colours wonderful? Welcome back, Mother.'

Elizabeth settled herself in the chair, sighing. 'It's so lovely,' she said. 'I'm so glad to be back.'

Richard nodded in perfect understanding. Hetty heard the last remark and wondered for a minute and then she realised what Elizabeth meant. It was as though she had been on a long journey.

'Go along then, Richard, back to your horse. And you too, Hetty, I know you have work to do.' Elizabeth picked up the novel Hetty had brought down with the shawl and opened it. 'Go on, then, I shall be quite all right here on my own without either of you fussing over me.'

'I suppose I can leave the door open,' Hetty said doubtfully. 'Then someone will hear if you call out for anything. And I can check on you every now and again.'

'Don't fuss so, it's time I learned to be more independent,' said Elizabeth. 'Go on, both of you.'

Richard raised his eyebrows at Hetty and backed away into the doorway. 'I'm going, I'm going,' he said, laughing.

But when they were out of earshot he turned to her. 'I'll stick close by in case you need me,' he said. 'She'll probably tire quite soon as this is her first day and then I'll carry her upstairs.' He took hold of Hetty's arm and drew her to the side of the hall, into the shadow cast by the great staircase.

She looked up at him, her eyes large and questioning, and he bent his head and kissed her gently on the mouth. His lips were warm and firm yet soft on hers at the same time.

'Oh!'

'Dear Hetty,' he whispered. 'I'm so grateful for what you are doing for my mother.' He walked away quickly and she gazed after him, still feeling his lips on hers. She put a hand up to her mouth and felt the place with her fingertips, sure it would feel different, but apart from a slight tremble it was the same. Fleetingly she remembered the night Matthew had kissed a girl in that self-same spot; his kiss had been so different though. She wasn't sure whether she wished Richard's kiss had been – not like Matthew's exactly but not quite so brotherly. Shaking her head, she went into the kitchen for the floor polish and cloths. She would clean the hall now rather than later so that she could keep an ear open for Mrs Hope.

'The mistress came down then,' said Mrs Peel. 'Do you know, I'm not sure you should have encouraged her. Not when the master's out.'

Hetty considered this. Surely the master would be pleased? She was assailed with doubt, though. Perhaps he wouldn't be. She remembered the last time she had had to go into the village to get Mrs Hope's prescription filled. It had been just after Havelock Hope had been closeted with his wife for a whole morning. Hetty had taken a tray up to the bedroom at lunchtime and hesitated for she could hear the murmur of his voice behind the closed door, rising once until she could hear the actual words.

'You're such a bloody fool, Elizabeth!' he had shouted. Hetty had retreated, not wanting them to think she had been eavesdropping, but then she went forward again and knocked loudly on the door and opened it.

'I've brought you some lunch,' she had said brightly,

advancing into the room. Havelock was standing by the window, red-faced with anger, and Elizabeth too was flushed, her eyes sparkling with tears.

'Put it down, girl, and get out. Don't you know enough ot to interrupt when I'm talking to my wife?'

'I . . . didn't know . . .' Hetty had faltered before concern for Elizabeth emboldened her. 'Are you all right, Mrs Hope?' she had asked.

'Get out!' Havelock Hope had shouted, making her jump.

'I'm fine, Hetty, thank you,' Elizabeth had said. 'Just go, my dear.' So Hetty went. That afternoon she had had to make a trip to the chemist's in the village and bring back the bottle of medicine for Elizabeth.

'I wish I knew what it was,' she had said to Ethel. But Ethel was getting married in October and could think of nothing else.

'Don't worry,' she had said. 'It's only a mixture for her nerves.'

'Well, I know, you've said that before. But really, I think she would be better without it. Look how much stronger she's been since she stopped taking it. I'm sorry she's started again.'

Ethel smiled. 'Nay, Hetty, you can't take everybody's worries on your shoulders. Let it be, lass, let it be.' She had started to hum a jazzy tune, bright and fast, as she attacked the dust on the banister rails, rubbing vigorously. 'Did I tell you I'm going in to Harrogate for my wedding dress?'

'Yes, you told me.' Hetty grinned. 'Once or twice you told me.'

Now, though, Mrs Hope had stopped using the bottle. Why, it must be almost a month ago that it had gone from the bedside cabinet. And she was so much better. Hetty couldn't believe her husband would not be pleased.

'I don't think he'll mind . . . Anyway, Master Richard helped me get her down and she wanted to come herself. In fact, it was her suggestion. Surely she can decide for herself, Mrs Peel?'

'Hmm.' It was all the housekeeper answered but it was enough to give Hetty a niggle of apprehension. She polished the floor in the hall, getting up from her knees every few

47

minutes to check on Mrs Hope. The last time she saw that Elizabeth had fallen asleep, her head on a cushion to one side. A little colour tinged her cheeks and she looked younger somehow, the book fallen to the ground, her hands laid palm upwards in her lap, delicate and white. Hetty glanced ruefully at her own hands, red and roughened through being too often immersed in hot water, the nails cut short because they broke so often through contact with harsh cleaners. Oh, well, she thought, she would rub in some olive oil and sugar tonight if she could beg the oil from Mrs Peel.

Hetty turned from the door and picked up her polish and polishing cloths. She would just have time to wash the cloths before helping Mrs Peel with the lunch. She was opening the door to the kitchen when she heard Havelock's voice, roaring from the garden.

'Elizabeth! What the hell do you think you're doing?'

Hetty dropped the polish and turned and through the open door saw Elizabeth, startled from sleep, rise from her chair and stumble forward, toppling down the steps into the garden. Then it was all confusion, Hetty and Mrs Peel running to pick her up, Havelock Hope standing, arms akimbo, shouting and swearing but making no attempt to help. Then Richard was there, taking his mother in his arms and carrying her into the house to place her on the couch in the hall.

'Shut up, Father,' he said, and amazingly Havelock Hope stopped shouting though he went on muttering that it was all Hetty's fault, she was as big a fool as her mistress.

'Shut up, Father,' Richard said again. 'If it's anyone's fault it is mine. *I* helped Mother down the stairs. Now don't you think we should be attending to her rather than shouting at each other?'

'I'm all right, son,' said Elizabeth shakily. She sat up and leaned against the arm of the couch, holding her head. 'I just got a bit of a shock. I was asleep, you see. The fresh air, I think. But I'm all right, no harm done, not to me anyway. Though one or two of the dahlias are looking a bit forlorn. You may as well pick them, Hetty, the stems are broken. Bring them up to my room, they're such a lovely colour. Richard, I think I'll go up now.'

48

Chapter 6

'It's a lovely day for the wedding,' commented Mrs Peel, and the group sitting round the table in the kitchen at Hope Hall nodded and murmured agreement – all except Sam whose mouth was too full of fried bread for him to murmur anything. Ethel was to marry her Bert at two o'clock in the afternoon and all the staff had the afternoon off to go to the wedding which was to be held in the stone church on the edge of the village.

Hetty looked at Ethel's empty chair. By, she thought, Ethel's going to be missed round here even though she's going no further than a mile or so. Havelock Hope had surprised them all by letting one of his tied cottages to the young couple. Hetty remembered the morning Mrs Hope had been downstairs; Mr Hope had called Hetty in to the study shortly afterwards. She had thought she was for it that day all right. But the master seemed to have forgotten all about the incident, he wanted to discuss something else altogether.

'Now then, Hetty,' he had said. 'You know Ethel is leaving us. I wondered if you could recommend anyone from your home town to replace her?'

Hetty thought immediately of Dorothy. Oh, wouldn't it have been grand to have Dorothy working in the same house? But Dorothy was gone ... A shaft of pain shot through her so that she couldn't answer for a moment. She stared at the carpet on the floor, seeing a piece of fluff by the leg of the desk; Ethel must have missed it this morning when she cleaned the study. Hetty dropped the hanky she

49

had been holding tightly in her hand and bent down to pick it up, surreptitiously picking up the fluff with it before Mr Hope saw it.

'Well, girl?'

He was impatient, the irritation there in his voice. Hetty swallowed. 'I haven't been home this year, sir, I don't know who is free. But I can write to my family and see if they know anybody.'

Mr Hope sighed. 'Oh, for goodness' sake, surely there's a lass there who would jump at the chance of a job?' He drummed his fingers on the desk. 'I've left it a bit late,' he said almost to himself. 'Look, Hetty, you can have the day off tomorrow, I'll give you your fare and you can go home and find someone. It will save me the bother of advertising.'

She gasped. 'In a day?'

Havelock Hope snorted. 'Good God, girl, this is the twentieth century. How long does it take to go into the next county?'

'I haven't had my holiday yet, sir.' Hetty had put it off all through summer, home wasn't the same without Cissy. Mam wasn't the same either. The last time Hetty had gone home Mam was very quiet and when Hetty had tried to kiss her she had turned her face away. And Mrs James, she looked straight through Hetty when they met in the street though at least she had stopped accusing her of being to blame for the accident.

'Well, we can't spare you for a week, not now. Go tomorrow and be back on Thursday. Two days will be enough, surely?' Havelock was saying.

'Yes, sir,' said Hetty. Though how was she going to let the family know she was coming? In the end she telephoned the post office in Morton Main and Mrs Atkinson, the postmistress, had grumbled about it but finally promised to send the boy up to Maggie Pearson's with a message.

Hetty didn't stay in Morton Main for the whole two days, she couldn't bear to, she felt like an unwelcome guest in the house where she had been born and brought up. Usually she sent her mother what she had managed to save out of her pay but this time, when Hetty offered her the two pounds ten shillings saved during the year, her mother just stared blankly.

'Best keep it,' said Maggie, and turned to open the oven door, checking the bread which she had checked only five minutes before.

'But why?' asked Hetty, startled. 'You could do with it, couldn't you? I know Dad's working, but . . .'

Maggie straightened up. 'I don't need your money,' she said. There was something in her voice which seared Hetty. She felt that she had done something offensive in offering her savings.

'Do you mean you don't want me to send any more either?' she asked.

'That's right.'

Hetty put the money in her pocket and walked to the door; she said no more. All she wanted to do was go. She had quickly found a girl, Havelock Hope had been right about that, there were plenty available. She had asked Sally Dunn who lived only a few doors away. Sally had just left school and jumped at the chance of a job, especially when Hetty would be there, someone she knew. So Sally Dunn was to arrive at Hope Hall on the Monday after Ethel's wedding.

Hetty made an excuse and travelled back to Yorkshire that same evening, stopping off in Saltburn-by-the-Sea. With the money her mother had rejected, she took a room in a small guesthouse in Ruby Street, on the top of the cliff where she could hear the roar of the waves as they gathered strength for the autumn storms. Next morning she walked along Marine Parade, deserted now the season was over, and sat down on a bench overlooking Huntcliffe with Old Saltburn tucked in beneath it, sheltering from the vast expanse of the sea. And there she allowed herself to cry: for Cissy and for herself and the childhood she had lost that winter's day.

'You're back then?' said Havelock Hope as he walked into the dining room that evening and noticed Hetty making up the fire beneath the ornate marble mantelshelf. 'Come on then, girl, did you have any success?' He had been away in Whitby all day and driven back over the moors in his

51

new Lagonda car. His cheeks were ruddy and bright against the silver of his hair.

'Yes, sir,' said Hetty. 'Her name is Sally Dunn and she will come a week on Monday.'

'I hope she's all right or I'll want to know the reason why,' warned Havelock, and sat down in a dining chair, spreading the evening paper over the table which was already set for the meal. He knocked over a wine glass so that it rocked and would have fallen if Hetty hadn't made a deft save. Havelock didn't appear to notice.

'Thank you, Hetty, for saving me the bother of finding another girl,' she said under her breath as she went back to the kitchen to help Mrs Peel serve the meal. 'Thanks I don't think!' But she was used to the master now. He was so uncouth in some ways and yet so sure of himself in others.

Hetty followed Ethel down the aisle in the little church, in an artificial silk dress she had made herself, using Mrs Oliver's sewing machine. 'Use it any time you like, Hetty,' Mrs Oliver had said, 'I don't have much use for it now. I'm too old, I can't be bothered.'

So Hetty had spent her free time in the little cottage, treadling away on the machine. Mrs Oliver had helped her with the cutting out and the fitting. The dress was rose pink and there was a lighter pink sash and round her neck she wore the small rope of artificial pearls which Bert had given her for a bridesmaid's gift.

Ethel looked lovely, she thought, pleased that she had gone into Whitby with her friend to choose the wedding gown. It was a creamy satin, full-length, and with a tiny train and a drape over one shoulder – very much in the mode, the salesgirl had assured them. A coronet of lilies-of-the-valley held the bridal veil on Ethel's head. She had had a Marcel wave only the day before and Hetty had combed it into place for her and fastened on the veil.

The organ rang out, played rather surprisingly well by Mr Jones, and as Bert stepped forward with Sam, his best man, Hetty took Ethel's bouquet of late roses. She noticed that the Hope family were there, even Matthew, though not Mrs

Hope, Hetty thought sadly. She was bedridden once again and the bottle had reappeared on her bedside table.

The reception was in the back room of the Moorcock Inn. Bert still hoped to take over a tenancy himself but for now he worked as a barman there. They ate ham and salad and the men drank ale with the meal and the women had a choice of lemonade or port wine. After a while Sam began to make eyes at Hetty and put his hand on her knee and let his gaze linger on the swell of her breast under the shiny material of her dress. She removed his hand and made an excuse to leave the room for a while, hoping he would cool down and get the message that she wasn't interested. But she had to come back when the speeches began and Ethel's father 'hoped all their troubles would be little ones', and Ethel blushed and the men roared with laughter. After that the remarks got wilder and the sexual references more pointed and at last Hetty managed to escape and go out into the autumn sunshine in the pub courtyard.

She walked over to the stone wall at the end and gazed out over the moors, enjoying the cool air for she felt a little light-headed after the glass of port wine she had been obliged to drink for the toasts. She moved into the lee of an outbuilding and leaned against the wall, feeling the roughness of the stone through her flimsy dress.

'Here you are then.'

Hetty jumped as Sam's voice cut into the quiet afternoon. He was standing by the corner of the building, swaying slightly, a glass of ale in his hand. His eyes were glassy and he nodded his head, grinning foolishly.

'Oh, Sam, go back inside and sit down before you fall down,' she said.

'Now you don't want me to go, not really,' he said, and lifted the glass and took a swig of beer, dribbling a little on his chin so that it splashed down on to his white shirt. 'Oops!' he said, and rubbed at it with the back of his hand.

'I do want you to go,' asserted Hetty. 'I think you've had enough to drink an' all.' She turned her back on him and gazed out over the moor. But Sam was not to be dismissed so easily. After a moment he put his hand on her shoulder and spun her round.

'I'll soon change your mind for you,' he said, slavering a little, his arms, strengthened by hard labour on the farm, slipping round her and holding her in a vice-like grip.

'Sam, let me go,' she said, not raising her voice, still sure she could keep control of the situation. Over his shoulder she could see where he had put down his glass of beer on the uneven top of the wall, balancing it precariously.

'I will when I'm ready,' he said, and bent his mouth to hers. She was overwhelmed with the stench of stale beer as he belched.

'Sam, let me go! I'm telling you, you'll be sorry . . .' Hetty said, louder now. She twisted her head to escape his searching lips and rasped her face on his badly shaven cheek. She tried to look over to the pub but somehow he had pushed her further behind the building and only a narrow strip of courtyard was visible. Suddenly, shockingly, his hand was on her breast, squeezing, pressing. Faintly she could hear the clip-clop of a horse. Oh, please God, she prayed in a split second, let whoever that is turn into the yard. But the clip-clopping faded away into the distance.

'Come on, Hetty, give us a bit of what you give Richard Hope,' Sam was saying, and she couldn't think what he was talking about – but then she wasn't thinking of anything except how to get away from the drunken beast who had hold of her. And still she didn't scream, didn't think of screaming. But she could get away, if only . . .

She stopped struggling and lifted her head as though giving in. 'All right, Sam,' she said, and he chuckled, relaxing, lifting one arm to the back of her neck – and in that instant she flung him away from her and he fell against the wall, knocking the beer glass off so that it shattered on the ground and beer splashed all over him. But Hetty didn't wait to see if he was all right. She ran out into the yard, pulling her dress together where his fingers had loosened the button at the neck.

Richard and Matthew were there, over the other side, by the back entrance to the pub. Evidently they had just arrived because Matthew's MG sports car was parked there. They looked at her, surprised, and Hetty stopped.

'Hetty,' said Richard. 'Are you all right?'

54

'Of course she is,' said Matthew.

Hetty felt dirty and dishevelled. She pulled her dress straight and ran her fingers through her hair, pushing it back from her forehead. She didn't look at Richard, she couldn't bear to. She wouldn't look at Matthew at all.

'Hetty?' Richard repeated.

She hesitated. If she said anything there was every likelihood that Sam would lose his job and where would he get another? Her childhood in Morton had shown her that for a man to lose his job was a terrible disaster. And after all, he hadn't really hurt her, had he?

'I'm all right,' she mumbled.

'Oh, dear, Richard, we seem to have interrupted something,' drawled Matthew, smiling sardonically. He was looking over her shoulder and as she turned she saw Sam stumbling across the yard, wisps of grass sticking to his brilliantined hair. There were beer stains all over his suit and shirt. He had grazed his cheek in his fall and blood had run down his jawline and dripped on to his collar.

Hetty wanted only to get away, not only from the amusement in Matthew's eyes but the unreadable look in Richard's. She walked past them to a door with a paper notice pinned to it reading 'Ladies'. It was a small outdoor lavatory with only a broken mirror on the whitewashed wall. She leaned against the door, trying to control her churned up feelings. The smell of disinfectant was the final straw. She bent forward and was violently sick into the bowl.

After a moment she wiped her mouth with a piece of hard scratchy toilet paper and pulled the chain. Peering at herself in the mirror, Hetty saw her face was pale but for one patch where it had rubbed against the stubble on Sam's chin. There was nothing she could do about that, she thought. She smoothed her hair behind her ear and, taking a deep breath, went back into the pub.

There was no sign of Sam, thank goodness. Richard and Matthew were standing by the bar, their backs to the room, and she prayed they wouldn't turn round and see her. Luckily they looked to be deep in an animated discussion about something.

'Where have you been?' asked Ethel. 'We're ready to go now, we've been waiting for you.'

'I just went out for a breath of fresh air,' Hetty replied.

Hetty climbed into bed that night, weary to her very bones and aching inside for her own folk. She couldn't sleep, the events of the day kept running through her mind ... the expression on Richard's face. Oh, she didn't care about Matthew, he could think what he liked. But Richard was different. He had been her friend, and now he wouldn't be. Ethel was gone, she had no one to confide in, not truly confide, tell all her thoughts. In the end she got out of bed and lit the candle and took paper and envelopes from the drawer. Pulling a blanket round her shoulders, she sat on the edge of the bed, feet dangling, and started to write, using a pencil for she couldn't afford to get ink on the sheets.

'Dear Gran,' she began, and chewed the end of her pencil. It was a long time since she had seen her gran, with not getting home so much this last year or the year before. She remembered how she had been used to pour out her troubles to her when she was little. But then, Gran had lived just up the street from them. When Granda died Gran had had to leave the colliery house and Morton Main and had moved five miles away to the other side of Auckland.

Hetty's brow creased as she tried to think what to say. Then she began to write, skirting round the subject of the family at home, concentrating on the wedding and how nice the church service had been though different from Chapel and describing her and Ethel's dresses in detail. And then she wrote down all her troubles of the day and how maybe they could have been her fault but she didn't think so, she hadn't led Sam on at all.

Hetty paused. She had heard something and it wasn't the usual rustling or creaking of the roof timbers. No, there was a step on the stairs. Suddenly she was aware that she was alone in the room, alone at the top of the house, and she had never been alone at night before. At home she had shared a bedroom with Cissy and here at Hope Hall there had always been Ethel.

'Don't be daft,' she murmured to herself. It was probably

56

the kitchen cat, prowling around looking for mice. Or if it was a person it wouldn't be a burglar, not up here, there was nothing to steal up here in the attics. But she put down her pencil and paper and scrambled under the bedclothes, pulling them up under her chin and staring at the door as it started to open.

'You're awake then, Hetty? Waiting for me, were you? You little witch, how did you know I would be coming?'

She heard the words but failed to take in their meaning. Surely this was a dream, a nightmare? She stared at Matthew Hope in the flickering light of the candle and shrank down into the bed even further.

'Go away!' she said. 'Go away. I'll tell your father about this.'

Matthew laughed softly. He sat down on the edge of the bed and cupped her chin with his hand. 'No, you won't, little witch. I know you. You're aching for it, do you think I can't tell? Now I'll just show you the difference between a boy and a man. Or a man and that peasant you were with this afternoon.' He pulled the bedclothes down to her waist and she jerked them back, holding them under her chin.

'Now don't be coy,' he said, 'I'm beginning to lose my patience. I've watched you flaunting yourself in front of Richard and me ever since I came home last month. Well, I don't know about Richard but I'm ready to oblige.'

'I didn't . . .' Hetty began, but Matthew had bent over her and put his mouth to hers, stopping her protest. His mouth was hard, pressing her lips bruisingly on to her teeth and she wriggled, trying to pull away from him.

'Oh, stop acting the innocent,' he snapped, lifting his head for a moment. 'Come on, Hetty, this can be fun for both of us, I don't like forcing a woman. Is it the light? I'll blow out the candle, that's it.'

As he sat up and reached over for the candlestick she managed to scramble out of bed and run for the door. Flinging it open, she was out on the landing which was lit only by a small window. But Hetty knew this part of the house so well, she raced for the stairs. Not fast enough, though. Matthew was behind her and caught her up, lifting

57

her off her feet, just as she reached the top of the main staircase.

'Not quick enough, my little witch,' he said, and buried his face in her neck. 'But you wanted to be caught, didn't you?' She kicked out with her bare feet and raised her hands to grab at his hair and pull him off her.

'Little bitch, not witch,' he said, but there was a savage amusement in his voice. And then the light came on on the landing below. For a minute neither of them noticed, they were so engrossed in their struggle. To Richard and his father, standing by the staircase gazing up at Matthew and Hetty with their arms around each other, they looked like two lovers, clinging to one another.

Chapter 7

'Get your things together. I don't want you in this house when I get back from Whitby,' said Havelock Hope. He held out a brown envelope to Hetty but she made no move to take it.

'But why? I haven't done anything,' she protested hopelessly. It was a phrase she had repeated over and over and no one in the house would listen to her, not even Elizabeth Hope. Hetty had tried to enter Elizabeth's room at nine o'clock as she regularly did but had found Mrs Peel barring her way.

'The mistress doesn't want you in here,' the housekeeper had said. She held on to the door with one hand and glanced behind into the darkened room before turning back to Hetty and hissing, 'Dirty bitch!'

Through the long sleepless night the only shred of comfort Hetty had been able to muster was that Elizabeth Hope would understand. Elizabeth and she were friends rather than mistress and servant, she would know Hetty wasn't the hussy that the master had called her. He had roared it out, there on the first landing, had fairly danced with rage until Richard had laid a restraining hand on his arm.

'Father, you'll wake everyone,' he had said.

'I don't bloody care if I wake the dead! There now, what do you think of that?' Havelock had answered and shook his arm free. 'A whore, that's what she is! Don't think I haven't seen her making sheep's eyes at you either, and now she's after Matthew. Well, she's not getting either one of my sons, I'll see you both in hell first, I swear to God I will.'

59

The words had burned into Hetty's brain and she'd lifted her head and taken a step forward. 'I didn't do anything,' she cried. 'I don't want—'

'Get out of my sight or I'll throw you out on to the moor in your nightgown,' Havelock interrupted.

'Matthew, tell him I didn't do anything,' she pleaded. But even as she said it she knew that there would be no help from him.

'Not this time, more's the pity,' he said, and grinned. His father took hold of him by the shoulder and, big as Matthew was, threw him down the stairs so that he cannoned into the wall on one side and back to the banister which he grabbed hold of and by some miracle arrested his fall.

'Get out of my sight!' yelled Havelock. Matthew opened his mouth in protest but thought better of it and went into his own room, banging the door behind him. Havelock turned back to the girl, standing with her arms crossed over her thin nightie, trembling with shock and humiliation.

Hetty looked at Richard, praying he would say a word in her defence. Surely he knew none of this was her fault? But the scene in the courtyard of the Moorcock that afternoon flashed through her mind and she could tell that he too was thinking of it. Turning, she walked back to her room. There was nothing more to say.

'I'll see you in the morning, girl,' Havelock shouted after her.

So here she was standing before his desk like a schoolgirl in the headmaster's study, and she knew there was nothing to be done at all. She held out her hand for the envelope. It was very light. For a moment panic struck her. She had three weeks' pay due, was she not even to get that? Havelock interpreted her expression correctly and smiled sardonically.

'Don't worry, there's two pounds in there. I don't want you hanging round here because you haven't the fare home. And don't forget to leave your uniform when you go. I made a mistake asking you to get another girl, she's likely to be no better than you are. But she's coming now and she can have a month's trial. I'm a fair man, I'll say that.' He rose to his feet and walked over to the door, holding it open. 'That's all. I don't want to see your face again.'

Hetty walked past him, her head up, determined not to let him see how hurt and humiliated she was. She went up to her room without looking back and packed her straw box. She took off the uniform and laid it on the bed. One last look round the attic bedroom and she was ready.

There was no one about when she went down the stairs. She hesitated a moment before taking the main staircase to the front hall. There were sounds in the kitchen, voices talking, the men were in for their mid-morning break. She could go through the kitchen and out of the back door, past the stable and on to the Olivers' cottage. Mrs Oliver had been good to her, maybe she would understand. But no, she didn't want to get the Olivers into trouble with the master.

Hetty thought of going into the village and seeing Ethel but she couldn't, not when it was just the morning after her wedding. She would write to her. But write from where? Where could she go with only two pounds in her pocket? She thought of the letter she had written to her gran, written but not posted. She thought of home, Morton Main. But even if home had been as it always used to be, she couldn't go back there, shame her mother and father before everyone.

Hetty had put her box down on the floor at the bottom of the stairs; now she picked it up and took it to the front door. The door was unlocked and she slipped out, closing it behind her.

As she walked through the orchard to the side of the property, Richard came out of the stables and suddenly they were face to face. He stood still, his face set, and gazed at her. He hadn't been able to put her out of his mind since that scene on the staircase, he couldn't believe it had been what it seemed. Yet she had been in Matthew's arms, dressed only in her nightgown, he could see no sign that she was struggling against his brother. The thought brought a sense of depression and loss which was almost physical and it swelled within him now.

Hetty shrank into herself when she saw his face, so cold, so condemning, she thought. 'Richard . . .' she faltered and looked about her, desperate to get away so she didn't have to see it. She could feel her face flush, her limbs trembled.

Richard read her feelings. 'You may well look away, can't face me, I suppose,' he said bitterly.

'No!' she cried. 'It's not like that! I didn't do anything! It was Matthew who . . .'

He laughed and the sound wasn't like Richard at all, but something which reminded her of his brother. A spark of anger lit in her and she flung her head up and shouted at him. All the pain and humiliation, the shame and degradation she felt she had suffered at the hands of his father and brother was there in her voice.

'Don't believe me then, I never expected you to! You are a *Hope* after all, why should you be different from the rest?' Turning, she ran to the gate and out on to the moor. She ran, humping her basket box so that it slapped painfully against her legs until she could run no more. Richard took a step after her, almost called out to her, worried about where she would go, if she had enough money. But he stopped. She had family after all, she would be all right. He crossed the yard to the kitchen door, the sad, lost feeling which had filled him since the night before, overwhelming him. He stopped at the back door. Maybe he wouldn't go in to breakfast, he wasn't hungry anyway.

Hetty walked along the track, head up, looking straight ahead. She would go to Saltburn, she thought suddenly, Saltburn-by-the-Sea. Surely she would get work there, in among all those hotels and boarding houses? Though she didn't have a reference, she reminded herself with some misgiving. Still, she would do anything: kitchen skivvying, casual work. At least she had some money in her pocket, enough to get her a bed for a while.

The thought of the jewel streets radiating out from the station to the cliff top beckoned her. Maybe she could start again there? And when she was back on her feet she would get in touch with the family, try to make it up to Mam for Cissy. It was only a couple of hours later, when she came to the main Guisborough to Whitby road which ran across the moor and she was tired and cold and hungry, that she remembered that this was the off-season in the seaside resorts. She would be very lucky indeed to find work in a hotel at this time of year.

Matthew Hope strode across the moor, his hands thrust deep in his trouser pockets, his overcoat open and blowing behind him in the wind. His trilby hat was pulled down over his forehead and below it his face glowered out at an equally glowering sky. A few spots of rain spattered down, the beginnings of a storm, but Matthew ignored the weather.

'My God, I need a drink,' he muttered to himself and stopped walking to glance around, hardly knowing where exactly he was. That was the trouble, he thought, that girl had got right under his skin. Why the hell could she not have just given him what he wanted? Maybe then he could have gone on his way, forgotten her like all the others.

He would never have thought of her if it hadn't been for the fact that there was no other choice at all on this wild moor, forsaken by God and man. If only the old tyrant would be more forthcoming with the wherewithal he would never have to go back there again. What was a fellow to do when there were only the maids to play with? Jenny, now, she'd been willing enough. Pity she hadn't been more careful, silly bitch. She'd thought she could trap him, though. Not likely!

Matthew decided on a path which he thought led to an inn he knew, one where the landlord took no heed of licensing laws. That's what he needed, a warm pub and a glass or two of brandy. The rain was coming down in sheets now, the wind gusting from all quarters, or so it seemed. Oh, well, he reckoned it could only be a mile or so to the Fox and Hounds.

Sitting by the log fire in the bar, watching the steam rising from his coat which was flung over the opposite chair, Matthew stretched out his long legs under the table and sipped from his brandy glass. He let his thoughts wander as the spirit trickled down his throat but they always returned to Hetty Pearson and how she had felt, soft in his arms, with nothing between his hands and her flesh but the thin material of her nightie.

Just another lass, he told himself, slipping from the

elevated English he had learned at school and Oxford into the local idiom. But who would have thought she would have changed so much in only a few years? He remembered the thin, pale, scrap of a girl she had been when she first came to Hope Hall. That was just after Jenny ... Matthew finished his brandy and shouted for another. The pub was empty but for a crony of the landlord's who was sitting at the bar discussing football with him. Both men stopped talking and glanced at Matthew then at each other. The landlord poured the brandy and brought it over to the table.

'That'll be two and a tanner,' he said, standing unsmiling waiting for his money.

'All right, all right,' Matthew snarled and fumbled in his trouser pocket for the money, bringing out three shillings. 'Keep the change.'

'Best not. You might be in want of it one of these nights,' the landlord said smoothly, and sauntered back to the bar.

Matthew glared after him. Who the hell did he think he was talking to? Maybe he had been short once or twice but the man had always got his money, hadn't he? But really, he wasn't in the mood for a fight, and anyway, there were two of them. He picked up the sixpence change from the table and put it in his pocket.

Hetty. Oh, she was a witch, that one. He got into a fever just thinking about her, that dark hair and those eyes. He remembered the feel of her lips: soft, enticing. Except that she had twisted away from him, he thought. Did she like that farm lad Sam better? He couldn't believe it. Yet she had been fastening her dress when she came out from behind the wall of the pub courtyard, hadn't she? Maybe she was just playing hard to get, like that one in Oxford, the one who had been the cause of his being sent down. Funny, he couldn't even remember her name now ...

Matthew sipped his brandy, staring moodily at the smouldering log in the grate. He supposed there would be hell to pay when he got back to the Hall. When Father came back from Whitby at least. There wasn't much chance of getting the old man to pay his debts now. He'd just have to stay in Yorkshire until he could get himself back into his father's good books.

64

There was still Mother, though. Did she have any money left of her own that Father hadn't yet got hold of? The thought was interesting anyway. Galvanised by it, Matthew threw back the last of his brandy and got to his feet. Reaching over the table, he took his topcoat and pulled it on, damned uncomfortable though it was, being still so wet.

The landlord and his friend watched as he strode out of the pub without so much as a glance in their direction let alone a goodbye.

'Arrogant bugger, isn't he?' said the friend.

'Arrogant nowt, that's what he is,' said the landlord.

It had begun to rain, coming down in buckets, soaking Hetty to the skin and her box too. But she was close to the turnoff for Moorsholm. If she could get there, surely she would get shelter, maybe something for her dinner at the village shop? She walked down the road, little more than a track, her feet squelching in the puddles it was impossible to avoid. A car was coming down the lane. Hetty looked about her; the track was so narrow she had to go on to the grass and press against the stone wall of a field to allow the car to pass. It wasn't until it was almost up to her and slowing down that she recognised it. Matthew's car, she thought dismally, the MG in which he roared about the roads, usually to and from Harrogate or Whitby.

She turned and pushed past the car, catching the wing mirror with her arm, almost taking with her the indicator finger which was jutting out and blinking yellow. She was in no mood for him, no mood at all. Besides she no longer worked for the Hopes; she didn't have to talk to him, be civil to him.

Matthew stared at her, the water dripping from her, her hair covered by a sodden scarf, her clothes plastered to her body. She was wet enough to have been fished out of the sea just a mile or so to the east. He couldn't believe it when he saw her. He had been driving around aimlessly in the rain. It suited his mood somehow. He'd tramped home after he'd left the pub and changed into dry clothes, made a sandwich of the crab salad Mrs Peel had put out for him in the dining room. His mother was asleep, he found, when

65

he went up to her room. It was impossible to waken her. Damn, he'd have to try later. He'd drunk some whisky from his father's decanter and then had gone out again and jumped into his car.

Bedraggled she was, he thought, half smiling. Yet in spite of it she was beautiful, her cheeks red with the cold, her eyes sparkling through the rain. Sparkling with anger, he thought, his grin widening, anger at him because he hadn't defended her before his father, told the truth. She had some spunk, that one, he thought, feeling an almost proprietary pride in her. He leaned over and opened the door on the passenger side.

'Get in, Hetty, I'll give you a lift,' he said. She did her best to ignore him. He called again: 'Hetty!' After a moment he got out of the car and went after her.

'Come on, Hetty, you've made your point. I'm sorry I didn't say anything to my father. But I'm in trouble enough with him, you've no idea how he went on after that business in Oxford—' He stopped abruptly as he realised that telling her about his escapade with a girl in Oxford was not going to help his cause. 'Anyway, come on, get in the car. I only mean to take you wherever it is you're going.'

He took hold of her arm and she stopped walking. At that moment the rain redoubled its ferocity and the wind howled through gaps in the hedge, blowing muddy water in waves across the road and spattering them both with dirty brown splashes. Hetty looked down at her coat. What a sight it was! How would anyone even consider hiring her to do anything at all, looking a scarecrow as she did? It was the final straw. She began to cry for the first time since this nightmare had begun, tears running down her cheeks and vying with the raindrops.

'Come on, Hetty, sit in the car. At least the hood's up and the seat is dry.' Matthew felt a rush of unaccustomed tenderness, surprising himself. He put an arm around her shoulders and led her to the car, sitting her down and closing the door after her. Hurrying round to the other side, he climbed into the driving seat and set off, before she could change her mind and get out.

Hetty's mind was numb, she couldn't think straight. She

66

searched in her pocket for a handkerchief, finding only the small scrap of one she had hemmed and embroidered herself, sending away to *Woman's Weekly* for the embroidery transfer which was on offer. It was for show, not for use, she thought ruefully, it was sopping wet in no time. But soon Matthew was handing over a large white square, one of those she herself had washed and ironed. Ages ago, it seemed now.

Hetty looked at him. 'Why are you helping me?' she asked, the bluntness of her question matched by the suspicion in her eyes.

He smiled. 'Why not?'

They were coming up to Moorsholm, the first cottages were just around the next bend. 'Let me out here, I want to get out,' she demanded.

Matthew looked down at her. 'Don't be a silly girl now,' he said. 'There's nothing here for you. Where are you heading, anyway?' He drove straight through the village. She watched the post office go by, there wasn't a soul about the place. Oh, well, she thought. He owes me something. But if he thinks he'll get what he wants in return for the ride, he's sadly mistaken!

Chapter 8

They drove through Brotton and on to the Saltburn road, the water streaming down the windscreen and splashing up on either side of the car and the wheels ploughing through puddles as Matthew swerved from side to side, his eyes more on Hetty than the road ahead. He laughed softly as he showed off his driving skills, watching her to see her reaction, the effects of the spirits he had drunk earlier in the day making him falsely sure of himself and his ability.

Hetty was oblivious to it all, lost in her own miserable thoughts, until, as they swerved along the narrow road and dropped steeply down to the left-hand turn where the road ran parallel with the sea wall and the waves came pounding up the beach to meet them, the surf rose high and roared so that she was jerked into awareness of the danger.

'Matthew! Slow down or we'll be into the sea!' she cried and pushed back in her seat as though she could restrain the car with her own strength. Just in front of them a brewery van trundled along the beach road and she had a brief glimpse of the driver as he turned his head and stared up at them and then was obscured by the rain.

'Matthew!'

The van was almost on top of them, green-painted it was, she saw as in a dream, and then it was past and Matthew had swung round it sharply left, missing the road and mounting the kerb of the promenade, coming to a halt inches from the sea wall.

He laughed. 'Had you worried there, girl,' he said. 'I bet

you thought we were for it, eh? Though I say it myself, I'm a hell of a driver, aren't I?'

Hetty didn't reply, for the minute she hadn't the breath. She sat up straight and looked out of the side window at the front of the Ship Inn. The van driver had stopped and was climbing out of his cab. He lifted his fist and shook it at the MG, mouth opening and closing as he took a few steps towards them before halting as though unsure whether to come on or not. Whatever he was shouting was drowned by the roar of the sea and the wind and the pounding of the surf. Carefully Hetty opened the car door and got out, standing for a moment as she braced herself against the wind. She reached for her box and pulled it out. Matthew put out a hand to stop her but she was too quick for him.

'Hey! Where are you going? Oh, come on, Hetty, get back in, don't be a fool. It was all right, nothing was going to happen. It was just a bit of fun. Do you know, I could have been a racing driver?' He grinned at her, his expression saying it all. She was a silly girl, frightened by nothing, he knew what he was doing.

'I'll walk from here.' She glared at him.

Matthew lost his grin. 'Get back in here when you're told,' he snapped. 'Now stop messing me around and do as I say, or I'll get out and make you. Who the hell—'

It was Hetty's turn to grin before she banged the door shut and headed along the promenade, crossing when she got to the cliff and going up on the other side of the road, taking the footpath behind the red-painted bathing huts, shuttered and all forlorn-looking. For she had seen the van driver make a move towards Matthew, a burly man not much taller than his prey but twice his weight. Judging by his expression his rage was mounting the more as Matthew ignored him. He stamped up to the MG and wrenched open the door. She heard his first words as he grabbed hold of Matthew by the throat, pulling him out of his seat as though he were a child, bending him over the sea wall.

'You bloody maniac!' he shouted. 'I've a good mind to—'

What he was going to do was lost to Hetty as she made for the footpath up the cliff. She looked back once as she passed the bathing huts and the two men were still there, struggling, and even as she watched a particularly strong wave flung spray into the air high over them and dropped on them with a force which made them stagger so that one of them fell. She hesitated. Were they all right? Oh, but of course they were, it wasn't a real fight, the van driver was just venting his feelings after the shock he'd got from the near crash. She turned back to the steep path, the wind at her back, pushing her on.

She stood at the top at last and looked back as she caught her breath. There was no sign of Matthew, the car was still askew on the promenade. Was Matthew all right? She hesitated for a moment. Oh, of course he was, he must have got back into his car, out of the rain.

Hetty changed her box to the other hand and crossed the road to Milton Street. She walked along it, not knowing what she was going to do or even where she was going. She came to a newsagent's and paused. There were notices in the window, advertisements, handwritten. For jobs perhaps, she thought, hope stirring in her, or maybe rooms to let.

The smell of fish and chips wafted to her and her stomach rumbled. It had been ages since the breakfast she had been unable to eat and she'd had no dinner. Before she did anything else she would have to have something to eat. But she couldn't afford to spend her money on fish and chips, no matter how hungry she was, she told herself. Even so, the fish shop was there, just a few doors away, and she couldn't stop herself from walking towards it and peering into the window. There were a couple of tables near the door covered with shiny red-checked oilcloth. A man was sitting at one of them, a plate in front of him with a huge battered fish on it, so huge the tail hung over the side of the plate. The chips which covered what was left of the plate stood in a golden crispy mound and Hetty was lost.

There was a notice on the wall she saw as she opened the door, and the bell clanged and the woman behind the counter looked up and smiled.

'Good afternoon, love,' she said, 'what weather, eh?' in the time-honoured way of starting a conversation. 'Come away in and shut the door, the draught's summat awful.

Now then, what'll you be having? You look as though you could do with something hot inside you.'

'I'll . . . I'll just have a pennorth of chips, thank you,' said Hetty. A pennorth of chips, and maybe tuppence for a cup of tea and bread, she could afford. But the notice said it was threepence for a piece of cod and fourpence for haddock. She put her box down by the empty table nearest the door and walked up to the counter. 'An' maybe a cup of tea and some bread and butter?'

The woman nodded understandingly. 'You sit down, pet, take off your coat and hang it up on a peg there. I'll bring it to you.'

There were more notices on a board by the row of pegs and Hetty studied them as she hung up her dripping coat. They were things for sale mostly – a wardrobe, a wedding dress, 'worn once only' – but no jobs, and no rooms to let either. She sat down at the table, facing the window where she could keep an eye out for Matthew, just in case he should be following her. The man at the next table looked up from his meal only for the space of time it took him to nod a greeting.

Her plate came piled high with chips and they were covered with scrapings, the bits of batter which dropped from the fish in the pan. There was even a small piece of fish and two slices of bread and butter. Well, no, Hetty reasoned to herself, not real butter, it was margarine, but all the same . . . 'Emm . . . I can't afford fish,' she said, looking up at the woman when she came back with her tea.

'No, well, you see, there won't be anyone else in to eat it now and I can't abide warmed up fish meself so I'm not serving it up tonight. Besides, it'll do you good, lass, you look as though you could do with it.' She eyed Hetty's box. 'Lost your place, have you?'

The woman's question was so unexpected and so accurate that it took Hetty off guard and she almost lost her composure. She stared at her plate and nodded.

'I thought as much. Blooming bosses, who do they think they are? Fancy turning a lass out in this weather!' She stood aside as the customer at the next table finished his meal and rose to his feet.

'Afternoon, Alice,' he said and rushed to the door, snatching a gaberdine raincoat from a peg and pulling it on even as he went.

'Afternoon, Mr Hutchins,' the woman said and turned back to Hetty. 'You look like a decent lass,' she observed, 'go on, eat up your dinner. You'll feel better after that.'

'Yes. Thank you,' said Hetty, and bent her head to her plate. A woman came in and Alice, as the man had called her, put fresh fish in the fryer, and the fat sizzled and smoked and the fug in the cafe thickened but Hetty didn't care. She cleared her plate and drank the strong sweet tea and the customer departed with a newspaper-wrapped parcel. Hetty sat on, making the tea last as long as she could, watching the raindrops run down the window and join into a tiny rivulet at the base.

'You don't know of any rooms to let, do you?' she asked at last, for Alice was leaning over the counter watching her.

She frowned in thought and shook her head. 'I don't, love,' she admitted. 'Here, I'll fetch you another cup of tea.' She picked up the large brown teapot and carried it to the table.

'No, no . . .' stammered Hetty.

'It's all right, it's on the house,' she said comfortably, and she paused before continuing. 'How old are you, love? If you don't mind me asking, that is?'

'Nineteen.'

'Are you really? You don't look it.'

'Well, I am. I've been working at the place I am now for nearly five years. Well, the place I was,' she added, remembering.

'If you were there for that long you can't have been a bad worker,' remarked Alice, looking thoughtful. Hetty knew Alice was curious to know why she had been dismissed, and also why she didn't go home to her folks, but she didn't comment. After a minute Alice went back behind her counter.

Hetty rose to her feet reluctantly and pulled on her coat. Picking up her box, she thanked the woman and went out into the street. The newsagent's window was full of cards, a few of them for rooms though most were articles for sale.

72

She began to feel more hopeful. Oh, surely she would get a room by the end of the afternoon, maybe even a job? A sports car turned into the street and she slipped inside the shop just in case it was Matthew and stood peering anxiously out between the cards. The car was green, a stranger sitting at the wheel, and she let out a sigh of relief.

'You want something?' asked the man behind the counter.

'Well . . . I was looking at the cards, I'm after a room.'

He looked her up and down. 'Plenty there. You read them from the outside, though,' he said, but his smile robbed his words of any ill will.

'Yes. Sorry.'

Hurriedly she went out, the bell tinkling as she closed the door behind her. The rain had stopped and, miraculously, the sun was coming out. She memorised a few addresses, at least she had a fair memory, she thought, and set off round the corner into Pearl Street. The road descended gently to the top of the cliff which bordered the beach and beyond she could see the sea sparkling, white waves rushing in towards the shore. Idly she wondered how the world could be round if she could see them when the cliff was so much higher than the sea, then she forgot about it as she turned into the narrow garden path which led to the front door of the first of her addresses.

By five o'clock her main worry was over; at least she had a room, a tiny attic room in Diamond Street, the third one she had tried. There was space only for a narrow bed, a chair and chest of drawers, but there was a curtained-off space in the corner where she could hang her best dress and coat. But, best of all, it overlooked the sea: she could see the pier and Huntcliff and even some of the fishing boats pulled up on the beach outside the Ship Inn.

Hetty finished unpacking her box and took out the note-paper and envelopes which were at the bottom. The letter to her gran too, she still hadn't posted it. Now she would have to write home and give Mam her new address. Not that she would care, Hetty thought sadly. The forlorn feeling rose in her, the one which always lay just below the surface of her thoughts ever since Cissy . . . No good thinking like that, no good at all. The best thing to do was go out and look for work. It was teatime already but places would still be open.

Perhaps it was because she was hungry again that she was drawn towards the kitchens of hotels and restaurants. She hadn't much hope of finding work in them but perhaps if she left her name and address now she had one, they would think of her should anyone be needed. Sixteen shillings she had paid her landlady, a month in advance, and a large chunk from her meagre store of money. In fact, one of her two pounds had gone already. She *had* to earn some money.

It was sheer luck that she approached the kitchen door of the George Hotel on Marine Parade just as a small figure dashed out, almost bumping into her.

'An' don't come back 'ere if you know what's good for you!' a loud angry voice shouted. 'Get the hell away from Saltburn before I have the law on you!' A man stood in the doorway dressed in a white apron and floppy chef's hat, his face red with fury.

The girl turned and shook her fist at him, though Hetty could see she took care to keep well out of his reach and was ready to dart away should she need to. 'Have the law on me? On *me*? Just because I ate a leftover chop which wasn't fit to eat anyroad? It's you that robs the customers blind, you thieving . . .'

He stepped out of the door and she retreated a few steps. 'Fit to eat or not, it's the last food you'll pinch from my kitchen! Now be off wi' you, or I'll give you a thrashing you won't forget. Bloody dishwasher! Not content wi' your supper, you have to pinch enough food for the whole day.'

'Did you hear that? Did you? Did you?' the girl appealed to Hetty. 'By, I'll fetch the polis I will. I will! I'll—' But the man was coming after her, raising his hand, and she fled round the corner of the hotel to the front and raced along Marine Parade, Hetty could hear her screeching fading away into the distance.

'An' what do you want, standing there gawping?' demanded the chef.

'I was looking for work, casual work'll do . . . washing up, anything,' stammered Hetty, standing well back from him just in case his anger should spill over on to her.

'Aye, well, it just so happens I could do wi' some help, now that cheeky young monkey's gone. Good riddance too. She's been eating us out of house an' home. Mind, I wouldn't be at all surprised if the lass has a tapeworm, but whatever, I can't afford to keep it for her. Well, come inside, let's have a proper look at you. I haven't got all night, you know, there's customers in the dining room.'

So within ten minutes Hetty was standing beside an enormous sink washing pots and pans and in between running to fetch and carry for the chef. It was only three hours' work, casual, no guarantee it would be every night, but it paid sixpence an hour and would keep her until something better turned up, especially now her lodging was paid for.

Mr Jordan, for that was the chef's name, wasn't a bad boss in spite of first impressions, Hetty realised. In fact, the rest of the kitchen staff and the waiters joked and laughed with him all evening.

She walked back to Diamond Street and her new home along the promenade after the washing up was done and the dishcloths washed and hung out to dry, the floor swept and mopped. The rain had blown away; down below the cliff she could hear the sea, quieter now. The only other people about seemed to be young couples, hand in hand or with their arms around each other, on their way home from the dance at the Alexandra Hotel, she fancied. Briefly she wondered what it would be like to be courting a lad, loving a lad who loved her too, someone like Richard.

What a fool she was! He wouldn't want her, especially after the events of last night. Last night? It was only twenty-four hours since it happened, she could hardly believe it. How miserable she had been this morning, how frightened of setting out on her own with nowhere to go and no job. Why, she had almost gone with Matthew Hope. If it hadn't been for that near-accident with the car she might have done. On impulse, Hetty walked over the grass to a vantage point where she could see the coast road, the place where the car had crashed into the sea wall. There was nothing to see, the van had gone. For a moment she wondered whether Matthew was all right, that van driver had been so angry . . . But of course he would be, she would have heard else.

'Hey, little lass, what's a nice girl like you doing out on your own? Want to get in here with us and we'll show you a good time?'

Hetty jumped. A car was crawling along the kerb, three young lads sitting there, grinning at her. She could smell the beer on their breath even though she was yards away.

'Howay, lovey, you want nowt on your own. Come for a ride, you can take your pick. Jack now, he's the handsome one, but don't be taken in by—'

'Leave me alone! Go on, or I'll call the polis!' Hetty found her voice and yelled at them. But she wasn't frightened, rather she'd been startled, she hadn't heard the car's approach. They were just a gang of boys from Middlesbrough on a night out.

'Aw, come on—'

Hetty ran across the road behind them to the entrance to Diamond Street. She was almost home now anyway. Inserting her key in the front door, she heard the car revving as they gave up and went in search of someone more willing. She was grinning to herself as she went upstairs, happier than she had been all day.

Chapter 9

'Did you see how there was a fellow washed up on the beach along by Hazel Grove?' Mr Jordan was asking one of the waiters. 'A right battering he'd had an' all. His head bashed in and his clothes in rags on him. They don't know whether he was washed off the deck of a boat or what. It was in the *Evening Gazette*, did you not see it?'

Bob the waiter said something in reply but Hetty couldn't hear him. Her hands stilled in the soapy water, still grasping a burnt-on oven dish. Her over-fertile imagination brought vivid pictures to mind. Could it be Matthew? If he had been stunned yesterday morning and then the sea had carried him out, he could have been washed back further along the beach towards Marske. She should have made sure he was all right, she thought. That van driver . . .

'Come on, lass, get on with it, there's another lot ready to do and nowhere to put them,' grumbled Mr Jordan. 'No time for day-dreaming here.'

'Yes, sorry.'

Hetty began scrubbing away at the dish, her head bent. No, of course it couldn't have been Matthew, she told herself. If it had been, the car would still have been there. Unless . . . unless the van driver shifted it, got rid of the evidence. She put the dish on the wooden draining board and picked up another. She had wondered why Matthew hadn't come after her. After all, it wasn't like him to give up just like that. All day yesterday she had been looking out for him, ready to dodge out of sight. And that van driver had been so enraged he'd looked capable of anything. Surely not murder though?

But he might have killed Matthew by accident, not really meant to go that far ... Hetty's imagination was running riot now and her imaginings could so easily be the truth. She carried on with the dishes, dipping them in the water, scrubbing away at burnt-on bits, rinsing them clean, and yet hardly knowing what she was doing. She felt that everything she touched turned into a disaster, why should this be any different?

Later on, when the work was finished and the staff were sitting round the newly scrubbed table eating the spaghetti Bolognese which the chef had made in an effort to extend his menu but which none of the customers had ordered, she casually picked up his copy of the *Gazette*. There on the front page was a picture of the beach by Hazel Grove and an article about the man who had been washed up there. There was nothing additional to what Mr Jordan had said; the police had no idea who the man was.

'Do you mind if I have my paper?' asked Mr Jordan, and Hetty handed it over. He gave her a keen glance. 'What's the matter with you? You're very solemn. Lost a shilling and found a penny?'

Hetty summoned a smile. 'Just a bit tired. I think I'll be on my way. Goodnight.' She abandoned the spaghetti and got to her feet.

'Goodnight. By the way, I won't be needing you until Friday. Not many in the hotel and only a few bookings for the evenings. Everybody's broke this time of year, I reckon.'

Hetty's heart plummeted. Friday! That was three nights without pay, what was she going to do? She walked home along the front miserably. She had to find something else, she had to! She thought about going home to Morton Main. The old, aching sense of loss, the terrible home-sickness, surged through her. Tears sprang to her eyes, blinding her. But she couldn't go. How could she explain losing her job? Dad might understand, he would put his trust in her. But Mam ... surely after these years since Cissy had died she was getting over the pain, surely she didn't still blame Hetty for taking the little girl out on the sledge that day? Hetty sighed and wiped her eyes. The wind blew bitterly cold off the North Sea, straight from the Arctic and Russia, Mr

Jordan said. If she thought any more about home the tears would freeze her eyelids together. Tucking her head down in her collar, she quickened her steps to Diamond Street.

And then there was the worry about Matthew . . .

Matthew was sprawled before the fire in the drawing room of Hope Hall, drinking whisky and soda. Richard sat opposite him, staring into the fire. Their father had retired early, saying he would sit with his wife for a while.

'Your mother isn't well this evening, I don't want you to disturb her.' Though he didn't say so, they all knew that Elizabeth had wept when he'd told her Hetty had been dismissed.

Richard was thinking about Hetty and his mother and how she hadn't been out of her room since the maid went. There was no doubt about it, Hetty had been good for her. Why, they had even been planning a trip to Harrogate when the weather improved. Of course that was all forgotten now. Richard himself had had to make a journey to the chemist's for his mother's medicine even though he had serious misgivings about it.

He glanced over at Matthew. His brother's face was flushed, his mouth slack, he'd dribbled some of his drink down the front of his shirt. All right for him, thought Richard, he hadn't lost his home and livelihood as Hetty had. What on earth did these girls see in his brother? he wondered. He really had thought Hetty was different but in the end she had been just like all the rest, and the knowledge of it was bitter.

The door opened and Sally Dunn came in. A thin slip of a girl, she reminded Richard of Hetty when she had first come to the Hall, four years ago, or was it five? He sighed. No doubt she was back with her family now, looking for work. Though she would have trouble, not having any references. He wondered what she would do. Truth was he was worried about her. He wished he had spoken to her when she was leaving, made absolutely sure she was all right. He sighed and stretched his legs in front of him, looked at his glass with distaste and put it down on the low table by his side.

Matthew was watching Sally as she bent over the fire, pulling the embers together and adding logs. He was frowning.

'Not like that, girl, don't be so bloody useless,' he snapped, and Sally jumped, the tongs in her hand knocking a log so that it fell to the hearth with a shower of hot ash. He snatched the tongs from her and mended the fire himself. 'Now clean that mess up. I suppose you're only used to coal fires, coming from Durham?' He said 'Durham' sneeringly and she flushed and opened her mouth to reply, but instead closed it again and picked up the hearth brush and shovel and swept up the ashes.

'Mucky, coaly Durham,' said Matthew, seeing he had upset her, a gleam of interest coming to his eyes as he continued baiting her.

'Leave her alone, Matthew, she's just a kid,' said Richard. 'Go on, Sally, we won't want anything else tonight, you can go to bed now.'

She nodded to him and mumbled a goodnight. She left the room with her head held high, though.

'Well, a girl like that, she's not worth her keep,' commented Matthew. He had sunk down into the chair again and held his whisky glass to his chest. 'There's nothing else to do in this hole anyway.'

'You could leave the maids alone at least. Especially a little girl like that.'

'Yes? And what about you? You're not exactly blameless in that department, little brother. I could see what was going on between you and Hetty.'

'There was nothing going on except in your dirty mind!' snapped Richard. 'If you had kept your hands off her she would still be here. She was working wonders with Mother, you know how good she was with her.'

'Good in bed too,' Matthew said, glancing maliciously at his brother. 'So you mean to say you really didn't have a go? Well, you missed a treat, I can tell you—'

Richard started to his feet. 'Shut your dirty mouth, I don't believe a word of it!' He stood over Matthew's chair, eyes flashing, fists opening and closing.

'Fisticuffs now, is it?' Matthew jeered. 'Don't be a fool,

Richard, I could thrash you with one hand tied behind my back. But I'm not going to fight over a maid. Though I have to admit she's no ordinary skivvy. Who would have thought that plain, thin little mouse we first saw would grow into a beauty like that? She's really got under my skin. I'll have her if it's the last thing I do . . .'

Richard forced himself to calm down. He went over to the window and drew the heavy curtain back, staring out over the dark moor. The moon appeared and disappeared between scudding clouds, a ring of frost surrounding it. Then he turned back to his brother.

'Does that mean you know where she is?' he asked.

'Where who is?' Matthew was being deliberately perverse. 'Oh, you mean Hetty Pearson? And why are you so interested, little brother? I thought you said there had been nothing between you?'

'There wasn't.' Richard looked impatient. What was the use of talking to Matthew when he was in this sort of mood? 'I'm thinking of Mother,' he said wearily. 'She would like to know Hetty is all right.'

'Well, I don't know where she is,' said Matthew, 'and I'm altogether sick of the subject.' He scowled into his glass.

Richard was sure he was lying but knew he was going to get nothing out of him on the subject, not now at least. 'I'm off to bed,' he said abruptly and went out of the room.

Matthew sat on, staring into the fire. Even though it was more than a week ago now, he still got furiously angry when he thought of that day in Saltburn, that oaf of a van driver daring to lay hands on *him*, Matthew Hope. Oh, but he had made the man pay! He remembered the feel of the stones and sand on the beach, the shock of the freezing cold water, the surprising strength of it. Most of all he remembered the humiliation rather than the pain when that lout had knocked him over the wall. Caught him unawares, of course. For a minute or two he had been dazed and when he came to his senses the man was holding him by his coat front and hauling him over the seawall. The salt water he had swallowed made him retch but still he had been able to join his hands together and bring them up in a mighty blow, catching his enemy under his chin and sending him over the wall in his turn. And Matthew had climbed over it after him, though he could hardly stand for the sea pounding on his back, and he had battered the man senseless.

Anyway, he reminded himself again, he'd made him pay. Not only for his damned impertinence but for the fact that when Matthew was finished with the fellow, Hetty was disappearing up the cliff path and Matthew was in no state to follow her, drenched as he was and in the teeth of a howling gale off the sea.

'Go then!' he had shouted after her, though she was too far away by then to hear anything he said. 'Go to perdition!'

He sat in his car, banged the door to and managed to start it and back it away from the wall and head back for Hope Hall, all without a thought for the driver he had knocked over the wall.

'Hell will freeze over before I'd look at that pitman's brat again!' he'd said aloud. Water dripped off his clothes and formed a puddle on the floor. Driving over the moors, he grew colder and colder in spite of the heater in the car.

As he turned into the gateway of Hope Hall the car stalled and wouldn't start again so he abandoned it and trudged up to the house, feet squelching all the way, sour bile rising in his gullet, a mixture of salt and whisky. He walked into the yard and Richard came out of the stable.

'What on earth happened to you?' he asked. 'You're like a drowned rat. Where's the car?'

'Damn' thing stalled,' Matthew answered shortly and strode into the house. But later, soaking in a hot bath, he thought about Richard, how concerned he had been when their father had sent Hetty packing. There had been something between him and Hetty, there surely had. And if Richard had had her, why not Matthew? It was only fair.

Oh yes, Matthew told himself that evening some time after the disastrous trip to Saltburn. It would be sweet to get one over on his brother. He didn't know where Hetty was; he would find her, though. He'd vowed he would have her and he wasn't going to be balked. Finding her would be something to do while he was forced to stay in Yorkshire because his father wouldn't subsidise him any further. His allowance was already overdrawn and the bank manager was threatening to tell the old man about his debts. Then there was that money-lender in Whitby... Matthew dismissed such unpleasant thoughts from his mind. No one was going to say anything to his father; after all, he was the heir to Havelock's fortune, wasn't he? The money men always had an eye to the future. Better to think of more pleasant things in any case.

He rose to his feet and stretched, yawning mightily. The wireless had forecast better weather for tomorrow. He might take a drive north. He would play detective, find Hetty Pearson. It was a diversion anyway.

Bishop Auckland, that was where she came from. Or at least, a village near Bishop Auckland. Matthew got the address from Sally Dunn, on the pretext that he had something of Hetty's he wanted to send on to her. He'd lain awake for most of the night, devising a plan of action, not even wondering to himself why he was so obsessed with finding Hetty.

Luckily, Havelock had gone to London on business and as usual his mother was confined to her room. Ethel had been persuaded to return temporarily to nurse Elizabeth, though she had been married little more than a week.

'Why don't you get a proper nurse up from Harrogate, Father?' Richard had protested when Havelock told them the new arrangement.

'A waste of money, that's why,' he had snapped. 'Anyway, your mother likes Ethel.'

She'd preferred Hetty, Richard thought. But he knew it was no good arguing with his father. He had looked across the table at Matthew. It was all his fault that their mother was suffering even more misery. But still, she was sleeping most of the time now, hardly had the energy to lift her head from the pillow when he went to see her. Not really suffering then, but it was very worrying; she should not be sleeping her life away.

Havelock had finished his breakfast and gone out into the hall. They could hear him shouting for Bill Oliver who was doing duty as chauffeur and driving him to York for the London train.

'I'm off too,' Matthew had said, patting his mouth with his napkin and pushing back his chair. Richard hadn't asked him where, he wasn't interested.

It wasn't until Matthew was well on the road north to Guisborough which was on the shortest route to Bishop Auckland, that he thought that Hetty might not have gone there after all. Hadn't she said she was bound for Saltburn when he'd driven her there? She hadn't mentioned going further, perhaps she had friends there? He might as well try there first, it was closer than going up to Durham. Besides it was a small place: if she was there he would soon find her.

Taking the turn off right, Matthew drove through Skelton and finally arrived on the road leading down into Saltburn, passing the ha'penny bridge and dropping down to the shore. As he went the smile left his face as he remembered the last time he had come this way, Hetty sitting beside him. He'd been a fool, handled it badly. Why on earth had he bothered to fight with that oaf of a van driver? He glanced over to the side of the road where the van had been parked. It was gone. Well, of course it was. But if it hadn't been for that van driver . . .

Forget about it, he told himself, this was another day and the sun was shining, it was warm, there were even people on the beach. The sands gleamed golden in the sunlight and seabirds wheeled around Huntcliff, claiming their nesting sites, no doubt, and their mates. He turned the corner at the bottom of Cat Nab, changing down a gear to drive up the steep hairpin bend.

It was as he turned into Milton Street that he saw her and a surge of triumph went through him. He hadn't even had to do any searching! She was standing by the news-agent's shop, reading the cards in the window. He slowed for a moment, almost stopped then changed his mind. Instead he drove along to where he could park his car out of the way and walked back up Pearl Street, approaching her slowly, studying her.

Hetty was hungry. She had eaten at breakfast time certainly,

84

but only a piece of bread spread with dripping. She was hungry and tired and almost ready to give up. There were no jobs available in Saltburn, none at all. For all the fine weather there were few visitors about, and visitors were Saltburn's livelihood. Already that morning she had trailed round all the hotels, all the shops, desperately seeking something, anything, which might bring in enough money to enable her to keep herself. But there was nothing.

'Not before Easter, love, maybe not even then,' people told her, shaking their heads. 'Whitsuntide more like.'

'Why don't you go into Redcar and see if there's anything going there?' Mr Jordan had said to her. 'Have you signed on at the Labour Exchange yet?'

'I . . . I might go into Redcar,' Hetty had answered, backing away. But she knew she wouldn't, not when she didn't have a reference to show any prospective employer. She had walked along the beach the few miles to Marske one day and answered an advertisement for a kitchen maid at Marske Hall, and been thoroughly humiliated when she was asked why she had no reference.

She read through the cards in the window yet again, hoping against hope that she had missed something. And as she turned away in despair there was Matthew, leaning against the corner post of the quaint Victorian canopy which ran the length of the street, grinning at her.

'Hello there, Hetty,' he said.

She was overcome with relief to find that after all he was not drowned and dead and the feeling of guilt she had carried all week was lifted from her. Radiantly she smiled at him, took a step towards him, held out her hand to him.

'Matthew!' she cried.

He could hardly believe his luck. This was a different Hetty, even more beautiful with her eyes sparkling and a touch of delicate pink in her cheeks. The thing was to take it easy, not be too eager, do his utmost to charm her.

'I was worried about you, Hetty,' he said. 'How are you? Come, let's find a place we can talk. Have you had lunch?'

Drawing her arm through his, he led her away from Milton Street, to a restaurant on Windsor Road. He still had a few sovereigns in his pocket. Not many but enough to dazzle an out-of-work maid.

Chapter 10

They ate crab salad and bread and butter in a small restaurant in Station Square and there was ice cream for pudding.

'If I'd known we would meet we could have gone to the Queen's Hotel, but I'm not dressed for it,' said Matthew, smiling regretfully.

'Oh, no, I like it here,' Hetty answered. 'I'm not dressed up neither.' She thought of her other dress and one jacket with its patched elbow hanging in her room in Diamond Street and almost laughed aloud, seeing the funny side. She was suddenly ravenous when the crab salad was placed before her but ate slowly, saying little except to offer Matthew the last slice of bread, taking it herself when he refused.

He barely tasted his ice cream while she nibbled away at the edges of hers, making it last, determined to do the meal full justice. He sat back and smoked a cigarette and watched her, a slight smile on his face.

His mouth was shaped like his brother's, she thought. Funny that Richard's should seem so much more friendly. But Matthew was being kind to her now, perhaps he had changed?

'Leopards don't change their spots,' Gran used to say. She had a picture of a leopard on the wall of her front room, a great fearsome face with sharp teeth which had frightened Cissy . . .

Hetty forced her thoughts back to Matthew and the problem at hand. Now she was no longer so hungry, she was well aware that she could be getting herself into a difficult situation.

'Finished?' He stubbed out his cigarette in the ash tray and called for the bill. Two shillings and threepence each, it was, Hetty could read the upside-down figures. That was a lot for a crab salad and ice cream, she thought, a little alarmed. Now she had really put herself in his debt.

'We'll walk down to the bottom esplanade, shall we?' he asked as they came out of the restaurant and walked along Dundas Street to the cliff top. He took her arm and she was startled. By, he was treating her as though she were a lady, not a servant, a pitman's daughter. Why was he so different? The time when she was fourteen and new to Hope Hall flashed through her mind, the day when he had caught her upstairs by the main bedrooms. 'A bundle of rags' he had called her. The memory still burned but she pushed it away; it was different now, she was no longer a servant in his house.

They walked along by the shore to where the path turned for Hazel Grove and Hetty was reminded of the man who had been washed up there and how she had thought it might be Matthew, and shivered.

'Cold?' he asked, his tone solicitous. 'Look, why don't I hire a beach hut? We can sit out of the wind.'

There *was* a cold wind blowing from the sea. Families on the beach were sheltering behind brightly striped windbreaks, and white-tops were forming on the waves and running in to break and spread in foamy bubbles on the sand.

Hetty looked at the red wooden huts. Quite a number had their doors open and people were sitting inside in deckchairs. There was nothing wrong in the two of them sitting in a beach hut too, was there?

He left her on a bench where she could watch the cliff lift going up and down, spilling out children with wooden spades and tin buckets and their mothers with laden bags of sandwiches and towels and bathing suits. The children ran down on to the sands, excited, calling to one another. It was the beginning of the season and cold but they didn't seem to notice.

Matthew had the key for a beach hut when he came back. He shivered theatrically.

'Come on then, let's get out of the wind,' he said, smiling at her. She went with him to the lines of bathing huts and people watched them curiously from those which were already occupied. Hetty didn't look at them, she felt too uncomfortable. Matthew opened the door of one which was in the middle of an unoccupied group and she was glad of that. Inside there was a tiny paraffin cooker and a tin kettle and teapot with thick white cups and saucers. And deck-chairs and a couch against one wall. Not much of a couch but still . . .

'Nice, isn't it?' asked Matthew. He stood watching her, a curious expression on his face.

'Yes, it's lovely,' she answered. The walls were distempered white and there was a framed beach scene on the wall: a woman in a bathing suit with a huge striped ball.

Matthew propped back the door and put up two of the deckchairs, close together. But they sat for only a short while before he got to his feet again and held out his hand to her. 'It's too cold, isn't it? I'll close the door, shall I, and light the stove? It will be all cosy in here then.' He helped her to her feet and they stood close together. She could feel the heat from his body and smell the maleness of him. She moved away and sat on the couch while he pulled the door to.

'Leave it open a little,' she said. 'We have to have some light.' So he left a narrow gap through which the sunlight sent a beam across the stone floor with its tiny rag mat.

Hetty didn't know how she felt. She told herself she was in control of the situation, she could leave at any time, there was nothing to worry about. When he sat down beside her and put his arm around her she felt perhaps she would let him kiss her and then she would make an excuse and go. But when he kissed her his lips were hard and demanding and in spite of herself she felt a response rising in her.

She had been so alone, she told herself afterwards, no one had shown her any affection for so long. So when Matthew murmured in her ear how pretty she was, how he loved her, how it was all right, nothing bad was going to happen to her, he would look after her, she knew she shouldn't believe him but she did. He covered her breast with his hand and she pushed it away, but he was firm, insistent.

'Everything's fine,' he said. 'Don't worry about anything. I know you want me as much as I want you. Just relax now, enjoy yourself.'

The strange thing was that she did. All the pent-up emotion in her was being released. He pulled her blouse free from her skirt and slid his hand beneath, and what he did then was sending such sensations through her whole body she could hardly breathe.

'I have to go,' she said once as he pushed her down on the damp-smelling couch.

'Have you?'

Matthew lifted his face from hers and gazed at her intently but not really seeing her; there was a faraway look in his eyes and he bent his head again, this time to her breast, touching his tongue to the nipple. His hands were busy where her skirt had ridden up.

'Please, Matthew,' she said weakly and it was hard to tell what she was asking him, but it didn't matter, he was beyond listening.

Afterwards, she tried to think of the point where she had been no longer in control or even believed herself in control. As she lay in her narrow bed in the attic room in Diamond Street, muscles she hadn't known she possessed aching, she went over it. How they had lain, uncomfortable on the couch, listening to the murmurs of the people in the other huts, the children shouting to each other on the beach, the seabirds crying.

Matthew had lain on her arm, breathing heavily, not quite asleep, and the arm became numb and then painful and she had had to move and disturb him. He had grunted and run his hand down her body, and she had stiffened. He didn't want to do it again, did he?

'Fetch me a drink of water, will you, love?' he said, and she thankfully eased herself off the couch and brought him a glass of water from the container by the stove. He sipped and grimaced and turned over on his back and watched as she pulled her clothes together hurriedly. Neither of them had actually undressed.

He reached to the floor for his jacket and took out his silver cigarette case with the lighter on the end and lit a cigarette, still watching her. Hetty was red-faced and fumbling.

'Oh, go on, take 'em off, let me see you,' he drawled. 'Go on, there's no one else to see here.'

She looked up at him quickly; even now she couldn't imagine taking her clothes off for him to see her. Seeing the lurking amusement in his eyes, her blushes deepened. She moved towards the door.

'I have to go,' she muttered. Her voice came out strangely; she felt outside herself, this couldn't really be happening.

'Oh no you don't!'

Matthew jumped to his feet and grabbed her arm. 'Come on now, don't be silly,' he said. 'It's too late for that anyway. Come on, sit down and wait for me.' He sat her down on the couch and put his arm around her, kissing her softly. 'You're not bad, do you know that?' he whispered in her ear. 'Definitely worth waiting for.' His hands were straying again and Hetty pulled herself away.

'I have to go, Matthew,' she said stubbornly, and he sighed.

'Oh, go on then,' he snapped. 'But don't come the prim little brat with me, not now.' It was a glimpse of the old Matthew and it broke the spell for her.

She rushed outside, past the people at the doors of their beach huts, most of whom were looking at her knowingly. Her face felt as though it were on fire, her sight was blurred. Up the cliff path she went, slowing down to a walk, beginning to pant as she reached the top. She looked behind then, but Matthew was not following her as far as she could see.

He hadn't even bothered to follow her, she thought, illogically, for only the minute before she had been praying he would not. The sun had gone behind a cloud and the wind strengthened, veering and blowing off the moors. She shivered. Catching sight of the cliff lift, she feared Matthew might be on it and began to run.

Reaching home, she crept upstairs to her room and lay on the bed with the coverlet over her, so tired her mind was blank. After a while she got up and brought a jug of hot water from the bathroom and washed herself all over. She thought longingly of the bath, how heavenly it would be simply to soak in hot soapy water, but a bath cost threepence extra and she couldn't afford it.

She had sold herself for a meal, she thought, a meal and a little show of affection. How could she have done it, especially with Matthew of all people? And now she couldn't go home. Always in the back of her mind she had thought she could go home even during the first years after Cissy died, for surely Mam would take her in? Her father would at least. Or she could go to Gran's. They would not want her to starve. But now she couldn't. Suppose she went home and they welcomed her back and then she found she had fallen wrong?

Fallen wrong! Was it possible, after only once? Could she be having a baby already? The thought was shocking, it had only just occurred to her, why hadn't she thought of it at the time? Why hadn't she thought of it before she went into the hut? a small voice asked sternly.

Oh God, she was letting her imagination run away with her again. If she stayed in this room much longer she would go mad.

'Anyroad,' she said aloud as she pulled on her coat and a drab brown beret over her hair, 'I'll have to find some work if I want to eat this week. "Sufficient unto the day is the evil thereof." ' As the minister back in Morton Main would say. A walk would take her mind off things, loosen her up, she felt all stiff and strange.

Locking her door, she went down the four flights of stairs to the main door and peeped out. The street was quiet, no sign of Matthew. She did her usual round of the hotels, asking for work, any sort of work, but there was none.

'I might have a few nights next weekend, love,' Mr Jordan said, and afterwards, when she turned away, he watched her go. The lass looked poor, pale and with shadows under her eyes, he thought. He shook his head, there was nothing he could do about it.

Alice was in the fish shop and waved as Hetty went by. They had become friendly in the short time Hetty had been in Saltburn. She went past and had a last look in the news-agent's window. Nothing. She walked back to see Alice.

'Can you not find anything, love?' Her friend was sympathetic. The shop was empty and she leaned over the counter, resting her arms comfortably on the pile of news-papers. She didn't wait for an answer. 'Look, I know a place for you. You remember that Mr Hutchins? Go on, you do, he was in that first day you came here when you'd lost your job. Well, he's been in here again, looking for a housekeeper – someone who will look after his children an' all. I've been watching for you. I told him – "I know just the girl for you, a decent girl," I said.'

'Housekeeper?'

'Yes. He's a widower, three children. You could manage three children, couldn't you? Mind, it's not in Saltburn, it's in Smuggler's Cove. He's a miner. A good chap, a chapel man. His last housekeeper has gone off. Here, I got the details. He said if you were interested to go there this after-noon, he's on early shift.'

'Own room, one afternoon free a week plus time off on Sundays,' the piece of paper read. 'Board and five shillings a week.'

Smuggler's Cove. Oh, it sounded lovely, a little village on the coast.

'Thanks, Alice. Oh, thank you,' cried Hetty, all her troubles forgotten for the minute. 'It'll be grand, won't it, a little village by the sea?'

'Well, it's not exactly – do you not know Smuggler's Cove?'

'No, but I know I can get a bus there from Station Square. I'll go now.'

Before Alice could say any more, Hetty was out of the shop and hurrying towards the bus stop.

Chapter 11

Richard drove through Darlington, stopping and starting and getting into jams for it was Monday, market day, and besides the market stalls were thronged with people. There were cattle trucks converging on the cattle mart and even a few farmers herding their own beasts. He'd made a mistake in trying to cut through the centre of the town, he thought wryly. But at last he reached Bondgate and found the road out to Bishop Auckland. It was a fine morning. At last there was a hint of warmth in the sun and buds on the trees were bursting green though the hedges still looked brown and barren. But underneath there were new shoots of grass and the occasional wildflower, a coltsfoot lifting its head to the sun, a few early daisies.

He wasn't sure where he was going, though he knew it was a village close to the little town, but he had the correct address from Sally, he would find it.

'Yes, sir, I know where Hetty's family live,' she had said, and had looked curiously at him. By, she would have a tale to tell when she wrote home! she thought. Though she was a poor writer and so far hadn't got around to writing even though there were such things to tell about Hetty Pearson, and her from a chapel family an' all. But she *would* write.

So Richard had the address in his top pocket, scribbled down on the back page of his appointments diary. He drove through Heighington and Shildon, where he had to wait by the Railway Waggon Works for the road was crossed by a railway line here and a waggon was being shunted up the line for a few yards and back again into the workshop. The smell from the engine got into the car, oily and sooty at the same time and reminiscent of stations, so that he closed the window.

As he sat, he thought about what he was going to say to Hetty when he got to her parents' house. 'I'm sorry I didn't support you,' he could say, but what would that mean? Hadn't he seen her with Matthew with his own eyes? Anyway, he couldn't say she could have her job back, only his father could do that and he would not. Even though Elizabeth was sinking back into a drugged lethargy now that Hetty was no longer there.

A car hooting behind him brought him back to the present. The gates were open. Richard put his own car into gear and went on to Bishop Auckland. Pulling into the kerb as he came out from South Church Road into Newgate Street, he took out the address Sally had given him and consulted his map. He'd come past the turn-off for Morton Main, he realised, and looked about him. The narrow street, so straight it must have been a Roman road originally, was very quiet in contrast with Darlington, though of course it had been market day there. The depression still held sway in this area, he thought. The few people there were poorly dressed housewives with shopping baskets looking into the windows of the Co-op.

Richard leaned out of the window to ask directions of a man wandering aimlessly along the path, his collarless neck wound in a white scarf, grey hair clipped very short except for a fringe across his brow – the typical miner's cut.

'Morton Main? Oh, aye, I can tell you that. I live out that way anyroad. You'll have to turn round and take the road out to South Church.'

'Thanks,' said Richard, and hesitated a minute. 'Would you like a lift home since I'm going that way?'

The man shook his head regretfully. 'No, I have to go to the Labour Exchange. It's signing on day, like.' Encouraged by Richard's friendliness, he went on, 'By, it's a grand motor you've got there though. A Riley, eh?'

'Yes. A Riley Monaco. Only a year old.' He glanced at the gleaming walnut dashboard with pride. 'Well, if you're sure . . . Look, would you like a cigarette?' He fished in the glove compartment and brought out a packet of Capstans.

'No, no, there's no need,' the miner answered, thrusting his hands deep into his jacket pockets though Richard caught the gleam of regret in his eyes. 'I have some tabs, thanks.' There was a half stub of a Woodbine behind his ear, Richard noticed.

'Well, take one anyway,' he insisted, and after a moment the man did. He leaned forward as Richard held out his lighter and lit the cigarette then stood and inhaled slowly.

'Are you looking for anybody in particular? If you'll excuse me asking, like.'

'That's all right. Yes, I am, the Pearson family, but I have the address: nine, Office Street.'

'Well, go through the old village and Office Street's right on the end of the rows, next to Chapel Row.'

Richard thanked him and started the car. Driving down the street, he turned round in the market place, by the entrance to the bishop's palace, catching a glimpse of the stone battlements of the old castle. Nothing shabby about that, he thought to himself.

The miners' rows, when he got there, were much like the ironstone miners' cottages in the villages on the North Yorkshire coast. Each house had its tin bath hanging on the wall in the yard; every step was sandstoned clean, even the yard steps. He found number nine Office Street without difficulty, hesitating before going in the back way, but as far as he could see there was no road to the front. Being the end row there were gardens there. So he walked up the yard and knocked on the back door. The dolly-dyed net curtain hung at the window didn't even twitch before the door was flung open.

'Oh! I thought it was the doctor's man. He's the only one who knocks around here.'

The woman who opened the door looked like an older version of Hetty; Richard would have realised who she was anywhere. She was drying her hands on her apron as she looked at him, her head held on one side enquiringly.

'Can I help you?'

'Who is it, Maggie?'

She turned her head to answer another woman's voice. 'I'll tell you when I know mesel', Mother.'

'Mrs Pearson? My name is Richard Hope, may I come in?'

'Oh, aye, of course. Come in, what am I thinking about?' said Maggie, standing back to allow him to pass into the kitchen.

Now he was here, Richard wasn't sure what he was going to say. There was no sign of Hetty, no doubt she had found work elsewhere. He looked around the room, taking in the gleaming black-leaded range, the cheap oilcloth on the floor covered with clipped rag mats, the bare table scrubbed white and with piles of wet washing on it and a scrubbing brush. In one corner of the kitchen was a zinc dolly tub complete with rubbing board. Of course, Monday, it was washing day.

An older woman was standing by it; obviously Richard had interrupted her labours. She too dried her hands on her apron and came forward, ushering him to a chair by the fire.

'Richard Hope, did you say? You mean from Hope Hall, where Hetty works? Has something happened to my granddaughter?'

'No, not exactly.' He hesitated, confused. He did not sit down for both the women were standing, looking anxious. 'Well, I mean, Hetty used to work for us . . . she left ten days ago. I thought she would be here.'

'Here? No, I haven't heard from her.' Maggie looked at her mother, flushing at the accusatory expression on her face.

'No, well, she wouldn't come here, would she? Not after the way you treated her. But why didn't she come to me?' There was a hurt expression on her face as the older woman turned to Richard. 'There wasn't anything wrong, was there? I mean, the bairn was all right, wasn't she?'

'Oh no, nothing wrong. I mean, she was quite well, Mrs . . .?'

'My mother, Mrs Wearmouth,' Maggie said belatedly. She sat down suddenly by the table, staring at nothing.

'Well, we'd best all sit down. Howay, lad.' She waited until Richard was settled before going on: 'She mebbe had another place to go to?'

'Not that I know of. I thought she might have found work here.' She had no references, he realised now. How could she get another post?

'She was turned off, wasn't she?' Mrs Pearson said, and it was a statement, not a question.

'Well—'

'So she'll have no character.'

Richard was inspired. He drew his pen from his inside pocket. 'Well, as it happens, we – my father and I, that is – we remembered that we had not given Hetty a reference. So I thought, as I was going to Durham today, I would call in and see if she needed one. I could write one out now, if you like? In case Hetty should come home.'

Mrs Pearson ignored this. 'What did she do?' she asked.

'Nothing. She served our family well. My mother thought very highly of her, you know. She misses Hetty terribly.'

The two women stared at him, faces blank.

'Then why no reference?'

'My mother is an invalid, she doesn't have much to do with the running of the house.' Richard was well aware that this sound lame. 'Shall I write a reference?' he asked.

'We haven't any good paper,' said Maggie. 'If you want to you can send one, though I doubt Hetty will come here. But she must have done something.'

'It was nothing to do with you, was it? You weren't after our lass? I've heard of that sort of thing. It happens all the time with our young girls when they go out to place. We tell them to be careful but it's the young gents, man, they think they have a right—'

'Mam!' ejaculated Maggie. 'That's enough now.'

The old lady subsided, though she pursed her lips and her face was red with anger.

'I think I'd better go,' said Richard, rising to his feet. He wished heartily he had never come. He felt flushed and embarrassed and didn't know what to say to defend himself. 'I will send a reference anyway. Good morning to you both.' He made as dignified an exit as he could manage.

'You see, our Maggie,' said Mrs Wearmouth as they watched him walk down the yard and round the corner. 'If you hadn't been so blooming hard, Hetty would have come home.'

'Mam, I wasn't meself. I haven't been since Cissy was killed.'

'Aye. Well, I know that right enough. When I think of that poor lass I get mad as hell, though, and that's swearing! I'm right fed up of you getting the dismals fretting over Cissy. No matter how much you grieve, you're not going to bring her back.'

'I know.' Maggie picked up the scrubbing brush and turned it over and over on the table, hardly aware of what she was doing. 'Thomas was stamping mad an' all when I told him what I'd said to Hetty last time she was here. He kept hoping she would come back but I doubt it. Eeh, Mam, I get such black moods on me and I don't care what I say when I do.'

'It's your time o' life,' commented Mrs Wearmouth. She got to her feet and went over to the rubbing board and began rubbing away at Thomas's pit shirt as though her life depended on it. 'But still, you had no right to speak to the lass like that. Now you've driven her away, and mind, you'll regret it when you're getting older an' you haven't got a daughter left. Sons isn't daughters, not by a long chalk.'

'I wonder where she's at? Have you any idea, Mam?'

Maggie too got to her feet and began going through the piles of washing on the table before throwing them in the tin bath underneath which was filled with blue water for rinsing. The habit of keeping on working no matter what was ingrained in the two women.

'No, I haven't. She hasn't written to me in many a long day. By, though, lasses! They're a worry to their mothers from the day they're born to the day they die,' said Mrs Wearmouth, illogically contradicting her previous comments on the subject.

Thomas came in from the pit which was working again, although the men were on short time, only three shifts a week. Maggie waited until he had had his dinner and bath before broaching the subject of the visitor.

'Richard Hope, it was,' she said. 'The lad, like.'

'A nice smart young lad an' all,' observed Mrs Wearmouth. She had washed and dried out the tin bath and now she filled it full of clothes. 'I'll just hang this lot out,' she said, making for the front door and the garden. As she always said, she was not one to interfere in her daughter's life; she'd be well out of the road while Maggie discussed it with her man.

He listened to what his wife had to say in silence. Then he went over to the high mantelshelf and took down his old pipe and Maggie, well used to his ways, waited.

'I don't believe my lass did anything wrong,' he said at last. 'Why, she's been at that place for years now, why would they keep her on if she hadn't a good character? No, I bet it was the lad was after her and his folks were frightened he would marry her. So Hetty had to suffer.'

Maggie stared at him. He had his pipe going to his satisfaction now and sat back in his chair, puffing at it, but his eyes were thoughtful.

'I was too hard on her,' said Maggie. 'She would have come home if I hadn't been too hard on her.'

'I said, didn't I? She was just a bairn, you can't blame her for what happened to Cissy. But there,' he added hastily as his wife showed signs of agitation, jumping up and going over to the window and back again, her face working, 'it's a while back now. It's the living bairn we have to see to, pet. And I tell you what – I'll have to find her. I'm laid off tomorrow, I'll go to look for her.'

'But where, man? We don't know where to look!'

'That's true. But I can take the train to Saltburn, mebbe ask around. You know how she always liked Saltburn.'

'A waste of money, I think,' declared Maggie. 'Why, man, you don't know where she is really, do you?'

Thomas gave her a hard stare. 'I'm going, woman,' he said. 'I won't be wasting any money, I'll go on me bike and you can make me up some bait. Just a sandwich will do.'

'Oh, I know you think it's all my fault,' cried Maggie. 'But I've told you, I couldn't help meself. Do you think I've never wished I could take back the words? Anyroad, hadaway if you want to. Not but what I don't think biking forty miles to Saltburn and forty miles back isn't too much, an' you having to go to work on Wednesday.'

'Look now,' Mrs Wearmouth intervened, for she had hung out the washing at breakneck speed and come back in with the empty basket, 'I have a bit put by. Take your fare home on the train at least. You can take the train, can't you?'

'Thanks, Ma,' said Thomas. He was still looking at Maggie as he spoke, his face grim. 'But as it happens, I have a bob or two meself. The cavil I'm on's a good 'un this quarter, even if I am only on short time – a really good seam. We've no bairns to keep, have we? Nothing to think on but ourselves.'

Rising to his stockinged feet, he tapped out his pipe on the bar of the fire and replaced it on the mantelshelf. 'I'm away to bed,' he declared. 'An' mind, Maggie, don't call me up for supper, not tonight. I want to be up as if for first shift in the morning, get a good start, like.'

He went upstairs and after a minute the women heard the bedsprings creak as he climbed in. Maggie looked at her mother, but Mrs Wearmouth merely shrugged and went back to the dolly tub to finish off the last of the weekly wash. 'I tell you, our Maggie, if your man gets it into his head to do something there's no use trying to stop him. Anyroad, he might find the lass. We'll wait and see.'

'Yes.' Maggie cleared the last of the washing from the table and dried it down. 'Mind,' she said after a long silence, 'our Cissy was a little angel, she was. Mebbe too good for this world.'

But her mother had heard her on the same theme so many times over the years she finally lost patience.

'Aye,' she said, her voice rising. 'An' so's our Hetty a lovely lass, and she didn't deserve what happened no more than you did. You know how she loved the bairn!'

'Mam—'

Whatever Maggie had been going to say, both women stopped glaring at each other and looked up at the ceiling. Thomas was hammering on the floor.

'Will you two had thee gobs and give a man some peace when he's come in from the pit? Or will I have to come downstairs an' shut them for you?'

The women subsided. Thomas had never raised a hand to any of his family in his life; it was not the threat which

101

silenced them. Both were pitmen's wives, they had been always used to having to creep around the house when their men were off shift. They looked guiltily at each other. It had come to a sorry pass when they had forgotten Thomas needed his sleep.

Chapter 12

Hetty descended from the bus in the village of Smuggler's Cove and looked around. It was far from the idyllic fishing village she had expected. Yet the fact cheered her somehow. There were the stone houses of an old village all right, but added on to them were rows of late-nineteenth century miners' houses, very like those at home in Morton Main. She could almost feel herself back there. Besides the two chapels she could see, there was a school and what looked like an inn though it proclaimed itself a coffee house on its faded sign.

The bus turned round and went back along the road past the mine buildings which stood at the entrance to the village. Hetty was alone in the square, apart from a group of urchins who appeared running along the bank of the stream, one with a gull's feather stuck behind his ear and a tiny home-made bow and arrow. The cowboys chasing him were screaming war-whoops and one was waving a crudely carved wooden gun. Suddenly a door opened and a young woman stepped out and shouted at the boys.

'Bobby! Jimmy! Come away from that beck. I've told you and told you not to play there – you'll fall in the water as sure as eggs is eggs!'

The leader of the cowboys, a boy of perhaps four years, stopped running. From across the stream, Hetty could see his deep sigh of impatience with women.

'But Mam—' he began, before his mother interrrupted.

'You do as I tell you, Bobby, or your dad'll tan the hide off you when he gets in from work. You know that beck's

103

mucky.' Hetty had noticed it was a bright orange colour, the banksides and stones stained with it. Everything looked rusty. From the iron workings, she thought, the way a stream by the pit at home was stained black with coal dust.

The boys trooped across a footbridge into the square. Hetty turned to ask the woman if she could direct her to Overmans Terrace, but she had disappeared inside again, the door firmly shut.

A car came into the square and the boys turned to stare; obviously cars were not too common in this little place. They made no effort to move from the middle of the road where they stood and to Hetty it seemed that the car wasn't slowing down either.

'Get off the road, boys!' she shouted, and they turned to stare at her. The car had pulled into the side by the inn. A man got out and went inside. Bobby stuck out his chin belligerently.

'I don't have to do what *you* say,' he said. 'You don't live here.' But at the same time, he looked over towards his home, obviously fearing his mother had heard. 'Come on then, lads,' he said to his followers who were clustered round him, 'let's go down on the beach and play.' He cast a baleful glance at Hetty.

'Wait a minute,' she said. 'Can you tell me where Overmans Terrace is?'

'You mean Hoss Muck Terrace,' stated Bobby. 'What do you want to know for?'

Before she could answer, one of the smaller boys spoke up, the one with the feather stuck behind his ear, the Indian of their game.

'I live in Hoss Muck Terrace, missus.'

Hetty smiled at him, a lad of no more than three or four, small and thin, one sock falling down where he'd lost his garter and a hole in the sleeve of his grubby jacket. His eyes were green with dark lashes, though his hair was fair. 'Will you show me where it is?'

'Yes, missus.'

'Aw, go on then, we didn't want to play with you anyroad,' said Bobby. He stepped forward and gave the lad a shove which sent him stumbling into the kerb. Before Hetty could say anything, Bobby and his gang were racing away, streaming along the path to the beach. An off-shift miner, walking down from the pigeon duckets which dotted the hillside, shouted at them, but they swerved round him and were away.

The boy left behind sniffed and wiped his hand across his nose. He stared after the others for a minute. Then he took the feather out of his hair and threw it on the ground. 'I didn't want to play with them anyroad.'

'I'm Hetty Pearson. What's your name?' she asked.

'Charlie Hutchins.'

Hetty held out a hand to him. 'Come on then, Charlie Hutchins, show me where you live.'

The boy thrust his hands into the pockets of his jacket, refusing to take hold of Hetty's. But he sniffed again and smiled.

'Down here,' he said, and led the way back along the bus route.

Hetty didn't know how she had missed it. The tin plate on the edge of the small terrace was plain to see: 'Overmans Terrace', it read, black on white. The houses were right by the entrance to the pit but were well-built with neat gardens at the front and clean, net-hung windows, sparkling in the sun.

'Who do you want?' asked Charlie as they approached. 'Our house is that one on the end.'

'I think I want your house, Charlie,' she said.

'Do you? Me dad's in, I'll tell him.' He ran ahead and opened the door. 'Dad, Dad, there's a lady—'

'All right, Charlie. Now go out and play. Only half an hour, mind, then your dinner will be ready.'

'Righto, Dad.' The lad flashed a grin at Hetty and walked down the path, swinging his bow against the dull grass at the side aimlessly.

'Come in. Alice said you might be here. Hetty Pearson, isn't it?'

Hetty stepped over the threshold and into a tiny vestibule with the staircase running straight off it and a door to the right leading into a living-room. The room was clean enough and the floor even had a square of proper carpet on it, brown with a fawn floral pattern. There was a chenille cloth on the table with an empty vase in the middle. There were clean but nondescript curtains hanging at the window and a bright fire in the grate. As she entered, a man rose from a well-worn leather armchair by the range. Mr Hutchins, of course. Yet he looked different somehow, younger, in a Fair Isle pullover and corduroy trousers.

'Sit down, Hetty Pearson,' he said, indicating the chair on the opposite side of the fireplace, a rocker with a flowered cushion on it, just like her dad's. He wasted no time in getting down to business. 'It's a housekeeper I want, you know that? Five shillings a week and your board. If you take the job I'll expect you to see to the house and the little 'uns. Make my meals when I come in from the pit. Do you think you can do all that? You're not very old.' He looked doubtful, and she hastened to reassure him that she was old enough.

'I can do it. I'm nineteen. My dad's a miner – a coal miner, that is. I'm used to the men doing shift work.'

'Of course, Alice said. Well, I'm on night shift all the time,' he said, 'so it is quite all right for you to sleep here. At present a girl from the village does that but she's going to train as a nurse. Next week, in fact.' He regarded her solemnly and she looked steadily back. He had green eyes, remarkably similar to Charlie's.

'Well, that's good,' she said. 'I'm sure I can manage the work.'

'You haven't asked about the older children yet,' he reminded her. 'They're at school at the minute, though they'll be in shortly. There's Peter, he's ten, and Audrey, she's seven. You can stay and have a bite with us if you like, meet them? If you decide to come, when can you start?'

Hetty realised the job was hers, it had been as simple as that. Of course, Alice had talked to him about her. And he evidently didn't have much time to look about, he had to have someone to stay with the children when he was at work. Briefly she wondered what had happened to his wife.

'I'll have to give notice at my lodging. A week, I think.'

'Can you start tomorrow? I'll square it with your landlady.'

106

Hetty felt as though she was being rushed along too swiftly. 'Well—'

'Make up your mind, don't waste my time.'

'Yes, I can start tomorrow. And really, there's no need to speak to my landlady. The rent is paid up till the end of the week.'

After all, she would be lucky to get anything else without references, she had found that out since she'd left Hope Hall. He seemed a decent man, and Alice knew him. Though he was a bit abrupt.

Riding home on the bus, Hetty had few misgivings. After all, most of the day Mr Hutchins would be in bed; he had only stayed up today to meet her and see to the children's dinner. But she did regret leaving Saltburn, regretted it greatly as the bus drove down the hill by Cat Nab, the conical hill right next to the beach. It had been used as an ancient burial ground, Mr Jordan had told her. He was very knowledgeable about local history. She looked up at the imposing buildings on the very top of the cliff opposite, the 'new' Saltburn built in Victorian times, as opposed to the ancient Saltburn which had once been a haven for smugglers.

Oh, she would be sad to leave it, she would, the jewel streets radiating down to the horse-shoe-shaped cliff above the pounding North Sea. She was still downcast at the thought of leaving when she heard her name being called.

'Hetty! Where have you been? I've looked all over for you.'

For half a second she thought it was Richard's voice, but no, it was Matthew's. Her pulse raced uncomfortably. She blushed and looked down, remembering the beach hut.

'Hello, Matthew.'

'Is that all you have to say? No "Hello, my love, how pleased I am to see you"?' He took her arm and drew her into the doorway of the chemist's by the bus stop. 'I'm pleased to see you, Hetty. I've thought of nothing else but seeing you for days.'

Even as he said it, he realised it was true. Once he'd got what he wanted, he had thought he would be bored to death with her. Why, he thought he'd only come here today because he had nothing else to do and he enjoyed deceiving Richard. But seeing her again, he began to wonder.

Richard had pestered him to know where Hetty was, but Matthew had insisted he didn't know. Well, his brother was such a fool, he'd even gone up to Durham to look for the girl. It was rather fun keeping him guessing. But looking at Hetty now, he wanted her again. There was something about her that he couldn't fathom and certainly couldn't forget. At least, not yet.

'Shall I get a beach hut again?' he asked, confident of her answer, but she shook her head and backed away.

'No, Matthew, no!'

'Oh, come on, don't be coy,' he said, smiling his charming smile. He looked down at the curve of her breasts, outlined by the thin dress she was wearing, and ran his tongue over suddenly dry lips. He was impatient with her reluctance. Hell's bells, it was too late now for her to act the shy virgin!

'No, Matthew. I won't let it happen again. Please go away.' She turned and walked rapidly down the street, through the station yard and across the road to the chapel which stood at the top of Diamond Street. She looked behind her but there was no sign of him and she felt a surge of relief. But just in case, she walked along Milton Street to the next right turn, Emerald Street, and down it to Marine Parade. Two sharp lefts and she was back in Diamond Street. Thank goodness Matthew seemed to have taken her at her word, he had gone.

She was wrong. Inserting her key in the front door, she opened it and was just closing it after her when he came out of nowhere and put his foot in the door.

'Let me in, Hetty,' he insisted.

'No. Go away!' she whispered. She cast a swift glance behind her, fearing to see her landlady was about, but the hall was deserted. Matthew was quick to see her trepidation.

'Let me in or I'll raise a ruckus,' he said, and he wasn't smiling.

Hetty was desperate. At any moment the landlady might come, or another boarder. Of course, it didn't matter that she might lose her room now, she was going anyway. But she didn't want anyone to think she was anybody's 'fancy woman', as Morton Main called it. She opened the door wider and stood back reluctantly, feeling there was no help for it.

'All right then, hurry up,' she whispered. 'Right to the top of the house and don't make a noise, please don't.'

Once inside her bedroom she closed the door behind him and leaned on it. Automatically she said, 'Sit down,' and he moved towards the bed.

'Not there!' she said sharply. She pulled forward a small wooden chair and he shrugged, humouring her.

'What is the matter with you?' he demanded, voice booming in the little room so that she shushed him quickly.

'Not so loud!'

'We could speak quietly together if we sat on the bed,' he suggested. He was mad for her. Now that they were alone in a bedroom, poor though it was, he couldn't wait. He tried another tack. Sitting down on the chair, he sat back, tilting it on to the back legs and folding his arms.

'You look lovely when you're agitated like that,' he said. 'Lovely enough to eat.'

'Don't be silly, Matthew, I know you're trying to flannel me. Now, I don't know why you've come here—'

'Yes you do!'

Hetty felt herself blushing even more. She was beginning to realise she had made a mistake in allowing him into the house. 'Look,' she said, 'I've told you how I feel. I don't want you, I don't want to see you again, now will you go?'

She started to walk past him to open the door but as she passed he grabbed her arm and pulled her down on his knee.

'There! Isn't that better? Now come on, be a good girl, give me a kiss.' He held her easily with one hand and cupped the other round her chin. 'You little witch,' he murmured as he found her mouth. She struggled but his arms were like iron, his hands running over her. She was gasping for breath when he moved his lips to the hollow of her neck, one hand still firmly holding her, the fingers of the other fiddling with the fastening of her dress. But how could she scream or shout? It was her bedroom, she was trapped. And then it happened.

There was such an almighty crash the whole street must have heard it, let alone anyone in the house. The wooden chair had collapsed under them, smashed to bits. A round, carved leg rolled over the floor, the rest was in a heap under Matthew. Hetty herself was on her back, dazedly staring up at the stained ceiling, her dress up around her hips showing her stocking tops and knickers. The top button of her bodice was open.

'What in heaven's name is going on here?' demanded a harsh female voice. The door was open and the landlady stood there, legs apart, hands on hips, mouth agape as she took in the scene and jumped to her own conclusions about what it meant. The shock on her face turned to blind, blazing anger.

'You'd use my house for a brothel, would you? Would you? Why, I'll—'

Hetty scrambled to her feet, pulling her dress together, running a hand over her hair. 'It was the chair,' she said, almost crying. 'The chair broke.' She stared in astonishment at Matthew as he laughed. He stood up, taking his time. Why, he was actually enjoying this, she realised. He put an arm around her shoulders.

'Come on,' he said to the angry landlady. 'I was just waiting for Hetty, we were going out for a meal. Now be careful what you say or you could be in trouble yourself. After all, that was an unsafe chair. Look at it, not fit to sit on.'

The landlady exploded. 'It wasn't meant for two to sit on!' she shouted. 'You get out of my house. You've got a bloody nerve, you have, talking about the law. Go on, out!'

'I'll go when I'm ready, you stupid old hag,' he said pleasantly.

'Go on, Matthew,' Hetty implored him.

'Oh, well, if *you* want me to,' he answered. 'I'll wait on the front, shall I?'

Hetty wished the floor would open and swallow her, she couldn't look at the landlady. She nodded dumbly, couldn't trust herself to say anymore.

'You do that. This baggage will not be more than five

minutes, I guarantee that.' The landlady was white with anger now.

Hetty got out her straw box and began packing her few things under the baleful glare of the older woman. She fastened the leather belt which held it together and pulled on her coat. Summoning as much dignity as she could muster, she brushed past her, dropping the keys in her outstretched palm and walked down the stairs and out of the front door.

Matthew was there. She could see him sitting on a seat facing the sea, his back to her. Resolutely she turned the other way though she hadn't an idea where she was going. The bane of her life he was, she thought as she trudged up the street. He spoilt everything; she was hard put to make a living because of him.

Then why did she feel such a response when he made love to her? Why, when she hated him? She could still feel his lips on hers, his hands on her body, her treacherous body.

'Hetty, Hetty, you're going the wrong way.' Matthew was running after her. She tried to run too but was hampered by her box and he caught her and swung her round to face him.

'Matthew,' she cried, 'please leave me alone! Go away, and leave me alone.'

He dropped her arm and stood back. The look on her face was one of such despair and loathing that it penetrated even his self-confidence. She ran off up the street and he watched her go. He was confused. Oh God, he was confused! Hetty was the only girl who had ever made him feel like this. He'd thought, once he'd broken down her defences, she would be like all the others – hanging on to him until he was sick to death of her.

Hetty rounded the corner and went off somewhere, he didn't know where. After a moment he walked slowly up the road too, through the station yard to where he had parked his car. What a mess he had made of today, just because of a pitman's brat, a skivvy from his father's kitchen. He called her everything ugly he could think of but in his heart he knew they were empty words. She was well and truly under his skin. He had never thought it could happen

111

to him and yet of all the girls in the world it had to be her who conquered him.

Frowning savagely, Matthew crossed over to his car and started the engine, turning to back up Windsor Road and return to the moors where no doubt his father would be waiting, ready to lash out with his tongue once again for Matthew's supposed failings. As he passed the bus stop his attention was drawn to the queue just moving on to the bus for Smuggler's Cove. And there was Hetty, heaving her box on before her. He braked sharply, causing the car behind him to toot loudly in protest. Then, smiling broadly, he drove on.

Chapter 13

Thomas Pearson arrived at Hope Hall at one o'clock in the afternoon. He had decided to go there first to try to find out more about why Hetty had been dismissed, obviously he hadn't been told the whole story. Also, he might be wrong in thinking she would go to Saltburn. Surely someone at Hope Hall would know where she had gone? He had walked the last few miles from the main road where he had alighted from the bus and now strode across the heather, the studs in the soles of his pitboots striking sparks off the occasional patch of rock bared by the grazing sheep.

'Me boots'll stand up to the walking best,' he had said to Maggie when she'd objected to his wearing them. 'Anyroad, we can't afford to have my shoes soled and heeled again.'

All the way he had worried about Hetty. Where was the lass? He blamed himself for it all. Maybe she would have come straight home when she got into trouble if only he'd been more firm with Maggie.

'I said nowt,' he told a peewit, startled from its nest by his approach and skimming over the heather crying plaintively. 'I say nowt when I should speak out and too much when I ought te keep me mouth shut.'

But how could he have said anything to Maggie when she was nigh out of her mind about losing the little 'un? He'd let it go, thinking he would wait until she was calmer, more rational, like. Then the months, nay years just went, and there never was a good time. Though he had tried. Oh aye. But Maggie got that upset, she was past herself. He'd thought it best to let it lie, especially when Hetty was away in a good job that fed her and gave her a roof over her head.

'I always intended to come and see her, try to explain to the bairn,' he said to himself now. But there was no denying the guilt which rose in him when he thought about Hetty. He had come to the top of a rise in the ground; there was a road of sorts, though unmade. He looked up at the sky, breathing deeply. By, he could really have enjoyed this day out in the open air. The moor was grand, stretching away on all sides, with ridges and banks and distant wooded patches. These last few years while times were bad he'd spent his time in the open air just looking to snare a rabbit for the pot or maybe even a hare.

He thought of the pit: the low seams, some of them only two feet six inches, pressing on him as he lay on his side wielding a pick, or taking the skin off his back as he crawled backwards through the goaf, the part from which the coal had already been won, at the end of the shift. But he loved the pit; friend and enemy at the same time it was.

'Obsessed you men are, and with a flaming hole in the ground,' Maggie would say. 'It's all you can talk about.' It was true, he admitted to himself. Off shift they would gather at the corner end and squat on their hunkers and talk of the pit, the bitchy seams as well as the good ones. It was a brotherhood.

Yet he loved the sky and the fresh air, though there was nearly too much here for a pit lad like him. He grinned at the thought then frowned as he realised he had almost forgotten why he was here: he had to find his bairn.

Richard Hope was crossing the farmyard leading his horse when Thomas came striding across the cobbles, scattering a gander and his geese before him. Thomas ignored them though the gander honked and threatened to no avail. Richard murmured to his horse and stood waiting, his heart sinking for there was no mistaking who this was. Hetty could have been no one's child but Thomas's; they had the same dark hair and eyes and fresh complexion, though his was marked with blue scars from the coal.

'Good afternoon,' said Richard and waited, thinking it

114

was a good job his father was at Harrogate yet again and so couldn't confront or be confronted by Hetty's father.

'Afternoon,' said Thomas, who had yet to eat the sandwiches which Maggie had put up for him. They were still in his bait tin in the pocket of his jacket. 'I came to find out where our Hetty is,' he began without preamble. He surveyed Richard from the toes of his polished boots to the top of his head. 'It was you, wasn't it? I mean who came up to Morton Main yesterday?'

'It was,' admitted Richard. 'Look, if you wait until I've stabled my horse, we could go inside. I'm sure you could do with a spot of lunch or something after such a long walk?'

'I've got me bait, thank you,' said Thomas. 'What I want to know is, where's my lass? An' why was she sent off? I know our Hetty an' I don't think for a minute she did anything wrong.'

Richard looked about him and saw Sam over by the cow byres. He called him over and gave the horse to him before answering Thomas.

'Look, Mr Pearson, I think we should go inside. We can talk quietly there.'

'Well, if you like,' conceded Thomas, and followed him through the kitchen door. Richard was for going straight through to the front of the house but Thomas spied Sally Dunn, who was sitting at the kitchen table finishing off her meal.

'Sally?' he said, pulling up short. 'Do you know owt about this? Or where our Hetty is now?'

She shot Richard a quick glance and blushed a fiery red. 'No, Mr Pearson, I don't,' she mumbled. 'I wasn't here, like.'

'We'll go through, Mr Pearson,' Richard insisted. 'Sally can't tell you anything as she says. She wasn't even here at the time.'

Sally stared at the remains of her dinner, thinking, By, but I could! She could tell Mr Pearson, a chapel man an' all, how his precious daughter had been caught with Matthew Hope in the middle of the night. Shameless she was! But just then one of the bells rang, the one from Mrs Hope's bedroom, and Sally had to rush upstairs to attend to it.

115

Richard took Thomas into the sitting room and offered him a chair.

'I'll stand, thanks,' said Thomas, stiff and unbending. He held his cap in his hands before him and as Richard regarded him he thought that the miner had a pride about him, and an honest, open expression which reminded him yet again of Hetty.

'Sit down, man,' he said gently. 'Have a drink, for goodness' sake.' Though he wondered just what his father or Matthew would have to say if they should come home and find a labouring man ensconced in their sitting room. But thankfully Matthew was out today also and unlikely to come home for hours.

Thomas hesitated before nodding his head and sitting on the edge of a comfortable leather armchair, and succeeding in looking very uncomfortable indeed.

'Have a drink?'

Richard went to the tantalus and held up the whisky decanter but put it down hastily when Thomas glared at him.

'In the middle of the day? Not that I drink anyroad. I've heard of men that go so far as to drink in the daytime, as though night time wasn't bad enough.'

'Em . . . yes. Well.' Richard almost said he wasn't a drinker himself but instead continued, 'I'm sorry, we don't know where Hetty is. I'm afraid my father was so furious when he saw her with Mat— when he saw she had someone upstairs with her, that he sent her packing. I'm afraid—'

'For goodness' sake, man, don't be so afraid all the time!' snapped Thomas. 'You're sorry and you're afraid but that doesn't tell me where my lass is, does it? What were you doing, letting a young lass go off on her own like that with nowhere to go if you were afraid for her? An' what's more I don't believe a word of what you're telling me. If there was a man upstairs with our Hetty, then I'm telling you, it was none of her doing. He must have gone up there after her.'

'I didn't know she had nowhere to go,' Richard pointed out, stung. 'I thought she would go home to you.'

'Aye, well . . .' Thomas went brick red and looked down

at the steel toecaps of his pitboots. 'I'm not saying we're not at fault,' he said after a minute's silence. 'But I am saying that the lass is missing and she's got to be found. I know she's been more or less on her own for five years but she's nobbut nineteen yet. An' I thought she was living in a respectable house. I thought you were concerned about her when you came up to Morton, like.'

'I am. Of course I am. That's why I came. She was good to my mother and I thought she deserved a reference. Besides, I wanted to make sure she was all right. I even went to Saltburn and looked for her but I couldn't find any sign of her.'

In fact Richard had come home from Saltburn to find his brother Matthew in a rare good mood, humming, 'Oh, I Do Like to be Beside the Seaside.' He thought of it now. He'd told Matthew where he'd been and his brother had laughed and said he was wasting his time.

'Saltburn? Saltburn-by-the-Sea, do you mean? I did wonder if she was there.'

'Oh, I don't know, she used to go there sometimes,' said Richard lamely. It was true. He knew Hetty and Ethel had liked to there on the rare afternoons they had off together.

Thomas got to his feet and glanced at the door. 'Your father's not at home?'

'No, I'm afraid he isn't.' Richard bit his lip. There he was, being afraid again. It was obvious this man was not afraid of much; he didn't have the usual attitude of the servant class. Come to think of it, neither had Hetty. She stood as erect as her father and looked everyone straight in the eye. Oh, why hadn't he been more thorough in his search of Saltburn at least? He turned his attention back to Thomas.

'Look,' he said, on impulse, 'I'll give you a lift to Saltburn, if you like? We could look around together. I know the place quite well.'

'Why should you do that?' demanded Thomas. 'Feeling guilty, are you? Is that why you came to Morton then?'

He was very shrewd, Richard thought, and said aloud, 'I like Hetty, I've told you that. It will only take me a minute or two to change.'

117

'Aye.' Thomas considered. 'Go on then. I haven't got all day. And I'd be grateful for a lift.'

Within twenty minutes they were in the car and heading for the coast road. Richard parked beside the sea on Marine Parade and turned to his passenger.

'I think we should ask at the post office first, don't you?' said Thomas, and Richard cursed inwardly. Why hadn't he thought of that himself last time he was here?

'A good idea.'

They walked up Amber Street and round to the post office but the postmistress shook her head.

'Unless she's a householder, I can't help you.'

'Hetty would be a lodger if she was here at all,' said Richard. They stood on the pavement and considered their next move. Seeing the worry on Thomas's face, Richard blamed himself. Somehow he had not thought of Hetty as part of a family, one which worried about her. Which was ridiculous, he told himself. She was the same as most other girls.

'We could try asking at the hotels. Someone might have seen her, she would be needing to work,' said Thomas. 'But look, there's no need for you come with me. It was very good of you to bring me here.'

'I'll come with you,' said Richard. He did not say that dressed as he was in a good suit and shoes his enquiries would carry more weight with hotel managers.

They tried the Zetland first, it was the biggest and hence would employ more staff, then the Alexandra, before striking lucky at the George Hotel. Mr Jordan was there, talking to the manager.

'Hetty Pearson? Yes, I know the lass,' he said. 'Why do you want to know? You her father?' He nodded to Thomas. 'I wouldn't tell any Dick or Harry where a lass was living, mind.' He looked suspiciously at Richard.

'I'm her father, aye,' said Thomas.

'Lost touch, have you? You should keep better watch on a young lass,' observed Mr Jordan. 'Though she's not in any trouble so far as I know. She works for me sometimes, casual like.' He stared up at the ornate ceiling of the reception hall while Thomas pressed his lips together to stifle an angry retort. 'Diamond Street, that's where she lives. The end by the sea.'

Thomas strode along the front so that Richard had to quicken his pace to keep up with him. The house they wanted was easy to find.

'Does Hetty Pearson live here?' Richard asked, a second before Thomas.

'No, she damn' well does not!' retorted the woman who answered the door. 'This is a respectable house, I won't have such as her in it. You should be ashamed of yourselves, coming after a young lass as is no better than she should be!'

'Hey, what do you mean? My lass is a respectable lass, don't you be telling such lies about her!' Thomas stepped forward, his face darkening, but Richard put a restraining hand on his arm.

'Wait, Mr Pearson,' he said. The landlady took hold of the door as though about to slam it in their faces but she did not as Richard spoke again. 'This is Miss Pearson's father and I am her employer. I don't know why you should malign her like that but if you could give us some information as to her whereabouts, we would be very grateful.' He put his hand inside his jacket suggesting that he would make it worth her while. Behind him, Thomas fumed and grunted angrily.

The woman looked him up and down. 'Her father, eh? Well, she has a look of you. It's a bit late to be worrying about her though, isn't it? I tell you, I don't know what girls is coming to, I don't, and she's a fast one all right. Had a man in her room she did, wrecked one of my best chairs too. Are you going to pay for it?' She looked at Richard's wallet which he had taken out and was holding in his hand. 'Belonged to my gran that chair did, a nursing chair it was. Smashed to bits with their carrying on, Lord knows what they were up to! Aye, she lived here all right, for a couple of weeks or so until I found out what she was like. Quiet as a mouse at first. Sly, I'd say . . .'

'Stop your blathering, woman, and tell us where she is now,' Thomas interposed. He thrust his hands deep inside his jacket pockets; they were clenched into fists and his eyes flashed dangerously.

The woman folded her arms and glared at him. 'How would I know that? The last I saw of them was when I threw the baggage out of the door, and her fancy man with her.' She looked again at Richard's wallet and changed her manner. 'I'm sorry to have to be the one to tell you.' Her smile was ingratiating. 'I would think the chair could have brought as much as thirty shillings in the salerooms. It was antique. A lovely bit of beechwood.'

And getting more valuable by the minute, thought Richard grimly. He took a ten-shilling note out of his wallet and handed it to her. 'Oh, I think ten shillings is fair,' he said. 'Well, thank you for your help.' She took the note though the smile left her face.

'Now I come to think of it, the man she was carrying on with looked a bit like you. Same la-di-da voice he had. Well, I'm glad to see the back of them, I can tell you. Folks like that get a house a bad name.' She stepped back inside and slammed the door shut. They could hear the key turning in the lock.

'Bloody woman!' Thomas all but snarled. 'God forgive me for swearing, but for two pins I could burst that door open and break another few chairs for her. When I think—'

'Come on now, let's walk up into Milton Street, someone else might know where she is,' Richard interrupted and Thomas nodded.

'Aye, you're right.' He glanced at the younger man. 'Do you not have to be getting along now? I'll look for meself, you've done enough for me. But I'm right shamed to hear my lass talked about like that. I don't know, if she has gone wrong, it's my fault . . . I can see it all. I should have done something, I should have—'

'I'll stay a little longer. In fact, I can take you into Middlesborough for the bus to Darlington, that will make it much easier for you.' He looked at Thomas's grim expression and went on, 'Don't believe it all. I've known Hetty a long time and she never once gave us reason to think she wasn't a respectable girl. Not until the last, that is . . .' The scene in the pub yard on Ethel's wedding day flashed through his mind, and the other, the one that really hurt though there was no reason on earth why it should. The time his father switched on the light on the staircase landing and there was Hetty, clasped in his brother's arms. Richard shook his head. 'That was probably a mistake,' he told Thomas. 'Hetty never had the chance to explain herself.'

They had reached the Wesleyan Church on the corner and turned into Milton Street to consider their next move. In the end they walked past the picture house to the Milton Club, enquiring in the butcher's and the greengrocer's but to no avail. All they received in reply to their queries were nods of denial and blank expressions.

Walking back they came to a fish shop and cafe and looked in, but there was a crowd at the counter and the tables were all filled. The woman serving the steaming pieces of fish looked hot and harassed.

'I'll go in,' said Richard. 'Excuse me, excuse me,' he said as he pushed his way through the crowd to the counter.

'Take your turn!' angry voices shouted.

'I just want to ask the whereabouts of someone.'

Alice looked up briefly. 'You'll have to wait, can't you see I'm busy?'

He turned back to the door. It was unlikely that the woman knew anything about Hetty, he thought. No one else seemed to. It wasn't worth waiting, it was getting late.

'A waste of time,' he said to Thomas who was standing on the pavement looking through the window.

'I can see that,' he answered. At that moment Alice looked up again and saw the two men standing outside. There was something about the older man which was familiar, she thought, something about the eyes.

'Two cod and chips, please,' said a customer and she nodded her head and got on with serving.

Richard took Thomas into Middlesborough, despite the older man's protest about there being no need. Afterwards he drove home across the moors. The darkness was closing in and the spring evening was cold. He felt for Hetty's father in his distress; was depressed at their lack of success in finding her. He wouldn't mind betting that Matthew knew something about her, he thought suddenly. He pondered on

121

his brother, how cheerful he had been last time Richard had spoken to him, the sly grin on his face. Yes, he would have to have a serious talk with his brother.

Chapter 14

Hetty got on well with Peter and Charlie Hutchins though she found the girl, Audrey, more reserved. Though only seven, she was the one who seemed to remember her mother the best.

'Mam used Rinso,' she said to Hetty the very first time she was busy with the washing. 'She said it was much bettter than that stuff.'

Hetty looked down at the packet of washing powder she held, the sort which had been in use at Hope Hall. She smiled at the little girl just in from school for dinner. Audrey had a disapproving look about her, undermined by the fact that one leg of her navy blue bloomers hung halfway down her thigh, the elastic broken, probably from the usual schoolgirl's habit of sticking her hanky up it.

'Rinso, eh?' said Hetty. 'I'll have to get some when I go for the messages. Though maybe I should wait until I've used this up. Now go and get your dinner, it's on the table, pet. Then I'll fix the elastic in your bloomers.'

'Knickers, my mam called them. They're not bloomers. That's old-fashioned.' But Audrey's tone was not so aggressive this time.

'Knickers then. Hurry up and eat your dinner, the bell will be going before you've finished if you don't.'

Hetty shook some powder into the washer – the very latest it was, a zinc tub with a hand-turned paddle and wringer attached. Audrey had informed Hetty that her daddy had bought it for her mam when she was poorly. Poor little Audrey, missing her mother, reflected Hetty, and felt a

123

pang for her own, back in Morton. She left the pit clothes to steep while she ate.

It was nice working here, she thought as she took up her spoon and began to eat the thick barley broth she had made with the remains of yesterday's joint of boiled ham. Mr Hutchins was a quiet man who allowed her to get on with her work as she pleased and ate whatever was put before him so long as it was hot and nourishing. And Charlie was a little pet, looking at her with big green eyes which reminded her of Cissy's. He was always trying to please her and in the evening, when he came out of the tin bath, he loved her to wrap him in a towel and hold him on her knees for a while. They would listen to the wireless, turned down low because Mr Hutchins was usually still in bed, having to go out to the pit at midnight.

Peter and Audrey would sit with them, and gradually Audrey relaxed and stopped comparing everything Hetty did with the way her mother had done it. Oh yes, it was nice. There was the sea so close and she could walk on the sands just as she had done at Saltburn. If she kept her eyes averted from the land she could even imagine herself there among the jewel streets. Not that Smuggler's Cove was so bad, she had to admit, built as it was at the mouth of a steep ravine with the hills rising on both sides – dotted with pigeon crees it was true, but wooded and bonny on a fine day.

Hetty remembered the story of how Saltburn had been built by the railway pioneers, mostly Quakers, on the model of the holy city, the new Jerusalem to come, described in the *Revelations of Saint John*. Though the streets were just named after precious stones, not actually built of them. And now, seventy years later, some of the houses were shabby and in need of repair. Oh yes, the story was fanciful but she liked it. She had practically been thrown out of Saltburn but she would show them, she thought, she would be back. And when she was, she would have an hotel, or maybe a boarding house. But even if it was just a boarding house she would make it the best, she would supply the nicest food, make it the best value for money in the town.

'Charlie is asleep,' observed Audrey and Hetty forgot her dreaming and looked down at the short-cropped head

124

against her breast. Charlie was indeed asleep. 'Now you'll wake him up to put his nightshirt on,' said Audrey. 'And he'll cry.'

'No, he won't,' said Hetty. She stood up and pulled down the nightshirt which had been warming on the brass line above the fireplace, holding Charlie deftly in her left arm. He might be four, but he was thin and light, she thought. She would have to try to build him up. He opened his eyes only once before she had him ready and she took him upstairs to the double bed the boys slept in.

After the older children were in bed, Hetty tidied up the kitchen and then sat by the fire. There was some dance music on the wireless, 'Little Old Lady' was the tune and she hummed along with it. At least, she mused, Matthew didn't know she was here. The thought of him confused her now. Why, oh why, had she gone with him into that hut? Yet she knew why really. She had allowed herself to be fooled by his charm because she was so hungry for affection. And if she was honest, he held a dark attraction for her; for all she had hated him for so long, she had wanted him too in a way. Or was it that she had wanted a man, any man? Was she a bad woman at heart, as the landlady in Diamond Street had implied? Or was it because he was like Richard in some ways at least and oh, how she'd wanted Richard!

Hetty got up and turned off the wireless. It was time to prepare a meal for Mr Hutchins and make him up some sandwiches. Then she would rouse him so he wouldn't be late for work. Though he had never insisted on it, she always waited up to see to him before he went out, just as her own mother did when one of the men was on that shift.

At least Mr Hutchins was very correct, never suggesting she use his first name, careful for her reputation. At weekends, when he was home from work, he went to visit his mother in Saltburn so he and Hetty should not be in the house together overnight. She thought that a bit over careful, but then, he had to visit the old lady sometimes, didn't he? And after all, that was how she'd come to get the job, through his association with Saltburn.

One afternoon after the older children had gone back to school, a bright breezy afternoon with the sun shining on the waves so that the sea looked as blue as the Mediterranean, Hetty took a walk up the path by the edge of the cliff, taking Charlie with her. It wound on up steeply and when they reached the top they were both out of breath.

'Let's sit on the grass,' she suggested and they flopped down, Charlie lying full-length and gasping, pretending an exhaustion worse than he actually felt. Hetty smiled down at him; she had become fond of him in these last few weeks, very fond. Her brow puckered, she wondered why he was such a solitary boy, rarely playing with the other children, and why when he did he always had to be the Indian to their cowboys or the German to their brave English tommies. If they were playing a team game, Charlie was always picked, if not last, that place being reserved for the fat boy of the village whose mother had the grocery shop, then next to last. Yet he was an appealing little boy, always anxious to please. Maybe that was the trouble.

Hetty looked away and out over the sea, such a great expanse of it from this height. The great dome of the sky came down to meet it, the blues intermingling on the horizon in a haze which could turn into a sea fret, or haar, but at the moment was stationary. In the distance a coaster chugged southwards. A collier perhaps from the Tyne, she wasn't sure, Hetty knew little about ships. Or were they boats?

' "Dirty British coaster with a salt-caked stack, butting through the channel in the mad March days",' she said. It brought back memories of school in Morton Main. John Masefield, she thought, they had had to learn many of his poems off by heart along with those of Wordsworth and Keats and so many others. And take turns to repeat them in class, the sing-song voices making nonsense of the poetry. She remembered how her hands had stung when she'd faltered halfway through that one; Miss Nelson always punished faulty memories with three hard raps across the palm with a wooden ruler.

'Come on,' said Charlie, breaking into her reverie. He looked up at her with those great green eyes. 'Are we going a bit further?'

'Will you not get too tired? We have to walk back, you know.'

'I'm not tired,' he said stoutly.

'You could have fooled me a minute or so back,' she laughed. Rising to her feet, she took his hand and they walked on. The sun was warm on their backs though it was only early May and for once the breeze was from the land and warm. She picked a blade of grass and showed Charlie how to whistle with it and he walked on happily, blowing out his cheeks until they were red and making funny little noises for all his efforts.

At least her period had come, after a few anxious waiting days for it was late. What a feeling of relief that had been! Never again, she had vowed, never, never again would she take such a chance. She watched the gulls swooping above the cliffs, calling to each other, their cries raucous. So different they were from the miners' pigeons with their soft cooing. Da had pigeons.

The thought struck her with an almost physical pain; after all this time she had thought she was over her home-sickness. Da used to take her down to the pigeon cree: to get the pigeons used to her, he would say. She loved the sound of their cooing, the way they always came back unerringly to their home after a race, the wonder of it never went away. Da. Why had he not defended her? she thought for the thousandth time.

'Are you going to be our new mam?' asked Charlie, the question such a surprise to Hetty that she stopped in her tracks and stared at him.

'Your new mam?'

'Yes. Jimmy Tate said his mam says you will be. Are you?'

'Nowt of t' sort!' Hetty lapsed into her native dialect in her surprise. 'That's nothing but tittle-tattle. Jimmy Tate's mother is a go—' She bit off the word before she said it, Charlie was only a bairn and he might repeat it to Jimmy. But after all Mr Hutchins's efforts to stop any gossip, it seemed hard.

'Howay, Charlie, I bet I can beat you back home!' And the pair of them set off, running down the track, Charlie's thin legs in their leather boots with steel segs in the heels and toecaps beating a sharp rat-tat on the stones. Hetty

127

dropped behind slightly as they reached the village so he got there first.

'I won!' he shouted, then looked anxious. 'I did, didn't I? You never let me?'

'No, I didn't let you, I'm fair worn out,' she answered, taking his hand. 'We'll go to the shop, eh? You can have a halfpenny to spend on what you like.'

Thankfully there was no sign of Mrs Tate or Jimmy as they entered the shop. Just as well, thought Hetty. She was angry enough to give that one a piece of her mind!

They walked along the road past the school. The sound of children repeating the three times table came out of an open window and, to Hetty's surprise, Charlie joined in.

'Three times four is twelve,' he called out in a good imitation of the sing-song voices within. Then he stuck the lollipop he had bought with his halfpenny back in his mouth.

Hetty looked at him, her eyebrows raised. 'How do you know that?' she asked.

'I don't know.'

'Can you say any more?'

''Course I can.' And he recited the whole lot, following on with the four times table for good measure.

'But where did you learn that, Charlie?'

'Aw, just hanging about. I can hear them, they do it every day. I wish I was at school, Hetty.'

He was clever, she thought, looking at him. He was small and thin but he had a good brain – not that she was any judge really. Was that why he wasn't so popular with the other boys? Was he too clever for them? She would have a word with his father, she decided.

All thoughts of Charlie and his intellect were driven from her mind, however, as they rounded the bend into Overmans Terrace. For there, lounging against the gate, was Matthew Hope.

'Afternoon, Hetty,' he said and grinned. Lazily he straightened up and ceremoniously opened the gate for her. She ignored the gesture.

'What are you doing here?' she demanded. Suddenly her stomach was churning, making her feel sick.

'Looking for you, of course, what else?'

128

Matthew looked around him as though to say that there was nothing else about the village that could possibly bring him here.

'Go away, Matthew, I don't want anything to do with you ever again,' Hetty said, her voice rising slightly. She bit her lip and glanced anxiously at the house, afraid that Mr Hutchins might come out to investigate. 'Go away, Matthew. Please, go away,' she repeated more quietly.

'Go away, Hetty doesn't want you here. I'll get my dad if you don't.' Charlie stepped forward, his little chin stuck out pugnaciously. He stood squarely in front of her as though his small body was some sort of shield.

'Fetch your dad, will you? You go and do that, kid, I'd like to see the man my girl is living with.'

'I'm not your girl and I'm not living with anyone, I work here—' Charlie was going through the gate, taking Matthew at his word, and Hetty panicked. 'No, don't, Charlie! Don't disturb your dad, he'll be asleep. Don't, pet.'

'But . . .' said Charlie, stopping and looking doubtfully at her.

'I'm all right, really I am. My . . . friend just wants to talk to me.'

'He's not your friend. If he's your friend why did you tell him to go away?'

'Oh, I don't know, I was just angry at him. Look, Charlie, why don't you go back to the school and meet Audrey and Peter? It's almost time for the bell.'

He looked uncertainly from her to Matthew.

'Yes, go on, kid, run along and play,' said Matthew. He put an arm round Hetty's shoulders and she stepped quickly forward as though his touch burned her. He laughed softly.

'Do I have to go?' Charlie asked her.

'Yes, go on, pet. We're just going to have a talk.' Out of the corner of her eye, she saw the lace curtain of the neighbouring house twitch. She had to get Matthew away from there before he did or said something outrageous. 'Go on, Charlie, it's all right.'

He headed off down the road, his whole body registering reluctance to go. After a few yards he stopped and looked round at her reproachfully and she smiled and nodded, willing him to go. He went on, head down dejectedly.

'Come on, walk up the road then,' she said to Matthew and he fell in beside her. Oh God, she thought, there's his car. People are going to notice, it sticks out like a sore thumb. She quickened her pace until they rounded a bend and were out of sight of the village altogether then she turned and faced him.

'Leave me alone, Matthew,' she said. She crossed her arms in front of her as some sort of shield.

He laughed. 'You don't want me to really. Tell the truth, you're gasping for it!' He took hold of her upper arms and pulled her to him, holding her against him. His hands slid down to her wrists and forced her arms open, lifting them around his neck. His eyes darkened as he bent his face to hers. The next minute he had stepped back, an angry curse springing from his lips.

'Bloody hell! What did you do that for?' There were four flaming marks on his cheek which she had raked with her finger nails. He stepped back automatically and put a hand up to his cheek, the fingers coming away tinged with blood.

'Now will you let me alone?' she cried, and turned and ran back to the village. She'd forgotten his car again. Oh Lord, he had to come back for his car.

Her chest was heaving as though she had run for miles. Standing behind the net curtains she watched as he came into view. Don't let him come to the house, she prayed, and slipped to the door and turned the key in the lock. But even as she went back to the window, the car's engine started and in a second or two it was roaring off on its way to the main road.

Chapter 15

Matthew drove away from Smuggler's Cove full of anger and strange emotions he couldn't put a name to and which he refused to acknowledge. Who did she think she was? Nothing but a pitman's brat, a skivvy in his father's house she had been. He had seduced her, hadn't he? It had been easy. Why didn't she fall into his arms now, grateful that he still sought her out?

Why *did* he seek her out? That was the real question which nagged at the back of his mind. Of all the women he had known she was the only one to obsess him like this.

Matthew swerved to avoid a farm tractor. 'Hell's bells!' he snarled. He was so distracted he had almost crashed the car. He forced himself to keep his attention on the road but his unruly thoughts were beyond control. He almost turned the car round when he got to the crossroads; the road was wide enough. He would go back and force his way into that hovel, drag her out by her hair. He saw red when he thought of her there with a man, a bloody miner and his brats. Randy lot, the miners, look at all the kids they had. But he went on, arriving at Hope Hall eventually and stopping the car just anyhow in the drive. He stalked into the house, ignoring the shout from his brother who was cantering towards him on that great black horse of his.

Thank God, Richard would be back at York next week. Matthew was sick to death of his questions, his accusations. Richard had been seeking Hetty, had said so.

'You know something. I'd say you know where she is,'

Richard had said. 'You'd better tell me where. Her family don't even know, and they're worried about her.'

Matthew had smiled. He smiled now at the memory of it. Goody-goody Richard, sanctimonious Richard, so upright, so bloody hypocritical! Why was he really looking for Hetty? Because he wanted her himself, that was why. Matthew flung himself on his bed, heedless of the dust on his shoes smearing the snowy counterpane. He picked up the packet of cigarettes from the bedside table and lit one, flicking it so that a red spark from the end fell on the whiteness and flickered and died, leaving a small, blackened hole. He smoked furiously, blowing the smoke up to the ceiling, then suddenly swung his legs off the bed and stubbed out the cigarette in an ash tray.

Whitby, that was where he would go, find himself someone willing. Some girl who knew her trade, someone who could take away the tension and ask only money in return. He strode out of the room not ten minutes after he had entered. He hesitated for a moment; he was short of cash. He tapped on a door further along the corridor but there was no reply. He opened the door quietly and went in. His mother was asleep.

'Mother?'

He looked at the form on the bed, so still, so white. She wasn't dead, was she? He stepped closer. No, her mouth was open and a small soft snore came from her. She wasn't going to wake up, he could tell. No doubt that stuff his father got for her would see to that. Going over to the dressing table, he began to search through the drawers – the piles of silk underwear, the chiffon scarves. He knew what was there, had often seen his father doing the self-same thing as he was doing now. Ah, well. He permitted himself a sardonic grin. They said the chip never fell far from the block.

He had found it, the chequebook with three or four cheques already signed. Elizabeth Hope. Oh, yes, his father was a sly 'un all right, getting her to sign blank cheques when she was dopey with sleep. Dopey was the word! Carefully he tore a cheque from the book, taking the stub with it, not the next one in line but the last one which was signed.

Glancing over to the bed he saw that his mother hadn't changed her position.

'Thanks, Ma,' he said and went out, closing the door softly behind him. Now for Whitby.

'Where are you going?' demanded Havelock, who was standing on the lawns having a word with Bill Oliver. 'Start on the boundary wall then, Bill, check it's in good repair.' He walked over to Matthew who was climbing into his car.

'Whitby,' he said. Stupid old sod! What the hell did it matter to his father where he was going?

'I don't suppose you've been to see your mother?' asked Havelock. 'Get out of that car, I want to speak to you. It's time you settled down, got yourself a wife – someone who will curb your wild ways. I've been thinking . . . that Joan Hunter, she's just the one for you. We'll ask her to dinner – hey, where're you going?'

Matthew had revved the car and was off, almost causing his father who had been leaning on the nearside door to fall into the gravel. As Matthew looked in his rear-view mirror he could see Havelock waving his arms in the air, stamping with rage. His figure grew smaller and somehow more grotesque until it disappeared as Matthew rounded the bend.

Get wed indeed! Not bloody likely. He remembered Joan Hunter, the daughter of a neighbouring landowner. Though there was some money there, he supposed. The thought gave him pause but not for long. Joan was a plain woman with wispy fair hair and a petulant mouth. Still, if it had not been for Hetty he might have considered her. He smiled grimly to himself. God, what *was* the matter with him? Marriage to Joan was just what he needed. With all her money he would be free of his blasted father. And he certainly had no intention of marrying Hetty, no indeed. But he wanted her . . . oh yes, he wanted her. He would give her a little time, enough for her to sicken of slaving after a working man and his brood. God help that peasant if he was trying to get into Hetty's bed! The very thought brought on a black ugly mood. Matthew couldn't bear to think of it.

Now, he told himself as he turned on to the Whitby road and increased his speed, he would find himself a woman to take away the urgency of his need for Hetty.

* * *

133

Hetty was anything but fed up with her life in Overmans Terrace. She was happy to look after the little house, which reminded her so much of home, and the children too. Charlie especially was carving himself a niche in her affections.

'If only . . .' she said aloud a few days later. She paused from working up a batch of flour for bread and brushed a stray lock of hair away from her forehead.

'If only what?' asked Charlie. It was a lovely day but he was sitting under the table playing with a wooden engine and waggon which his father had carved for him. Mr Hutchins was quite a hand at making such small things out of wood.

'Oh, nothing,' said Hetty. 'I was just thinking aloud.'

Charlie conidered this gravely, his brow puckered. 'I didn't know you could think aloud?' he said.

'No, well, you can't. I mean, I had a thought and said it aloud,' she explained. Charlie nodded and went back to his game. She watched him for a minute. He was a worry sometimes, she thought. Why didn't he go out and play more? He was thin and pale too. But he seemed happy enough.

Her thoughts returned to her own problems. Every day she dreaded to hear a car, expecting it would be Matthew come back. When she'd been out and came into sight of the little terrace of houses she could hardly look at them in case she should see him lounging against the gate once again. Not that she was afraid of him now, oh no. But she was afraid that he would say something to Mr Hutchins, and she didn't want to lose this job.

Hetty finished pounding the dough and put a clean cloth over the bowl. Carrying it to the hearth, she set it on the fender to rise. It was time to get in the washing from the garden at the back of the house, then there was the ironing. Ironing was very different here from in her mother's house. Electricity had been put in recently and Mr Hutchins had bought an electric iron which was a delight to use.

A car drove up to the terrace and her heart jumped into her mouth. But it was only Mr Watts, the tenant of the house at the other end. He had recently bought a second-

134

hand Austin 7 to replace his motorcycle and side car, and was the envy of the village.

Hetty need not have worried that Matthew would come that day, he was on his way to Whitby once again. He parked his car down by the harbour and walked to a door tucked away between two shops in a street just off the front. He did not have to ring the bell, he had a key for the door. Inside there was a flight of steps covered with a dusty carpet which had once been red. At the top there was another door and he opened it and stepped inside.

'Harry! Don't you ever knock?' The woman who turned from contemplation of her reflection in the wall mirror hid her irritation in seconds but not before he had noted it.

'What's the matter with you?' he growled. 'Don't I pay you enough?' He surveyed her. She had curling rags in her hair even though it was already the middle of the afternoon and a cigarette hung from the corner of her mouth. She was wearing a chenille dressing gown, unbelted and open, showing a lacy petticoat over which her bust bulged. Nothing else as far as he could see. Certainly no knickers.

'Just as well you're not dressed, Diana,' said Matthew. 'You can go straight back to bed.' Already he was pulling off his tie, the familiar urge hastening his actions.

Diana giggled. 'My, Harry! You are in a hurry, aren't you? Have I not time to finish my fag, then?' But she was walking into the bedroom as she spoke, her ample buttocks swaying below her surprisingly slim waist. He grinned. Diana was as likely to be her real name as Harry was his.

At least she was clean and so was the bed, he thought as he flung off the last of his clothes and slid under the sheet. And she knew a thing or two about how to please a man, not like that little bitch from Durham.

Afterwards he flung himself off her and lay back on the pillows. Diana curled up against him and he moved irritably.

'You don't have to pretend any feeling for me,' he said. 'That's not what I pay you for.'

'Oh, Harry.' She pouted. 'Don't you like me a little bit?'

He blew out a long line of smoke and considered her critically. At least she had taken those bloody curlers out before she joined him in bed. Her lipstick was smeared, going over the line of her thin lips; it didn't matter that it was he who had done the smearing. There was a smell of sweat from her, mingled with Evening in Paris scent. He knew it was Evening in Paris, the bottle stood on her dressing table and he had seen her dab some behind her ears. Cheap, he thought, common.

Hetty now ... Hetty smelled of household soap and water, and something else, indefinable, exciting, something he could drown in.

'What's the matter, Harry?' the girl asked. She felt uncomfortable, he was staring at her so coldly, his eyes hard and unreadable. 'What are you looking at?' she cried when he didn't answer.

'Not much.'

Matthew swung his legs out of the bed and went to the wash basin, pouring water into the bowl. He washed himself carefully and she watched, knowing he was trying to wash away all traces of their coupling. She got out of bed and pulled on her dressing gown, feeling the need to cover herself. She was humiliated, angry.

'You shouldn't say things like that, Harry,' she said.

'I can say what I like, damn you!' he replied. 'Don't think I didn't notice you weren't exactly pleased to see me.'

He dressed quickly, pulling on his clothes roughly, using a comb he took from his breast pocket. Then he went to the door, not bothering to look at her where she stood at the foot of the bed, face red with impotent anger.

'Don't forget my money,' she shouted at him as he opened the door.

'There's your money,' he snapped, pulling a note out of his pocket, one of those he had drawn not half an hour ago on his mother's cheque. He threw it at her and it fell on the floor.

Slamming the door behind him, he ran down the stairs and into the fresh air. Even the smell of fish on the quay was welcome to him after the atmosphere of the room he had just left. Pushing his way through the early holiday makers, he found his car and drove back to the Hall. His father was just coming out of the door of his study.

136

'You're back then,' he said. 'Come in here, my lad, I want to talk to you.'

Matthew lifted his eyes to the ornate ceiling in a long-suffering glance but behind his father's back. He followed the older man into the study and flung himself down in a leather armchair. Havelock went behind his desk and father and son glared at one another, and never was the similarity between them more startling. The same cold eyes, the same thin line of the lips, the same set to their jaws. Even the way they held their heads was similar though Matthew lounged in his chair, one leg slung over the arm, while Havelock sat straight as a ramrod in his swivel chair.

'I won't tolerate your insolence any more,' he started. His voice swiftly rose in anger. 'Sit up straight in that chair when I'm talking to you!' he bellowed and, surprising himself, Matthew did just that.

'Steady on, Father,' he said, and tried an amused smile which Havelock totally ignored.

'You will smile on the other side of your face if you don't mend your ways!'

Matthew's smile slipped. He crossed his legs, still trying to appear uncaring, nonchalant.

'You've been back here for weeks after your disgraceful behaviour at Oxford. I've waited for you to do something with yourself, I've given you every chance, but you seem to think the world owes you a living. You'll get no more money from me, I have decided.'

Matthew's eyebrows lifted. 'My allowance comes through Mother, from my grandfather,' he reminded Havelock, and his father went purple.

'And when did you live on your allowance from your grandfather? You live here, in my house, dependent on me, and don't you forget it, lad. I can throw you out any time I wish to, and I don't mind telling you, I'm beginning to think about it.'

Matthew was silent, his confidence seeping away. He had complained often and bitterly about the old man but knew he would do badly without him now, in spite of his allowance from his grandfather. He thought of the forty pounds in his pocket, all that was left from his mother's cheque. It wouldn't get him very far and certainly wouldn't pay off any of his debts.

'I was in a hurry this morning, Father, sorry,' he tried on a conciliatory note.

'Hmm.' Havelock stared at his elder son, not in the least mollified. Nothing but a waster, he thought bleakly. But, by God, the lad would mend his ways or he would disown him, he swore he would. 'I'll tell you what you must do if you don't want to be thrown out on your ear,' he said. 'I want no argument from you either. You will do as I say from now on.'

'Yes, Father.'

'Now, I have invited the Hunters and their daughter Joan here for dinner tonight and I want you to be present. I not only want you to be present, I want you to let them all know you are attracted to Joan. Don't say you can't do it, I know very well what you can do with a young girl if you get the chance. You can make her believe anything. Well, you'll have to convince her parents too, for you'll marry this one. I tell you you will.'

138

Chapter 16

Charlie had the measles. For the time being, Hetty forgot about Matthew and everything else except the little boy. He had been fretful all day, hanging round her skirts, more like a two year old than four going on five.

'Have you had the disease yourself?' asked the doctor, looking at her over his spectacles. She seemed so young in her enveloping floral pinny, he thought, like a girl playing at house.

'Yes, Doctor,' she answered. Her mind flitted back to the time she and little Cissy had lain together in the double bed in the front bedroom at Morton Main. It was her parents' bedroom, the largest one and airy, and from the window opposite the bed she could see the hill rising up to Shildon on the summit, the bankside wooded and green. Then her mother had drawn the curtains against the light.

'It's bad for your eyes,' Maggie had explained when Hetty had protested.

In Overmans Terrace, the view was restricted to the side of the ravine which closed in the village. Still, it was green and wooded too. Charlie had not protested when she had drawn his curtains, though.

She gazed anxiously at him, his little face bright with blotchy spots. He had fallen asleep before his father left for Saltburn and when he awoke there were the spots. He was feverish, his eyes half-closed against the light even though the curtains were drawn.

'Plenty of fluids,' said Doctor Gray. 'Do you know if the other children have had the measles?'

139

Hetty had to admit she didn't. Of course, there was the question of quarantine. Luckily it was Saturday, and the children weren't at school. But though Audrey was sitting on the top stair just outside the door, waiting anxiously, Peter was out on the beach with his friends, searching for shellfish.

'Well, don't worry. If they're going to get it they're probably infected by now. But try to keep them away from the other children for a few days.' Doctor Gray closed his Gladstone bag with a snap. 'Where's their father?'

'Gone to Saltburn to see his mother,' said Hetty. Wouldn't it just be a Saturday evening? Oh, why hadn't she called the doctor earlier, when Mr Hutchins was still at home? It had been no good consulting him, he had just said she should use her own judgement.

'It's likely something he has eaten, you know what children are like. He'll be better by this evening.' Mr Hutchins had been distracted, his mind already on his mother who was suffering from the arthritis which usually plagued her more in the spring than the wintertime.

Now Doctor Gray pursed his lips. 'I would have thought he would have stayed at home when the boy was out of sorts. He must have been off colour earlier. When did the spots appear?'

'Only after Mr Hutchins had gone. He goes every Saturday.'

'Well, is there anyone you can send down to the surgery? I'll give you some tablets for him.'

As Hetty was assuring him she would find someone the door burst open and Audrey came in, stopping short just inside the room. She looked suddenly guilty, knowing she had let it out that she had been eavesdropping.

'I'll go,' she offered nevertheless. 'I'll run all the way there and all the way back.'

'Little girls who listen at doors hear things they don't want to hear,' observed Doctor Gray. But he smiled at her. 'Come on then, I'll give you a lift down then you only have to run all the way back. I bet you like to ride in motor cars?'

After they had gone, Hetty brought in some tepid water and sponged Charlie down. He was fretful and wanted to hold her hand. She gave him one of the tablets when Audrey returned and after a while, looking a little cooler, he dropped off to sleep. Going to the window, she drew the curtain aside slightly and looked out on to the road and the hill beyond. Should she alert Mr Hutchins? she pondered. But after all, he would be back tomorrow and there was little he could do for now.

Then she noticed the car parked not quite out of sight along the road out of the village. Was it Matthew's? She opened the window and leaned out. It *was* Matthew. There he was, sitting at the wheel; he saw her and waved, smiling cheerfully. She withdrew her head sharply and closed the window. Glancing at the bed and seeing Charlie was still asleep, she went downstairs and locked the front door.

Audrey was sitting at the kitchen table, colouring in a picture she had drawn of the sea with some unlikely-looking boats and stick children playing in the waves.

'Why did you lock the door, Hetty?' she asked, blue pencil poised. 'My dad never locks the door until it's night.'

'I don't want Peter to bring his friends in,' said Hetty, thinking fast. 'If he has to knock, I'll let him in on his own. We don't want to spread the measles all over the village, do we?'

Audrey looked puzzled, as though she was going to say more, but in the end she bent over her colouring book again. Hetty sat down by the fire, expecting a knock on the door at any moment. But Matthew did not come. After about half an hour she heard his car engine start up and go off, the sound dying away up the road.

Audrey brought her picture for Hetty to see and she admired it and pinned it on the wall. Then she went upstairs and fastened an old towel round the light fixture. It was growing darker already and a bright light would hurt Charlie's eyes. She resolved not to think any more about Matthew, she had enough to do. She made some barley water and flavoured it with sugar and a few drops of lemon essence for she had no fresh lemons. Peter came to the door and she let him in, explaining about his brother and the measles. She made the children's suppers and they went to bed – and all the time she listened for the engine of

Matthew's car approaching in spite of her resolution to forget him.

Hetty went up to check on Charlie and then sat for a while, over tea and Welsh rarebit she had prepared and now found she couldn't eat, then she too went to bed. Her night was disturbed, not only by dreams of Matthew chasing her along the cliff top at Saltburn but by the waking nightmares which plagued Charlie. He would cry out for her and she would get up and change his damp nightshirt and sponge his face with cool water and give him barley water to drink.

'You don't look well yourself,' observed her neighbour. Hetty had washed Charlie's nightclothes and was hanging them out to dry in the back garden. Mrs Timms, the neighbour, came nearer to the fence. 'You don't want to let Mr Hutchins catch you washing on a Sunday,' she said. 'Not hanging it out, anyway.'

'Well, they have to be washed and I can't hang them in the house when they dry so quickly in the garden.' Hetty was tired, her arms felt heavy as she lifted them to peg out the nightshirts. At the moment she didn't care what Mr Hutchins thought about her breaking the Sabbath.

Her dreams of the night before were still vivid in her mind. She was racing along the cliff at Saltburn, looking back fearfully over her shoulder as Matthew drew nearer and nearer until she got too near the edge and fell, rolling over and over down the almost vertical slope, crying out as she neared the boulders at the bottom with the angry waves smashing themselves to pieces on them.

'Da!' she had shouted in her dream. 'Richard!' But when she awoke and sat up in bed, trembling, it was quiet, Audrey slept soundly in her little bed in the corner and grey light was just beginning to enter through a gap in the curtains.

Mr Hutchins came home. 'Another time you should ring Alice from the callbox,' he said, but mildly. 'Still, you did the right thing calling the doctor.' He went upstairs and sat with Charlie, releasing Hetty from the need to stay near and listen for the boy. She walked up the cliff path and sat on the grass, far from any chance of hearing Matthew's car.

* * *

142

Matthew himself was walking sedately around a small copse on the estate of their neighbours, the Hunters, in company with their daughter Joan. He looked sideways at her now; her normally pale complexion showed spots of colour on her narrow cheekbones and her light blue eyes sparkled. He held her arm as they came to a rather steep part of the path and could feel the tremor just beneath her skin. She was beginning to be fat, he thought, the flesh bulged under the puff sleeves of her pink flowered dress. She had a large bust, though, startlingly large even for her round, solid body, surprising against the narrowness of her face and small head.

They came to a stile and he climbed over first and held out his arms for her gallantly. Joan giggled as she put her hands in his – hands which were tiny, like her face. Her short pink dress blew high as she jumped down, showing a paler pink petticoat and an expanse of plump thighs.

'Oh, you're so polite,' she breathed. He held on to her hand as they walked on; it amused him to do so.

'To think you've been home all these weeks and last night was the first time you have had dinner with us,' said Joan. Matthew had his answer ready.

'Well, you know, I like to dine with Mother when I can. It's the highlight of her day.' He sighed. 'Poor Mother.'

'Oh yes, how is Mrs Hope? She has been ill for a long time, and it's such a shame. Mother asked to see her, of course, but we quite understand that her condition prevents her from mixing with people.' She hesitated. 'What exactly *is* the matter with Mrs Hope? I'm afraid I never really knew.' Joan stopped walking and looked up at Matthew, a direct gaze.

Phenobarbitone and codeine, prescribed by Father's friend, the village doctor, was the answer which came to mind, Matthew thought. Amused, he allowed himself to laugh into those repellently light eyes and Joan fell even deeper under his spell.

'She has been an invalid since Richard's birth,' he said, allowing the smile to slip into sadness. 'I'm not sure of the precise term . . . a woman's thing.'

'Oh yes, of course,' said Joan, nodding her head as though she understood very well when in fact she was mystified.

143

They walked on for a few minutes in silence. At least she didn't chatter, thought Matthew.

When the men were left alone to their port the previous evening, Mr Hunter had been quite open about Joan's prospects.

'She will get the lot when I go,' he said. 'Not that the lass needs it, she has a fair inheritance from her grandfather. He was a mill-owner over Bradford way.' He had looked directly at Matthew.

'Yes, anyone who weds my girl will find she doesn't come empty-handed. Though most of it's tied up pretty well – I'm old-fashioned about women and money. They need someone to look after it for them.'

Oh, I could do that for her, thought Matthew. But he couldn't help comparing Joan with Hetty, amazing himself yet again that he should even hesitate when Joan had all that money.

'You'll be comfortable enough there,' said Havelock as their guests departed. 'Just as well her money's tied up, though, or you'd be through it in a year. I just hope to God Hunter doesn't hear more of your wretched reputation before the knot is tied.'

Perhaps he had heard something, Matthew mused, that could be the real reason that Joan's money was tied up. He wouldn't mind guessing that he wasn't Hunter's first choice for her. But it was obvious that she wanted him and the old man couldn't deny her anything. Oh yes, it would be easy to manipulate Joan Hunter to his own ends and desires.

He squeezed her hand gently, almost imperceptibly, and she turned to him eagerly. Drawing her to the side of the path, into the shade of an oak tree, he pulled her to him and kissed her. Her breasts pushed into his chest, the brassiere she wore tight and restraining, almost like armour. Blast the things! Whoever invented brassieres wanted shooting, he thought. Her lips were soft and wet and primly together. Experimentally, almost clinically, he put the tip of his tongue between them. Joan drew back.

'Don't do that,' she said. 'Why, we hardly know each other! I don't think a girl should permit any liberties at all until she's engaged. Men don't respect a girl if she does.'

144

'It was just a kiss,' said Matthew.

'One thing leads to another,' declared Joan. She walked on a few paces and looked back provocatively. 'You're not angry with me, are you?'

Matthew did his best to look disappointed though in truth he was relieved. Her mouth had tasted slightly of the onions she had eaten for lunch, and something else, something sour. Though he would have to get used to that if he was going to marry her. He felt depressed, suddenly.

'Shall we turn back now?' he suggested.

'Oh, but I though we would walk over to Hope Hall. I would love to see it, I haven't seen it in daylight since I came home from finishing school.'

Finishing school! Matthew wondered how much old Hunter had paid for that. Whatever, it was too much. He smiled at her, widening his eyes, flicking his head so that a lock of hair fell over his forehead. He knew it affected the women. Hadn't he proved it over and over again? Like putty in his hands they were.

'I'm sorry, Joan. Perhaps at the weekend? I have some urgent business this afternoon. I meant to tell you earlier . . . I'm not going home now, I have an appointment with a colleague.' Thankfully she didn't ask any more questions, though she pouted.

'Oh, very well,' she said. 'I know you men are always rushing off on business.'

They walked back to her house where Matthew had left his car. He was filled with an overpowering desire to escape, it took all his will-power not to leave her standing, to run back to his car and drive off. He managed to see her into the house and promised to telephone her later to arrange something for the weekend.

'Now don't forget, will you?' she said as she closed the door.

Matthew was at last free to go and roared away down the drive and out on to the open moor. At first he hardly cared where he went so long as it was away from Joan Hunter but inevitably he found himself taking the small byroad which led to Smuggler's Cove. He parked on the bend once again as he had done every day for four days. There was no one

145

about. It was the middle of the afternoon and no doubt the men were at work and the women in their houses for the previously sunny day had turned overcast and there were a few spots of rain already falling.

Hetty. She was the reason why he was here. He was trying to wear her down, get her to see he was not going to give up so she might as well give in to him. It was part of his plan, he told himself.

Bloody Joan Hunter! he thought savagely. He wouldn't touch her, he'd be blowed if he would. He remembered the taste of her mouth with disgust. He felt like washing his own mouth out. Felt like a drink now he came to think of it, a couple of whiskies would do the trick. But he didn't want to go back to the pub on the main road, neither was there anywhere to go in Smuggler's Cove, not without making himself conspicuous. Still, he could use Joan's money. The girl was loaded, or her father was. Spoilt rotten too. She obviously thought that anything she wanted was hers for the taking and she wanted him, Matthew Hope. He should be flattered. Instead he badly wanted to march up to that cottage in – what was it called? – Overmans Terrace, that was it. He would march up to that mean front door and kick it in and drag Hetty out by her hair.

He became lost in an erotic dream. He would keep her in a place on the cliff edge, miles from anywhere else, somewhere where she couldn't get away until she was well and truly his slave. And she would be, he had no doubt about that. He supposed he could marry Joan Hunter, keep his father sweet, get all the money he wanted from her, for she was besotted with him, he knew that now. And he could still keep Hetty, at least until she had lost her looks, and then when the witch lost her power over him he would throw her out, get his revenge . . .

'What are you doing? You're blocking the road. Don't you know this is a working mine?'

The irate voice brought him out of his reverie and he looked up, startled. 'What? I'll park where I damn' well like. Who the hell are you to tell me what to do?' Matthew soon recovered from his surprise and spoke with all his natural

146

arrogance. He climbed out of the car, ready to argue the point.

The man frowned impatiently. He wasn't a common workman, Matthew saw now, but some sort of official, probably the mine manager.

'You're blocking the entrance to the mine, man! Now come on, shift this car or I'll have it shifted.'

At that moment, Hetty opened the door and stepped out into the road. She had a basket over her arm, she was headed for the Co-op to buy groceries. She heard and saw Matthew arguing with the manager and didn't wait for him to see her but turned and ran round the bend to the village square.

Dear Lord, she prayed as she waited her turn to be served at the butcher's counter, please let him be gone when I have to go back. When she did walk back it was with tremendous relief that she saw the road was empty. The altercation was over, the manager must have won. Oh Lord, why wouldn't Matthew leave her alone? Every day she saw him, even though she hadn't been out of the village. Why was he doing it? He was like a cat stalking a mouse.

Chapter 17

'At least you're getting it over with quickly,' said Mrs Timms. 'All three together is better than one after the other.'

Hetty smiled wearily. There might be something in what her neighbour said but this last couple of weeks had been a nightmare for her as first Audrey and then Peter had gone down with the measles after Charlie. She couldn't remember when she had last slept for more than an hour at a time and now her movements were automatic, her head felt full of cotton wool.

'That's true,' she said wearily. 'I don't know what I would have done without you, though.'

'Well,' said Mrs Timms, 'I did what I could.' She placed the pile of ironing she had just brought back from her own house on the table and pushed back a strand of crinkled grey hair, the result of a bad perm. 'I remember what it was like when I had my brood at home.'

All except one of her own children were living away from home, Hetty remembered. The exception, a man in his forties, worked at the ironworks in Skinningrove. He was a bachelor and lived with his parents, Mr Timms being a retired overman.

'I'll keep an eye on them this afternoon, if you like?' Mrs Timms said now. 'You look as though you could do with some fresh air. Take yourself off on the bus for a ride out. Go to Guisborough, it's market day there. It'll do you good.'

'Oh, I can't. Mr Hutchins—'

''Course you can. You'll be there and back before the

148

man gets out of his bed. Wonderful how far you can go these days with the buses.'

'But the children . . . I can't leave you with the children,' said Hetty. But there was a longing in her voice which did not escape her neighbour.

'Oh, but you can,' she replied. 'Do you think I've forgotten how to look after them? Go on, get yourself ready, there's a bus in fifteen minutes.' She paused. 'You've got the fare, haven't you?'

'Oh, aye, yes, I have,' Hetty assured her. Her heart lifted at the idea of a day out, she had not been to Guisborough before.

'Go on then. I'll see to the dinners. Catch that bus.'

'I will.' Hetty made up her mind.

Travelling along the country road, the fields all green with the coming of summer and the leaves on the trees new and fresh, a surge of happiness welled up in her. By, she liked this job, she did. Even when the bairns were bad, she liked it. The fresh air coming in the open window beside her had blown away the cotton-wool feeling from her mind and her tiredness was forgotten. For she would not be turning round in Guisborough and seeing Matthew yet again, thank the Lord for that. She could relax.

The little town was bathed in sunshine; women with shopping baskets over their arms were thronging around the market stalls which straggled out from Market Place into Westgate. The sun was warm on Hetty's back and she was glad she had put on her blue cotton dress even though this was the third summer for it. But it was fresh-washed and starched to a crisp smoothness which felt good against her bare arms and legs. Most of the women were wearing waisted cotton dresses, she saw. The straight up and down fashion of the last decade had finally been superseded by more feminine styles.

Hetty bought oranges for the children, lucky bags and gobstoppers too. By, it was nice not to have to turn every penny over twice, nice to be able to afford treats for the bairns. She thought of Cissy. Not many treats in her young life. But it was a passing sadness, nothing was going to be allowed to spoil her perfect day. She bought a pork roll from a butcher's shop in Westgate and took it into the priory gardens for her own dinner. Sitting on a low wooden bench and gazing at the great stone arch still standing after all these centuries, she ate heartily and threw the crumbs to the birds. Leaning back, she closed her eyes and let the sun play on her face. By, it was grand here, it was. It may have been her lack of sleep and the peace of this place away from the bustle of the market but she drifted off into a doze.

'Hetty, I've been looking for you all over.' The voice was close to her ear. For a moment she thought it was a dream, or a nightmare more like. She tried to jump up, disoriented, but there was a restraining hand on her arm, holding her back.

'Matthew, let me go,' she whispered, defeated.

'Oh no, my love, I'll never let you go.'

He put an arm around her shoulders and kissed her on the lips. To Richard, just passing by the priory gates on his way to a business lunch at the Seven Stars Hotel in Westgate, the scene looked like two lovers happy in each other's company. Home from university for a couple of weeks, his father was initiating Richard into the business.

'For I've just about given up on Matthew,' he had said grimly. Richard couldn't help but sympathise with him, especially now, this minute.

Two lovers, taking advantage of a quiet garden . . . it took a second or two for it to dawn on him who they were. When it did, he saw red and strode into the garden to confront them.

'Hetty! Where have you been? Do you know your father has been looking all over North Yorkshire for you?' Richard was white with anger, could hardly control himself as he glared at his brother, sitting there his arm around her, smirking too, my God! All the time he had insisted he didn't know where Hetty was and all the time he had been carrying on with her. It made Richard so furious he wanted to spit!

Hetty jumped up, her head thumping, the shopping basket with the oranges and the lucky bags rolling off the bench on to the path.

'Richard, it's not like it seems, really it isn't,' she pleaded, her face red, her hands shaking. She had a terrible feeling

150

that this was all inevitable; it had happened before, it would happen again for Matthew made it happen. No matter where she went he found her.

'Is it not?' He looked at her and her heart dropped; his expression was so cold, his mouth such a thin hard line. She dropped her eyes, just couldn't bear to see that look on his face. She picked up her basket and retrieved the oranges, thankful for something to do with her hands. He turned away, addressing himself to Matthew. 'What are you doing here anyway? I thought you were going to the Hunters' place? Isn't Joan expecting you this afternoon?'

'It's no business of yours where I go,' returned Matthew. 'There's plenty of time in any case.' He glanced at Hetty to see if she had picked up on the reference to Joan. Girls could be so damnably jealous. But Hetty didn't appear to have heard.

Richard turned on his heel and walked away then stopped and turned back to address Hetty. 'You should get in touch with your family. They're worried about you. I told your father I would let him know if I saw you. Will you give me your address so that I can send it on?' He spoke impersonally, barely looking at her.

'I will get in touch myself,' she answered.

'But will you?'

'I promise I will.'

Matthew laughed, obviously amused by the exchange. Richard transferred his gaze to his brother for a long moment then strode off.

'Pompous sod,' said Matthew cheerfully. 'You do what you like, Hetty.'

She didn't answer. She was sunk in such misery that even the sunny day seemed to have darkened. 'I have to go for the bus,' she said.

'No, you're coming with me,' said Matthew. He took hold of her arm in a grip of iron and though she struggled to free herself, she couldn't. A couple strolling by turned their heads; the woman looked concerned and whispered something to her companion.

'Are you all right, miss?' he asked, stepping forward.

Matthew answered for her, smiling at them while he held

her to him. 'Just a little tiff, nothing to worry about. My wife will be all right when I get her home.'

The man stepped back uncertainly and they hurried away.

All the fight had drained from Hetty. What was the use of fighting anyway? No matter where she went, Matthew was there ready to pounce on her. She might as well just give in. She was at such a low ebb, so tired, aching with tiredness. The days and nights spent nursing the children had taken it out of her.

Matthew knew he had won. 'Come on, love, the car's just around the corner,' he said, unable to keep the excitement out of his voice. He led her away, holding her close to him by her arm, the movement of her body against his exciting him even further. Joan Hunter and her dumpy little body could not have been further from his thoughts at that moment.

He did not ask her where she wanted to go, did not offer to take her back to Smuggler's Cove. Not yet at least. He handed her into the car and climbed in beside her and drove out into the hills, up to the top of the moor. The air here was fresh and clear and the view stunning but Hetty gave no indication of seeing it. She made no objection when he stopped by the roadside and led her to a quiet grassy hollow behind a low stone wall where he began to undo the buttons of her cheap cotton dress.

Hetty pulled herself out of her lethargy when he began to fondle her bare breast, sinking his head into the hollow of her neck, and groaning. She started to pull away from him but it was too late. Savagely he pulled her back and took her roughly. It was all over in a couple of minutes. Afterwards he lay back, panting heavily.

Hetty ached. Oh, how she ached. Her thighs felt as though they had been rubbed red raw, there was a soreness inside which throbbed and stung. She moved to sit up and saw that her right breast had a red place which was rapidly turning into a bruise. Oh, Richard, she thought achingly, you would never have forced yourself on me. With a shuddering sigh she sat up and covered herself, fastening her dress and smoothing back her hair. Feeling Matthew's eyes upon her, she looked down at him. He raised a hand to finger a lock of her hair.

'So silky,' he murmured, rolling a curl between his finger and thumb. His eyes glazed slightly and he pulled her down beside him, holding her head against his cheek. 'You are a little witch,' he said into her hair. 'How do you do it?' There was genuine wonderment in his voice.

'I didn't do anything.'

'You cast a spell on me.'

He rose on one elbow and gazed at her in puzzlement. 'Of all the girls I've ever had, only you make me feel like this.' He shook his head. 'A skivvy, too,' he said, almost to himself.

Hetty tried to get to her feet but he was having none of it. His arm went round her waist and held her fast. 'I'm not going to let you get away, you know,' he said. 'You are always going to belong to me. We'll find a place, a cottage perhaps, somewhere you will always be waiting for me—'

Hetty managed to throw off his arm and got to her feet. 'I have to go,' she said, brushing bits of grass from her dress. There was a green stain on it, she saw with dismay.

'Righto,' he said. 'We'll find a cottage. In fact, I know just the place. In Runswick Bay it is.' He was warming to the idea. With Joan Hunter's money, he would be able to keep Hetty, of course he would, she wasn't the sort of girl who demanded presents all the time. And there was the little cottage in Runswick Bay where his mother used to take his brother and him for a week or two in the summer. It had been empty since she had been ill.

'No, I have to go back. The children will be needing me. Mr Hutchins will be getting up, he has to go to work.'

Matthew frowned. 'That's another thing. I don't want you staying in that house with another man. You'll have to leave.'

Until then Hetty had been in a haze of unreality. Now she was jolted into awareness. 'No, I can't. I'm not going to leave, Matthew. The children need me, especially little Charlie. Besides, I have to earn a living.'

'I won't have you in that house with him.' Matthew said the words mildly enough but she could tell he was adamant.

'Oh, Matthew, it's no good. I can't run away with you. I

153

can't leave Charlie and Audrey and Peter, I can't, not now. Not when they've been bad. And Mr Hutchins – he never touches me, he wouldn't.'

'Ill! Not bad, ill. My God, I'm going to have to teach you how to speak English,' he exploded, and walked to the top of the rise to stare out over the moor, his face set. Hetty watched him anxiously, suddenly realising how far away they were from human contact. If he got violent – but then, he wouldn't hurt her, not really. He loved her, didn't he? Though he hadn't actually said so. In fact, she didn't know how he felt about her really.

Matthew strode back to her. 'Come on, we're going.'

'Are you taking me back to Smuggler's Cove? Please, Matthew. If you take me back, I'll go out with you. I'll marry you and we'll live in . . . Runswick Bay, did you say?'

Matthew laughed. 'Marry me?' he said. 'Did I ask you to marry me?'

Hetty looked at him, nonplussed. 'I thought—'

'Don't be a fool, Hetty, I can't marry you!'

She flared angrily: 'Go away then, get out of my sight! I never want to see you again, do you hear me?'

Matthew laughed. 'All right, I will,' he replied. He began to walk away, still laughing cruelly. 'The miner's brat thinks she can marry the boss's son? What does she think this is, a fairy tale? Just because I fancied a bit of skirt . . .'

His voice faded as he crested the rise and was lost to view on the other side. After a moment she heard the car's engine as it started and roared away up the road. Well, she would just have to walk until she found a village, she thought dully. Once again she had made a fool of herself. Smoothing down her dress, sadly wrinkled now, she walked on in the direction she thought would bring her to the nearest village.

The memory of Richard and the way he had looked at her made her burn with shame. Oh, she might have been innocent at one time but now she was everything he'd thought she was. Fooling herself an' all, telling herself she wouldn't let Matthew make love to her again, then doing just that. Weak-willed she was, stupid and weak-willed.

She trudged along the road, nothing in sight except for a few sheep and their lambs which scuttled away from the

154

road as she approached. Richard . . . He had said her dad was looking for her. Oh, Da, she thought. Oh, Da. What would he say if he knew what sort of a pickle she was in now? She thought of the letter in her box, the one to Gran which she had written ages ago and never sent.

First chance she had, she would go home, she resolved, the very first chance. If she managed to get back to Smuggler's Cove and still keep her job, that was. She thought of Mr Hutchins, and his elaborate arrangements not to be in the house overnight with her to protect her reputation. Her reputation! Now that was funny. She even managed a smile. What did it matter anyway? No man would have her now except Matthew and he didn't want to marry her. But she'd be blowed if she'd go to live with him in Runswick Bay!

She wiped her forehead with a handkerchief. She was hot and sticky and sorely in need of a bath, a proper bath like the ones at Hope Hall. A car came up behind her, slowed, and the driver inclined his head towards her, mouthing a question. Did she need a lift? She breathed a sigh of relief and nodded, stepping back on to the verge so that he could pull in.

'Where do you want to go?' asked the driver, a farmer by the look of him. He leaned across the seat to open the passenger door for her. She knew he was wondering what on earth she was doing, walking along a moorland road miles from anywhere.

'The nearest bus stop,' she answered, and his eyebrows rose.

'Well, there's one in—' The farmer stopped and looked over her shoulder. A car had raced up to them and was drawing to a halt, raising a cloud of dust. Matthew. She knew it was him before she turned round.

'You want to be careful, driving through the moor at that speed,' said the farmer. 'If you hit a sheep or a lamb—'

'I'll drive how I like,' snarled Matthew. He glared at the farmer who looked prepared to argue but Matthew went on: 'Get about your business, man, and leave my girl alone.'

The farmer glanced from him to Hetty, shrugged and drove away, obviously thinking it wasn't wise to interfere in a lovers' tiff. He felt sorry for the girl though, she seemed so miserable and the chap was so angry. He watched in his rear-view mirror and saw them both get into the car and it drive away.

'I only came back because I thought you would be stranded on the moor.' Matthew didn't know why he was explaining his actions. He was confused, angry, had felt a burst of fury when he saw that lout of a farmer trying to pick Hetty up. For the thousandth time he wondered why he had let the want of her take over his life like this. Always before he had been in control, could take them or drop them without a moment's regret. But that thought was fleeting, his mind was filled with Hetty. He looked down at her and remembered the feel of her body, the silkiness of her skin, and passion rose in him again, mingled with a baffled fury.

Hetty stared at him. 'You needn't have bothered, I was managing fine.'

'Yes, I might have known you would find yourself a man to help you, even here on the moor.'

She said nothing, there didn't seem to be any point. She stared out of the window as the moor gave way to green fields and hedges white with May blossom. They were entering Guisborough again, she noticed all of a sudden.

'Let me out here,' she demanded, and was surprised when he slowed to a stop. 'Thank you,' she said formally, for all the world as though things were normal between them.

'I'll be seeing you,' he answered. 'Don't forget your basket.' The trouble was, she thought numbly as she climbed on to the bus which was waiting at the stop, he most likely would.

The light was falling by the time the bus drew into the stop on the main road. This one did not go into Smuggler's Cove and she had to walk down the narrow side road to Overmans Terrace. She walked in a haze of misery. The day which had started out so well had turned into a nightmare. She slipped in something soft and disgusting and righted herself only at the cost of the oranges jumping out of her basket once again. She scrambled after them, just making them out in the gloom, feeling like yelling out her anger and frustration at the sky. The lights of the pit yard twinkled on one side. She was nearly back at any rate. Wiping her

156

shoe on the grass, she hurried on to Overmans Terrace. Hoss Muck Terrace, the children called it. Hetty smiled wryly.

Chapter 18

'Hetty, I want you to meet my future wife,' said Mr Hutchins. The woman with him stepped forward – a large, plump woman with middling brown hair and a fair, freckled skin and horn-rimmed glasses. Her eyes were light brown, almost green, and looked unnaturally large behind the thick glasses.

'Anne Appleby, soon to be Anne Hutchins,' said her employer. 'Next week in fact, Saturday, in the Methodist church in Saltburn. Two o'clock.'

Hetty suddenly realised her mouth had dropped open in surprise. She closed it as she got to her feet and took the woman's outstretched hand. 'Pleased to meet you,' she murmured automatically, though her head was in a whirl.

'I'm glad to meet you too,' said Anne Appleby, giving her a keen glance. 'John has told me all about you. I'm sure we're very grateful to you for looking after the little ones when they had the measles.' She looked round the kitchen: at the gleaming range, the brass rail twinkling above it, the highly polished press and crisply clean curtains at the window, and nodded. Hetty had the feeling that she had missed nothing at all, especially not the mark on the mat which Peter had left when he came in for his dinner.

Though it was mid-June and a warm day, the fire was burning in the grate as it was the only means of cooking and the back door was standing open to stop the room getting over-heated. It was Sunday and the children were in Sunday School, giving Hetty a welcome break.

'Well,' she said, 'I didn't know . . . I mean, congratulations, I hope you will be very happy. Both of you.'

'Of course we will,' said Anne, 'but thank you.' She smiled at Mr Hutchins as though there could be no question but that they would be happy and he reddened slightly and smiled back.

'I . . . we thought that it was best to be married quickly once we had made up our minds,' said Mr Hutchins. 'Best get on with it.'

So they could save her wages, thought Hetty, panic-stricken. What was she going to do? She remembered the half-written letter on the table and picked it up quickly, slipping it into the pocket of her apron. She could go home, she thought. Oh yes, she could go home now. She had been answering a letter from her father, which was in turn a reply to her own letter telling him where she was. Her father wanted her to go home and, what was more, insisted her mother wanted it too. A warm feeling began to replace the mild panic which Mr Hutchins's announcement had brought.

'Of course, we will give you proper notice,' said Anne. 'A week, isn't it? That will just work in nicely for us all.'

'A week?'

Mr Hutchins intervened. 'Of course, if you have nowhere to go, you—'

'Don't be silly, John. Of course Hetty will have some-where she can go. You have, haven't you, Hetty?' Anne sounded quite sharp.

'Of course,' she said. 'I will go to see my family. They'll be delighted to have me.'

Anne nodded and smiled. Everything was working out as she wished. Hetty felt a desperate need to get away, to be on her own for a spell. She needed time to take in the sudden change in her position. She was losing control over her life once again and the thought frightened her.

'I think I'll just take a walk now you're here,' she said. 'You don't mind?'

'Not at all,' Mr Hutchins replied. 'Fresh air will do you good, you look a bit peaky.' He was patently relieved that all had gone well.

Hetty walked to the cliff path, climbed to the top and gazed out to sea. Though she could go home, there was still the fact that she had to earn a living one way or another.

159

And there was Charlie, little Charlie, so alone in spite of his brother and sister. She suspected he would be a loner all his life. Yet he had taken to her, even today had wanted to stay with her rather than go off with Peter. Now she had to leave him. She could weep for him.

She wasn't sorry to be getting away from Matthew, though. He was still there most days, parked close to the house for at least a couple of hours. Even the neighbours had stopped commenting on it now. She had developed a policy of never looking up the road to where he might be whenever she went out of the house. They seemed to have come to some sort of truce since that day on the moors above Guisborough. He no longer tried to force her to do anything, simply sat in his car. On the rare occasions she did look directly at him, he gazed back without expression. He wouldn't be able to do it in Morton Main, her da and Frank wouldn't stand for it. That was one good thing about the situation for the feeling of being watched all the time was sometimes unbearable.

Hetty sighed. She had better get back, it was almost tea-time and the children would be home from Sunday School. This was the last time she would think that, she thought sadly, and a picture of Anne Appleby came to mind. There was something cold about her eyes behind those thick glasses. Poor bairns. She hoped Anne wasn't at all like the storybook idea of a step-mother.

Mrs Timms was at her door when Mr Hutchins was setting Anne Appleby to the bus stop for her journey back to Saltburn that evening, and of course had to be introduced. Next morning, as she and Hetty were hanging out washing in the narrow gardens, she was forthright about the change coming to her neighbour.

'Mark my words, she's a hard one, that,' she said, mumbling through the pegs held in her mouth as she struggled with a sheet in the wind. She managed to peg the sheet out and stuck a prop in the line to lift it higher, stepping back as it flapped noisily. She took the remaining peg out of her mouth. 'It's Charlie I feel sorry for.'

Hetty couldn't speak. She picked up the washing basket and fled indoors where she cried bitterly over the washing machine, tears mingling with the suds as she pushed the handle forward and back, forward and back. Her own back ached and she stood up straight and rubbed it with both hands. Then she dried her eyes with the kitchen towel and got on, trying to think of nothing except her work. The children would be in for their dinner shortly, she needed to get the piles of washing off the table in order to lay it for the meal.

There was a letter from her father in the eleven o'clock post.

' . . . Of course you must come home, lass,' he wrote, and she could almost hear his voice as she read the words. 'Mind, I must warn you, there are some rumours in the place about you and why you had to leave Hope Hall. Sally Dunn has been home and I reckon she's been spreading a bit of poison, God forgive her. But I said to your mam, we'll wait and hear what Hetty has to say for herself.'

But the best thing was, there was a note on the end of his letter from Mam. 'Just a line,' she'd written. She always put that on every letter she ever penned, thought Hetty, smiling to herself. 'I'm looking forward to seeing you, pet. Until next Saturday then, we're all that excited.' And best of all, she had signed it 'Love, Mam'.

Mam had finally forgiven her for Cissy's death. Hetty was overwhelmed with happiness. What a morning it had been for emotions! This was the second time she had been in tears only this time it was different. Oh, Mam! Hetty attacked her work with renewed vigour, even singing under her breath as she brought in the washing basket after the last of the washing and laid the table for dinner. Then she went to look for Charlie. Where was he? It wasn't like him to disappear like this.

Charlie was sitting in Matthew's car, pretending to drive. Anger swept through Hetty when she saw the boy, with Matthew next to him, grinning.

'Come out of there, Charlie,' she called as she hurried up to the car. She didn't look at Matthew. 'Come on, get out. Your dinner's ready. You should never get in anyone's car!'

Charlie, crestfallen, let go of the steering wheel and climbed out of the car. 'I wasn't doing anything wrong,' he

161

said, his bottom lip jutting. 'I was only playing, I wasn't going to *go* anywhere. I can't make it go, I can't reach the pedals.'

'Hello, Hetty,' Matthew put in. 'I thought that might change your mind about ignoring me.'

Hetty took hold of Charlie's hand. 'No, I know,' she said. 'But don't do it again, will you? Look, I'm not cross. Go on now, Peter and Audrey will be home in a minute.'

Charlie ran off down the road and Hetty turned to Matthew. 'You can sit there as often as you like, you can stay as long as you like, I don't care. But don't you touch Charlie or any of the bairns, do you hear me?'

'Dear me, in a temper, are we?' Matthew laughed. Hetty turned on her heel and walked away. After a minute or two, Matthew started the car and turned it round in the entrance to the pit, going off towards the main road.

'Did you talk to the man, Charlie?' Hetty asked when she got back to the house. 'What did you say?'

Charlie considered. 'I said that it was a nice car and he said: would you like to sit in it? That's all.'

'You're sure that was all you said?'

Charlie nodded. 'Then he let me sit in his seat and play with the steering wheel. When I grow up, I'll have a car like that.'

Hetty was relieved. At least Charlie hadn't told Matthew she was going away. Let him find out for himself, then if he couldn't find her he might give up pestering her all the time.

Hetty sat on the end of the pew in Saltburn Methodist Church, Peter and Charlie beside her, dressed in their Sunday suits with white shirts and bow ties. They were very quiet, looking around them at the rows of empty pews on their side and the ones on the other side of the church filled with men in suits and women in flowery dresses and smart hats. In the pew in front sat Mr Hutchins, his hair slicked back from his forehead with pomade. The smell of the pomade rose above even the scent of the roses on the altar.

Hetty's box was at the railway station, only fifty yards from the church. Her sadness at leaving the children was tempered by excitement for she was going home as soon as the service was over.

'You will be able to sit with the children during the service, won't you?' Anne Appleby had asked. 'I mean, in the church. I know you will be anxious to get home or I would invite you to the reception.'

'Oh, surely she can come to the reception, dear?' Mr Hutchins had said.

Anne shook her head at him. 'Don't be silly, dear,' she had replied. 'Of course Hetty would rather be on her way as soon as the service is over. In any case, I have booked only for the immediate family.'

Hetty had assured them she would make up sandwiches, and would rather be on her way.

'There's a train at twelve o'clock,' said Anne. 'I looked it up.'

The clock in the church said eleven o'clock now and right on cue the organ began to play the 'Here Comes the Bride' and Anne came down the aisle on her father's arm, followed closely by an anxious-looking Audrey, dressed in pink artificial silk with layers of frills on the skirt. She had artificial pink carnations fastened to her hairband and Hetty felt for her. Pink was definitely not the colour for the little girl, it made her look sallow-faced. But Anne had insisted on pink. She herself wore a cream suit with a blue chiffon scarf and blue hat.

The congregation was standing and Hetty hurriedly got to her feet and motioned to the boys to do the same. Charlie was white and looked as though he might be sick. Hetty prayed that he wouldn't.

'It would be best if you just slipped away, Hetty,' Anne had said earlier. 'Better for the children. I don't want tears, not on my wedding day.'

Hetty hadn't argued, she knew it would do no good. Anne was a very forceful woman. She hoped Mr Hutchins knew what he was about.

As the service began her thoughts wandered to Matthew. She thought, she hoped, she had succeeded in fooling him, bringing her box in on the bus the evening before after he had gone and leaving it at the left luggage office. She looked

163

up at the ceiling as the minister intoned the wedding service. Please God, she prayed, please don't let him come after me. Dear God, how did you let me get into this mess?

The congregation was standing again, the organist playing 'Love Divine, All Loves Excelling', Charlie was holding his hymn book out to her so she would find the number for him.

'Hetty?' he asked. His eyelashes were damp as though he was holding in tears but he didn't actually cry.

'Are you all right, pet?' she asked him and he nodded. Oh, poor Charlie. She vowed there and then she would keep in touch with him no matter what.

The service was over, now was the time for her to slip out while the bride and groom were in the vestry signing the register.

'Sit still, boys,' she whispered. 'I have to see to something.' Peter looked solemnly at her and nodded. Hetty pressed Charlie's hand, not daring to kiss him in case he realised she was not coming back. Then she slipped out of the church.

The journey up to Darlington passed in a blur of tears. Every few minutes she was trying to guess what Charlie was doing now, how he was behaving, how he was feeling. For she was well aware that his new mother would stand for no 'bad behaviour', or even questions. And Audrey, Hetty prayed she would not make a scene either. Especially not in front of her new step-mother's relations or Anne would make her pay for it later when they got home. For the family was going back to Smuggler's Cove that afternoon, straight after the wedding breakfast. Mr Hutchins had not taken any time away from his work, neither he nor Anne deeming it necessary.

At Darlington Hetty dried her eyes before getting off the train. Then she went into the rest room and splashed her face with cold water. She stared at herself in the fly-spotted mirror, feeling calmer. It was no good weeping over the children, she told herself sternly. She couldn't help what had happened. Though she knew that Anne had no real regard for them, surely Mr Hutchins would not allow her to hurt them? No, of course not. He would see they were treated decently.

164

With this cheering thought Hetty boarded the train for Bishop Auckland. Though it was Saturday afternoon, the compartment was almost empty but for a young girl with a laden shopping basket who, after smiling shyly at Hetty, sat in a corner and buried her head in a copy of *Woman's Weekly*. Of course, Hetty reminded herself, most of the shoppers came in and out by bus these days.

Feeling suddenly hungry, she brought out the packet of sandwiches which she had made up in Smuggler's Cove and forgotten all about on the Saltburn train. By the time she had munched her way through them and drunk the small bottle of ginger beer she had put in the bag with them, the train was already drawing into Shildon station. The girl got out and walked up the incline to the road. Hetty thought she herself could have got off the train and walked the two miles to Morton Main, it would have saved her half an hour. But the nearer she drew to Morton, the more nervous she became. Nervous and excited. Anxious to get there yet dreading her arrival.

The train entered Shildon tunnel and the lights flickered on and then suddenly they were out in the daylight again and almost before she knew it were steaming into the station.

'Bishop Auckland! Bishop Auckland!' shouted a porter and a great lump settled in her throat for there, on the platform, were her da and her gran. And though at first she thought her eyes were playing tricks on her, there were her mother and Frank too.

Chapter 19

'You're not going back to Yorkshire then?'

The family were walking down Newgate Street to the stop where the bus came in for Morton Main. The late-afternoon sun cast the street into areas of light and shadow and struck a prism from the clock on top of the Wesleyan Church tower. The familiar street, said to have first been built by the Romans and straight as a die, stretched out before them in a gentle slope down to the market place at the other end. Hetty's heart was full as she gazed down the length of it: the same Wilkinson's department store where her mother bought the materials for her sewing, the same Holden's with the windows full of toys. How she and Cissy had loved to gaze into them!

'Hetty? What's the matter? You've not gone off in a dream, have you? By, as I remember you were always doing that, lived more in dreams that you did in life.' Frank looked down at her as they walked along the sunny side of the street. Her box was on his shoulder and he carried it as though it was as light as a feather.

'Our Hetty always was one for going off into a dream, all right,' said Da from behind where he was walking with Mam on one side and Gran on the other. Hetty joined in the general laughter.

'Eeh, I'm sorry, Frank, what did you say?'

'I asked if you were going back to Smuggler's Cove?'

'I don't know. We'll have to wait and see. Now Mr Hutchins is married they don't need me,' she replied and a cloud of worry dimmed her happiness for a moment. By, she hoped the bairns didn't need her either, she thought. Charlie and Audrey at least.

The bus for Morton Main was standing there and they all piled in, to curious glances from the other passengers. For a second or two Hetty quailed, thinking that she saw Mrs James near the back, but she was mistaken.

They settled in the rear seat so that they could talk easily together, though Maggie was quiet. Hetty gazed at her, wondering if after all Mam was still going to be reserved with her, though her kiss on the station platform had been warm enough. But Maggie smiled lovingly back and Hetty's heart lifted.

'Mind, you'll see a lot of changes, our Hetty,' said Gran, nodding her head to emphasise her words. She was a little more bent with her arthritis than she had been and the whole family kept their pace down to hers.

'Aye,' said Frank. His smile slipped a little and he looked searchingly at Hetty. 'A lot of people have moved away. The Jameses now, they've emigrated to Canada to be with their son. He's farming in Alberta and they say he's doing grand.'

Well, at least she didn't have to fear bumping into Mrs James, thought Hetty, relieved. Aye, but the woman had a right to hate the sight of her, she admitted to herself as a vivid vision of Dorothy, lying so still in the snow, invaded her mind. But it hadn't been all her fault! No, it had not.

'Have you not got a lad, Hetty? A bonny lass like you, you're not going to land on the shelf, are you?'

'I'm only nineteen, Gran,' she protested, laughing. But for a fleeting moment an image of Richard flashed into her mind. But that particular dream was finished, Matthew had seen to that.

'No, I haven't got a lad,' she said. 'I don't want one, neither, I'm happy on me own.'

'I wish I had a sixpence for every lass as said that before they met the right one and got wed,' Gran observed.

Morton Main wasn't so much changed though, thought Hetty as she got off the bus and walked past the chapel on the end of Chapel Row. There was still that air of deprivation and poverty about in spite of the yard steps scrubbed white and marked out with sandstone, the dolly-dyed cream

167

curtains at the windows in the backyards. The same tin baths hung on the walls beside the windows too and it could almost have been the same knots of miners, whether they were out of work or simply off-shift, Hetty didn't know, sitting on their hunkers at the gable ends of the rows, discussing the pit and the conditions in it.

'I tell you, man, the water's seeping in that bad in the seam I come home wringing wet every blessed day,' one was saying. It could have been the same conversation she had overheard the last time she was home, Hetty thought.

Some of the women hanging out washing in the back lanes looked sideways at her but most greeted her civilly enough.

'That Sally Dunn was spreading lies about you,' said Mam when she saw Hetty's face. 'Take no notice, pet. If they're talking about you, they're leaving other folks alone.'

Hetty's smile lit up her face. Praise the Lord, she thought. Mam was taking her side. She was all right again, must have forgiven Hetty for Cissy's death.

Maggie had baked and all. There was bacon and egg pie, and rhubarb tart and custard, even fresh lettuce from the cold frame on Da's allotment, and tomatoes and pease pudding from the Co-op. By, her mam had gone to a bit of trouble to welcome her home!

'Oh, Mam!' said Hetty, and her eyes filled with tears. She put her arms around her mother and hugged her.

'Howay now, none o' that,' Maggie said softly. 'You're home now, me bairn, an' I'm right sorry it's taken me all this time to see sense. I was off me head, likely. The change, I reckon, but I'm over it now.'

The men had seen what was going on and retired into the front room out of the way. Not Gran, however. She had gone into the pantry to fill the kettle from the tap there. Now she came out and settled it firmly on the fire.

'I gave her a good talking to, our Hetty,' Gran said now. 'Why, aye, I know it's hard losing a bairn, especially a little 'un like Cissy, bless her heart, but mebbe she's better out of the troubles of this world. Mebbe—'

'Mother,' Maggie butted in, 'don't go on, please.' She turned back to Hetty and smiled as Gran muttered something under her breath about not being allowed to have her say, and what was the world coming to? Time was when a bit of respect was shown to your elders, but not these days.

'I'll say this now and then we'll not speak of it again,' Maggie said to her daughter. 'I did blame you for Cissy's death as you well know, pet. But I was out of my head and I let it prey on me mind for far too long. I know you loved the bairn, Hetty—'

'Eeh, I did, I did,' she said.

'Aye, well, it was an accident, I know that now. An' I'm sorry I blamed you, Hetty, it was wrong of me. I felt I had to have somebody to blame but I was wrong. Forgive me, pet?'

'I'm sorry too, Mam,' Hetty said softly. Behind them, Gran grunted.

'Right, now that's over, let's get the dinner on the table. By, I'm fair clemmed for a bite to eat.'

The kettle began to sing and the table was soon laid. It was as good as a party, thought Hetty, her family all around her. And afterwards they all went off to the picture house on top of the Workingmen's Club, which was run by the club committee. They watched Douglas Fairbanks swashbuckle his way across an unlikely landscape and cheered mightily when he came out triumphant. And the committee men shone their torches and shouted for order and threatened to put out some of the more unruly lads and lasses in the twopenny end who promptly sat down quietly for they knew the committee men meant what they said and they didn't want to miss the ending. And Hetty remembered sitting on the benches at the front herself when she was a bairn, and grinned. She had always been as good as gold, as her mother used to say, for it would be dreadful to be put out before the picture ended.

They walkd back home arm in arm across the road. The air was fresh and clear and there was a cool breeze coming from the fields in front of the village and no one noticed the smell from the coke works except Hetty. She supposed she had forgotten it.

'Hadaway, man,' said Da, grinning at her when she

wrinkled her nose. 'It's good for you that smell, kills all the germs that does.' Which she could well believe.

By, it had been a lovely day, she thought as she lay in bed that night, a lovely, lovely day. And tomorrow she would make the Yorkshire pudding for her mother to go with the joint of beef which sat in the pantry under a gauze cover, and peel the potatoes and turnip. And afterwards she would go for a walk and discover all the old secret places she and Frank used to have when they were little. And after that she would go to chapel with her mam and da. She didn't care if anyone looked sideways at her, no, she didn't.

Monday, though, Monday she would have to start looking for a job, she couldn't expect her family to keep her forever. They were eating well this weekend but she knew it was a special effort and had probably made a big hole in Mam's emergency fund, which she kept in an old teapot on the top shelf of the pantry.

'Please, God,' she prayed, closing her eyes tightly as she had done when she was little, 'please let me find a job so that I can stay here for a bit. And don't let Matthew find me or even come looking for me. Let him forget all about me and I promise I'll never be so wicked again as I was with him.'

Joan Hunter sat before her dressing table, gazing at her reflection. She looked well, she decided. Maybe a little too plump but Daddy assured her that men liked a bit of flesh on a girl. And Matthew did like her, she was sure of it, and she would make sure he married her, yes, she would. Joan nodded to herself in the mirror, pleased with the way her hair, marcel-waved and dressed just like that German film star's, Marlene Dietrich, held close to her head, not a hair disturbed by the movement.

Maybe her cheeks were a little too red . . . she picked up a fluffy powder puff and dusted her face heavily with the cream-coloured powder. There, she was ready. She felt a thrill of excitement. Tonight, she had decided, was the night Matthew would ask her to marry him. She had it all planned. She would take him into the conservatory after dinner and

170

they would sit on the cushioned basketwork sofa where she would allow him a small liberty or two.

He was a man, wasn't he? He wouldn't be able to help himself. And afterwards, well, he would feel compelled to ask her to marry him for she was a young lady, unused to the ways of men, and would act the frightened virgin, just like Pauline in the *Perils of Pauline*, and he would feel like a cad if he didn't offer for her. Joan grinned at her reflection. If all she'd heard was true, Matthew had been a cad and worse, but that was all to the good. He must be experienced in *it*. Anyway she would change him when they were married, indeed she would. No husband of hers would get away with being a philanderer!

Pulling on her elbow-length blue silk gloves, which matched her blue silk dress, low-cut to show off her magnificent bosom, she gave her hair a final pat and made for the stairs. Matthew must have been waiting ten minutes at least, best not let him get too impatient. It might be a good idea, she thought as she reached the bottom stair, to have Daddy come into the conservatory at just the right time and catch Matthew with his hand in her dress or something like that. Then he would have no choice but to act the gentleman. Breathing in, for the blue silk dress was a little tight, she went into the drawing room.

Matthew and his father were standing before the fire with her father, and her mother was sitting straight-backed on the edge of the settee. All turned and smiled at her as she came in.

'So you have decided to come down then, have you?' said Mr Hunter. 'Come along, come along, we're all starving to death waiting for you.'

'Nonsense, darling,' said Mrs Hunter primly. She was thin and angular and Joan looked at her critically. There was no doubt her mother had a certain elegance but, as her father said, a man liked something to get hold of and Mother hadn't an ounce of fat on her.

Complacently, Joan turned to Matthew and smiled brilliantly before addressing his father. 'I'm truly sorry to have kept you waiting, Mr Hope,' she said, giving him her hand.

'No, not at all,' Havelock answered. As she turned to

171

Matthew he could not help seeing the way her dress pulled across her ample hips. An unfortunate choice, he thought. He had seen the strain in Matthew's smile for an instant before it was covered up. Bless the lad, at least he was an excellent actor. Havelock would have a quick word with him if he could get him on his own for a minute during the evening, remind him that a large dowry made up for a multitude of sins. In any case, women were all the same in the dark. Who looked at the chimney when they were stirring the fire? And Joan looked to be a strong-minded girl, would keep Matthew on the straight and narrow, he was sure of it.

The dinner was good and the company ate heartily: salmon caught in the Tweed and smoked locally was followed by a saddle of lamb from their own moor. Joan ate daintily, Matthew was amused to see, tiny little bites from the end of her fork, her brightly painted mouth showing only glimpses of small teeth. Yet her plate was cleared at every course and when the chocolate mousse appeared she eyed it greedily and had a second helping.

Matthew would have enjoyed the evening, found it highly amusing, if only he'd known where Hetty was now. He had gone down to Smuggler's Cove every day for a week but was well used to her hiding from him. The feeling of power that had given him was intoxicating. But she couldn't possibly hide away all this time, and besides, that other woman was going in and out of the house now. So only today he had knocked on the door and asked for Hetty.

The door was opened by the sprat, as Matthew thought of Charlie. He had gazed up at Matthew with woebegone eyes. Miserable as sin, the kid looked.

'Who is it, Charles?'

The woman's voice was harsh, impatient, and the boy had jumped and stammered as he answered: 'It's . . . it's that man, the one . . . the one who . . . who sits in the car up the road.'

'Mother!' shouted the voice. 'How many times do I have to tell you?'

Charlie looked down at his boots. 'Mother,' he mumbled.

'What? What did you say?'

'Mother,' said Charlie, louder this time. 'It's the man who . . .'

'Yes, I heard you, go inside.'

The woman came to the door, her face set, and cuffed the boy, none too gently across the head. 'Remember what you have to call me another time.' He disappeared inside and she looked at Matthew enquiringly. 'Well? What do you want?'

Matthew looked down his nose at her in the way which Hetty would have recognised and quailed before in her days at Hope Hall.

'I'm looking for Miss Pearson,' he stated.

'Are you now?' retorted Anne. 'Well, that's too bad, isn't it? She doesn't live here anymore.' She started to close the door but Matthew slipped his foot in the opening to prevent her.

'Don't close the door on me,' he warned her, and she snorted. 'I'm telling you, don't do it or you'll be sorry.'

Anne looked uncertain. 'I've told you, she's gone,' she said, but quieter now.

'Well, can you tell me where?'

'No, I can't. I'm not interested.' She looked behind him and took courage. 'You'd best not threaten me either, mister, here's me man coming and he'll sort you out.'

Matthew looked down the road. A group of men were walking up, Mr Hutchins among them. 'Damn!' he swore and stamped off up the road to his car. Behind him Anne had opened the door wide and come out into the road.

'Don't you come back here, do you hear me?' she shouted. Matthew turned his head to retaliate but saw Mr Hutchins detach himself from the group and hurry up to his wife, taking her arm and hurrying her inside. Matthew grinned. Evidently Mr Hutchins didn't like any unseemly shouting in the street. He drove up to the main road and across it in a furious temper for all that. Now he had to find Hetty again, he *had* to, and he must face the prospect of not seeing her until he did and that thought was anathema to him.

'Don't forget we're going over to the Hunters' tonight,'

173

Havelock had growled at him the moment he came in at the door.

'Bugger it all!' Matthew had snarled.

'What did you say?' snapped his father. 'You're going to have to take a different attitude to that, my lad, and you're going to have to get a move on about it too. Now away up to your room and get ready.'

'Oh, dear, I'm so hot,' said Joan, bringing Matthew's mind back to the reality of his tedious evening with the Hunters. She gazed at Matthew meaningfully. He looked away for a minute, couldn't stand to see that fat white hand waving a handkerchief over the vast expanse of exposed bosom. Like a slug, it was, that hand.

The smile slipped from Joan's face for an instant, but only for an instant, as she decided that the momentary disgust he had showed could not possibly be aimed at her.

'Why don't you young people take a turn in the garden?' suggested Mr Hunter. 'Or sit in the conservatory, perhaps?'

'Oh, that's a good idea,' Joan exclaimed, jumping to her feet. 'Are you coming, Matthew?' That was one thing about Daddy, he cottoned on to an idea immediately. A word in his ear as they were leaving the dining room had been sufficient. Matthew walked to the window and looked out over the dark garden. He didn't appear to have heard the small exchange.

'Matthew? Matthew!' The sharp note in his father's voice roused him and he turned, summoning a smile.

'I think it will be chilly in the garden, Joan,' he said.

'The conservatory then,' she replied. The two fathers looked at each other indulgently though Havelock only just restrained himself from telling Matthew to behave himself.

The conservatory was poorly lit by a couple of imitation Victorian street lamps. There was a great deal of cast iron-work and an Italian tiled floor and tall frondy plants in ornate pots. Joan put her arm through Matthew's and looked up at him admiringly.

'Oh, Matthew, isn't this nice and private? We can sit and talk in here, can't we? Look, let's sit on this little sofa here.' She pulled him down on to the cushions. The sofa was indeed small and he was squashed in between her bulk and the equally fat, overstuffed cushions.

Oh, well, he may as well play his part, Matthew thought. She was a girl, wasn't she? He was never one to refuse something offered on a plate. He leaned over her and smiled brilliantly before dropping a light kiss on her cheek. He was so close to her that her perfume was overpowering and he pulled his head back sharply.

'Is something the matter?'

'No, of course not, but I don't want to offend you.'

He put one arm around her waist and picked up her hand (the slug) with his free one and brought it to his lips.

'Oh, you're so romantic!' squealed Joan, but softly so as not to be heard by the others. Matthew drew a deep breath and kissed her on the lips. After all, he was getting used to her perfume. If they did marry he would soon wean her off that, he thought abstractedly. For in spite of his aversion he was beginning to feel aroused. The pressure of her tightly restrained breasts against his chest encouraged him.

'Oh, Matthew, Matthew,' she murmured, and her mouth opened slightly, just enough for him to insert an experimental tongue. She tasted of chocolate mousse and wine. He could feel the rapid beating of her heart even through her corset. He ran his fingers down her spine. The corset ended just below her bust, he reckoned, and, yes, there was the fastening of her brassiere. Damn! It was broad, there must be at least a dozen hooks and eyes. Oh, well. Matthew began to kiss the nape of her neck, then lower down to the top of her breast.

Joan sank back on the cushions. He pulled the top of her dress down a little and kissed the exposed skin. Joan moaned but made no move to stop him. He kissed her eyes, her lips, and pulled the dress a little lower over one breast – and suddenly it popped out! There it was in all its glory. Though the light was dim he could see it, like the figure head on the prow of an old sailing ship, white and firm and with a rosy-tipped, surprisingly small nipple. He bent his head to taste it and his hand slid down to her thighs.

'Matthew! What are you doing to my little girl?'

The centre light had been switched on and there stood

Mr Hunter, looking extremely shocked, and Havelock behind him, barely able to contain his mirth.

Chapter 20

Hetty picked up her mop and bucket and took it down the hall to the caretaker's room. There was a big sink in the corner and she tipped the dirty water down the drain, rinsed out the bucket and washed the mop under the tap before putting it away in the corner. She dried her hands on the hessian apron which she had tied round herself before starting on the floor. It was almost dark outside, she noted. Well, another half an hour and she would be finished for the night.

Taking a duster out of her pocket, she went to the head-mistress's study and began to dust and tidy the desk. Mr Cooper, the caretaker, popped his head round the door.

'Nearly knocking off time, lass, you about finished?'

'Yes, Mr Cooper, I've just the dusting in here to do,' she replied.

'Well, when you're ready you can get off home.'

He went off down the corridor, whistling tunelessly. He was a nice man, she thought. Oh, aye, a grand man. Always scrupulous about sharing the work out between the cleaners, always making sure they got off at the due time. He was a retired miner, a friend of her da's. He'd been injured in the pit and walked with a limp yet he was always bright and cheerful and the bairns loved him. Hetty remembered the year before she herself had left school and Mr Cooper had taken over from the previous caretaker.

'You're a ray of sunshine,' Miss High, the headmistress, used to say to him. Hetty finished her dusting and shook the duster outside in the school yard before putting it away.

She stood for a moment, remembering the days when she herself had attended the school. In those days she'd had ambitions to be a head teacher herself. What a shock and disappointment it had been when she'd realised that the family couldn't afford for her to go to the grammar school even though she had won a scholarship.

Hetty shook her head as though to rid herself of old memories. She was doing fine, wasn't she? Of course she was. She had been lucky to get this job only a matter of yards from Office Street so she could help her mam during the day. By, she had been shocked to find how easily Mam tired these days. She would have to go and see Dr Richardson, maybe she needed a tonic. Da paid his fourpence a week to the panel for the doctor, didn't he? And Doctor Richardson was nice, though there had been some talk about his wife, she forgot what. But then, folks would talk about anybody if they had nothing better to do.

Walking home, Hetty reflected on how lucky she was. For Matthew hadn't been near Morton Main. By, she was thankful for that! But there was the other . . . she hadn't needed her clouts for almost two months. It was likely just the upset of the move, she told herself. But, oh, she wished it would come soon, for Mam was sure to notice the clouts were missing from the wash else.

She paused at the gate, her hand on the sneck. Maybe she should go and see Dr Richardson herself? But she quailed at the idea. No, she would wait a while. Likely it was too early to tell anyroad.

'Howay in, our Hetty, an' hurry up,' said Frank as she closed the door after her. 'Mam insists on waiting for you before she sets out the supper. An' here am I, perished with hunger!'

' "Rescue the perishing, care for the dying . . ." ' sang Hetty as she took off her coat. 'Go on, Mam, feed the greedy brute or he might cry.'

'Less of your lip, my lass,' said Frank. 'Or I won't give you the message I have for you.'

Hetty's heart missed a beat. Message? She didn't know whether she had said it aloud or not. Dear God, not Matthew! He hadn't found her, had he?

'There was a letter in the afternoon post an' all,' Maggie observed. She was ladling out platefuls of panhaggalty from the dish she had taken out of the oven. The smell of the potatoes and onions cooked with strips of belly bacon wafted about the kitchen but Hetty had lost her appetite. She glanced sharply over to the sewing machine which stood by the window. Mam always propped letters there on top of the cover. The writing on the envelope was round and childish, however, certainly not Matthew's. For a moment she forgot him as delight flooded through her. It was a letter from the bairns! Oh yes, it had to be, the stamp was franked Smuggler's Cove. Well, at least the new Mrs Hutchins had allowed them to write to her.

'It's from Peter and Audrey. And look, even Charlie has printed his name. Oh, and there's a picture, he's done a drawing. Look, it's the beach. Oh, he's good he is, it looks just like the sands and the cliff.'

Hetty had opened the envelope and there was a letter written by Peter, and a little bit by Audrey who was just starting joined up writing, and a row of kisses from Charlie, beside his printed name.

Tears sprang to Hetty's eyes. For the last part, half printed by Audrey, read: 'Charlie and me miss yu. Wen are yu cuming home?' And underneath in Peter's stronger hand, 'Don't tell my dad's new wife about this letter.'

' "My dad's new wife". Not "our mother", not even "our step-mother",' Hetty said aloud.

'Eeh, the poor bairns,' Maggie said softly. 'Them poor, poor bairns.'

'Maggie,' said Thomas, 'they're not the only bairns to have to get used to a step-mother.'

But Hetty's appetite was gone. She went up to bed as soon as she could and lay in the dark, staring out of the gap between the thin curtains. There was moonlight but clouds scudded across the dark sky so that the light came and went, came and went. She would have to find a place nearer Smuggler's Cove, she told herself, so that she could at least watch out for the bairns. By, she knew what that woman was like, she might even bray them. Not that she had ever seen Anne hit them but then, when she was in the house on her own with them, well, it certainly looked as though she might.

That's your imagination running riot, she told herself, you really don't know that Anne is cruel to them. There was no evidence, as the detectives in the pictures would say. Hetty turned on her side and closed her eyes, trying to sleep. From below she could hear the murmur of voices as the family finished supper and no doubt speculated about that other household in Smuggler's Cove.

There were footsteps on the stairs and a tap on the bedroom door.

'Hetty? Are you awake? Make yourself decent and I'll come in. I forgot to give you that message.'

'Aye, I'm decent,' said Hetty, pulling the sheet up under her chin as Frank opened the door and came in. He didn't bother to turn up the gas jet on the wall but walked over to her bed and sat down on the end of it. She looked at him, resigned to more bad news. Somehow, she had a feeling that was what it was.

'I was in Bishop at the football match this tea-time. You know, it was a replay from last Saturday's that was a draw,' Frank began. 'There was this fellow – Richard, he said his name was.'

'Richard?' Hetty sat up in surprise, pulling the sheet modestly after her. 'You said Richard? Richard Hope?'

'Well, he never told me his surname. You see, the Bishops were playing Skelton and he was a supporter. I don't know how he knew who I was. Anyway, he said for you to meet him tomorrow at the King's Hall cafe. He's staying over like. Business, he said.'

'Richard said for me to meet him?' Hetty was still unbelieving.

'Now, our Hetty, you're not going deaf as well as daft, are you?'

'But why? I mean, why didn't he just come here? Mam said he came before.'

'Aye, so she told me. I don't know, Hetty. Mebbe he hasn't the time. Me, I'm just a pitman, I don't know what these businessmen do.'

'He's not a businessman, he's a student—' Hetty stopped. Of course, Richard was leaving university this summer.

'Well, I've told you, now I'll leave you in peace.' Frank rose from the bed and went to the door, pausing before he opened it. 'He's sweet on you, I think, Hetty,' he said.

'Hadaway!' she exclaimed in disbelief. Well, she thought, she could meet him at the King's Hall all right, it was Saturday tomorrow. A thought struck her as her brother began to close the door after him. 'Frank? What time did he say?'

'Eeh, I'm a fool, I am. Fancy forgetting to tell you the time! Four o'clock, that was it. After he got his business finished.' A shaft of moonlight illuminated his face and Hetty saw he was grinning. 'Well, *I* think he's sweet on you, a gent an' all he is. You be careful, our Hetty, I'm not sure I like toffs coming after you. Don't worry, though, I won't tell me mam.' And before she could retort, he was clattering down the oilcloth-covered stairs.

Hetty took the quarter to four bus into Bishop Auckland the next day. It was almost empty for most of the miners' wives would have been in much earlier in the day. All day she had waited for it and now at last it was time to go.

'You look very bonny today, lass,' the conductor commented as he took her tuppence and handed her a ticket. 'Got a date, have you?' He smiled and moved on, to show that he was just being pleasant, not really prying.

Not a date, not really, Hetty mused as she looked at her reflection in the grimy window. But she did look nice, she knew it. She was wearing a soft pale green dress, linen, with a nipped in waist and short sleeves.

'Carry a cardigan, just in case,' Mam had insisted so she had a white cardigan over her arm which she had no intention of wearing even if the temperature dropped to zero for it was past its best, the ribbing on it sagging. But still, it was grand to have her mam fussing over her like she did, Hetty had quite got out of the way of it.

'He was here once, you know,' Mam had told her after she had badgered Hetty to say whom she was meeting. 'A

181

canny lad.' But there had been a concerned look in her eyes nevertheless.

The bus arrived in the small town and Hetty alighted and walked to Newgate Street. The clock on the Wesleyan Church tower said three minutes to four, right time to walk to the King's Hall cafe for four o'clock.

He wasn't there, she couldn't see him among the few people sitting drinking tea and eating toasted teacakes and fancies. Hetty hesitated in the doorway.

'A table for one, madam?'

She turned to the waitress standing there in her black dress and frilly white apron and cap. Oh, it was a posh cafe all right.

'No, for two,' she said. By, she hoped he wouldn't be long! She didn't like the idea of sitting on her own while folk cast curious glances in her direction. She picked up the menu and studied it. A pot of tea and fancies, one and sixpence. Toasted buttered teacakes, fourpence each. Mind, it wasn't cheap. No wonder the waitresses got to wear smart uniforms.

She was sitting with her back to the door so the shock was all the greater when a hand landed on her shoulder, a firm hand which held her in her seat. She would have jumped up and run out of the cafe if it hadn't.

'Hello, Hetty,' said Matthew.

She was dumb as she stared at him, her mind wouldn't work somehow. 'Where's Richard? Frank said it was Richard wanted to meet me!'

The disappointment crushed Hetty. Matthew's face swam before her in a black mist and she closed her eyes for a second. Please God, it's my mind playing tricks, she thought frantically, the face, so like Richard's, was Matthew's all right. Irrationally she felt Frank had misled her deliberately, how could he?

'Frank said it was Richard!' she said again.

'Did he?' Matthew sat down in the chair beside her rather than the chair opposite his hand slid down her arm and held her hand. He dropped a featherlight kiss on her cheek. To the other diners it must look as though they were lovers, Hetty thought dully.

'Waitress!'

182

With his easy manner, ever the gentleman, Matthew had simply to hold up his other hand and the waitress scurried to his command.

'Tea for two, I think, don't you darling?' He smiled from the waitress to Hetty. 'And you can bring your tray of fancies, just in case my friend would like one.'

'Yes, sir.' The waitress rushed away; the other diners turned their attention to their own business.

'Why did you tell Frank you were Richard?' she whispered furiously. 'And leave go of my hand, leave go or I'll . . . I'll show you up before everybody here, I will! I'll . . . I'll call the polis!'

Matthew laughed fondly. 'No, no, darling,' he said, then leaned forward and lowered his voice to match hers. 'You won't. For one thing, if you believe I care what these people think you're sadly mistaken. And as for the "polis", as you call them, what am I doing wrong exactly? Apart from having tea with my girl on a Saturday afternoon. It's you with your working-class mentality who doesn't want to be shown up. I couldn't care less, I assure you.'

Hetty stared at him, defeated. 'How did you find me?' she asked.

'Don't be silly, Hetty, your home address is in Father's desk along with details of all the other maids we've ever had. Besides, there's Sally Dunn.'

Oh yes, she rued the day she had brought Sally Dunn to Hope Hall, Hetty thought bitterly.

The waitress returned with the tray of tea and fancy cakes and Matthew made a show of helping Hetty choose one. He let go of her hand but she could still feel the pressure of his fingers there.

'Shall I pour, dear?' asked Matthew. He was enjoying himself, she could tell he was, there was a triumphant expression in his eyes. She looked down at the custard slice on her plate, feeling sick.

'Always put the milk in afterwards, Hetty, only the lower classes put it in first,' he was saying as he poured the tea and handed her her cup and saucer.

'I'll have to go,' she said suddenly, and rushed across the cafe to the ladies' room.

183

'Wait!'

But she was beyond waiting, the bile was rising in her throat. In the lavatory, Hetty retched and retched though there was nothing in her stomach but bile.

'Are you all right in there? 'Cos I'm waiting. There's only one lavvy, you know, and I've got a little lass here wetting her britches.'

Hetty flushed the bowl and opened the door from the lavatory cubicle to the slightly larger one with the washbasin. The woman waiting with the little girl hopping from foot to foot rushed past her.

'Sorry, pet,' she said, as she sat the toddler on the seat, 'When bairns have to go, they have to go.' She left the door of the cubicle open and came out and leaned against the wall, watching Hetty as she ran cold water in the basin and splashed it on her overheated face.

'Eeh,' said the woman, 'never mind me. I know what it's like. How far are you on? Two months, is it? Well, like I always say, the first three months is the worst.'

Hetty managed to smile weakly but her thoughts were in an uproar. Dear God, no! Dear God, it couldn't be. Yet hadn't this been the dark fear at the back of her mind for what seemed long enough? The woman and the little girl went out and Hetty was on her own. But the door had not closed properly and she could hear Matthew's voice. She moved closer to the door and heard him asking the woman if she was still inside.

'Aye, she is,' was the reply. 'Spewing her tea up again, a waste of money it's been. But that's what it's like when you start a bairn.'

Oh, dear God, thought Hetty. She caught hold of the roller towel to wipe her hands but the next minute she was seized and spun round to face Matthew.

'It's mine, isn't it? It's not that miner fellow's – what's his name, Hutchins? For if it is, I'll swing for you both, I swear it!'

'Matthew, let go! You can't come in here, they'll throw you out of the place,' she cried.

'Can I not then? I'd like to see them try! Now tell me, tell me!'

'I'm not having a bairn, Matthew. I'm not, honest I'm not. Something disagreed with me, that's all.'

'Mine or his?' demanded Matthew implacably. 'If it's his, I'll kick it out of you, I promise you that.'

'Here now, this is the ladies', you can't stay in here,' said a scandalised voice from the doorway. An elderly lady stood there looking shocked to the core. Matthew swore again and dragged Hetty out with an iron grip on her upper arm, pushing the old lady out of the way, throwing a ten-shilling note at the manager when he tried to stop them going. All Hetty saw was a sea of upturned faces as the whole cafe stopped eating and talking, and watched open-mouthed. She was drowning in embarrassment and mortification. All of Bishop and the pit villages would be talking about her tomorrow.

Matthew dragged her outside and up the alleyway to Kingsway. There were few people about and he pushed her against the wall of the Labour Exchange and held her there.

'Well?' he demanded again.

'I'm not having a baby,' Hetty insisted, then quailed at the terrible look in his eyes. 'But if I am,' she added hastily, 'then it can only be yours, Matthew. Nobody else has touched me. Nobody.'

He stared hard at her, holding her gaze. Then, apparently satisfied, his manner relaxed. He loosed his hold of her and took a handkerchief out of his pocket and handed it to her.

'A bloody good job for you too,' he said, but quietly now. 'Now, come on, is there anywhere in this godforsaken town where we can talk without folks gawping at us?'

'Matthew, I want to go home,' she said. She fought for composure and began to feel better, her stomach settled, her racing pulse slowed. 'I don't want to talk to you, I just want you to leave me alone.'

'A shame that, for I'm not going to,' he said grimly, and taking hold of her arm, set off towards the market place. She had no choice but to follow. 'If you can't think of anywhere we'll take the car, it's up by the market stalls. We can go up the dale. I remember Teesdale from when I was at school in Barnard Castle.'

185

'No, Matthew, we can go down to the park, the bishop's park. I don't want—'

'Stop telling me what you don't want to do!' said Matthew. But he carried on past his car and went over Durham Road to the Norman arch which was the entrance to the bishop's palace. The long drive stretched ahead of them, the battlements of the castle showing above the high walls to their left, the formal flower beds to one side until they got to the ancient iron cattle gate which led into the park proper. He led her to a seat away from the main paths and sat her down, seating himself beside her.

'Now then,' he said, 'I'll tell you what you're going to do . . .'

Chapter 21

The notice of the forthcoming wedding was in the *Yorkshire Post*, just a week after the fateful dinner party at the Hunters' house.

'There now,' Havelock had said with some satisfaction, 'you can't get out of it, not when it's public. You'll show willing and wed the lass and think yourself lucky the Hunters don't know the half of your wild carryings on – or if they do, they're prepared to forget them. Do you hear me, my lad?'

'Yes, yes, I've said I'll marry her, haven't I?'

Matthew, who was helping himself to grilled kidneys and bacon at the sideboard, carried his plate to the table and sat down. He stared at the food, his appetite deserting him. How the hell he'd got into this mess he didn't know. The thought of being tied to Joan Hunter for the rest of his life was anathema to him. He wondered at himself, told himself to think of her money, which could make him independent of his father. If he could wrest any of the stuff from the girl. Trouble was, this last week Joan had shown a surprisingly strong will.

'Of course,' she had said, 'we will live here with Mummy and Daddy. There's loads of room, it's bigger than Hope Hall.'

'But Father will expect us to live with him. After all, I'll be working with him,' Matthew had replied, but Joan had shaken her head, flatly dismissing the idea.

He sighed and pushed his plate away. Taking his cigarette

case out of his pocket, he lit one and his father rustled the newspaper irritably.

'Anyone would think it was your funeral being arranged, not a wedding,' he growled.

'Might as well be,' muttered Matthew under his breath. Havelock threw the paper on to the table and glared at his son.

'Damnation, Matthew! I don't know what's the matter with you. I've never known you to turn up your nose at money, not when it's there for the taking. You have to get married some time, haven't you? Here's a local girl, daughter of the richest man in North Yorkshire, panting to marry you, though I cannot for the life of me think why. More, her father is prepared to indulge her, God help him. I'm telling you, you'll marry her and put a good face on it or I'll know the reason why! You've led a wild life until now, but it's time you settled down. You'll thank me for it in the future.'

Will I? thought Matthew. Will I really? Oh yes, the future looks rosy – rosy as hell. He stubbed the cigarette out on his plate, savagely pressing the end into the congealing bacon fat.

'And use an ash tray!' yelled Havelock. 'Anyone would think you had never been taught how to behave. All the money it's cost me for your education . . .'

'My mother's money,' snarled Matthew, rising to his feet and striding to the door.

His father spluttered, face red as beetroot. 'What did you say? Why, you young pup—'

Matthew turned back from the open door. 'All right, all right, I'll marry the girl! I said I would, didn't I? Now, for God's sake, leave me alone, will you?'

He strode through the hall and out of the front door, his father's voice ringing in his ears. Getting into his car, he started the engine, misfiring twice before the wheels spun on the gravel and he was away. Not to the Hunters' place, nor anywhere near it, though Joan was expecting him to discuss wedding plans. Wedding plans, be blowed! No, he was going to enjoy his last bit of freedom, he was certain of that. He thought of going into Whitby but the idea didn't appeal.

In the end he drove across the moors recklessly, not caring where he went, only sure he had to satisfy this craving for Hetty, he had to find her, even if he only sat in his car and watched her. Oh yes, there was something about simply watching her, it was like a drug, he could watch her for hours. Even watch the house where she was, sometimes it was enough that she was inside. But this time he would be ready when he found her. He fingered the tablets in his jacket pocket. His mother's. The doctor had begun prescribing them on top of the mixture she usually took at his father's suggestion.

'She doesn't sleep properly,' Havelock had said.

Matthew had had some idea they might come in handy to subdue Hetty, bring her round to his way of thinking.

A week later his father, going out in a hurry, left the key to his desk in the lock, something which never usually happened for Havelock Hope was very close about his business. Matthew had soon found the folder with the names and home addresses of the domestic staff. Hetty's was confirmed when Sally Dunn came back from her annual holiday and Matthew asked her how Morton Main was getting along. Sally had mumbled something and scuttled into the kitchen, the baize door swinging behind her. By, she didn't want Master Matthew to take an interest in *her*, she had thought fearfully.

'I'll look after you, Hetty,' said Matthew now as he sat, his arm around her, in the park. 'We'll go away today, now. I'll take you to Staithes.'

'I can't, man, what about me family?'

He was going to have to do something about her grammar and that dreadful Durham accent, Matthew told himself. He held his tongue with difficulty. Careful now, careful, he must gentle her along.

'What do you want to do then?'

Hetty could hardly think straight. Matthew's hand was clasped around her wrist, his arm felt like an iron band on her. She should get up and go, shake him off, run. She stole a glance at him, catching a hard, intent light in his blue eyes, quickly masked when he saw her looking.

'I don't know,' she said nervously, pleating her skirt with trembling fingers. Oh, she had just found her family after so many years, she didn't want to lose them! But she imagined what they would think if she went home and announced she was having a bairn. By, no, she couldn't imagine it, it was too nightmarish. If she'd been getting married now, they could maybe forgive that, but not her with a fatherless bairn, no. Especially not after all the rumours and gossip which had gone the rounds of the pit rows of Morton Main about her. Mam and Da would never be able to hold their heads up in chapel again. But neither could she just walk out and break her mother's heart all over again.

Hetty stared across the park, at the oak trees casting dark shadows now with the sun behind them. A mother and two young children came up the path, the youngest one wailing with tiredness. The mother had a bag with a towel sticking out of the top. They must have been plodging in the Gaunless, she thought abstractedly. The mother took her child's hand and spoke softly to him. Hetty guessed they were going home to make the father's tea, a nice ordinary family. She felt a stab of envy.

'Well then, I'll have to make up your mind for you,' said Matthew, bringing her attention back to her own tangled life.

'What do you mean?' God help me, she cried silently, for I can't help myself. A malaise was creeping over her. When Matthew was with her, holding her, touching her, all she could feel was his power over her. His dark power. She actually felt a stirring within her, a need for him. But how could it be love? She didn't even like him. She tried to pull away from him, ineffectually. Oh Richard, where are you, she cried silently.

'I'll come home with you, I'll talk to them.' Matthew's voice was soft, persuasive.

Hetty was filled with horror at the thought. 'No, don't do that, please!'

He laughed. 'Come now, Hetty, if you don't tell them, I will.'

'I . . . I will. Don't you go. I'll tell them, I promise.'

'All right then.'

Matthew released his hold on her, and she got to her feet and walked rapidly away through the darkening park. He sat for a moment, thinking, then went after her, catching up with her at the entrance.

'I'll run you home,' he said, and she shook her head.

'No, I'll get the bus.' She had to get away, she could think on the bus. Her head was aching, the market place seemed unreal somehow.

'It's all right, I won't go near the house.' He was keeping pace with her. She tried to hurry but he took hold of her arm and turned her towards him. 'You're not going to get rid of me this time,' he warned. 'You weren't thinking of hiding away from me again, were you, Hetty? You love me, and now you need me. And so does the kid. Every kid needs a father.'

Matthew almost laughed aloud as he mouthed the trite words. Words from a picture he had seen at the flicks, in London that had been. But he could see that Hetty was gazing at him with new respect. That was the way then, appeal on behalf of her unborn brat.

She stopped walking and began swaying alarmingly. He had to hold her firmly to keep her upright. The market stalls were packing up and pieces of paper were blowing about in the wind which had sprung up. A brown carrier bag blew against her leg and was held there for a minute before lifting in a sudden eddy and spiralling across the pavement. Hetty put back her head the better to see him; his face swam before her eyes.

'I . . . feel giddy,' she gasped, and with a small moan collapsed altogether. Luckily, they were very close to the car. He picked her up in his arms, elation surging through him.

'What's up?' asked the nearest stall holder. 'You need any help there, mate?'

'I can manage,' said Matthew and, propping her up against the car, managed to open the passenger door and get her in. She lay against the seat, her head back. 'Can you get a drink of water for my wife?' he asked the stall holder. 'You know how it is, she's in the family way.'

191

He watched as the man took the top of a flask over to the tap by the town hall. Well, some things were meant to be, thought Matthew exultantly. He fingered the top pocket of his jacket, found the two phenobarbitone tablets he had filched from his mother's drawer with some half-formed idea of drugging Hetty. The man brought back the cup just as she began to struggle to sit up properly.

'Thanks, mate,' said Matthew.

'No trouble,' said the stall holder. 'My old woman flakes out all the time when she's starting a babby, I know what it's like.'

It was easy to get the tablets into Hetty's open mouth and support her while he poured the water down her throat. She spluttered a little but drank the water and he was fairly sure the tablets were gone.

'Hey, what's that you're giving her?' asked the man, and Matthew turned to find him still standing by the car, looking concerned.

'Oh, mind your own bloody business!' yelled Matthew and threw the cup at him. Then he laid Hetty back against the seat again and started the car. The man jumped back and Matthew drove out of the market place and down Newgate Street, roaring away, making pedestrians leap for the pavement and other motorists swerve and honk their horns at him. A policeman stepped into the road and held up an authoritative hand then had to leap back as Matthew ignored him. They would be out of the town before the stupid 'polis', as Hetty called them, could do anything about it, Matthew exulted.

'Morton Main be buggered!' he chuckled, and glanced quickly at Hetty's pale face, the dark lashes sweeping her cheeks and sparkling intermittently as flashes of light came and went from the newly lit street lamps. He laughed aloud as he took the Darlington road out of town. Two hours, he calculated. No, an hour and a half at the most to get to Staithes. He wasn't sure how strong the tablets were but she would sleep for that length of time, surely? After all, look what the drug did to his mother.

Chapter 22

Hetty sat at the kitchen table in the tiny wooden bungalow. The day was overcast and there was a cold wind blowing in from the sea. She shivered. She had been writing a letter but now she put down her pen and went over to the door and out into the garden so that she could see if Matthew was coming along the path. There was no sign of him, but then she had not really expected him until after dark; he was usually quite late getting back. Only a few holiday makers were down on the beach, sheltering behind wind-breaks. There were other bungalows like theirs dotted about the sandy hill which rose from the beach, most of them belonging to folk from the mill towns inland.

Pulling her cardigan round her, Hetty picked up the hoe which leant against the side of the bungalow and began weeding where she had left off the day before. Putting the garden in order was something she could do to occupy herself and at least the work kept her warm.

For this wasn't Staithes, it wasn't a village at all, just a collection of holiday cottages without water or electricity or any modern conveniences. Matthew brought in the supplies they needed from Staithes which was further along the coast.

Hetty worked steadily until her back began to ache, clearing the weeds which were choking the few clumps of flowers growing in the neglected garden. Gradually, she was bringing some order to it, though she wasn't sure why she bothered. Matthew had said he would marry her, hadn't he? Well then, they would soon be moving to Hope Hall. He had told her it was just a matter of time before his father came round.

'Stay quietly here, Hetty,' he had told her. 'It's not for long.'

Mind, she thought, arching her back to ease the ache, she had her doubts about Havelock Hope accepting her into the family. She had begun to say so to Matthew but he had quelled her with a savage look. She laid a hand on her belly. Oh, you, she said silently to the little 'un inside. I wouldn't be here if it weren't for you. But she didn't blame the babby really. No, it was her own fault, all of it.

Hetty wasn't even sure how she came to be on this lonely hillside, miles away from her own folk. She had only a hazy recollection of getting here though she must have agreed to it. She'd been so queasy that day, she remembered that all right.

She should have been at home in Morton Main now, surrounded by her family, knitting tiny vests and bootees and cutting up a blanket and hemming it to make cot blankets. She should have been sitting with her mam and her gran, and all looking forward to the baby, and Gran and Mam would be free with their advice as their hands worked the needles. How sweet that would be! For a minute Hetty felt such an acute sense of loss she thought she couldn't bear it.

'What can't be cured must be endured,' Gran used to say. Hetty knew the true meaning of that now.

She gazed along the path. No sign of Matthew yet. She put down the hoe and went inside, closing the door behind her though the wind still whistled round its warped frame. She tipped water out of the bucket into the basin and washed her hands. Better fill the bucket before Matthew got home, he hated having to fetch it himself.

'After all,' he said, 'you're used to hard work, it won't hurt you, but I've not been brought up to it the way you have.'

Sitting down and picking up her pen, she carried on with the letter she was writing.

'It's lovely here looking over the sea,' she wrote. 'Though we are only staying here for the summer, we intend to move

194

inland when the weather turns this autumn. Oh, Mam, I'm sorry we couldn't have told you about us before. I'm sorry I couldn't have a proper wedding at the chapel and a wedding reception in the Sunday School. But we are going to get married, just as soon as we can. The baby will have Matthew's name.' Hetty paused before continuing, doubt assailing her. But Matthew had promised, hadn't he? 'Please write back, I miss you all.' She signed the letter 'All my love, Hetty', with a row of x's, before putting it into an envelope and addressing it.

She propped it on the battered chest of drawers, Matthew would take it to the post tomorrow, as he had done the other three she had written. Neither Mam nor Da nor Gran had written back, not even Frank. But Hetty knew how she had hurt them. Sometimes she cried about it. And maybe they would get in touch after she was married. After all, she must be a great shame to them living in sin as she was. If only she had been able to go home and explain to them herself that day instead of rushing away with Matthew the way she had. She couldn't talk to him about it, though. He didn't understand.

'You need no one but me,' he always said. 'Forget it now, you're like a baby crying for your mother. Your life is with me.' And Hetty had learned not to cross him, never to upset him.

By the time she heard footsteps coming up the garden path, she had the paraffin stove working and a stew and vegetables cooking on the top. The room was warmer because of the lit stove and she had regained her spirits. She was sure the family would write back to this letter, or if not then to the next she sent which should be an invitation to the wedding.

'Matthew! The meal is almost read—'

Hetty's greeting was cut short as he saw it was not Matthew at the door but his father. 'Mr Hope! Oh, I'm so glad to see you. Matthew has told you everything, has he? Oh, forgive me, do come in. I'm forgetting my manners, have a seat.'

Havelock's lip curled. 'I'll come in, all right, seeing as this is *my* cottage. It's you that will be getting out, you young trollop, you! You're trespassing here and you're lucky I don't have the police on you.'

The harshness hit Hetty like a blow. She stared at him, the gladness changing rapidly to a sick dismay. 'But . . . has Matthew not spoken to you? I'm not trespassing, Mr Hope, Matthew brought me here.'

'Aye, I thought as much.' Havelock nodded his head as though confirming something. 'A love nest, is it? Did you never think I'd have someone watching the place for me? The first thing Tommy Charlton did when he came and found someone was living here was let me know. A young woman, he said, and a man comes after dark. Well, it didn't take much to know there was something going on, and I thought it might be Matthew, especially when the key was gone from my study.' He stood before Hetty, hands on his hips, eyes like pebbles in his furious face.

Tommy Charlton. She'd heard the mother of that family on the beach call her husband Tommy. They had a bungalow a hundred yards further along the hillside.

'But surely, Matthew—'

'Matthew thought he had me fooled all right,' snarled his father. 'But he'll have to get up a lot earlier in the morning to catch me napping.'

Darkness had almost enveloped the small kitchen except for the glow from the paraffin stove. Havelock moved with long familiarity to pick up the lamp from the table, taking off the globe and putting a match to the wick. The light lit up Hetty's white face, her dark eyes large and staring. Something in her face must have touched even Havelock's hard heart for he softened his tone.

'Look, lass,' he said in a gentler voice, 'get away back to your own folk. I'm telling you, there's no future here for you. Matthew is going to marry Joan Hunter. I'll give you time to pack your things and I'll take you up to the main road. I can't say fairer than that, can I?'

Joan Hunter? No, there was some mistake. 'No, it's not true. Mr Hope, I can't go. I can't! I'm carrying Matthew's bairn. It's your grandchild, Mr Hope. He is going to marry me, not Joan Hunter.'

Havelock sighed. 'I might have known. He's been spinning you a yarn, has he? Well, you're not the first to have his by-blow as you must have heard when you lived in my house.' He strode to the door. 'I've told you, lass,' he went on with a return to his former attitude. 'I can't help it if you don't believe me. And if you won't come with me, you can walk to the main road. I'll be sending Oliver and Sam round in the morning, and if you're not out they will have instructions to throw you out.'

Hetty stared after him from the doorway as he disappeared along the path into the gloom. Oh Lord, what have I done? What am I going to do? she wondered. She stood there with the wind biting into her. At last she came to a decision. Going back into the house, she turned off the paraffin stove and ladled herself out a plateful of stew. First of all she had to eat, she couldn't go out and face the world with an empty stomach. She ate methodically though she had to force the food down, then poured a little water into the bowl and washed her plate and fork.

There was nothing much to pack for she had brought nothing with her when she came. Matthew had bought her a change of clothes and though the skirt was already tight it would do. She changed into clean clothes and bundled up the ones she had been wearing and wrapped them in the brown paper the new ones had come in. She was ready. She considered leaving Matthew a note but decided against it. Now she had to get to a village. Maybe she could even catch a bus to Saltburn.

Though she only had the four shillings she had taken with her that day she met Matthew in Bishop Auckland. Well, she would manage for she couldn't stay where she was. Not for poor Mr Oliver to have to come and evict her in the morning. She could not embarrass him in that way. She turned off the lamp and, not even glancing behind her, went out of the door and along the path. There was a moon luckily, and after a few minutes her eyes grew used to the moonlight and she could see the way quite clearly. Her parcel under her arm, she walked along, keeping a weather eye open for Matthew. But the path was deserted. At that time of the evening most people were indoors eating their evening meal, she supposed.

The last stretch of the path widened until it became a track and then an unmade road. And at last she was at the top, breathing heavily but at the side of the main road, the Whitby to Saltburn main road, she surmised.

Turning right, she trudged along in the dark but for the headlights of the few cars which drove past her, illuminating her way, and the few coming in the opposite direction, almost blinding her with their lights. She felt she didn't care if she had to walk the whole way to Saltburn or perhaps Loftus, that was nearer, wasn't it? Was there a lodging house in Loftus? She didn't know, she knew very little about the place except that it was an old mining town. Well, she would find out when she got there.

She refused to think about Matthew or his father or the situation she had found herself in. She only knew she had to find herself a place to stay and tomorrow she had to find work. And then, she thought bleakly, she would have to find a mother and baby home for the time when she couldn't work. There were a few months left to her. If she worked and saved as hard as she could she would be able to pay a little and then she would not have to go into the workhouse.

Matthew was stamping angry, so angry he could have killed Hetty. How dare she up and leave him like this? Didn't she know how much he was giving up for her? Only that afternoon, Joan bloody Hunter, proper madam that she was, had issued him with an ultimatum.

'Don't you ever do that to me again!' she had shouted at him. For a minute he couldn't remember what it was he had done but she wasn't slow in reminding him. 'Those were my friends we were supposed to be lunching with. I won't be stood up again, do you hear me, Matthew Hope? What sort of a fool do you think I looked?'

Matthew had been tempted to reply to that one: 'No bigger fool than you already are, and an ugly one at that,' but he managed to bite the words back. What he had done was turn on his heel and walk out. So God knows what sort of temper his father would be in when he went home, for no doubt he had heard all about his son's shortcomings from old man Hunter's little darling. He'd forgotten about the lunch date. These days his mind was filled only with Hetty. He could hardly believe she was finally his, had to tell himself constantly she was there waiting in the cotttage for him.

Except that she wasn't. There was a smell of cooking. He lifted the lid of the pan which stood on the paraffin stove, it was still warm. So she hadn't been gone long. Damn! If he'd only got here earlier he would probably have caught her. But it wasn't safe coming in daylight, it might get back to his father where exactly he was disappearing every evening.

Rage welled up in him. When he found the bitch he'd show her who was boss. He'd beat her until she begged for mercy. Banging the door to after him, he stalked out of the bungalow, making for his car which was parked discreetly on a layby on the main road.

Once there he debated where she would go. Whitby? But no, she knew no one there. More likely she'd make for her usual bolthole, Saltburn. He roared through Loftus and on to Saltburn, only realising when he got there that she wouldn't have got so far, not on foot, and if there had been a bus he would have passed it. Turning back, he drove more slowly, watching for her.

Hetty was at the bus stop in Loftus when he found her. The last bus for Saltburn had just come in and she was about to board when Matthew took her arm.

'There you are, darling,' he said, and the passenger in front turned his head and grinned when he saw the young toff holding the girl with a bulky brown paper parcel in her arms.

Hetty opened her mouth to protest but Matthew bent and spoke softly in her ear. 'You don't want a scene here, do you?' He slid his hand to the back of her neck under her hair and gripped it, drawing her away from the queue. The pain was so excruciating she had to follow.

'Good girl,' he said quietly. He led her to the car and they got in. Only then did he release his grip. Hetty sat back in the seat, her parcel on her lap. If she hadn't been taken by surprise . . . What? What would she have done? She couldn't

199

think any more, she was too tired. Her legs ached; there was another dull ache in the small of her back.

'It's no good, Matthew,' she said. 'Your father came to see me.'

'Father?' How in hell had he found out about her?

'He said you would never marry me. He said that he was sending Mr Oliver and Sam in the morning, and if I wasn't out by then they would throw me out. I told him about the baby but he only laughed. He said—'

'Never mind what he said,' Matthew snarled. 'I'll do what I bloody well like, I don't have to ask him!' He sounded like a rebellious schoolboy, she thought. But he was far from that. Hetty sat there, bone weary. She stared out of the window at black nothingness. She didn't bother to reply.

'He didn't tell you anything else, did he?'

'You mean about Joan Hunter?'

'It's not true, you know, I won't marry her,' said Matthew. And in that moment he knew it was the case. No matter if the Hunters owned the crown jewels. And he wondered at himself, even laughed inwardly at his own stupidity. He glanced down at Hetty. She was lying against the seat in just the same position she had been in when he'd brought her down from Durham. Her eyes were closed, in the faint light from the dash he could see that. She was fast asleep.

Matthew turned the car round once again and set off. Not for Saltburn but Redcar, there were plenty of boarding houses there. He would face his father in the morning.

When Hetty woke next day, it was a minute or two before she could think where she was. A strange bed, a strange room, cheap dark furniture, a rickety wardrobe, a wash stand with a jug and bowl sitting on it. There was the sound of the sea, waves beating against the beach. It must be high tide, she thought fuzzily. Memory came flooding back to her. She turned her head to the pillow next to hers but Matthew had gone. She remembered waking up as the car pulled up. Oh, she must have been truly exhausted to follow him to this house, let him book a room. Where were they? This wasn't Saltburn, the sea was too near, not at the bottom of a cliff. Getting out of bed, she went to the window and looked out. It was Redcar. There was the pier, the familiar beach. They were on the front at Redcar. Well, now was her chance, while Matthew was away.

The door was locked! She couldn't believe it, it must have stuck. She rattled the door knob, but it wouldn't budge. She bent and peered at the lock. It was locked all right.

'Hey!' she cried. 'Let me out, somebody, let me out!'

After a few minutes there were footsteps on the stairs, stopping outside her door. 'Stop that racket, Mrs Smith, you're upsetting my other tenants. Your husband says you have to stay in there. You're not well, Mrs Smith, I could see that when you came in last night. Now behave yourself or I'll be sorry I took you in. It was against my usual practice anyhow.'

Hetty stepped back from the door. She couldn't believe what she was hearing. 'Let me out, please,' she said again but in a normal voice which it took all of her will-power to achieve. 'There's nothing the matter with me.'

'Now be a good girl, Mrs Smith,' the woman said. 'It won't be long before your husband is back and then he'll take you out for a nice dinner. He told me to tell you that. "Important business," he said. Only a couple of hours, and that was nine o'clock. It's half-past eleven now, he'll be coming any minute.'

'Please, I'm not his wife, I want to go home, let me out!' said Hetty.

'He told me you would say that,' said the voice, and Hetty heard footsteps retreating down the stairs. She sat down on the bed, anger raging within her. By, Matthew had done some terrible things to her in the past but this beat cock-fighting! She went to the window but it was too high. She couldn't get out anyway. When she tried it, it was stuck solid.

201

Chapter 23

'Come in here at once, Matthew.'

The order was barked at him the moment he entered the front door of Hope Hall. Groaning, he went into the study to face his father. But there was not only his father, there was Mr Hunter too. Both men had got to their feet and were standing together, faces red with anger.

'Explain yourself, and by Harry, it had better be good or you will never see my daughter again!' said Mr Hunter.

'Is that a promise?' Matthew almost said it aloud. For a minute he thought he had but it was only in his mind. He dragged his thoughts away from Hetty, the worry that she might somehow escape before he got back to Redcar. His head throbbed. On the way here he had called in at a pub and taken a few glasses of whisky, to fortify himself for the coming interview with his father. Suddenly he couldn't care less about any of them. What did he care if he never saw Joan again? Never was too soon in his opinion.

Mr Hunter spluttered, going even more purple if that was possible. 'You young pup, I said explain yourself!' he repeated.

Matthew smiled. 'Sorry, I'm afraid I'm not quite sure what it is I have to explain?' he said, in his most charming voice. If he needled the old fellow long enough, he might have an apoplexy.

'Matthew!'

That was his own father shouting now. Matthew studied him. Unfortunately Havelock did not look very likely to have a stroke. Pity, that would have solved so many problems. Matthew was his heir, wasn't he?

'Yes, Father? If Mr Hunter means I missed a lunch date with his daughter then it's quite true, I did. Pressure of business, I'm afraid.' He could do with another drink. He noted that the others both had glasses in their hands. 'May I?' he asked, and went over to the drinks tray and poured himself a stiff one, downing it in one swallow.

'And may I ask what business caused you to miss the theatre last night too?' Old Hunter's voice was tight, his fists clenched. Matthew felt it his duty to warn him.

'Take it easy, old man,' he said with a show of concern. 'You don't want to have a stroke, do you?'

'You insolent, drunken . . .' Hunter was fairly choking over his words. He turned on Havelock. 'This is the end, you realise that? If you think I would let my girl marry a ne'er-do-well like him . . . why, I'd see her in hell first!'

'Look, he's joking, really—'

Havelock's words were lost on Joan's outraged father. Mr Hunter strode out of the room. 'I'll see myself out,' he snapped from the doorway.

Matthew grinned and went to the tray to pour himself another drink. 'Only trying to help,' he mumbled.

'Put that glass down,' said his father. Matthew was so startled by his cold and quiet tone when he had been expecting a shouting match that he replaced the glass on the tray and lifted his gaze to meet Havelock's.

'Now get out of my house and don't come back again. I never want to see or hear from you again.'

'Oh, come on, Father, you don't mean that?' said Matthew, stretching his hand to the tray again.

'Oh, but I do. You can pack your things and go.' Havelock sat down at his desk and took his chequebook out of a drawer. 'I won't cut you off without a penny, but this will be the last you get from me. And don't think you will get any from your mother. I will give orders that you are not to be let into the house again.'

As he lifted his head and stared at his father bleakly, it slowly dawned on Matthew that Havelock meant every word he said. He got to his feet. 'I'll make up with Joan. I'll—'

'You will not! Do you think you would even get the chance? If so you're a fool as well as a blackguard.'

'But what will I do?'

'I don't care what you do, but if you're not out of this house in ten minutes, I'll call the men and have you thrown out.'

Fifteen minutes later, Matthew was on his way across the moors, his entire worldly possessions in two suitcases in the boot of his car. There was the cheque from Havelock in his pocket. Fifty pounds, that was all. And of course the twenty-five pounds a month from his grandfather's estate. A measly twenty-five pounds! How was he supposed to live on that? Yet somehow, Hetty still occupied most of his thoughts. He hadn't even one left to spare for his own predicament.

He had thought to slip into his mother's room before leaving the Hall. She was snoring softly and he had opened the drawer of her dressing table but the chequebook was gone. He supposed his father had found one cheque missing and decided to put the rest in a safer place. Damn him! He could threaten Havelock, could tell the police about the drugs and the blank signed cheques. But what could he prove? Besides, his father would surely come round, eventually and welcome him home once more? He always had in the past. But for now he was going back to Hetty. His body tingled with excitement as he neared Redcar.

'You're still here, then?' said Matthew. He dropped his suitcases on the floor, closed the door behind him and clutched her to him.

'I could hardly go anywhere else,' she pointed out when she'd got her breath back. 'What did you tell the landlady? Did you say I was off my head?' She strained back from his embrace, glaring up into his face. And strangely, in that moment, she saw how like he was to Richard, something she didn't normally notice. Oh, Richard, she thought sadly, but suppressed the thought for now she was carrying Matthew's child, how could she possibly think of Richard?

She had had it all planned that as soon as he opened the door, as soon as he dropped his guard, even for a minute

204

or two, she would run down the stairs and out into the street, and nothing, nothing at all he could do would ever force her back into that room. She would shout for help to the holiday makers, she would call the polis, oh aye, she would. She gathered herself up to do it now the door wasn't locked. And then her gaze fell on the suitcases. She looked back at him in disbelief.

'Matthew? You've left home?' No, she thought, she was jumping to stupid conclusions again. She couldn't look at him, she knew there would be mockery all too clear in his eyes. Her face burned with anticipated humiliation at what she knew he would say. She braced herself.

Instead of speaking Matthew picked her up bodily and carried her to the bed. He was scrabbling at her clothes and his own and her heart dropped. He was going to force her again, oh, she didn't think she could stand the unlovingness of it. She tried to slip to the edge of the bed, away from him. She didn't care that she was half undressed, she couldn't stand it.

'No, Matthew,' she said.

'No?' He laughed softly and nuzzled her neck, and the unexpected gentleness of it took her breath away for the second time in the space of a minute. 'But I love you, don't you see?' he asked softly. 'You're all I have left. And I don't care, I want no one else. I've left home for you, we'll never be parted again.'

Her treacherous body responded to his. Maybe it was the deep need she had to be loved, to be wanted. Oh, she was well aware of her own weakness. She forgot her anger at being locked in, or at least it was dulled. This was the father of her baby and the bairn needed him. She had no right to deprive a child of his father. If only the father had been Richard.

Of course, the next day was different. It always was. Matthew's rapid changes of mood made her constantly apprehensive. 'Hurry up and get out of that bed,' he said, pulling back the eiderdown and letting the cold air which blew through the cracks in the window frame make her shiver. 'We're not staying here, I won't spend another night in this flea-ridden place.'

205

'Fleas? There aren't any fleas,' she replied, but dragged herself out of bed and began to wash in the water from the jug. Its coldness revived her a little. She stretched, thankful that today there were no stiff places or bruises from his lovemaking as there usually were. She felt better than she had for a long time; even his coldness failed to get her down.

Matthew waited for her, watching her every move impatiently. 'At last,' he commented when she was ready. 'We'll go and get something to eat then we'll find somewhere else to stay. Fetch me my jacket.'

It was not two strides away from where he was sitting but he enjoyed having her run after him. Hetty made no demur but opened the wardrobe door and took the jacket off its hanger. She bent to pick up his shoes from the floor of the wardrobe and as she did so a letter fell out of the jacket pocket. It was a letter from her to her family, and not the last one she had given him to post either.

Hetty stared at it then felt in the pocket. Sure enough, there were the other two. She was hidden by the open wardrobe door; she made no sound though she felt like shouting her anger at him. But she had learned to be more subtle and secretive than that.

'What the hell are you doing?' called Matthew. Quickly she replaced the letters in the pocket. If he was going to take her out, and it looked like it, she would find a way to post a letter herself, one way or another.

They ate bacon and egg and baked beans at a cafe on the sea front. Hetty was ravenous for she hadn't eaten at all the day before. She cleared her plate of the greasy food and took two slices of bread with it. Afterwards, they drove out of the town, through Marske and Saltburn, and on through the iron mining villages which dotted the hills and cliffs and valleys of Cleveland.

They drove past the entrance to Smuggler's Cove and Hetty gazed along the road, thinking of Peter and Audrey and little Charlie. How were they getting on with their stepmother now? she wondered. A lot of good she had been to them, she thought sadly. But she would get in touch as soon as she was able, she vowed to herself.

'Stop the car!' she called suddenly, and with a startled

glance at the strained whiteness of her face, he pulled into the side and she dashed out and behind a bush and threw up her breakfast. She stood for a moment, taking huge gulps of fresh air, her heart thudding and the sky and earth whirling round about her. At last the world righted itself and she walked shakily back to the car. Matthew had not moved from his seat. He watched her broodingly.

'Where are we going?' she asked as he started the car again.

'To see a friend of mine.'

For Matthew had remembered Jeremy. He hadn't seen him since they were at school together but didn't reckon that would matter. Jeremy had always been there on the edge of Matthew's crowd, a quiet, mousy boy. Matthew had used him to run errands, take messages to the girls of the town. Later he'd gone somewhere obscure, Matthew recalled, to study engineering. He remembered that especially as he had always assumed Jeremy would become a Latin teacher or something equally boring.

They were climbing now, out on the cliffs far above the sea. Hetty gazed out over the vast expanse, the haze on the horizon which could turn into a sea fret and roll inland or simply burn up in the sun, there was no telling. No telling, she thought, just like me and my life. Why can't I take control of my own future? But she had no answer for herself.

They turned inland, over the moor, and halted at an isolated house which lay on a fold of the moor. A stone house, foursquare and grand, with small-paned windows and a surprisingly imposing portico.

'Stay there,' commanded Matthew and she watched from the car as he strode up the path and rang the bell. The door opened and he disappeared inside while she sat on. Half an hour later when the door opened again she was still sitting there.

'You can come in now,' said Matthew. He glanced critically at her. 'And for goodness' sake, don't speak more than you have to. And comb your hair!'

Hetty tugged her comb through her wind-swept hair and fastened it back securely with a clip over her ear. Don't talk, she thought dully. That meant he was ashamed of her again.

207

'Mrs Hope? How nice to meet you, I'm Jeremy Painter.' The man waiting in the hall looked delighted to see them. That was something at least, she thought. Of course, Painter Iron Works. He must be one of the family which owned them. He was about Matthew's age though smaller built but there was an air of prosperity about him, from his highly polished shoes to his centre-parted hair, smoothed back over a high forehead. Hetty mumbled something and held out her hand which he took. His own was white and the nails were manicured, but the grip was firm.

'I'm delighted you decided to visit.'

'Well, we were near and I suddenly thought of you. Haven't seen you in years, old boy.' Matthew sounded hearty, pleased to see this friend of his, thought Hetty. Yet she had never heard of Jeremy Painter before; he had never been mentioned in Hope Hall, at least not in her presence.

'I'll have your luggage taken up. You'll stay for a few days at least, won't you? Or is there somewhere you have to be?'

'No, no, delighted to accept your invitation, old chap,' said Matthew.

Hetty followed a manservant up the stairs which were similar to the ones at Hope Hall. Everything felt unreal. In the grand bedroom with its panoramic view over the moors she stood by the window, unsure whether to unpack or not. How could she stay here? How would Matthew explain her lack of clothes? Even the few she had were cheap and shabby.

'Mrs Hope' Mr Painter had called her. Did that mean Matthew really would marry her? Not that she cared for herself, not now. But for the baby, she did care. She remembered a couple of illegitimate babies in Morton Main. Poor little mites. Right from the beginning they had been stared at, looked down on. She was determined that would not happen to her baby. She would not go home with a fatherless child, not ever.

'Haven't you even changed?'

Hetty jumped as the door opened and Matthew came in, frowning irritably at her.

'I haven't anything to change into,' she pointed out.

208

'Hell, no, nor you have.' He studied her for a moment then appeared to make up his mind. 'Come on then, we'll have to go into Whitby. It's all right, Jerry's gone off on business.' His lip curled in derision. 'He always was a good little boy. Still, he's come in handy this time. Makes up for all the times he trailed around after us when we were at school! I should think we'll be able to stay here at least a week, give me time to look around.'

In Whitby he bought her a couple of dresses: one a soft apricot wool which clung seductively to her figure and another in turquoise with skirts which swirled round her calves. Hetty had never had such expensive dresses in her life.

'They won't fit me for long,' she warned him regretfully. 'Shouldn't I have something fuller? The baby will show in a week or two.'

Matthew shrugged impatiently. 'It's now we have to think about,' he said. 'I have to go to the bank, you wait for me by the harbour.' Buying her clothes had made inroads into his money but his allowance was due. Anyway, he reasoned, he wouldn't be spending anything much this week, they would be living off good old Jerry. He would be drinking Jerry's whisky. Matthew grinned to himself as he sauntered into the bank. Things weren't so bad after all.

Five minutes later he was furiously angry. 'You must have made a mistake, you bloody fool!' he shouted at the manager sitting behind his desk. The self-satisfied man looking down his nose.

'No mistake, Mr Hope,' he said stiffly. 'In fact, your father was in only this morning to tell me your allowance has been cancelled. And I'm afraid we can't cash this cheque as your account is already overdrawn.'

Matthew stared at him. 'But he can't cancel my allowance,' he cried. 'It's from my grandfather!'

'I'm afraid he can, Mr Hope. He is the administrator of the trusts your grandfather set up for you and your brother.'

Nothing Matthew could say moved the manager. 'You're enjoying this, aren't you?' he snarled, and the manager shook his head politely.

'No, it's just a matter of business.' He pressed a button

on his desk and in only a second or two the door opened and two men were standing outside. 'Show Mr Hope out, will you?' Only when Matthew turned back from the door and glared at him did the manager permit himself an icy smile.

The vindictive old sod! Matthew thought savagely as he strode down the street, his face black with anger so that the people on the pavement hurriedly got out of his way. He didn't see Hetty at first and rage boiled up in him. If he had to go searching for her again, he would take a horse whip to her, he told himself. He did not wonder why even now the feeling of panic which accompanied his rage whenever she went missing made anything else that was happening to him fade into insignificance. He glared round at the passers-by. She was across the road, gazing into a shop window. He strode over, ignoring the hooting of traffic, and grabbed her arm.

'Where the hell have you been?' he demanded, and pulled her after him to the car. She didn't mind, had already posted the card she had bought from a pavement display. It was a picture of a fat woman and a skinny man in bed together but that didn't matter. It was on the back she had written her message.

Chapter 24

'Come on, pack our things,' said Matthew, closing the bedroom door after himself with a bang.

'Pack?'

Hetty sat up in bed feeling disoriented. She blinked for Matthew had switched on the light as he came in.

'I said pack, didn't I? You've not gone deaf, have you?'

He strode across to the window and opened the heavy curtains. The first flush of dawn was just lightening the sky.

'But where are we going?' Hetty dragged herself out of bed and began pulling on her clothes. Her legs and arms were heavy with slumber and her head ached in protest. Nevertheless she took the cases out of the closet and began to fill them.

'Never you mind. You're going where I go,' snapped Matthew. He was in a foul temper, having just lost the last of his cash to Jeremy in a card game. Jerry was not the lad he once was, Matthew thought grimly to himself. No, he was showing his true colours now. All evening Jerry had been needling him, reminding him of the slights Matthew and his friends had inflicted on him when they were at school. Hell, the fellow had a memory like an elephant! And now he had the upper hand. Oh yes, like a fool Matthew had played straight into Jerry's hands. Though to give the fellow his due, he had come up with a solution to their problems.

'You've been here a week now, Matthew,' Jeremy had said after scooping up the last pot of the night. 'What are your plans?'

Matthew hadn't any plans at all, that was the trouble.

211

And his mind was on the game. He had been willing Lady Luck to turn in his favour, was devastated when he lost. He had stared blankly at his host.

'Plans?'

Jeremy waited until he had taken the top off a cigar and lit it to his satisfaction. 'You don't have any, do you?'

'I . . . well, of course.'

'As I understand it, you are broke, old boy, with no hope of getting a sou from your father. Been a bit foolish, haven't you? But who wouldn't lose his head over a delectable bit like the one upstairs? Believe me, I envy you, old boy.'

Matthew glared at him. 'What do you know about my position?'

'Well, old boy.' Jeremy tapped the ash from his cigar tip and sat back more comfortably in his chair. 'You have tended to let drop most of it yourself when we've been chatting over a drink or two these evenings.'

'It's none of your bloody business!'

'No? But you're living in my house, my friend. My dear old school friend.' Jeremy paused and Matthew caught a glimpse of malice before the other dropped his eyes. Shifty little weasel that he was.

'Do you want us to go? I assure you, we can be out of the house in ten minutes if that's what you're leading up to.'

'Oh, calm down, Matthew, don't get on your high horse. What I am doing is offering you a job and a house into the bargain.' Jeremy smiled at him. Maybe he had been mistaken about the malice.

'A job? What sort of job?'

'Oh, nothing too tedious. I want a well-spoken front man for the office. One who knows the best places to take clients, overseas visitors, people like that. I've been doing most of it myself but I just haven't the time now. What do you say? There's a house goes with the job.'

Matthew was thinking rapidly. If he held down a job, even if it was only until he got back on his feet, his father would probably change his mind. 'What sort of house?'

'Oh, nothing beneath your status, old boy,' said Jeremy. 'My grandfather's house on the coast. Your . . . er . . . wife can look after it for me. I've been looking for a caretaker for it, a housekeeper really. In fact, you would be doing me a favour. I needn't bother advertising for one now. I'm afraid there'll be no other staff, though, she'll have to see to everything herself.'

'She's just what you've been looking for,' said Matthew, and rose to his feet. 'I accept. When do I start?'

'Oh, right away, old boy. Today, in fact. It's already morning. If you set off now you will be able to get there and drop Hetty off and still be in the office by eleven. I have a client from Holland coming for lunch. You can come with me to learn the ropes.'

'We haven't discussed my salary.' Matthew was beginning to feel better about the job now he had had time to get over his initial horror at the thought of work. This wasn't a job, really. He quite fancied himself visiting all the best places, and at Jeremy's expense.

'Oh, my accountant sees to such things. Don't worry, you won't be disappointed. Now, as I said, you could move today, it's already morning. Then I'll expect you at the office at nine.'

'Nine o'clock this morning? I thought you said eleven?' Matthew was genuinely horrified but Jeremy affected not to notice.

'That's right, nine. Eleven is a little late, I think,' he replied and stood up with the unmistakable air of an employer dismissing an employee. The effects of the whisky he had drunk were beginning to wear off Matthew. Maybe this wasn't such a good deal after all. But what choice did he have? Anyway, he didn't have to stay long, just until he had convinced his father that he had turned over a new leaf.

Hetty wandered out of the garden and across the expanse of grass which lay between it and the top of the cliff. There was no road, just a dirt track, and that was muddy with the rain that had fallen yesterday. By, the air was lovely up here, she thought, and it was grand to get out for a walk, to explore the area. Very like the cliffs above Smuggler's Cove. This was the land of cliffs. Alice had said that 'Cleveland' meant land of cliffs. Hetty thought sadly of Alice; how she would have loved to have her living near.

She looked back at the house, surrounded by a stone wall but the upper stories visible. A large house, very large, bigger even than Hope Hall. Hetty sighed. She was trying hard to get it back into some semblance of order but it was so big and she had no help. Matthew was out most of the day and even when he was home he expected her to wait on him, it did not occur to him to help her with anything.

She remembered the morning she had first seen the house, she couldn't believe it was where they were going to live. The rooms were so big and the grimy windows made it so gloomy, the dust lay thick on everything. Well, she had got most of the downstairs rooms cleaned up, simply by doing one room at a time. But so far she had done only one of the bedrooms, the one Matthew had elected they should sleep in.

Sitting down on the grass, she gazed out to sea where a line of steamers chugged their way north to the mouth of the Tees. Or maybe further on to the Tyne. As she did every day, she wondered if her card had reached her mother and father in Morton Main. But even if it had and Mam or Da replied, it would be to Jeremy Painter's house, that was the address she had put on the card.

Idly, Hetty began to make a daisy chain as she and Cissy had done so long ago on the grassy banks beyond the gardens of Office Street. She felt a flutter inside her belly and put a hand on it, startled. Surely it was too soon to feel the baby moving? Was it due sooner than she thought? Sighing, she wished she had another woman to confide in. It was a month since she had sent the card; she was beginning to fear that there was not going to be a reply.

Maybe she should begin to make preparations for the baby. Matthew wasn't interested, she would have to do everything herself. Now was the time, before she got too big and heavy. Rising to her feet, Hetty started to walk back to the house. The garden was wildly overgrown, she had to push branches aside from the path to reach the front door. Maybe next spring, when the baby came, he could sit out in the garden in his pram and she would be working near him, weeding the beds, planting flowers in the empty spaces where weeds had been.

She went into the house, noting with satisfaction the gleam of polished wood from the furniture, the glass dish on the hall table in which she had arranged sweet-smelling roses. Of course, when her gaze shifted to the stairs, she saw that they were once again covered in a film of dust. Dear Lord, she was tired. The more rooms she cleaned, the more time it took for her to keep them right before she could start somewhere else.

But it was three o'clock, she had a right to be tired, she had worked from dawn. She didn't want to start again, not now. Hetty thought of her baby again and had an idea. She would look for a nursery. Surely there was a nursery, and there might be something in it she could use for the baby? She made for the stairs with a new purpose. Surely Mr Painter wouldn't mind that?

There were wooden shutters over the tall windows of the first floor, making the rooms look even gloomier. But even with the furniture all covered with dust sheets, she could see that they were meant for adults, not one was a nursery, at least not like the nursery at Hope Hall. On the second floor there was one room with bars across the window that could have been meant for children but it was disappointingly empty. Hetty opened the shutters and the light flooded in. There was a print on the faded yellow wall, a picture of a teddy bear, but nothing else.

Well, she would try the attic. There were no electric lights in this house, no electricity at all, just candles and paraffin lamps which she was unable to use because Matthew always forgot to bring the paraffin. But at the bottom of the steep attic stairs, there was a candlestick with a stub of a candle and an ancient box of matches.

Hetty began to enjoy herself as she lit the candle and climbed the narrow flight to the attics. It reminded her of the times she and Ethel had giggled together in the attic bedroom at Hope Hall, but most of all it reminded her of a haunted house film she had seen once at the King's Hall in Bishop Auckland. By, it was funny.

Disappointingly, the candle wasn't necessary, there was plenty of light in the attics from windows let into the roof. Regretfully, she blew out the flame and left the candle by the door. There were lots of boxes in the attic, all dusty. She opened one and peeped inside. It was filled with books, old-fashioned books, leather bound with gold leaf on the edges of the pages. Some of them looked as though they had never been opened. She was just going to delve further into the box when she caught sight of a cradle, a lovely rocking cradle with a hood and frills and when she blew a little of the dust away she saw the material was satin. By, it would be grand if she could have it for the baby, aye, it would. She forgot about the books as she took the duster she had got into the habit of carrying around with her since she came to this house and carefully wiped away the dust.

Mind, she told herself, they won't let you have it. The cradle was a family one, handed down no doubt; she bet Jeremy and his father had slept in this cradle. Her hands caressed the polished rosewood of the frame regretfully. Her baby would have a dresser drawer for a cradle, just as she had had herself. Matthew wouldn't provide for the bairn, she was fairly sure of that, everything it had she would have to get. But what was wrong with a pillow in a drawer? Babbies didn't know the difference.

There was a sound downstairs, what was it? For a minute her heart thudded; they were such miles from anywhere and Matthew wouldn't be home for hours yet. The wind it would be, she told herself, aye. The wind was something shocking up here on the top of the cliff, it fair whistled through the house. And when it rained, the wind slashed across the windows so that it sounded like needles hitting the glass.

Nevertheless, Hetty went down the stairs to investigate, just in case anyone was there. Pausing at the mirror which stood on the first-floor landing, she rubbed a smudge of dust from her cheek and took off her apron, rolling it into a ball and leaving it there.

The main door was open, that was what it was, she must not have closed it properly. She ran across the hall and was about to close it when she heard a man's cough. Flinging the door wide, she stepped forward to confront who ever it was and found herself face to face with her father.

'Aye, we have the right house, Frank,' he called over his shoulder and there was her brother. 'Now then, Hetty,' he said and she flung herself on to her father, laughing and crying together.

'Oh, Da! Oh, Da!'

He hugged her awkwardly and then Frank stepped forward and kissed her cheek and swung her round off her feet. The sun shone and happiness bubbled up inside her and Da took off his cap and beamed at both of them.

'Aren't you asking us in, lass?' he said at last. 'By, we've been walking all afternoon, I'm ready for a sit down and a sup of tea.'

They sat in the kitchen around the table and Hetty made tea and took out a packet of shop-bought biscuits Matthew had brought with the groceries. Da looked dubiously at them and declined. They talked about how the pit had gone back on to three-day working and how Mam had had a bad cold but was getting better now and how Gran was failing and didn't get over to Morton Main as much as she used to do.

'We had some bother finding the place,' said Frank. 'It was Mr Painter who told us where you were. Why didn't you write sooner, Hetty?'

She looked at him. How could she say she had but that Matthew had kept her letters? So far they hadn't mentioned Matthew but he was in all of their minds, she could feel his presence like a physical thing. Da leaned back in his chair and planted both booted feet squarely on the red tiles of the floor.

'You fair broke your mother's heart when you went off like that without a word,' he said. 'Why did you do it, Hetty?'

'Matthew ... Matthew wanted ...' she began but her voice trailed off. She wasn't at all sure why she did it nor even what had happened that day.

'Aye, Matthew,' said Frank. 'Does he treat you right, Hetty?'

'Aye, he does,' she said, but there must have been something in her voice, some hesitation.

'You'll come home with us,' Da declared. 'Bairn or no bairn. You didn't think we'd just abandon you, did you?'

Hetty looked down at her hands, twisting in her lap. What about Mam? she wanted to ask. What about the shame, the

217

gossip in the rows, what about my baby brought up without a father? But she just couldn't manage to bring out the words.

'Where's the lad now, then?'

'He's at work. He works for Mr Painter. At the iron works. The office.'

Thomas thought about it. He didn't know much about the gentry but he was sure working in an office must be a comedown for one of them. He shrugged. 'Well, you can come with us now, leave him a note. If we go now we'll be back in time for first shift at the pit. Go on, Hetty, get your things together.'

'I can't, Da.'

Thomas exploded. He jumped to his feet, the studs in his pitboots ringing on the tiles. 'Damn it all, lass, what's the matter with you, have you got no backbone at all? Where's your pride? He's not going to marry you, can you not see that? Not when he can get all he wants without. An' what about your babby then, eh?'

'He's right, Hetty.' She looked over at Frank as he agreed with his father. His face was red, embarrassed but earnest. What was she doing to them?

'Matthew says we will be wed, Da,' she said. 'An' I want my bairn to have a name.'

'Aye, well, I understand that but—'

The sound of a car's engine cut across his words. All three of them looked towards the door. The front door banged and they heard footsteps as the new arrival marched through to the back of the house. Seconds later the door opened and Matthew stood there smiling grimly.

'Well,' he said, 'I thought I would find you all in the kitchen, it being your natural habitat, and I was right, wasn't I?'

'Matthew, this is my father and—'

'I know who they are, Hetty. Jeremy bloody Painter came back into the office especially to tell me about our visitors.'

Thomas and his son looked at each other and Thomas got to his feet. 'Hetty, Frank and me'd like a word with your man private like,' he said.

Hetty knew that tone from the few times in the past she

218

had heard her father use it and she turned to leave the kitchen.

'Stay where you are, Hetty, I'm sure your father has nothing to say you can't hear,' said Matthew.

She looked from him to her da. Matthew was still smiling, a cruel, contemptuous smile. Oh, she was used to that smile but she couldn't bear to see it used on her da. 'I'll just be upstairs,' she said and went out, not looking again at Matthew.

Thomas began straight away. 'I want Hetty to come home with us, we'll look after her,' he said.

Matthew felt a surge of rage so intense it burned. 'She is staying with me!' he snapped.

'Will you marry her?'

Matthew hesitated for only a second but it was enough. Frank stepped forward. 'You'll not, will you? No, you'll lead the lass on wi' promises an' such like and when you've finished wi' her you'll hoy her out.'

Matthew raised his eyes to the ceiling. With a great effort he managed to keep his rage in bounds as he said, with all the contempt he had for the lower classes, 'What the hell am I doing, standing here in a *kitchen* arguing with a pair of *pitmen*?'

'Why, man, lad,' said Thomas, his voice flat and even, 'why, man, we don't have to stay in the *kitchen*, do we?' He nodded to Frank and they moved in unison, Frank clasping his arms round Matthew's upper body and Thomas opening the door which led to a cobbled courtyard with stables opposite.

'Let me go, you oaf!' Matthew said through clenched teeth. He strove to free himself. He was a head taller than Frank and broad-shouldered from the rugby he had played at school and university but Frank was a coal hewer, with massive shoulders and forearms from wielding the pick in confined spaces.

'I'll let you go,' Frank said pleasantly once they were in the middle of the courtyard. 'Now, Da asked you a civil question and he wants a civil answer.' He moved back a pace so that the three of them were standing in a line, with Matthew in the middle.

219

He couldn't believe this was happening. After the rotten day he had had, to have such peasants lay their hands on him!

'Oh, go to hell,' he said. 'I'll do what I like, and if I don't like to marry her I bloody well won't. There's not a damn' thing you can do about it.'

'Is there not?'

Frank stepped forward and Matthew put up his fists to defend himself but Frank was too quick for him. With one swing of his fist he caught Matthew on the jaw and he fell back, not on the cobbles but into Thomas's arms. Thomas watched interestedly as blood began to well from Matthew's mouth.

'You broke my tooth, you—'

'Aye, he did,' commented Thomas. 'Now then, can you stand up by yourself, man?'

'By God, I swear I'll have you for assault,' he said savagely.

'Eeh, I think not,' said Frank. 'Not when the circumstances come out. But thanks for the warning like. Now, what were you saying about our Hetty?'

She had heard the commotion and was watching the confrontation from the back landing window. She couldn't believe it when Frank hit Matthew – Frank who was such a quiet, inoffensive man, Frank, who wouldn't hurt a fly. And what's more, it looked like he would do it again. Hetty rushed down the stairs and through the kitchen to the back door.

'Frank, Frank, don't do it!' she cried, just too late to stop the blow falling on Matthew's face, the blow which cut straight across his eyebrow and closed his eye. Thomas deftly caught him again and lowered him to the ground gently for Matthew was knocked out.

'Jack Dempsey couldn't have done better,' he observed, giving his son an admiring glance.

'Frank! Eeh, Frank, what have you done?' Her father and brother drew back as Hetty ran across the cobbles, sobbing, and flung herself down beside Matthew. Anxiously she was checking his pulse. Oh, thank God he was not dead. What would she do if they put her da and Frank in Durham

Gaol? And it would be all her fault . . . what would Mam do without her menfolk? Dear God, please God, she prayed, let him be all right.

To Thomas and Frank, as they watched her distraught state, it looked as though it was all due to her feeling for Matthew. She must love the bloke, really, Frank thought, depression falling on him.

'Come on, Da,' he said. 'I don't think we're wanted here.'

Chapter 25

Hetty sat in the attic, listening anxiously for any noise which would show that Matthew was waking up.

'Get away from me, woman!' he had shouted at her when he had come round, lying on the cobbles with the stink of ancient horse manure in his nostrils. He had sat up, gagging, his head screaming in protest at the sudden movement.

'I'll help you up,' Hetty said, holding out her hand.

'I can get up myself,' he roared, or thought he'd roared; it came out pathetically quiet. That was what it had been: pathetic, humiliating. Where were they? He'd kill them, he'd take a horse whip to them, he'd . . . The courtyard was empty but for Hetty, standing over him, her eyes large and anxious.

'You won't set the polis on them, will you?' she asked.

Matthew staggered to his feet and lurched for the doorway. 'Set the police on them? I'll have them for attempted murder, I will. I swear I will,' he snarled.

'No! No don't, please don't,' she begged. They were in the hall now, she following him as he stumbled inside, refusing to let her help him.

'You're not really hurt, Matthew, not really, are you?'

Her anxious questions maddened him. He turned on her suddenly, his fist lifted, and she fled to the staircase. He started after her but stopped after only a few steps, his hands on his head. 'Just you wait,' he said thickly, 'when I catch you, I'll—'

But Hetty didn't wait to find out what he would do. She raced up the stairs, all the way to the top of the house, to the attics. She had sat there on a dusty trunk until everything below her was quiet then she crept downstairs. Matthew was asleep in an armchair in the drawing room, a whisky glass in his hand. She stared at him searchingly, wanting to make sure he was just asleep, not ill, not injured. Matthew awakened abruptly and saw her and a deep rumbling started in his throat. Hetty fled back to the attic, fastening the door at the head of the narrow stairs behind her with the hook and eye latch she found on the inside.

It was beginning to grow dark but she stayed where she was. Best wait until tomorrow, she thought, Matthew would have to go to work tomorrow. It wasn't that she was frightened for herself but if he got hold of her while he was in a rage he might hurt the baby. The shadows stretched across the boarded floor; the sun must be almost down now, the air was cooler. She began to look around for something to wrap herself in. There were shawls in one of the trunks, not warm woollen shawls but silky embroidered shawls, no good at all for her purpose. But in one old press there were blankets, moth-eaten but woollen, and she pulled them out gratefully.

She made herself a sort of bed with them, using one rolled up as a pillow. Then she lit the candle and delved in the box of books. If she had something to read it would pass the time for she didn't want to think about Da just now, or Frank, it hurt too much. They were old books, perhaps a hundred years old, some of them more. She turned the pages curiously. There was a set of books on *Household Management for the New Bride*. She fell asleep reading the section on 'How to Manage Servants'.

The telephone woke her, the one which Mr Painter had insisted on having installed only a week ago. The poles holding the wire marched across the fields, looking alien, out of place. For a minute she didn't know what it was and jumped up in alarm, hardly knowing where she was. She went to the door and opened it a little, anxiously wondering if Matthew had heard it. He had. There was his voice answering it though she couldn't hear what he was saying.

Then he was shouting through the house for her, calling up the stairs and out by the kitchen. 'Hetty? Hetty, where the hell are you?' She waited, holding her breath, though there was no possible way he could have heard it down three flights of stairs.

'I know you're there, Hetty. When I come back I'll find you,' he threatened. Then she heard the front door bang and the engine of his car start up. He was gone. Thankfully she descended to the kitchen and cut herself a slice from the loaf and took a lump of cheese from the pantry. She sat at the table and forced herself to eat, washing it down with cold water from the tap and listening all the time for the return of the engine.

At last she could allow herself to think of the ache inside her, it was almost a physical sensation. Why had Da and Frank gone away so quickly? She couldn't understand it. One minute she had been looking and feeling to see if Matthew was dead, terrified that if he were, her father and brother would be taken by the police, and then when she'd looked up they had gone. She felt utterly deserted. What if Matthew had been dead and she had been left alone to face the consequences? If they were so afraid of going to gaol, why did they do it in the first place?

She remembered the fight that had broken out one night outside The Black Boy in Morton. A man had died then and two miners had disappeared and were never seen again. Da and Frank wouldn't just disappear, would they? No, no, her imagination was running riot again, what a fool she was.

Suddenly she felt so tired, so bone weary, that she had to go to bed. A proper bed, not the shake down she had made up in the attic. She would wake when Matthew came in, she told herself, she always did when she heard the car. She went upstairs and washed in the ornately old-fashioned bathroom which had garlands of painted roses on the handbasin and around the bowl of the water closet. Then she took off her dress and got into bed, too tired even to remove her petticoat. Yet she tossed and turned for a while before she fell into an exhausted sleep.

Matthew rang the bell on the door of Ridgeways, Jeremy Painter's house. He scowled, waiting on the step like some damned tradesman, he thought savagely. In fact, Jeremy Painter was beginning seriously to annoy him. Matthew

224

grinned mirthlessly – an understatement if ever there was one. Just you wait, Jeremy bloody Painter, don't think you can get away with this! Wait until my father comes to his senses, I am his heir after all. Then you may look out, I don't forget insults. And the way he'd been treated since he came to work for Painter had been more than an insult, it had been a flaming outrage. Like a messenger boy, in fact, the merest factotum. Once, he'd even been asked to make the tea.

'My secretary is busy, old chap,' Painter had said. Old chap! Smarmy sod. Matthew put out a hand to ring the bell again. Why didn't he just walk in? It was open. Because Painter had made it plain the one time he did that that it wasn't the behaviour of an employee.

'Yes?'

The door had opened and Painter's manservant stood there, looking down his nose. Matthew's patience was at an end. He pushed past the man into the hall.

'Where's your master?' he demanded. It was ten o'clock in the evening and Matthew's head ached. He put up a hand and felt the bruise over his eye; his tongue gingerly probed his broken tooth. He needed a drink.

'Ah, there you are, Matthew. Come into the study, will you?' Painter was there at the door of his study. He nodded to the manservant. 'It's all right, Parker, you can go to bed now.'

Matthew followed him into the room where there was an aroma of good cigars and malt whisky. He stared at the tray. The decanter was half full but there was no spare glass. He wasn't going to be offered a drink then. Bile settled on his stomach, bitter and burning.

'Good God, Matthew, what have you done to your face?' Jeremy was standing by the fire. He picked up his glass and drained it before putting it down on the tray.

'I walked into a door,' he said, and his need overcame his pride. 'Are you going to offer me a drink, Jerry?'

Jeremy looked regretful. 'Oh, I'm sorry, Matthew, better not. I want you to go to Thirsk and pick up a client – he's on the midnight train from King's Cross. Señor Allemany, from Barcelona. Do you think you can manage that?' He looked Matthew over critically and Matthew was within an ace of telling him to pick up his own client and walking out. To hell with him. But the thought that all his humiliations over the last few weeks might then go for nothing stopped him.

'Thirsk, you said? How will I know him?'

'Oh, you'll know him, I think. There shouldn't be many Spanish businessmen getting off the train at Thirsk.'

Matthew turned for the door but Jeremy was not finished with him yet. 'By the way,' he said, 'I'd rather you didn't call me Jerry. Well, it doesn't sound right in front of clients, does it? I am, after all, owner as well as managing director of the firm. Better call me Mr Painter. Oh, and Matthew, while we are on the subject of names, do you prefer to be called Matt? Well, do go and clean your face up a little better than you have done. You can use the bathroom at the head of the stairs.'

Matthew went out, not trusting himself to reply. It was a wonder to him he didn't smash *Mr* Painter's head in. In the bathroom, he studied his face in the mirror; the bruises on it were turning purple. He patted a little talcum powder into them, wincing as he did so. That looked better. Well, at least he had remembered to change before he came out, though he'd had the devil of a job to find his clean shirts. Where the hell had Hetty got to? When he got back he'd have to teach her a lesson she wouldn't forget in a hurry.

Hetty woke with a start. It was morning, a chink of light came through the heavy velvet curtains. What was it she had heard? Jumping out of bed, she went to the window and drew back the curtains. Matthew's car was there, he was just getting out of it. Hurriedly she grabbed her clothes and ran. She was already opening the door of the attic when he came into the house.

'Hetty? Hetty, where the hell are you?' His voice was slurred but belligerent. She held still, her hand on the door knob. He mumbled obscenities and went into one of the downstairs rooms, getting himself a drink, she supposed. She slipped inside the attic and fastened the door.

The house fell quiet. She supposed he had gone to sleep

in an armchair, that was what he usually did. She pulled on her clothes, thinking longingly of the bathroom. Dare she go down to it? She would have to. Carefully, silently, she opened the door and crept down the stairs in her bare feet. She closed the bathroom door after herself, bolted it and leaned against it, sighing with relief. By, the bliss of washing herself all over, even if it was in cold water. She daren't start the ancient boiler, it rumbled and thumped alarmingly and might wake him. She left flushing the lavatory until the last minute then ran like a hare for the attic again.

This was no good, she told herself. Where was her backbone? She had to go out and face him, she had to. But when she heard his step on the stairs, he had indeed heard her in the bathroom, she panicked and shrank back deeper into the attic, deeper than she had been before, looking for somewhere to hide. The latch would not hold against his shoulder, she was sure of it. She stood by the side of what looked like an ancient painted chest, peeping round at the door.

'You in there, Hetty?' he shouted. He tried the door. Luckily he did not test the strength of the hook which held it. After a minute, mumbling something inaudible to Hetty, he started down the narrow stairs which led to the broader staircase below. She could hear him wandering about the house then there was quiet. She was fairly sure he would not have gone out. She would have heard the front door, she thought. Well, she would just wait.

Going back to her nest of blankets, Hetty rummaged in the box of old books, looking for something to read apart from the antiquated books on household management. Right at the bottom of the box was a pile of yellowing bills, all written in a copperplate hand. The top one was worn and thin and the ink so pale that she couldn't read it but the others were in better condition. November 9th, in the year of our Lord 1793, she read. Provisions for the sloop *Primrose*. Pickled herrings, 1/- a barrel, flour, 4d a stone, salt . . . Hetty forgot all about Matthew as she turned them over.

At the bottom was a larger sheet, folded, the paper along

the folds broken with age. Carefully she opened it out. It was a map of a small bay, but there were no names written on it. But it was a dotted line drawn from the bay which interested her: it led up to a house. This house, she was sure it was. Not only up to the house but to the very top of the house. It was intriguing.

Hetty sat back on her heels. Dowstairs she could hear Matthew moving about again. She stared at the map, trying to figure it out. The line went up the back of the house, along the line of the chimneys. The place where the chimneys converged was at this side of the house behind the old cabinet. The chimneys were big, but surely not big enough to hold a secret passage? But perhaps it wasn't really so fanciful. She remembered tales of the smugglers who used to abound on this part of the coast: John Andrews, for instance, who ran a band from the old Ship Inn in Saltburn until the revenue men rounded them up. Smuggler's Cove too. There were tales of houses there with secret passages. She went over to have a closer look at the wall by the chimneys but she could see no sign of a door.

There was a distant thud. The front door – Matthew must have gone out again. Hetty forgot about secret passages and smugglers. Her imagination running riot again, she thought ruefully, when there was a great deal of work to do. She made her way down to the first landing and through the window saw Matthew getting into his car again. Relief flooded through her. Now she could get on with the work of cleaning the house. She had a suspicion that Mr Painter would be coming to have a look at it one of these days.

Hetty worked all morning, going over the rooms she had already done, dusting and mopping and polishing, and then began on the second bedroom on the first floor. Dust lay thickly over everything; there had been a fall of soot in the fireplace and it had billowed out on to the carpet. It was three o'clock when she decided to have a break. She made herself a sandwich and took it outside, going beyond the garden and making for the cliffs. She sat on the grass and ate the sandwich, thinking about the map she had found in the attic. Looking back at the house, she wondered about the people who had lived there so long ago – a crony of John

Andrews, perhaps, and his family. It could have been money made from smuggling which had built the house, or at least given the family a start. They could be ancestors of Jeremy Painter and look where *he* was today.

Hetty went to the edge of the cliff. By, it was high. There was a small beach but it was uneven with piles of waste which had been tipped there from some long worked-out mine; there were old workings all along the coast. She walked along the cliff top and after a while found a sort of dip in the edge. There was a path down and another small beach. Hetty followed the path down; it wound its way between dunes that could have been man-made or not. In any case, the path led her to the bay.

By, it was lovely. She took off her shoes and buried her toes in the fine sand. So warm it was on her toes. The cliffs rose high beside her, gulls swooped about and a crab walked determinedly along the water's edge. She thought of taking him up, they could have dressed crab for supper, but changed her mind. The crab knew where he was going, who was she to stop him? She smiled to herself. Anyroad, she couldn't kill him and she didn't want to.

This wasn't the beach of the map, or she didn't think it was. She walked along the water's edge, back towards the spoilt beach near the house. She had to climb over rocks to get round a small headland, keeping a weather eye on the tide as she did so, but it didn't seem on the turn. The beach when she came to it was a hideous mess, with piles of rusty rocks and small pools of stained water. But it could be the one on the map. She studied the cliff face but most of the bottom half was hidden under rubble. There was nothing to see.

Hetty began to walk back to the path, disappointed. It was when she skirted round a pile of boulders that she saw what looked like an opening to a cave, half hidden by rubble. If she hadn't been on the alert for something of the sort she would have walked past it. As it was she paused and bent down to peer inside. There was nothing to see, it was so dark inside. But nevertheless she bent even lower and went in. After a moment her eyes adjusted to the dimness and she saw it was quite a big cave and at the other end was a lighter area – light coming in from above. Hesitating for only a second, Hetty moved forward and began to climb.

By, it was a long way. Her legs began to ache, her back too. Hetty thought of the poor miners of long ago who had had to climb ladders up the shafts with baskets of coal on their backs, women too and little lads. No wonder they had celebrated when the first winding engine and cages were installed at Haswell Colliery. And she wasn't carrying anything! She paused and looked down. The cave bottom was a very long way away but she could see the glitter of water. The tide must have come in. Well then, she had to go on up, she couldn't go down.

The door at the top was behind the painted cabinet. She had to use all her strength to get it open, leaning her back into it and pushing the cabinet away. For a while she thought she wasn't going to do it but suddenly the cabinet shifted, almost toppling over but steadying and allowing her just room enough to squeeze through into the attic.

'Hetty? Hetty? Oh, come out, Hetty, will you, I'm not going to hurt you. I won't lay a finger on you.'

Matthew was on the stairs. She had a painful stitch in her side but managed to push the cabinet back to hide the gap and ran across to the door to the stairs. She had to face him some time.

Chapter 26

Hetty sat in the armchair on the opposite side of the fireplace to where Matthew sprawled, legs stretched out in front of him. He clasped a glass in his hand but his eyes were closed. He snored gently. The curtains were pulled against the sea fret which had rolled in soon after she had returned to the house. His mouth was open slightly; his mouth . . . so like his brother's yet different somehow, slacker, weaker. Hetty smiled gently as she thought of Richard smiling down at her from his horse. By, those had been happy days. Even though Richard was the Master's son and she was the maid, he had always treated her with respect. The smile faded and she stared into the fire, her hands stilled over the sewing in her lap, a petticoat she was mending. What did Richard think of her now? she wondered.

Matthew snored a little louder and she glanced at him. He was on the point of dropping the almost empty glass, she saw. Putting her sewing down, she tried to ease it from his hand but Matthew stirred and opened his eyes.

'Leave me alone, woman,' he growled. A fog horn sounded out on the sea, the sound muted by the heavy curtains. She let go of the glass.

'I thought you were going to drop it,' she said. 'You were asleep.'

'I was not asleep,' he snapped, and poured himself another drink from the bottle on the occasional table beside him. He nodded his head blearily and glared across at her where she had settled back into her chair. He looked as though he would take it further but in the end decided not to bother.

231

He swallowed half the glass of whisky thirstily and stared over at her.

'You look tired,' said Hetty. 'Why don't you go to bed?'

'Fancying coming with me, are you?' he leered, and drank again.

'You didn't get any sleep last night,' she reminded him.

'No, thanks to Mr Jeremy bloody Painter.' Matthew scowled blackly. 'But, by God, I'll get my own back, I'll be damned if I don't! Sending me off to Thirsk on a wild goose chase. I wouldn't be surprised if Señor Allemany or whatever the dago was called wasn't supposed to be coming after all. There I was, waiting on Thirsk station, and not a bloody soul got off the train. A wild goose chase, I tell you. Then this morning *Mr* bloody Painter – *Mr* indeed – tells me he had a phone call after I left. The damned fellow wasn't coming at all!'

Matthew rarely talked to Hetty about his work. Now she felt a glimmer of sympathy for him. By, how he must hate working for his old school chum. She watched as he drank again from the glass; the bottle was almost empty and she was pretty sure it had been full only half an hour ago.

He had been sitting here when she had descended from the attic. At first she had hovered warily out of his reach, just in case he was going to knock her about. But Matthew had stayed in his chair, contenting himself with glaring at her in his usual manner.

'So you've decided to make an appearance, have you?' he'd said, and filled his glass with whisky, splashing a tiny amount of water in after it. He looked dispirited somehow, not himself at all, more human perhaps.

'Come to bed,' she said again now.

Matthew looked at his empty glass. He picked up the bottle but it too was empty. Cursing, he threw it on the hearth. Luckily it did not break, simply knocked down the long poker with a clatter on the hearth. Hetty picked up the glass and stood it on the tray.

'I'm coming,' he decided with a sudden change of mood. 'Help me up, Hetty.' He staggered to his feet, holding on to her arm, then leaned on her as they made their way to the door.

232

He tripped over the bottom stair, falling heavily against her, but, cursing and panting, he righted himself and they were almost to the top when he tripped again and this time they both fell, Hetty managing to save herself from falling all the way by hanging on to the banister, but Matthew – and she was to remember the scene in nightmarish detail ever after – went rolling over and over to the bottom where he hit his head on the claw foot of a side table and lay still.

He'd passed out, she told herself, refusing to believe it was worse. Of course he'd just passed out. Everyone knew drunks never hurt themselves. Why, Matthew drove home pallatic drunk practically every night, didn't he?

'Matthew?' she said, then louder, 'Matthew?' She was frozen in position where she half sat, half lay against the banister, her fist clenched around the square dolly rail. It was the telephone, shrilling out shockingly loud and insistent, that made her aware of the pain where the sharp angle of the rail bit into her hand. She got to her feet carefully and walked down to the hall, stepping carefully to the side of Matthew, not looking at him. Gingerly she lifted the receiver from its rest.

'Yes?'

'Who is that? I can't hear you. Is that you, Hetty?'

'Yes.'

'Speak up, woman, do! Is Matthew there? This is Jeremy Painter.'

'Yes.'

'Can you not say anything else? I asked you if Matthew was there?'

'Yes. I mean, yes, he is here, Mr Painter. But he can't come to the telephone.' She looked over to Matthew for the first time. His eyes were open, as was his mouth, hanging slackly. There was a dark patch on the carpet beside his head. Oh yes, he was dead. She had seen men dead before, brought out of the pit after an accident at Morton Main. She had seen them. Oh yes, she knew what death looked like. Her mind shied away from a sudden image of Cissy, dead in the snow.

'Don't be stupid, girl, I wish to speak to him.'

233

She tore her gaze from Matthew's face. 'Matthew can't speak to you, Mr Painter. He's dead.'

Afterwards Hetty couldn't remember how it was the police were informed, or Havelock Hope. She sat in the kitchen, away from the gaze of Matthew's dead eyes and eventually a police car drew up, followed by an ambulance.

'It's too late for the ambulance,' she observed calmly as she opened the door to them and the policeman looked sharply at her. Shock, he decided, the poor woman, and in the family way too. He took her into the drawing room and sat her down in the wrong chair for it was Matthew's usual armchair and she stood up quickly.

'I'll make you some tea,' he said, but she declined.

'No, I'll make it.' And he understood that she had to be doing. He was a man of middle age and experienced in these things.

'Take it easy, missus,' he advised. 'You've had a nasty shock.' She nodded her agreement. There were sounds from the hall and she understood the ambulance men were moving Matthew. Oh, well, she thought dimly, there's that bloodstain on the carpet, I'll have to clean it before Mr Painter gets here. But she didn't, she went back into the kitchen and sat down. The policeman came in and there were questions and she answered them truthfully and he seemed to be satisfied. Mr Painter came and was talking to the policeman; he said Matthew had drunk a lot at luncheon.

'He had a disturbed night, officer,' he said. 'Had to meet a client of ours off the midnight train. Then with the whisky—' And Mr Painter shrugged.

'I'm sorry about the stain on the carpet, Mr Painter,' said Hetty suddenly, and both men looked at her, startled.

'Perhaps we had better ask the doctor to have a look at her?' suggested the policeman.

'No, I think I'll just go to bed, I'm all right,' said Hetty.

She fell asleep the moment she got into bed, a deep heavy sleep with no dreams, and woke the next morning with a throbbing headache. But at least her thoughts were not so muddled. Matthew was dead, she was on her own again. No, not on her own, she had the baby to think about. She washed and dressed in a plain brown dress, the nearest she had to black for her mam would be scandalised if she didn't show some respect for the dead. She brushed her hair and pinned it back behind her ears with hair-clips, then looked at herself in the glass. She was decent.

Havelock Hope was downstairs, talking on the telephone. As Hetty came down, carefully not looking at the place where Matthew had lain, he said, 'I have to go now. I'll ring you back.'

He put down the telephone and stared at her. 'You're awake then,' he said. 'My lad's dead, but you can sleep like a baby.'

'Good morning, Mr Hope,' said Hetty.

'I expect you've got your things packed,' he replied.

Hetty was startled. She couldn't go yet, what about the funeral? Anyroad, she had nowhere to go. Surely Mr Painter wouldn't throw her out today?

'Because if you haven't, you can go and do it now!'

'This isn't your house.'

'No, it isn't, but I want you gone. And I'm sure Mr Painter will agree with me.'

The animosity he felt towards her was plain to see, she could even feel it. 'I'm going now, I don't expect to see you again. And don't think you'll get a penny from us because of that.' He indicated her stomach and she put a protective arm around it almost as if she feared a blow.

'What about the funeral?' she asked, and he laughed.

'You don't think you'll be welcome at the funeral, do you? Get yourself away, girl, as far away as possible. The Antipodes won't be far enough for me!'

Hetty did not reply but turned to the stairs; she would not give him the satisfaction of seeing her cry. She went up to the bedroom and began to pack. She heard Havelock drive away and the house fell silent. She brought her few belongings down into the hall and hesitated. By, but she should be at the funeral. Matthew would have wanted her there. It wasn't right just to leave, she should show her last respects. Even though she hadn't respected him in life. Hetty sighed. Should she just leave or should she get in touch with Mr Painter? She eyed the telephone doubtfully. She had never made a telephone call in her life. But it looked like no one was coming to the house today.

As though to prove her wrong there was the sound of a car drawing up at the gate. She waited, bracing herself for more insults, but it was Mr Painter who came in the door.

'Hetty? You're not going?'

'Well, I'm not sure what to do, Mr Painter, and Mr Hope said—'

'Never mind what he said. You must stay until after the inquest anyway.' He looked around the hall with an approving air. 'You wouldn't like to stay anyway, would you? I can see what a difference you have made to this place. Stay for a while, at least. I don't want to have to sell the house and any tenants will have to be special. Will you stay? Finish cleaning it up? Until such time as I do find tenants, that is.'

Hetty stared at him. She needed somewhere to stay, of course. He was different since Matthew had died, she realised, more human, not so much the boss. He actually smiled at her. But she couldn't live on air, she had no money. As if he knew what was going through her mind, he said, 'I will pay you, of course. Three pounds a week? And the cost of any cleaning materials you need?'

It was good pay but she would have to work for it. But what about when the baby came? Still, it was now she needed a place.

'I'll stay,' she said.

It was good living in the house all by herself: no listening for the sound of Matthew's car stopping outside the front door, no wondering whether he had been drinking, or what sort of a mood he was in. Mind, she was grateful to Mr Painter for giving her the job, she told herself every day. And she could live on a pound a week if she was careful and save the other two for when the baby came.

Hetty worked hard all morning in the house, gradually going through the rooms, making her own pace. She began to take a pride in seeing the house emerge from its pall of dust, discovering what it must have been like in the old days. Most of the furniture was of rosewood, very old, and

236

polishing it was rewarding for it had a patina to it which always came up glowing. She rolled up the carpet in the hall. No matter how she tried, she couldn't get rid of the stain upon it, so she put it away in an empty room and scrubbed the black and white tiles which covered the floor.

At one o'clock, she would have a rest in the kitchen, eat a sandwich or make scrambled eggs. She had made friends with the farmer's wife from the farm about half a mile away, along the cliff. There was a row of miners' cottages near the farm and though the mine was closed now, there were still a few people living in the cottages and they were friendly, though curious about her. A travelling shop called twice a week on the cottages and the owner was only too willing to call on her and even bring her items such as baby wool from the Co-op in Staithes. There was really no need for her to go into the village for weeks on end and she didn't, content to work about the house in the mornings and sit before the fire in the evenings knitting and sewing for the baby.

'Don't you get very lonely?' Susan asked more than once. Susan was the farmer's wife who supplied Hetty with eggs and milk and cheese. She was a woman in her thirties with three children, all at school. They walked three miles every day to school through the fields, and three miles back, unless their father happened to be in the village for supplies when they had a lift back in his ancient car.

'No, I'm not lonely,' Hetty would reply to her. 'I know I can come over here and visit you if I want company.' But she didn't, not often anyhow. Funny, she would muse. When Matthew was alive she had thought there was no one within miles of the house and yet all the time there had been people so near. Then she had been lonely but now she was happy messing about on her own. 'Nantling' her gran used to call it.

In the afternoons Hetty would weed the garden, though she was finding it harder to stoop now that the baby was getting bigger. That was another thing. It was all right to stay here until the baby was born, for there was a telephone at the farm and Susan would help her. Susan had even arranged for the midwife to call on her.

237

'You'll like her, she's a grand lass,' Susan said, and Hetty did like the midwife, a Nurse Bainbridge, when she called in.

Sometimes in the afternoons, if it was fine and the wind from the sea not too strong, Hetty would walk down the path to the bay at the bottom and sit and listen to the birds wheeling and crying above her. No one else ever went there and she didn't mention it to Susan or the women in the row of pit houses.

Once she watched seals dipping and diving, once saw dolphins playing in the waves and went home happy and at peace with the world. By, she loved that little bay, she thought. Sometimes she walked over to the other bay, the spoiled one, but she only tried climbing up to the house by the passage once. She was too big now, she thought ruefully as she collapsed on to the floor in the attic. For a minute or two she had thought she wouldn't make it.

Her wages arrived every week on Fridays, usually by the postman who wound his way over the tracks on his bicycle. On the day they failed to arrive, Mr Painter rang to say that he was coming himself, to expect him at four o'clock. Hetty gave the downstairs rooms an extra dusting and put a bowl of dahlias on the table for it was autumn already.

'Good afternoon, Hetty,' he greeted her as she stood on the doorstep. She had opened the door when she heard the car, had been listening for it for half an hour. Was he going to tell her she had to go? Would Susan take her in for a day or two until she could make arrrangements? Was it fair to ask her friend? Her head was full of questions.

'Havelock Hope wants me to send you packing,' said Mr Painter. He watched her face keenly. Pregnancy suited the girl, he thought. She had a bloom on her cheeks overlaid with a slight tan, no doubt from the sun and wind but very attractive. There was a radiance about her. The shadow which had seemed to hang over her when he'd first met her had disappeared. Her dark hair was brushed and shining. She had it pinned back behind her ear but round her neck it fell in waves. It made him begin to understand why Matthew Hope had acted as he did.

'Will I be packing my bag then?' asked Hetty. She bit her lip. He was going to send her away.

238

'Not unless you want to go,' said Mr Painter. Perhaps if he bided his time, until after the baby was born at least, she would be grateful to him, show him some favour. He hadn't thought of it before, but after all, this house was isolated. He could keep her here for as long as he wished.

'I would like to stay,' Hetty said simply. She coloured and looked at the floor. For a minute she had thought she saw something else in his eyes but of course she was wrong, the light was not too good in the hall.

'That's all right then,' said Mr Painter. He took hold of her elbow. The flesh was firm though soft to the touch. 'Now I would like to see the rest of the house.'

Chapter 27

Hetty was working in the garden, pushing an old hoe she had found in the shed between clumps of Michaelmas daisies, trying to clear the bed of couch grass, when she had another visitor. She had heard the car approaching but didn't look up, supposing it must be going on along the track. Frustrated at the tenaciousness of the weed in clinging to the ground no matter how hard she pushed the hoe, she threw the implement down and got down on her hands and knees in spite of her bulk, leaning forward awkwardly to pull it up by hand.

The weeds weren't the only things making her frustrated. She was trying to make plans for what she could do after this baby finally decided to come into the world. Two pounds had seemed such a lot to be able to save every week at first, but if she left as soon after the birth as she could she reckoned she would only have between thirty and forty pounds, hardly enough money to keep them both for long. It was a nagging worry to her.

For she couldn't stay, she knew that. Mr Painter fancied her. Oh, she had tried to tell herself it was her imagination running riot yet again but she knew it was true. He came almost every Friday now; he made remarks, some of which made her blush; when he handed her her money, his fingers lingered on hers. And eeh, by, she wasn't going to get mixed up with another toff, not for anything, not even for the sake of the bairn. Especially not for the sake of the bairn. She had got herself into enough of a mess now. How could she embarrass a bairn, a little lad maybe, let him grow up

240

knowing his mother was a— The thought was interrupted by the clanging of the front gate. She realised that the car hadn't gone by at all, it had stopped. Oh, mebbe it was Susan and her man. Sometimes he dropped her off so that they could have a nice chinwag.

'I'll make a cup of tea, Susan. Hold on a minute, while I get to my feet,' she said.

'Here, let me help you. I really don't think you should be doing that in your condition.'

It was a man's voice. A man's hand was under her arm, helping her to her feet. A well-kept man's hand, not a labourer's but capable-looking. And the voice was familiar. Hetty straightened her back with some difficulty and looked up at him. He was against the sun and what with her hair all over the place, for a second or two she couldn't see who it was. She pushed back her hair from her eyes.

'Richard,' she said. Of course she had known it was him but she couldn't let herself believe it. All summer she had thought he might come, if only to see how she was. But when he didn't she'd asked herself, why should he? She was nothing to him. He had been disgusted with the way he thought she had behaved, she had seen it in his eyes. Yet gladness filled her at the sight of him. He was broader now, she noted, his mouth and eyes so like Matthew's yet they were more open, smiling, the mouth firmer.

'Father said you were still here,' he said. 'I wanted to see how you were.'

Hetty was suddenly conscious of what a mess she must look. Even apart from her enormous bump she felt fat and plain and her face was burnt with the sun. She had on her oldest dress. She had let it out as far as it would go and then put an insertion in the side which didn't quite match, and besides there was a smear of damp soil across the skirt. Her fingernails were black with earth. The contrast between them couldn't have been more marked, Richard so smart in grey flannels and a navy blue blazer with a badge on the pocket.

'Em . . . come into the house,' she stammered. Her old shoes were caked with damp soil. She had to take them off at the door and all her movements were heavy and awkward.

241

'I'll help you,' he said, holding out a hand, but she shrank from it.

'I can manage,' she answered and did. 'I'll just wash my hands.' She went up to the bathroom in her bare feet. Seeing herself in the glass, she was mortified. There was mud on her brow where she had pushed her hair back and the insert in her dress had given way as she had bent forward over the weeding, showing her petticoat. Her face was red with exertion and something had gone wrong with her breathing.

When she came back down the stairs ten minutes later she was washed and dressed in her brown, her hair brushed back from her forehead. She had even got most of the dirt from under her nails.

She stopped at the bottom of the stairs and took a few deep breaths to steady herself. He hasn't come to see you for yourself, she told herself sternly. It's because he's so good, he likes to make sure everyone is all right. He's not interested in you, not really.

'I'm in here,' he called, and she saw he was standing by the kitchen door. He had put on the kettle and the teapot was warming on the hearth. 'I thought you would be ready for some tea after all that hard work,' he said. It was so unlike anything his brother would have done that it brought tears to her eyes.

'Come on, sit down.' He came to her side and led her to a seat by the table. 'It looks like you're doing too much. You must be careful with the baby on the way.'

He poured her tea and watched while she drank it and all the time she wanted to shout at him, 'Where've you been? Where were you when your brother was killed, where were you when your father tried to get me thrown out of here, where were you, Richard?' But she knew she had no right. After all, he was not in love with her, not as she was with him. For she was, oh yes, she loved him, she had always loved him and never was she more aware of her love than now when he had reappeared so unexpectedly after so long.

As if in answer to her unspoken questions, he said, 'I went abroad with a friend from university. I was in Africa when Matthew died. I didn't find out for weeks and then I came home as soon as I could. I was worried about you,

Hetty, especially since my father told me you were pregnant. But I see you are all right, really. You are, aren't you?'

'Yes, I am.'

'I thought, if you weren't happy, you would go home to Morton Main. But I see there was no need.' He looked down at his hands, suddenly embarrassed. For he was remembering Havelock's words that morning, how his father had said she was already up to something with Painter. 'Don't be so soft, lad,' his father had said, 'she's the type that falls on her feet. There's always some man daft enough to keep that sort. I tell you, why else would he let her stay in that great house?'

'I daresay she's earning her keep looking after the place. And the baby is your grandchild,' Richard had said. 'It is our duty to make sure Hetty is all right.'

'Duty be blowed,' Havelock had retorted. 'If I had to look after all Matthew's by-blows, I'd be bankrupt.'

Nevertheless, Richard thought now, even if his father were right about Hetty and Jeremy Painter, he had to make sure that she was being looked after. If only for Matthew's sake, he told himself, it had nothing to do with how he himself felt about her. But would his brother even have cared?

'Who is this, Hetty?'

Both Richard and Hetty jumped as Jeremy Painter stepped through the door from the hall. They had been so engrossed they had not heard him come in the front door. She started to her feet with a cry of surprise but Richard was before her.

'I'm Richard Hope, how do you do?' He held out a hand to the newcomer. 'I take it you are Jeremy Painter? Yes, of course you are, I remember you from school. You were a year or two ahead of me. Same age as Matthew, aren't you?'

Jeremy shook his hand but his eyes were cold. 'Yes, of course, I remember you now. Well, what can I do for you?'

Richard looked surprised. 'Well, er . . . nothing really. I came to make sure Hetty was all right, that's all. I've just come back from abroad.'

Jeremy pursed his lips. When he had entered the house he had expected to find Hetty on her own. He had no intention of letting her get under his skin as she had done with Matthew Hope, but still, he had looked forward to seeing her – and here she was with another Hope brother. He had to think about that. In the meantime he turned to her.

'Hetty, what are you doing? Why didn't you take Mr Hope into the drawing room?' he asked coldly. 'The kitchen is hardly the place for visitors.'

'It was my idea,' said Richard quickly, hearing the censure in Jeremy's voice.

He looked pointedly at Richard's empty tea cup. 'Well, perhaps you will excuse us now. You have seen for yourself that Hetty is not taking any harm. And I haven't much time to spare.'

Richard rose to his feet, flushing slightly. 'I must be on my way in any case,' he replied.

'I'll walk with you to the car,' she said quickly, ignoring Jeremy's frown.

'No need, Hetty. We don't want to hold Mr Painter up any longer than need be.'

Hetty was left staring after him as he strode across the kitchen and out into the hall. The front door opened and closed and shortly afterwards his car started and faded into the distance. I won't see him again, thought Hetty. She was crushed. Why, oh why, did Mr Painter have to come today? It wasn't even Friday. For a minute or two she had really thought the old feeling was back between her and Richard, then Mr Painter had come in and everything had changed. She began to collect the tea things, briefly holding the cup Richard had used before putting it on the tray.

'Leave those alone, Hetty,' said Mr Painter. 'Come and sit down.' She left the tray on the table and sat down opposite him.

'I have a proposition for you, Hetty.'

Not now! Oh no, she didn't want to hear what he had to say. 'I'm very tired, Mr Painter, I was working in the garden this afternoon and I have to clear away the tools yet,' she said. She didn't want to look at him so stared at the cups and saucers on the table.

'They can wait.' He was insistent. He leaned forward and cupped her chin in his hand, forcing her to look at him. It took a supreme effort of will for her not to shrink from him, to pull away and go out into the garden, along to the cliff top, anywhere she could feel the clean, cold wind from the sea.

'Mr Painter?'

His eyes were a pale blue, glittering behind his glasses. He had a thin mouth, she noticed, pale hair and eyelashes.

'Have you considered what you are going to do after the birth?'

Yes, she had considered it but could find no solution to her problem. But she wasn't going to tell him that.

'I have friends in Saltburn.' She had, there was Alice.

'You could stay here. I have thought of using this house for entertaining clients. Of course, I would employ other staff, I wouldn't want you to do the work.'

'What would I do, Mr Painter?' She wanted him to say it. She wanted to be able to refuse him. She wanted him to leave so that she could go upstairs and lie down on her bed and cry and cry.

'I think you know what I want,' he said. 'You would be my hostess, Hetty. Think what it would mean – security for you and your child.' He put out a hand and touched her breast and he thought, this is Matthew's woman, Matthew's child, and I have them now. Matthew, his old enemy. There was triumph in it. He smiled thinly at the thought.

Hetty jumped to her feet, brushing his hand away, and the smile faded. 'I'm sorry, Mr Painter, I can't do that,' she said. He would tell her to go now, she thought, panic-stricken. Would Susan take her in? Just for tonight?

But he had recovered himself. The smile had gone and he coughed, holding his hand up to his mouth. 'I must go,' he said, for all the world as though they had been discussing the weather. 'I must congratulate you on the way the house is looking. Quite takes me back to my grandfather's day.' He walked to the door to the hall before turning back to speak again. Now he will tell me to go, she thought, but he did not.

'I shouldn't have mentioned it. I know all you will be able to think of now is the birth of your baby. I won't speak of

245

it until after that. I think then you will come to see it will be for the best, for you and the baby.'

After he had gone Hetty pulled on her coat and tied a scarf around her head. She felt stifled, she must have some fresh air. It was already turning to dusk outside but she walked along the track to the edge of the cliff and stared out to sea. A light winked on the horizon, and another, further along. The gulls were quiet now, they must have bedded down for the night. She walked along to the path which led down to the little bay but it was too late in the day to wander down it so she turned back reluctantly.

She would have to go as soon as her baby was born. The family would take her in, of course they would. But there was the memory of that last time Da and Frank had come to see her. They had just gone, not said goodbye or anything, because of Matthew.

Next morning, Hetty woke with a headache and aching limbs. She had had a night of bad dreams, dreams where her baby and Cissy were in danger and she had to protect them. Anxious, hectic dreams. She decided she would walk along to see Susan. Her life was so normal, she was such a sensible girl, Susan would never have made such a mess of her life as Hetty had.

She got as far as the farm gate before she remembered that Susan would be out; she was going into Whitby with her husband today. Hetty would walk down to the bay then. It would be the last time before the baby was born, probably the last time she would walk down there at all for soon she wouldn't be here. The day was overcast and the sea covered in whitecaps, but at least it wasn't raining. She could easily get down the path to the bay, she told herself.

Once there, she walked in the shelter of the cliff. The wind was from the land for a change, a west wind. She noticed a large shell. She would look for more, she thought, with some idea of making a mobile to hang over the baby's cot when she was a little older. It would be a girl, she thought, a girl like Cissy, a girl she would cherish and never allow out on a sledge, never.

Hetty found half a dozen shells, pretty pink and white on

246

the outside with shining cream-coloured insides. Just what she wanted. She sat on a rock and laid them out before her. A hot needle would make holes in them, she reckoned, so she could thread them on strong crocheting cotton.

There was a spot of rain. She looked up and saw the clouds had changed to black; rain was spattering on her shells. The waves were thundering now, coming close to her feet. What a fool she was! She had lived by the sea, knew well what it could do in a storm. Gathering her shells together, she turned for the path – but no, the waves were almost up to the cliff along that way. The cave was the answer, the only way she was going to make it back to the house. It sloped gently at first but rose above the highest seas as it turned into the smugglers' passage.

It was only five minutes to the cave but by the time she got there the rain was coming down in sheets and her feet were wet where she'd had to wade through the oncoming tide. But she reached the cave and ducked into the entrance and waited for her eyes to accustom themselves to the gloom. The water was over her feet. Thank goodness she had had the presence of mind to string her shoes round her neck. Her feet sank into the soft, wet sand but she could see that the water extended for only a few feet into the cave.

Carefully, Hetty picked her way between rocks and boulders to the back of the cave and began to climb. The way wasn't very steep near the bottom and she didn't find it too strenuous to reach a point above the high water mark. There was a sort of platform, hollowed out by the smugglers of long ago, she thought. She rested on it, looking back to where she had climbed. The water came swirling in. Already it was creeping up behind her. She could see the white froth on the waves but not much else. The light which had filtered in from above the last time she was here was poor today. Of course, the sky outside was black, she reminded herself.

She debated whether to try to climb up to the house, or wait until the storm blew itself out and the water went down. It could be hours and hours, she knew that. But the floor was level and there was even a sort of platform where she could sit with some comfort at least. Hetty sat down and leaned her back against the wall of the cave. Suddenly she was tired, so tired. She closed her eyes and listened to the storm. There was a sort of music in it, crashing and reverberating about the walls of the cave and being channelled up through the tunnel, coming out in this wider part. She listened, too weary to worry about anything anymore, and after a while she slept.

Chapter 28

Hetty woke with a start. She was cold and wet. Disoriented, she stared up at the dark shadows of the roof, shifting to the patch where light filtered down, very little light, barely enough to lighten the gloom. Her back ached, her shoulder was painful where a pebble had been digging into it.

She was in the tunnel, the passage which led up to the house. Memory returned as a wave washed over her, making her gasp and splutter and scramble to her feet. The water was washing over the platform. Even as she watched another wave swept across it and receded. Down below, the cave bottom was awash, the mark left by previous high tides already underwater. The baby moved restlessly within her, turning. There was a small pain as it kicked her ribs. Hetty put her hand over the spot and felt the bump of its foot or knee. Something, anyway.

Straightening up, she caught the back of her head against a projection from the wall and sat down suddenly on a rock, feeling sick, letting the water wash over her feet and recede. She had to go on up. No matter how hard it was, there was no other way. The next wave might not recede at all and then there would be more. With an effort of will, she gathered herself together, got back on her feet and walked over to the source of light, the place where the tunnel led up from the platform. Somehow she had to reach the top. She was wet and shivering. Even if the tide rose no further the cold would get her, she thought.

At the bottom of the shaft, her foot slipped against something hard and though the toes were numb with the cold, the pain as she caught her little toe was excruciating. 'Blast it!' she shouted, bending down and feeling it gingerly. It was then that she saw, as yet another wave receded, a gleam of something . . . she didn't know what. Despite the cold and the wet and the threat of the sea, she was instantly curious. She scrabbled in the sand around it and revealed a draw-string bag, a purse maybe, rotten with age for even as she tried to pick it up the leather burst and there was the chink of metal as coins fell to the floor.

Her imagination had really run riot now, she told herself, she was seeing things! This wasn't a fairy tale, this was hard reality. A person didn't just find treasure in a cave except in books, not even a smugglers' cave. She was going daft in the head. Another wave came, washing round her legs as she knelt on the ground, moving the bits of leather that had come off the bag, even moving some of the coins.

Hetty was galvanised into action. She picked up the purse and as many of the coins as she could and thrust them into the pocket of her dress until it bulged then lifted more and put them on a ledge, as high up as she could reach. But the water was swirling round her knees now and she had to go. She stepped up and began to climb away from the platform.

Her knees ached. She struggled higher and higher and thought her back would break in two. She couldn't catch her breath. There was a terrible pain in her side, the weight in her pocket pulled her down and at last she had to stop and lean against the wall of the passage. After a while she looked up at the light filtering down from the chimneys and somewhere else, she couldn't fathom where. She was little more than halfway up. She would have to leave the coins, or most of them. She lifted a stone and hollowed out a hole with her hands for them though why she didn't know, she was fairly sure no one came near the passage.

Climbing on slowly, taking her time, she took frequent rests, but the ache in her back was turning to a pain, recurrent, insistent. When finally she reached the door to the attic she thought she was dying. She fell on to the dusty boards and closed her eyes. The light from the skylight shone red through her eyelids, she could feel her heart racing.

Please God, she prayed, please God, let me reach the

telephone. Don't let the baby come here, please God. Susan . . . she had to telephone Susan. After a while she recovered enough to get to her hands and knees and crawl slowly, oh so slowly and carefully, down the stairs, pausing and doubling into a crouch when the pains came. They came ever faster, the intervals between less and less. But she reached the telephone and huddled over it, panting.

'Come on, howay man!' she cried into it when the operator was slow to answer but at last she heard Susan's voice at the other end of the line. She sank down on to the floor of the hall. She could hand over the responsibility for the day to Susan now, could stop resisting and let nature carry her away. There was one more thing though, she'd almost forgotten. She delved into her pocket and found the two coins still there. She pushed her handkerchief over them, deep down in the pocket. Then she forgot all about them in the urgency of the moment.

It was a girl, not born until the middle of the night. 'There's plenty of time for Nurse Bainbridge to get here,' Susan had assured her, and there had been. Next morning, as Hetty lay in the bed she had shared with Matthew, her baby in the cradle which she had brought down from the attic only a week before, she remembered the coins. Susan had gone home to see to her own family but had brought in a fourteen-year-old girl from the miners' cottages.

'I can manage,' Hetty had said, but Susan had laughed.

'Don't be silly,' she replied. 'You need someone here, especially the first week.' She had paused. 'You can afford it, can't you? Sylvia won't want much.'

There was the money she had saved to make a new start for her and the baby, thought Hetty. It was then she remembered the coins from the cave. But it was so unreal, had she dreamed it? Pushing back the bedclothes, she found the dress she had been wearing, ruined with salt water now, shrunken and stained. But there, in the pocket, were the coins. Hetty drew them out and got back into bed. There was a gold coin and a silver one. She stared at them. They didn't look to be worth much. The silver one had 'four pence' round the edge, and a head on it she didn't recognise.

But the gold one was a sovereign, or at least she thought it was. She had seen sovereigns before but this was very old and it hadn't the head of Queen Victoria on it either. She rubbed it with her thumb. The date on it was 1792.

She lay back on the pillow imagining that time so long ago. A smuggler could have dropped the bag – by, they must have made a mint of money with their smuggling! Fancy ordinary working people with all that money. Or no, perhaps it was that John Andrews, the Scot who had lived at Saltburn. They said he'd run all the smuggling on the coast. Perhaps the revenue men had been after them, mebbe they had run into the cave to get away and then one of them dropped the bag in his hurry to escape the law.

Hetty smiled to herself. Sometimes the real world was more fantastic than her imagination. The smugglers must have been there. After all, there was the passage and the leather purse, rotten with age. But the money wasn't rotten, it was here and it was Hetty Pearson who had found it.

'I'll make good use of it an' all,' she whispered to her baby. 'John Andrews won't miss it now.' Penny, she'd call the bairn, after the first coin. Well, she could hardly call her fourpence now, could she? The baby whimpered and she leaned over from the bed and picked her up, cuddling her into her breast. Penny snuffled blindly into the softness, searching for the nipple.

How much was a gold sovereign worth now? She had seen some old coins in the curio shop in Saltburn. The older ones were worth a mint, they were an' all. Penny whimpered in frustration and Hetty bared her breast and put the baby to the nipple and Penny hung on like a leech. By, it was sweet, it was. A wave of love swept over her.

'Whisht, babby,' she whispered, bending her head and kissing the soft down on Penny's. 'Whisht, babby, Mammy's going to buy you the world.' She laughed softly to herself. Here she was with a few old coins, she didn't even know what they were worth, and she was talking as though she was rich. But surely she could use them to establish herself, and then she could go home and hold her head up high. She could show them the baby, and Mam and Da would fall in love with Penny straight away. She fell asleep, the baby at her breast, still making plans for the future, a future which had changed dramatically in the last few hours.

Exactly three weeks later, Hetty stood outside the curio shop in Saltburn, heart beating so fast she felt as though she was suffocating. She clutched her handbag. Imitation leather it was in dark green and some of the outside had worn, showing the cloth underneath. But inside there were the coins, or at least a selection of them. There had been pennies as well as fourpenny and sixpenny pieces, sovereigns and even guineas. Not exactly a hoard but a nice lot, Alice said when she saw them. For Hetty had thought she would burst if she didn't confide in someone and Susan lived too near her little bay. She didn't want anyone, not even her friends, to walk in *her* bay, maybe even find the cave and the passage up to the house. And Alice had been so pleased for her, not a bit of envy in her.

'I don't know, love,' she had said doubtfully when Hetty said she was going to take them to Mr Martin's shop. 'I'm sure he's an honest man but you can't be too careful. Why don't you look around? There are other places that sell such things. I'll mind Penny for you.'

Hetty hadn't time to look around, she needed money now. Taking a deep breath, she opened the shop door and went in. Mr Martin was a dapper little man with pince-nez and rosy cheeks. When he saw the half dozen coins which she brought out of her bag, he drew in his breath sharply.

'But, young lady, where did you get these?'

'I . . . my grandmother left them to me, they were her grandmother's. They've come down in the family,' said Hetty. Now why had she lied? she asked herself. But she knew why, she was frightened she might have the coins taken from her.

'And now you have to sell them? What a shame.' But Mr Martin had accepted her explanation and was examining the coins closely now and Hetty could tell he was excited about them even though he was murmuring about old coins not being worth as much as people thought.

'I can take them into Middlesbrough, or perhaps Whitby,' she said. She caught sight of a trade magazine, *The Coin*

Collector, lying to one side of the counter. She picked it up and rifled through the pages, her confidence growing as she saw that there were many advertisements. People all over the country were asking for old coins! 'Or I could write away—' she began. But Mr Martin looked up from his scrutiny of the coins, frowning as he saw what she was doing, the frown turning to an easy smile.

'I can see you are a businesslike young lady,' he said. 'But I assure you, I can give you as good a price as you are likely to get anywhere.' When Hetty came out of the shop, she had his cheque in her bag for eighty-five pounds.

'Well! Who would have believed it!' said Alice when Hetty went back in triumph, and picking up little Penny, danced around the cafe, which luckily was empty, it being too early in the morning for the dinner time rush.

'And do you know what I'm going to do?' asked Hetty. 'I'm going to buy a house in the jewel streets, I'm going to have my own boarding house. What do you think of that?'

'Oh, but will there be enough?' asked Alice doubtfully.

'For a deposit at least,' Hetty assured her. She was filled with a new determination. Fate had given her this windfall and she was going to do something with it, for the sake of her daughter. It was a chance, something people waited years for, and now she had it she was going to take hold of it and do something with it. And if she got as much for the rest of the coins as she had for the odd half dozen she had sold to Mr Martin, she would make about six hundred pounds. Six hundred pounds! It was a fortune, one to work with.

Customers came in and Alice was soon busy serving them. The cafe tables began to fill up and Hetty took Penny into Alice's front room and fed and changed her. This was the time she loved, a time of communion between her and her daughter. She spent at least an hour with her, rocking Penny to sleep when she had finished. Then she took her back into the cafe and put her down in the pram. By, it was going to come in handy, that pram.

When Alice turned to her, Hetty was putting on her coat. 'You're off again?' Alice asked, surprised.

254

'Do you mind? I'll take Penny. I thought I'd go to see Mr Jordan. You know, the chef at the George.'

Alice helped her out with the old deep-bottomed pram she had picked up at the salerooms the day before and watched her walk down Milton Street until she turned the corner. Then went back behind her counter, shaking her head.

How she had worried about the girl when Mr Hutchins had told her Hetty had been turned off because he had married. She had wondered why Hetty hadn't come back to Saltburn, though she had heard a nasty rumour put about by that woman from Diamond Street who had been her landlady. Alice didn't believe the story anyway. She felt guilty that she hadn't made more of an effort to find out where her friend had gone. It was obvious she had been taken down and the baby was the result. But the lass deserved a chance, she really did. Alice wished her all the luck in the world. And if Hetty didn't want to talk about what had happened to her, then she for one wasn't going to ask.

Hetty took the pram round to the back of the George Hotel and parked it outside the kitchen door. Penny was fast asleep so she went in and found Mr Jordan, there by the stove as she had expected.

'Now then, lass, it's a while since we saw you,' he greeted her. 'Have you come looking for a job?'

'Not exactly, Mr Jordan,' she answered, ridiculously grateful that he had remembered her from the short time she had worked for him. 'I've come to ask for your advice on a matter of business, but I see you're busy. I can come back another time.'

'Business advice? What about?' He was intrigued and showed it.

'I'm thinking of starting a small hotel.'

'Go on! You're pulling my leg.'

'No, I've come into a bit of money and that's what I want to do.'

Mr Jordan studied her thoughtfully and made up his mind that she was serious. 'Well, I don't rightly know as I'm the

255

one to advise you, lass,' he said. 'But never mind, come on, we'll find a quiet corner and you can tell me all about it.'

They walked along Marine Parade with Hetty wheeling the pram. He never asked about the baby's father, though his eyes had widened for a moment when he saw the pram.

He had peeped inside. 'A little lass, is it?' And as Hetty nodded, 'A bonny one too.' They walked as far as the Italian gardens.

'I could do with the fresh air after being in the kitchen all morning,' he said. 'I usually take a bit of air in the afternoons.' They sat on a bench in the gardens and Hetty told him her idea.

'I thought just a small hotel, mebbe in one of the jewel streets. Do you think it's daft? I was looking in the window of that estate agent's in the square. There's one in Ruby Street for £750. I haven't got that but I could raise £600. Do you think I could get a mortgage for the rest?'

Mr Jordan looked out over the rose beds where a gardener was busy clipping the last of the year's flowers. £600! It was a fortune. He had been saving all his life yet he hadn't £600. But still, it was maybe not quite enough for what she wanted. And looking at her, she seemed no more than sixteen, her cheeks flushed with the sea air, her dark hair framing her face. 'I don't know, lass, I think you might be too young. But I can make enquiries for you, if you like? I tell you what, I'll do that.'

Hetty was filled with a terrible disappointment as she walked back to Alice's house with Penny, for Alice had said she could stay with her at least for a short while.

'It'll be grand having a baby in the house again,' she had said. Her own two boys had emigrated to New Zealand and she heard very little of them. Lately the loneliness had grown worse, especially since Tom, her husband, had died last year.

Next morning, before the cafe opened at eleven o'clock, there was a knock on the door. Hetty had been bathing Penny before the fire when Alice showed in Mr Jordan then tactfully left them alone.

'I've been thinking, Hetty,' he said. 'And I have a proposition for you.'

She laid Penny to sleep in the pram which took up one side of Alice's small living room, thinking she would have to find somewhere else to live, it just wasn't fair on her friend. Now she gave Mr Jordan the whole of her attention.

'A proposition?'

'Yes. Why ask for a mortgage? As I said, you aren't likely to qualify, being under twenty-one. But I have a bit of a nest egg put by for when I retire and I've been thinking more and more of doing that lately.'

'You mean, you would lend me the money?' Hetty showed her surprise. Why, Mr Jordan didn't know her *that* well. But he was shaking his head.

'No, not exactly. But why can't we be partners? I wouldn't be putting as much in as you – say the £150 you're short of the purchase price, plus another £200 to start us off.'

'Eeh, I don't know,' said Hetty. 'I hadn't thought of taking a partner.'

'No, but I've always dreamed of having my own little restaurant. You know I've a reputation in these parts for my cooking. You could run the hotel and I could run the restaurant. I know that place in Ruby Street, there's ample room, and being a boarding house already, it must have the proper licences.'

Hetty watched his face. It was animated, full of enthusiasm. And there was no doubt he was a good chef. People came from Middlesbrough and Stockton to eat at the George. But still, to have a partner? Even Mr Jordan. Yet there were advantages to having an older man as partner . . .

'What does your wife say?'

'I'm a widower. I'm on my own completely. Look, you would be the senior partner, we could get an agreement drawn up. After all, you would be putting more money towards it.'

'Well, I don't know . . .'

Mr Jordan rose to his feet. 'I have to go to work now. But promise me you'll think about it at least?'

'Oh yes, I will.'

After he had gone, Hetty took Penny out for an airing, walking down Ruby Street and looking closely at the boarding house from the outside at least. It was double-fronted, three stories high and with imposing bay windows angled to look over the sea, though they could do with a coat of paint. Oh yes, it could be upgraded to the status of a small hotel, it could indeed. But she would need to find more extra money than she was likely to get from the sale of the coins. Thoughtfully she carried on walking, going up to Station Square and pausing outside the estate agent's. There in the window was the notice about the house. Ten bedrooms, one bathroom, large reception rooms and kitchens.

It was the place for her, she knew it. Turning the pram round, she walked down to Marine Parade and the George Hotel. As she went, her imagination streaked ahead of her. She was already planning what she would do with the place, how she would make it more attractive than any other small hotel. She would put in another bathroom as a priority, maybe handbasins in the rooms if the budget would run to it. Pearson's, she would call it. Just that, no fancy names. And Mr Jordan would make the restaurant famous too. And who knows? Pearson's might be just the first of many such hotels, maybe a hotel in each of the jewel streets, and Penny would never, never have to go to place in some strange house where she was treated worse than dirt. Her daughter would have the best of everything.

Hetty laughed at herself as she turned into the side of the George Hotel. By, it was good to have a dream but it was even better to have the means to make that dream come true! Or at least to make it take shape.

Mr Jordan was working hard, putting the finishing touches to plates of hor d'oeuvres. He looked up and his hand, holding a piece of lettuce, stayed in the air.

'Well, lass?'

'It's a deal,' said Hetty.

PART TWO

Chapter 29

Penny stared out of her window, high up in Pearson's Hotel in Ruby Street. From her vantage point she could see part of Marine Parade, and the sea to her left, and the junction of Ruby Street and Milton Street to her right – but either way, there was no sign of her mam yet.

'I promise I'll be back on Saturday morning,' Mam had said before she went away on Thursday.

'Let me come,' Penny had begged. 'I don't like it here on my own.'

'You're not on your own,' Mam had pointed out. 'You'll be at school tomorrow, and over the weekend there's Nanny, and you'll have Alice and Mr Jordan. But promise me you won't bother him when he's busy in the restaurant?'

'I won't,' Penny had said, but she put her hand behind her back and crossed her fingers. 'Cause sometimes, if he wasn't too busy, Mr Jordan would allow her to eat in the restaurant. She would sit at a special table by the window and the waiters would ask what madam would like and she would read from the menu backed in red leather with gold lettering on it. She could read everything on the menu, even though she was only five.

Penny looked down the street and up the street, searching for Mam's red car turning the corner. It was an Alvis. 'A sports saloon,' Steve had told her. Steve was one of the waiters and he loved cars, talked about them all the time. Penny liked Steve. Sometimes he was the one who walked her to school when everyone else was busy.

Mam was always busy, she thought as she leaned forward

for yet another look out of the window. Her thick dark hair fell forward, the slide holding it unequal to its task. She pushed it behind her ear impatiently. There was the car, just turning in from Marine Parade! Penny jumped down from the window seat.

'Mammy's here! Mammy's here!' she cried, and rushed to the door.

'Be careful on the stairs, Penny,' called Nanny, putting down the school dress she had been shortening and starting after her. 'Penny! Not so fast.'

But she was already on to the next landing, racing down the stairs, and when Hetty picked her weekend case out of the car and started up the steps to the hotel, Penny was there on the top step waiting for her. Hetty dropped the case and opened her arms wide and Penny jumped into them, almost knocking her mother over with the momentum.

'Mam, where've you been? I've been waiting for ages and ages,' she shouted as she wrapped her thin legs round her mother's waist and buried her face in Hetty's neck, breathing in the perfume which was her mother's alone.

'I came as soon as I could, pet,' Hetty said and kissed the top of Penny's head. 'Come on now, let's go inside, I'm famished. I set off before breakfast so I could have it with you.'

Penny jumped down and picked up the weekend case, holding it with both hands, heaving it up the steps. Steve came out into the hall and took it from her.

'Good morning, Mrs Pearson,' he said. 'Did you have a pleasant trip?' He smiled at Hetty and then looked beyond her to the Alvis parked at the roadside, his glance anxious. But as far as he could see there were no bumps or dents in the gleaming bodywork. Hetty smiled. She knew well enough that Steve didn't trust women drivers to treat cars with respect.

'Morning, Steve. Yes, thank you, a very pleasant and successful trip. Will you bring breakfast up for us now, please?'

Penny grinned at him as he nodded assent, and, still grasping her mother's hand, she led the way up the stairs to their private rooms. Hetty allowed herself to be practically

262

pulled up the staircase, listening as Penny told her all about what had happened at school the day before and how she had to read her composition aloud before the whole class.

'It was supposed to be about our house, Mam, but I had to say we didn't have a house, just rooms in the hotel, and Gladys Poole said everybody had a house unless they were very poor.' She stopped her progress up the stairs and turned her clear grey gaze on her mother, and once again Hetty was struck by how like Richard's her eyes were, and the way she tilted her head to one side when she was talking. Somehow Penny seemed to have nothing of Matthew in her yet it was strange how like she was to Richard. Hetty shook her head. It was ages since she had seen him, not since that day before Penny was born. Six years in fact.

'Mam? We're not poor, are we, Mam?'

Hetty laughed. 'No, pet, we're not poor. Come on, I'm starving.'

Penny danced away into the flat where the table was already laid for breakfast. It wasn't really a flat, their rooms were on two floors now. Two years ago Hetty had bought the George Hotel on Marine Parade and turned it into Pearson's Marine Hotel. Pearson's Ruby had been altered to turn the rooms into more spacious accommodation for the family. Now the restaurant occupied all of the ground floor and Mr Jordan reigned supreme over it.

A wave of love washed over Hetty as she watched and listened to her daughter as she chatted on as though her mother had been gone for a month. She was so pretty, Hetty thought. Even though she was her mother and could be expected to think that, it was true. Penny was going to be a beauty, she knew it. But she was going to have the best education there was. She would never have to rely on men for her living. Never, never, never. No, Penny would go to university, she was clever. Why, she could even go to Oxford or Cambridge, why not?

Steve came in with a tray of crisp bacon and scrambled eggs, light and fluffy and with just that extra something which Mr Jordan gave to them and which he vowed was a secret he would tell no one until Penny was old enough to be told. Nanny served the food and poured tea for Hetty

263

and herself and milk for Penny. Nanny always ate with them. She had been with them practically from the beginning. In fact, it was only six months after Pearson's was opened that Hetty had sent for her, for Nanny was Sylvia, the girl from the miners' cottages near the house where Penny had been born, the girl who had helped Hetty as she'd recovered from Penny's birth. She had fallen in love with the baby and though she was now nineteen years old, a plain girl with a motherly figure in spite of her youth, she still doted on Penny.

'Eat your eggs, Penny,' Sylvia was saying now. 'Stop talking and eat your breakfast or you'll be hungry again before dinner.'

Hetty's thoughts wandered, rambling over the last couple of days. Her trip had been successful, very successful. She had been after an hotel in Whitby, a modest place, little more than a boarding house but in a good position over-looking the harbour and with potential for improvement, just as Pearson's Ruby had when she'd acquired it. But she had other things to think about this weekend, unconnected with business. She picked up the letter which lay beside her plate, the only letter in a cheap, handwritten envelope. There were several others but they were businesslike missives, buff envelopes typewritten.

Hetty knew who it was from, of course, but she had put off opening it, terrified that it might be the final rejection. For never in all these six long years had she been back to Durham to see her family. The longer she had put it off, the harder it had seemed to her, actually to get into the car and go. But Penny had been asking about her family lately.

'All the other girls have grans and granddads, Mam,' she had said only last Wednesday evening. 'But I told them, I've got Mr Jordan, haven't I? He's as good, isn't he, Mam?' Penny had looked up at her with those clear grey eyes and Hetty had been smitten with guilt.

She had no right to deprive her daughter of her grand-parents, no right at all, Hetty told herself. And after Penny had gone to bed she had written a letter to her parents. She had sat up long into the night with it, rejecting draft after draft until at last, in desperation, she didn't even read

264

the last one through but had thrust it into an envelope, stamped it and had gone out there and then and slipped it into the post box in Milton Street. And immediately wished it back. Here was the answer, her mother's handwriting on the envelope and a Bishop Auckland postmark. The last time she had seen that was when she had sent a five-pound note in a Christmas card and Da had sent it back on Boxing Day with a curt note saying they didn't need it. It had hurt, oh yes, it had hurt. And now she had to open the letter and read it. Hetty put down her knife and fork and picked up the letter, hurrying to get it open now and the rejection over with.

Dear Hetty,
I was so pleased to get your letter, I thought you had forgotten all about us. You will be very welcome to come home, you always have been, I thought you knew that? Sunday is a good day. We will be looking forward to seeing Penny.
Yours faithfully,
Mam

Hetty carefully put the letter in its envelope and placed it beside her plate. She picked up her cup and drank some tea. Then she looked across at her daughter and said, 'Penny, we're going on an outing tomorrow. You needn't go to Sunday School, we'll be setting off at ten o'clock.'

Penny beamed. 'Where? Where to, Mam?' She jumped up and down in her seat until Nanny had to put a restraining hand on her arm.

'Wait and see, it's a surprise,' said Hetty.

A knock on the door heralded Mr Jordan. Penny jumped down from her chair and ran to him and he swung her up in his arms and she giggled in delight. He looks younger now than he did when we started, thought Hetty. How old is he? Over seventy at the very least.

'Well, sparrow,' he said as he put the girl down. 'Happy now you have your mother back home?'

'Oh yes. Yes, I am, Mr Jordan,' Penny said breathlessly. 'And guess what? We're going on an outing tomorrow. A surprise outing!'

'You're a lucky little girl, do you know that?'

'Oh, I am, I am, I know I am, Mr Jordan.'

Hetty watched the two of them together, smiling. It was funny but no one knew what Mr Jordan's Christian name was even after all these years. Even she didn't know. He signed documents with an initial E, but what it stood for was a mystery. Now she couldn't imagine his being called anything other than Mr Jordan.

'Come on, Penny, we'll go for a walk along the sands. Maybe we'll get as far as Marske this time and have a lemonade in the cafe and catch the bus back, would you like that?' Sylvia pushed back her chair and held out a hand to Penny.

She was only too eager. After they had gone Hetty poured a fresh cup of tea for Mr Jordan and they went to sit in the comfortable armchairs to either side of the fireplace. The fireplace was of Frosterley marble, the black lightened by the myriad small white fossilised sea creatures in it. Every time Hetty looked at it she marvelled that the sea must once have covered Frosterley, now high up in Weardale, miles from the coast. Inset there were pretty tiles decorated with marine life, and the chairs were covered in blue and white cretonne which matched the summer curtains. Every time Hetty came home to this room it lightened her mood, it was so bright and cheerful.

They discussed the acquisition of the hotel in Whitby, Hetty going over the business details for him meticulously, though he always left such things to her, apart from the restaurant.

'You have a good head for business, Hetty, much better than mine,' he always said.

When they had finished, she leaned back in her chair and regarded him. 'Have you thought of taking on another chef, Mr Jordan? You know we discussed it last week.'

His smile faded. 'I don't see the need. So long as I have enough assistance in the kitchens, well, I'm still capable—'

'Oh yes, I know, and of course the reputation Pearson's has is built on your skills, there's no one to touch you, not in this area anyway.'

'Not in Whitby or Scarborough neither,' he said, not boastfully, just stating a fact.

Hetty nodded her agreement. 'I get worried, though, in case you do too much. The restaurant here and supervising the kitchens at Pearson's Marine – it's a lot of work and we can afford for you to take it easier now.'

'A lot of work for an old man, you mean? Well, I don't feel like an old man. In fact, I think I'm fitter than I've been for years.'

Hetty admitted defeat. Maybe he was right to go on. Some people lived for their work and Mr Jordan was one of them. 'I think you are,' she assured him. She almost said more but decided to drop the subject. After all, if he wanted to go on, why shouldn't he?

He finished his tea and got to his feet, tall and upright with that spark of vitality so often absent in old men. For goodness' sake, she said to herself, you're worrying about nothing. After he had gone back to his flat at the top of Pearson's Marine for a break until it was time to return for the lunchtime rush, she put it out of her mind.

Going back to the table, she picked up the letter from Mam. It was so brief, she thought. The handwriting which she had learned at the British School was a copperplate, strong and perfectly formed, Mam had told Hetty once how she and her sisters had wept over the learning of it, the knuckle-rapping with a ruler they had had to endure until it was right. Not that they had learned anything else much at the school, apart from simple arithmetic and reading and how great was the British Empire with most of the globe shaded pink.

Not a shadow of emotion had been allowed to come through in the letter. Even the beginning, when Mam wrote 'I was so pleased—', even that meant nothing to her for Mam would never say that normally, not to family, only to strangers. She was a stranger now, Hetty told herself, and it was her own fault, most of it.

Steve came and cleared away the tray and she settled back into her chair, relaxing for a brief period for she had had a busy day yesterday and an early start this morning. She had come a long way since she had found the coins in the back of the cave. Her cave, as she thought of it now. She thanked God for them and the unknown smuggler who had dropped them so long ago. She had sold them to dealers in Harrogate and Leeds; £800 they had brought her altogether, and for a while she had regretted the fact that she had taken Mr Jordan as a partner. But now she knew it was one of the best things she had ever done. They were firm friends and trusted each other completely, and there was no doubt that he adored Penny as she adored him.

Sometimes, not often now, she went back to her bay and always looked about for anything else the smugglers might have dropped, laughing at herself for doing it when she found nothing. But never again had she gone up the secret passage to the house. She shivered now as she remembered that last time, with all the pain and the stitch in her side and the fear that the baby could come there, in the dusty passage, that or she would fall and die and no one would ever find her body.

The clock struck eleven and Hetty started out of her chair. She must have dozed off and she had an appointment with her bank manager at half-past the hour. Still, that was one thing about Saltburn, everything was close by, even the bank. As she showered and changed quickly into a pale lemon suit with the new squared shoulders and neatly fitting waist, her mind wasn't on the coming interview at the bank, where nowadays she was always greeted deferentially, but on that other interview tomorrow, with her family in Morton Main.

Chapter 30

Richard Hope stood at the rail of the great liner, staring ahead as though he could already see the docks at South-ampton though in fact they were still more than twenty-four hours away from England. It was five years since he had been back, five years which had been spent in the diplomatic service in Nairobi. He had preferred it that way, spending his annual leave in Egypt or once in Mexico, for his greatest interest was archaeology.

This year he had made tentative plans to visit Greece, strangely the one place in Europe he had not seen. He supposed in the back of his mind he had been saving it, something to look forward to. This year was the year he had been going to Greece, he had booked into an hotel within sight of the Acropolis. Until he got the cablegram from his mother.

Richard stood straighter, stretched his back and resumed his stroll around the deck, enjoying the breeze against his face, colder now that they travelled further north. His mother was better now, much better than she had been five years ago. She must be to have sent a cable. It was his father who was ill. Richard found it hard to grasp that. Havelock Hope, strong in mind and body, the man who despised illness. And he had been stricken with a heart attack and left an invalid. So now Richard was on his way home.

Thoughts of home had brought back memories, memories he didn't wish to think about. His brother Matthew and his pointless death. His brother Matthew and Hetty Pearson, the memory of that night when he and his father had seen them at the top of the stairs, locked in each other's arms. The shock, the emotion which had risen within him and which he now recognised as jealousy. And the other one, the scene in that lonely house at the top of the cliff, so aptly named Cliff House.

Hetty had looked so beautiful in her pregnancy, so vulnerable too. He had wanted to put his arms around her and take her away, anywhere he could cherish her and her baby and let his father do what he would about it. He had been on the point of suggesting it when Jeremy Painter had come and saved him from his own folly.

'The strumpet will always find someone fool enough to keep her, mark my words, Matthew is hardly cold in his grave and there she is, making eyes at that Painter fellow,' his father had said to him and he hadn't believed it until then. What a fool he had been!

In one of his rare letters, Havelock had told him something of Hetty's rise in the world: ' . . . running a string of hotels now, would you believe,' Havelock had written. 'I reckon she got her start from Painter; even if she didn't steal something from Cliff House she must have milked the fellow for all she could get.'

Richard walked on restlessly. No, he thought. No, surely not, none of this squared with the Hetty he had known, the timid little girl who had come to Hope Hall, her dark eyes large in her white face, her skinny little figure and mop of black curls which refused to stay under her housemaid's cap.

The light was fading now. Shaking his head he made his way back to his cabin to bathe and change for dinner. Tomorrow evening they would dock, he would take the overnight train north.

'How far is it now?' demanded Penny as Hetty stopped the car at the junction with the Great North road at Rushyford and waited while a lorry lumbered past going south and a couple of cars and a van went on their way north to Durham.

'This is a bad time to talk to me,' said Hetty, 'just when I'm busy.' She found a longish gap in the traffic and crossed over into the village, driving past the Eden Arms and out on to the relatively quieter road to Bishop Auckland. 'Now, what did you say?'

'How far is it, I said, Mam, how far is it to Grandma's house?'

'Not far now, about six miles,' Hetty said absently. She had opened the window and the air was rushing in. She drove past the entrance to Windlestone Hall, then had to wait a while as a herd of cows made their slow progress across the road to an open field gate, seeming to know exactly where they were going without any help from the farmer who waved his stick nevertheless and called, 'Cush! Cush!'

'What does cush mean, Mam?' demanded Penny. But the next minute she was asking about the marsh marigolds which lifted their brilliant cups to the morning sun in the water meadow further along.

'I used to pick them when I was a girl,' said Hetty and smiled, a happy reminiscent sort of smile.

'Can we pick them now, can we, Mam?'

So they stopped the car and picked a handful of the flowers.

'We can give them to Grandma, can't we, Mam?' said Penny and Hetty rememberd the Mothering Sundays when she and Frank would get up early and pick flowers to take to their mam, it felt like a lifetime ago. They got back into the car, Penny clutching the bunch of flowers, and went on their way. As they turned off on to the lane which led to Morton, Penny grew quieter. She stared out of the window at the enormous slagheap, the towering winding wheel of the pit. They had gone through the pretty old village of Morton but now were in the colliery village of Morton Main and Penny stared solemnly at the colliery rows, the chapel on the end of Chapel Row, listened hard to the sound of children singing which was coming from the chapel.

Hetty stopped the car at the end of Office Street. In fact the narrow back lane would have been completely blocked off if she had taken the car up to her mother's gate and there was no road to the front of the cottages, only narrow gardens.

'This is it, Penny.' She looked at her daughter and smiled at her disbelieving expression. 'It is, really,' she added.

'Come on, they will be waiting for us.' At that moment Hetty was glad that she had her daughter with her, almost as an ally. The gate was closed, there was no one about the back street, everything looked smaller and meaner than she remembered. Well, at least there was no smell from the coke works, it being Sunday, she thought. Penny took hold of her hand and held on tightly. She might have been in the African bush, the place was so strange to her, thought Hetty.

'Now then, lass, you've come home.'

Hetty whirled round and there was Da, standing by the now open gate. He looked older, dressed in his Sunday suit with a neat blue tie, as though expecting company. I'm not company, she wanted to cry to him, I'm Hetty, I'm family! But she didn't. She stepped forward and kissed his cheek and he made an automatic move to put his arms around her then stopped.

'Yes, Da, I've come home,' she said. And then, 'Penny, this is your grandda,' to the little girl who was now clinging to her leg. And Da sank down on to his hunkers, in the position which Hetty remembered so well for it was the one in which he was the most comfortable, the one in which he had swung a pick for years in the narrow coal seams. His eyes were now on a level with Penny's and he reached out a hand to her while his face lit up like a Christmas tree.

'Well, now, Penny, is it?' he asked. 'You're a grand lass, aren't you? Will we go in the house now and meet your grandma? Then I'll take you to see the pigeons. You like pigeons, do you?'

Penny loosed her hold on Hetty's leg and put her hand in his. 'I don't like to eat them,' she said. 'Mr Jordan cooks them in white wine sometimes but I like to see them flying about in the air the best.'

'Oh aye, I do an' all,' said Thomas. 'My pigeons are champion flyers. We don't like to eat them neither. Besides, some of them have babies. Do you like to *see* baby pigeons?'

'Oh yes.' Penny sighed with relief and trotted by his side up the yard and into the kitchen with Hetty trailing behind.

The kitchen smelled of the roast beef cooking in the oven just as it always did on Sundays when there was enough money coming into the house to buy beef. Maggie stood by the kitchen table, beating Yorkshire pudding mix in a bowl with a large metal spoon. She paused and looked at her daughter, unsmiling, the spoon held up in the air.

'Hello, Mam,' said Hetty. The clock on the wall ticked loudly; on the bar an iron pan settled on to the fire with a slight hiss of spilled water. Penny stood still, her hand in her grandfather's, and looked anxiously from her mother to the grey-haired woman mixing something with a metal spoon when Mr Jordan said you should always use a wooden one. 'Are you my mam's mam?' she asked.

Thank the Lord for Penny, thought Hetty afterwards as they all sat round the table eating great chunks of Yorkshire pudding with onion gravy and then followed it with roast beef and mushy peas with potatoes and turnip creamed together. There was even a sweet rice pudding with a brown coating of nutmeg and cinnamon so Hetty knew there must be good money coming in, Da and Frank in work.

There were other signs too. New lace at the windows, shiny linoleum covering the stone floor. But still the proddy mats that Mam made in the evenings. Hetty and Frank used to amuse themselves picking out from which discarded garment each patch of colour came. She looked at the one by the hearth now, sad that she recognised none of it.

Penny sat next to Da, her eyes bright as she chattered away to him, eating her rice pudding without a single moan, though usually she would reject it with a grimace. Both Thomas and Maggie watched her with fond expressions and Hetty felt a twinge of remorse that she had not brought her here sooner. They had a right to know their grandchild, even if they were at odds with her mother.

And they were at odds with Hetty. When she had kissed Mam there had been a coolness about her, a coolness which Hetty had known on most occasions they had met since Cissy died. But how could she blame her mother? She could hardly bear to think of the time she had disappeared without a word, gone off with Matthew straight from Bishop Auckland to Cleveland without even letting her parents know. The remembrance of that time was hazy to her, she didn't know how it had happened at all, but surely she should have been able to stop it happening?

'Where's Frank?' Hetty broke into Penny's account of school and how much she liked it except for that Gladys Poole who was mean and Mam said she should just try to keep out of her way. Thomas and Maggie were listening, making suitable noises of sympathy where appropriate, all their attention on the child. They had said very little to Hetty so she had been quiet too but she had been wondering about Frank.

Mam looked at her, a different way altogether from the way she had been loooking at Penny. 'Frank? Why, where would he be? He's down at the club like he is every Sunday from twelve o'clock. Didn't you see me put his dinner in the oven to keep warm?'

'He'll be back about half-past two,' put in Da.

'He's not courting then? I thought he might be.'

Mam laughed shortly. 'Not our Frank. No, I reckon he's too comfortable here with us. No, I cannot see our Frank getting wed.'

After dinner, Thomas took Penny off to see the pigeons and Hetty helped her mother clear away and wash up. There was no sink, the washing up was still done in an enamel dish on the kitchen table, and the dishes piled on a tin tray. They worked quietly, saying nothing until the dish was emptied in the drain in the yard and the table dried and covered with a red chenille cloth. Hetty kept stealing a glance at her mother's composed face until in the end she felt she had to say something about what was on both their minds.

'Mam, I'm sorry I didn't bring Penny to see you sooner.'

'Aye,' said Maggie, nodding her head.

'I wasn't sure whether we would be welcome,' Hetty tried again.

Maggie's head shot up. 'Me own grandbairn not welcome? Whatever gave you that idea?' Hetty could have said that she herself hadn't felt welcome and she was Maggie's daughter but she didn't.

'Well, you sent back my Christmas present.'

Maggie took the dish cloth over to the fireplace and flung it over the brass line which hung above. For a minute she held on to the line and stared down into the fire then she turned back to Hetty.

'Your da was working, Frank an' all. Besides, we didn't want the money you got from your fancy man.'

Hetty gasped. 'I didn't! Mam, I didn't! I worked for it, every penny, I did. I got nothing from Matthew when he died, nothing at all. Everything I've got now, I have worked for.' She was desperately trying to hang on to her self-control, trying to keep her voice normal but it was hard.

'Not him, not that Matthew Hope, I never meant him though he was bad enough. That other one, the one you took up with when he was barely cold in his grave.' Maggie sat down suddenly in the rocker by the fire, rocking herself back and forth convulsively, taking a hanky out of the pocket of her pinny and blowing into it furiously.

Hetty stared at her and she too sat down, in the opposite chair. The emotion between them was tangible, heavy, fraught.

'I didn't, Mam, honest I didn't,' she said, and something in her voice made her mother search her face doubtfully. But then she shrugged and shook her head.

'Don't you tell me lies, our Hetty,' she snapped. 'You never used to tell lies but you must have got the money from somewhere for what you've done. An' we *know* what you've done.'

'How can you know what isn't true?' cried Hetty.

'It's true you're a big businesswoman now, isn't it? It's true that even though you had a little babby to keep, you've managed to buy all sorts of property, isn't it? Do you think we live in such an out of the way place that we wouldn't find out what you were doing? Why, man, you know even the Sunday School trips go to Redcar and Saltburn, not to mention the bairns' outing from the Club. Thirty buses went to Saltburn last year. Surely you must have met some of those folk?'

'I didn't, Mam. I don't know why. Though wait a minute, I was away a lot last summer, to do with work. And the people from here, well, not many of them would be using a restaurant like Pearson's.' Most of them would have sandwiches and bottles of pop, she thought, and eat them on the sands.

Maggie snorted. 'They might not go in for a meal but

275

they'd walk past it, wouldn't they? Why, man, you know what folks're like. When our Frank hurt his back in the pit last year—'

'Our Frank hurt his back and you didn't tell me?'

Maggie just gave her a look. 'When our Frank hurt his back last year,' she repeated, 'the Club wanted to send him to their convalescent home, you know, the one in Saltburn. But he wouldn't go because of you. No, he went to the union one instead, and you know he loves the sea.'

'How is his back?'

'Better. But he's come off the hewing, he couldn't do that. He's a deputy now, working for his overman's ticket an' all.'

They sat in silence, both women staring at the fire. Then Hetty said, 'Mam, I haven't got a fancy man. I never had anyone after Matthew.'

'Will you stop telling your lies!' Maggie jumped up, shrieking. 'I tell you, I know. I wasn't going to show you this but I will now.'

She went over to the mahogany press which stood against the wall and, opening a drawer, took out a letter and handed it to her daughter.

Hetty stared at it in disbelief. It was in Havelock Hope's writing. She remembered it well from her days at Hope Hall. Slowly she unfolded it and smoothed it out while her mother stood over her, quivering.

Dear Mr Pearson,
In answer to your query concerning the whereabouts of your daughter, I have to tell you that I do not have the faintest idea of her address though I understand she and her bastard are living in some affluence in Saltburn. What I do know is that before my son, over whom she had cast her evil spell, was barely cold in his grave she had taken up with another man, the owner of the house she was living in. No doubt it is his money which set her up in Saltburn.

The letter was signed 'Havelock Hope'. Hetty, unable to look at the hateful words any longer, thrust it into the fire and watched as it flared up and sank back to black ashes which lifted and fell into the embers and was gone.

'The dirty, vindictive, bloody rotten liar!' she whispered.

'Hmm, watch your language, our Hetty,' said Mam. 'And burning it won't do any good, like, will it?'

'But it's not true, Mam. Really it isn't. I swear it's not. I'll swear on the bible, if you like?'

Maggie sat down again, gazing earnestly at her, and Hetty knew she was wavering. She even reached out a hand to her daughter and was about to speak when the door opened and Frank came in, followed after a moment by Thomas and Penny.

'Mam, Mam, the pigeons are lovely, and there's some baby ones but I could only have a peek because Grandda says we haven't to disturb them, not when they're in the nest 'cause the mother bird doesn't like it . . .' The child stopped as she noticed Frank, who had come to a halt just inside the door. He and her mother were looking at each other strangely. Penny took hold of Thomas's hand and stared at Frank.

'Penny,' said her grandfather, lifting her up so that her face was on a level with Frank's. 'Penny, this is your Uncle Frank.'

'How do you do?' said Penny, evidently remembering the lesson in polite introductions she had learned at school. She held out her small hand. Frank appeared not to have heard, he was still staring at Hetty.

'Frank!' barked his father, and he turned and saw the child's proffered hand.

'Hello, Penny,' he said, and took it in his.

'You smell funny,' she observed and Thomas snorted.

'Aye, he does, doesn't he? It's the beer.'

'Now, Thomas, don't start,' Maggie interjected. 'The lad has a right to do what he likes, he works hard all week.'

'Aye, well,' said Thomas, 'mebbe so.'

'Hello, Frank,' said Hetty. 'How are you now? I hear you had an accident to your back.'

'I'm all right,' he answered. 'How's yourself?'

Maggie had laid a cloth over one end of the table and was bringing Frank's dinner from the oven. 'Sit down, lad, eat it afore it's spoiled altogether. As it is the pudding's kizened. Where've you been since the Club shut?'

'Just walking with the lads.' He hadn't, he had been

playing pitch and toss with pennies round behind the slag heap, but Da would only play war if he told them. 'Don't fuss, Mam, I like me dinner all kizened up.'

'What does kizened mean, Uncle Frank?' Surprisingly, Penny was standing at his elbow, watching him as he ate.

'Did you not teach the bairn the language, our Hetty?' asked Frank, and Hetty had to smile and a little of the stiffness between them melted away. He looked down at his niece. 'Well now, kizened means dried up, overdone, see. Like this gravy.' He pointed to a brown patch on his plate.

'I like it like that,' declared Penny. 'But Mr Jordan, he says it's a disgrace to serve anything overdone.'

'Does he now? Well, I'm like you, I like it.'

Thank the Lord for Penny, thought Hetty yet again. Frank finished his meal. Sitting back in his chair, he lit a cigarette and began to cough, a harsh, rattling cough.

'By, I wish you wouldn't smoke those filthy things,' said Mam.

'They clear me tubes, I couldn't do without them,' he replied when he managed to catch his breath.

'You do without them down the pit, why not here?' she countered.

'Aw, Mam, give over, hold your whisht,' he said wearily and pulled once more on the cigarette with such force that it burned almost halfway down.

They sat on for a few minutes, saying little except to the child who wanted to know about everything. Hetty wanted to say to them that it wasn't Painter's money which had given her a start, she wanted to tell them all about it. But she knew how daft it would sound to say she'd found treasure in a cave, they would never believe her at all then. She was quiet, looking into the fire, thinking desperately how she could tell them but saying nothing because she was so worried they wouldn't believe her.

The men started to talk about the pit as they always did and Penny chatted to her grandmother. After a while, the women made tea and then it was time for Hetty to take Penny home and still nothing had been said.

Chapter 31

Hetty drew the Alvis up to the front of Pearson's Ruby and switched off the engine. Penny was asleep in the back seat. She had had a momentous day, meeting her new relations. On the way back she had chatted the whole time about them, her grandda and her grandma and Uncle Frank.

'Wait until I see Gladys Poole,' she said, 'won't *she* be surprised?' And, 'Can we go back next Sunday, Mam? Grandda says the baby birds might be flying by then, I want to see them fly.' She thought for a moment. 'The gulls won't get them, will they?'

'There are no gulls in Bishop Auckland,' her mother assured her. 'They only go inland if there's a big storm.'

'There won't be a big storm?'

'No, pet, not this time of year. Not until the pigeon chicks are old enough to look after themselves.' And Penny was reassured. Dusk began to creep over the land, the Cleveland hills came into view on the horizon and Penny slumped in her seat and nodded off. Hetty stopped the car and made her comfortable. She was just small enough to fit on to the back seat lying down.

There had been no chance to talk seriously to her parents or Frank with the child there. The afternoon was soon gone and she had to get back, she explained. 'It takes an hour and a half,' she said, and they had nodded their understanding.

'You'll come back, though?' said Da. 'Now we've met our granddaughter, we don't want to lose her.'

'Why don't you come through to see us?' asked Penny

279

eagerly. 'We've got plenty of rooms, haven't we, Mam? You can stay for a holiday. You can meet Mr Jordan and Steve.'

'We'll see, we'll see,' Maggie temporised.

'Mind, you like this Mr Jordan, don't you?' asked Thomas. 'Who did you say he was?'

'Why,' said Penny, 'he's Mr Jordan, that's all. He's the chef.'

'He's more than that,' said Hetty. 'He's my partner.'

Da's eyebrows lifted. 'Oh, aye? I never knew you had a partner. And do you like him as much as Penny does?'

Hetty laughed. 'I do indeed, I don't know what I'd do without him. But it's not like you think. Mr Jordan is older than you, Da, he runs the restaurant. Put his life savings into it.'

They had reached the end of the street and there was the Alvis, a gang of small boys around it. 'Can we have a ride, missus? Can we? Dr Richardson always gives us a ride round the rows when he has time.'

Hetty hesitated. 'Oh, go on, lass,' said Frank. 'Can you not remember what it was like to have a ride round the rows in old Dr Short's motor car?'

'Come on then, but mind, keep your feet off the seats,' she said to the boys. Penny turned suddenly shy and hung back, clinging on to her grandfather's hand as though she had known him all her life.

'I don't want to go round the rows,' she said, almost in tears. 'I don't know where they are anyway.'

'No? Well then, lass, you will stay with us,' said Thomas and swung her up on to his shoulders where she sat, clinging to his forehead, delighted with herself. She was just beginning to look a little worried when the Alvis came round the corner and stopped in front of them once again.

'Thanks, missus. Eeh, thanks, missus,' cried the lads and tumbled out. 'By, your car's smashing, loads better than Dr Richardson's.'

'I'll keep in touch,' said Hetty as Penny climbed into the back seat.

'Aye, and mind you do this time,' said Da.

Well, now it was over, she had at last been home. For always, no matter where she was or how happy she might be or how long she had been away, County Durham, and Morton in particular, was home to her.

'Come on, Penny, wake up, pet,' she said. 'We're back, time for bed. Here's Nanny for you.' Sylvia was descending the front steps. She lifted Penny out of the car and held her over her shoulder. Penny murmured something and snuggled in.

'Did you enjoy yourself, Penny?' Sylvia asked.

'Oh aye, I did,' she lifted her head to say.

Oh dear, thought Hetty. She'd already picked up the speech. From her grandfather, no doubt.

The next few weeks were busy ones for Hetty. There was the hotel in Whitby to refurbish in readiness for the season and she liked to be there to supervise this critical time in the opening of any venture. It was her first step outside Saltburn and Redcar and the twenty-mile journey back and forth added time to her day she begrudged, for it often meant she was away before Penny was up and sometimes returned long after her daughter's bedtime. But she tried hard to keep Saturday afternoons free so they could be together. This Saturday they were going to pick up Charlie Hutchins and go to the fun fair at Redcar.

Hetty's brow wrinkled as she thought of Charlie. He was ten years old now, a thin, clever boy always growing out of his clothes and with horn-rimmed glasses perched on his nose, usually twisted out of shape. It was when Penny was a year old and still in her pram that Hetty had met him again, in Alice's fish cafe, the place where she had first met his father.

At first Hetty hadn't noticed them, sitting in a corner eating plates of cod and chips and mushy peas. She was busy negotiating the pram into a place where it wouldn't be in the way of the customers, putting on the brake, sitting Penny up so she could see everything that went on. The child hated not to be able to see everything.

'Hetty! Hetty!'

She looked up in surprise and there was Charlie, jumping up and down in a seat next to his father, his thin face beaming a welcome.

'Charlie! Oh, Charlie, it's lovely to see you,' she cried and held out her arms to him and they hugged each other. Penny looked on, her eyes wide, not sure if she liked her mother hugging someone else.

'How are you, Hetty?' asked Mr Hutchins. 'I've often wondered how you got on. Won't you sit down?' He glanced at the pram but said nothing about it.

'You didn't come to see us,' Charlie said, and was obviously waiting for an explanation.

'No, well, I've been away. I've been very busy,' said Hetty, and even as she said it she knew it sounded lame, just an excuse. 'What are you doing in Saltburn?' she asked, by way of changing the subject.

'Visiting Gran,' said Charlie.

Alice brought her a cup of tea and then, as the cafe wasn't busy, she took Penny from the pram and behind the counter, the baby crowing and laughing as Alice made a fuss of her.

'How is your mother?' Hetty asked. Mr Hutchins looked tired, she thought, tired and unhappy. Charlie too. His little face was pinched somehow and his wrists stuck out of his too-short sleeves, bony and thin. His collar was frayed too, she noticed.

'Oh, bearing up, bearing up,' said Mr Hutchins.

'You'll be at school now, Charlie, do you like school?' Hetty smiled at the boy and he brightened again. 'Oh yes, I do, school's lovely,' he declared.

Hetty would have asked more but just at that moment Penny decided her mother had been talking to these strangers long enough and started to wail and at the same time, the door opened and a stream of customers came in. So she got no further than enquiring after the rest of the family and receiving a rather perfunctory answer before she had to take Penny and leave the cafe.

'I'll see you again,' she said to Charlie, 'I promise I'll come down to Smuggler's Cove as soon as I have the chance.' Both Charlie and his father looked a little guarded about that and Hetty had a good idea why. 'That woman,' she said savagely as she wheeled the pram round the corner into Ruby Street. 'By, I bet she has a lot to answer for, seeing the state of that poor lad.' Penny looked startled and then

282

her bottom lip turned down, 'Not you, pet,' her mother assured her, 'I'm not angry with you.'

On Alice's half day closing the following week, Hetty had left the baby with her and taken the bus to Smuggler's Cove. It was a warm day as she walked up to Overmans Terrace and most of the front doors stood open. Anne Hutchins sat in a chair by her front door, fanning herself with a newspaper she had been reading. She was fatter, Hetty noticed. She sat with her legs apart and her feet planted firmly on the ground. She gazed malevolently at Hetty.

'An' what brings you here, Hetty Pearson?' she demanded by way of greeting.

'Hello, Mrs Hutchins,' Hetty replied, determined to be pleasant. 'How are the children? I saw Charlie when he was in Saltburn with his dad. By, he's grown a lot. I suppose Audrey and Peter will have too. All right, are they?'

'What do you expect them to be? Do you think I don't do my duty and look after them properly? Well, let me tell you, those little hellions are the bane of my life. I rue the day I was soft enough to take them on, I can tell you. A slave to the three of them I am. And that Charlie . . . I'll skelp his behind for him when he gets in from school, I swear I will. Tell him not to do something and you can be sure it's the first thing he does do. Why—'

'I found him a nice, biddable little boy,' Hetty interrupted the tirade.

'Did you now? Well, all I can say is he must have changed a lot. Such a sly, deceitful lad I've never seen in my born days. Just stands there dumb as a donkey when I'm talking to him. I tell you, he was at the back of the queue when brains were handed out, that one.'

Hetty was standing by the gate as Mrs Hutchins had not asked her in. 'He was not!' she retorted, unable to listen to any more. 'He's a bright lad, he is! If you've been hitting him, I'll have the cruelty man on you. Anyroad, what does his dad say to that?'

'His dad? His dad?' Mrs Hutchins rose to her feet and picked up her chair. 'Like I tell him, he's at work most of the time, he's working double shifts since the pit went on to full-time. "It's all right for you," I tell him, "but I have the

283

bringing up of the little tyke." Now I'll thank you to mind your own business and leave me to mine.' At which she went in and banged the door to after her. Hetty was staring at it when Anne opened it again and came out, her arms akimbo. 'An' another thing,' she shouted. 'You bring the cruelty man here and I'll have you up for slander, I'm warning you! So get back to where you belong. By all accounts, you've nowt to be proud of yourself.'

Hetty was trembling with frustrated rage. She felt like battering down the door and giving the woman what for but she knew she couldn't.

'Hello, Hetty, why don't you come in and we'll have a nice cup of tea?' It was Mrs Timms from next door and as Hetty looked up she saw she wasn't the only woman who had come to the door and all were watching her with avid curiosity. Except for Mrs Timms, who was smiling a welcome. Hetty nodded thankfully and followed her inside.

'Take no notice of that woman next door,' said Mrs Timms when Hetty was settled in a comfortable chair and a cup of strong milky tea put in her hand. Mrs Timms offered her a plate of home-made ginger biscuits and took one herself.

'It's hard, though, to think she has charge of the bairns,' said Hetty. She sipped her tea and took a bite of the ginger biscuit, concentrating on it in an effort to prevent the tears. 'I should have been back sooner.'

'You wouldn't get in next door,' said Mrs Timms. 'None of the neighbours have been in. I offered to help one time when Charlie had the quinsy, but she told me to mind my own business.' Mrs Timms folded her arms and glared at the party wall between her house and the Hutchins', as though she would burn a hole through it.

'No, but I should have kept an eye on the children, Charlie at least.'

'Well, there's no doubt the poor lad bears the brunt of it. I don't know what his father's thinking of sometimes. She starts shouting at Charlie and lifts her hand to him, and what does that man do? He gets out of the way. He works all the hours God sends and I'm sure it's just to keep out of the house. By, I knew when she came here, all mealy-mouthed, it would be a different story after she'd managed

284

to wed him. Anyway, I don't know what we can do about it. Let's talk about you. How are you getting on? I heard you had a baby. A girl, wasn't it?'

'How did you hear – oh, never mind. Yes, a girl, Penny. Well, Penelope, but I always call her Penny.'

Mrs Timms looked pointedly at Hetty's third finger. 'That chap who used to be always angling after you, was it? I remember, he was a blooming nuisance to the waggons going in and out of the pit yard.'

'Penny's father was killed before she was born.'

'Eeh, I'm sorry, lass. Life's a devil, isn't it?'

'Don't be sorry, Mrs Timms,' she said. 'It was a while ago and I'm fine now. We have a nice place in Saltburn, Ruby Street. If you're ever there you must come in and see us.' She put down her cup and saucer and rose to her feet. 'I think I'll just walk down to the school, meet Charlie and Audrey as they come out.'

'Yes. But be careful, lass, you don't want to get him into more trouble.'

'More trouble?'

'Well, I mean she might take it out on him if she sees you with him.'

The children were just coming out of school in rows two by two, walking to the gate. Charlie was easily picked out, he was a head taller than the others in his class. His shoulders drooped, though, and his stick-like legs dragged along in boots which looked too heavy for him.

'Hetty! Have you come to see me?' he shouted, and beamed all over his face.

'Just you. You and Audrey, that is,' she replied as the girl came running up close behind him. Now about eight years old, she looked careworn. Her checked gingham dress was spotless and there was a tear in the skirt which had been mended but it was too short for her and one leg of her knickers was hanging down to her knee. On impulse, Hetty bent down and put an arm around each of them. She kissed them. 'By, how you've grown!' she cried. 'You're going to be as tall as houses if you go on.'

'We can't stop,' said Audrey worriedly. 'Mother will be angry if we don't go straight home.'

285

'Surely you can spare me a minute or two? I've brought you presents.'

Charlie began to jump up and down. 'Presents? Like it's Christmas, do you mean?'

Hetty took three small packages from her bag. 'One for you and one for you,' she said. 'But where's Peter?'

'He goes to the big school now, I can take his if you like?' Audrey answered. But most of her attention was on her package.

'You can unwrap it now, Audrey,' said Hetty, and the girl carefully removed the red tissue paper and revealed a hair slide with glittery stars in a row and a comb to match. Her face lit up.

'Eeh, thank you, Hetty,' she breathed and the careworn expression slid from her face until she looked like any other little girl of eight.

Charlie had a Dinky car and was already squatting on the pavement, running it up and down. 'Brumm-brumm,' he cried, totally absorbed.

'Say thank you to Hetty, Charlie,' said Audrey, and he mumbled his thanks. 'We'll have to go,' she went on. 'Mother will be cross, we must run.' He got to his feet reluctantly, clutching his toy car, and she took his hand and they were away, running up the road to Overmans Terrace. Charlie looked back once and shouted something about Hetty coming back and she waved and nodded her head. She followed more slowly and when she passed Overmans Terrace saw all the doors were closed, though Mrs Timms waved to her through the window. She walked to the road end to get the bus back to Saltburn, resolved that she would come back again. She would keep in touch with the children.

That had been the start. Five years later, as she finished off her correspondence and tidied her desk that Saturday morning before the promised outing to the fair at Redcar, she was thinking of how she had been waiting for Mr Hutchins the next time he had come into Saltburn. How she had persuaded him to bring the two younger children with him on Saturdays. She had been surprised at how easy it had been, had thought up every argument, but he had agreed to her suggestion straight away. And when the children came and she had taken them down to the shuggy boats and the roundabouts down on the sands, she found out why.

'Dad said we could come no matter what Mother said,' Charlie volunteered happily. 'We can come every week, he said.' He looked anxiously up at Hetty. 'You want us to come, don't you, Hetty?' When she assured him she did, he went off, a carefree little boy for the day at least, a penny clutched in his hand, for a ride on the roundabout.

Chapter 32

That day, it was Peter who brought Audrey and Charlie to Saltburn. An almost grown-up Peter, for he had left school the year before and was working in the mine now.

'Dad's working today,' he told Hetty. He was a tall boy, dark-haired and blue-eyed, his shoulders already beginning to broaden. He was the one of the Hutchins children she knew the least. Even when she had been living in their house he had been uncommunicative, spending most of his spare time with his friends, wrapped up in them. 'I'm going to call in on Gran and see if she's all right,' he said.

'We'll wait for you, Peter, if you like?' said Hetty. 'Come with us, it will be fun.'

'I will. I'll not be long,' he replied quite eagerly. He smiled and for the moment the grown-up was gone and there was a little boy again, looking forward to going to Redcar to the funfair.

Charlie and Audrey were sitting with Penny, all in a row on the couch in the sitting room. The three of them looked glum, Penny almost in tears. She jumped to her feet as Hetty came in.

'Mam! Oh, Mam, Audrey's going away. She's got a job in Harrogate. She's going to be a parlour maid. And, Mam, she doesn't want to go! She doesn't, Mam.' Penny looked hopefully at her mother, sure that she could do something, anything to stop it happening.

'Is it true?' Hetty asked Audrey and the fourteen-year-old girl nodded. 'Mother says I'm old enough now to leave home and make my own living. Peter has to go too. He's

288

got work in Northumberland, in a coal mine. Mother says it's only fair, she has done her duty by us and she's not our real parent.'

'Northumberland? But he has a job in Smuggler's Cove, hasn't he?' Hetty didn't trust herself to comment on Anne Hutchins's other remarks.

Audrey nodded. 'Yes. But Mother says there's not enough room for us all now we're growing up. She says it's time.'

Hetty remembered the day she had left home and gone to work in Hope Hall. But that had been so different. No matter how short of room they were, her family would never have let her go if it weren't that they couldn't afford to keep her. That was a time when the pits weren't working and the village had been in a deep depression. But the iron mine at Smuggler's Cove was working, Peter even had a job there. It was *that* woman of course. How could Mr Hutchins go along with it? But even as she thought it, she knew why he did. He was a weak man at bottom, dominated by his wife. And if she wanted the children out, she would work on it until she had her way.

'You don't want to go to Harrogate, Audrey? You know, you might be surprised, you might like it there. It's a big place, lots of nice shops, plenty to do.'

Audrey put an arm around her brother. 'I don't want to go. And if I do, what about Charlie?'

'He will be all right,' Hetty assured her, though she was far from sanguine about that. 'I'll keep an eye on him, and your dad will be there, won't he?' But not all the time he wouldn't, and who would there be to stick up for Charlie then? she thought, but didn't say it.

Audrey's expression showed what she thought of that argument, she wasn't impressed at all. 'He's sitting the scholarship for the grammar school this year, though, and I don't think she'll let him go. I'm worried about it. You know, she told Peter it was a waste of time him even sitting when he was eleven, he was going down the pit, and that's what happened. Peter didn't mind so much, but Charlie minds.'

Hetty looked at Charlie's flushed face. His glasses were slightly twisted and gave him an air of being even younger than he was. She sighed. What could she do? Apart from

289

being here, someone to bring their troubles to. But Penny was looking at her trustfully, she expected her mother to do something about it, thought Hetty was a miracle worker. Penny sat close to Charlie, her hands folded tightly in her lap, legs crossed and swinging in the air and gazed at her mother.

'Look,' said Hetty. 'Let's just go out and have a good time today. I'll talk to your dad the next time I see him, that's all I can say.' For it was no good giving the little family any false hope, she thought dismally as they all trooped down the stairs and out to the car.

They had a good time at the fair. Peter took them out on the boating lake and they went on the dodgems and the Noah's ark, and when they had had enough of the fair they went on the sands and played cricket with Peter directing the game and Charlie showing himself to be surprisingly athletic. Afterwards, breathless and happy, they ate ice cream and paddled in the waves just like the day trippers who were picnicking all around them.

Hetty watched Peter. He had always seemed so much older than the other two and more interested in his friends than them, but today he was being especially attentive to them, showing Charlie how to bowl a spinner and commiserating with Penny and Audrey when they missed the ball. He was just realising how much he would miss his family when he had to go, thought Hetty, and she determined she would definitely speak to Mr Hutchins when she got the chance.

That chance came the very next day when she met him in Station Square and asked if she could have a word with him.

'I'm on my way to my mother's,' he said, and glanced warily at her and away again. He was very distant and Hetty knew she was barging into something which, after all, was not her business but she persuaded him to go into a nearby cafe for a cup of tea with her so that they could at least discuss it.

'It's about Audrey, isn't it? She's told you about the job in Harrogate?' he asked as soon as they sat down. 'You know she's old enough now to go to work, and what work is there in Smuggler's Cove?'

'But to have to go as far as Harrogate, Mr Hutchins, when she doesn't want to go,' said Hetty. 'She could get work in Middlesbrough, or even Saltburn.

'Oh, Anne says she'll soon get used to it and love it there. Anne herself lived in Harrogate for a while. She says Audrey will be fine.'

'But the girl doesn't want to go, and she feels responsible for Charlie, she'll worry about him!' As soon as she said it Hetty knew she had gone too far. Mr Hutchins was standing up, signing to the waitress for the bill. He hadn't touched his tea. 'Really, Hetty,' he said, 'I don't want to be rude but don't you think you should attend to your own family and leave mine alone? My wife and I are quite capable of deciding what's best for our family and that includes Charlie. Now I have to go.'

Hetty could do nothing but watch him walk out of the cafe. She had said the wrong thing. What she should have said was that she would give Audrey a job. Why hadn't she thought of it before? She got hurriedly to her feet and ran after him.

'Mr Hutchins? Mr Hutchins, I'm sorry, I don't mean to interfere, but naturally I'm concerned—' She had caught up with him and put a hand impulsively on his arm. He stopped and turned a stern face to her.

'Miss Pearson—' he began, but she butted in impusively.

'No, I'm sorry. What I meant to say was that I am prepared to take Audrey on as a trainee in one of my hotels.' She paused for breath.

'I think she'll be better off further away,' Mr Hutchins said, and Hetty caught what he really meant immediately.

'Of course, she won't be able to live at home. There will be accommodation provided for her.' She watched his expression, feeling some hope. He was undecided, she could tell.

'I'll have to talk it over with my wife,' he said at last. 'I'm not promising anything. Anne really does think Audrey would be better off away on her own, where she can live her own life, not be thinking of others all the time.'

291

'But you will think of it? Audrey could have a good career with us, a real career, not just in service,' said Hetty, though she was thinking how clever it was of Mrs Hutchins to put forward that argument. The woman would do anything to be rid of the children, she thought, anything. Hetty was seething with indignation though she hid it from Mr Hutchins.

'Look, I know you still feel for my children,' he said. 'You have been good to them these last few years. But I must consider my wife in this. I'll let you know what we decide.'

With this, Hetty had to be content. He turned away and headed along Dundas Street towards his mother's house. Hetty watched him until he was out of sight. She wouldn't give up, she vowed. And Charlie? She would do her best to see that if he gained a scholarship to the grammar school, he would take up the place. Charlie wasn't for the pits, no he was not. He was a bright boy and probably had it in him to do well, go to university even. She felt a small pang of regret for Peter. She couldn't think what she could do for him. For now he might have to go to Northumberland. Somehow she didn't think Mrs Hutchins would give way on all three children. But, Hetty told herself as she turned the corner into Ruby Street, she wouldn't lose touch with the boy.

The following week, Hetty was waiting eagerly for Charlie's and Audrey's visit, not that they were going anywhere, but she expected Mr Hutchins to be bringing his decision. She hadn't had much chance to think about it during the week, she had been busy with the builders who were altering the hotel in Whitby, telling the decorators how she wanted it done, a thousand and one things which were needed to prepare the place.

There would be a restaurant too, she hoped, one to rival the restaurant in Pearson's Ruby, and Steve was to be in charge of it. Mr Jordan had been training him for two years, he was ready. Yet what she liked about Steve was that he was always keen to turn his hand to anything. He didn't ask any of the juniors to do anything he wasn't prepared to do himself. It was a good trait.

But it was Saturday afternoon and Hetty had trained herself to put aside the cares of the business and devote the weekends to relaxing with Penny. Not that she felt very relaxed at the moment, waiting for Mr Hutchins. Penny too was waiting. She stood in her place by the window and watched the street, the people streaming down from the coach park where the day trippers came in to the cliffs at the bottom of the jewel streets and the paths down to the lower promenade and beach. And there, in amongst them, were Audrey and Charlie.

'They're here! They're here!' she cried, and ran down the stairs to meet them, followed by her mother. Audrey had a letter in her hand which she handed to Hetty.

'Me dad's gone to Gran's. He said to give you this.'

It was permission for Audrey to come to work for her. A wave of thankfulness ran through Hetty. 'Dad had a row with Mother,' Audrey confided. 'I didn't know you had asked him to let me come here. Eeh, Hetty, I'm so grateful, I really am! Mother went mad, you know, but Dad didn't back down this time. He said there was no reason in the world why I shouldn't and she'd best keep quiet about it. And Mother went all red and shaking but she stopped arguing. So I'm to ask you when I can start?'

'How about Monday?' asked Hetty. 'The sooner the better.'

So it was arranged. Audrey was to come on Monday with her luggage and she had a room in Pearson's Marine Hotel, right up at the top. Not much different from the one Hetty herself had had in Hope Hall but Audrey seemed delighted with it. The only drawback was that Charlie was left alone at home for Peter had already gone to Northumberland's Wylam Colliery.

'He has nice lodgings,' Audrey reported, 'we had a letter from him. I don't think he hates it as much as he thought he would.'

Charlie said nothing, he was very quiet. Penny sensed how unhappy he was and stuck close by him in sympathy. To celebrate, Hetty took them all to the matinee at the pictures where *Snow White and the Seven Dwarfs* was playing, and afterwards they ate a huge tea in the restaurant.

All except Charlie, that is, who picked at his food. Hetty watched him anxiously but knew there was nothing she could do. And after all, he would be out at school for most of the day, and Audrey would go home to see him on her day off, and there was his father. But perhaps a film about a wicked step-mother had not been a good choice. It was Penny who made the connection and put it into words.

'Are all step-mothers wicked like Snow White's?' she whispered to Hetty.

'No, of course not, it was just a story,' Hetty replied, but Penny wasn't convinced.

'I don't ever want a step-mother,' she said, and gave her mother a swift kiss on the cheek. Shortly after, Mr Hutchins came to the door for Audrey and Charlie and another Saturday afternoon visit was over. Next time there would only be Charlie coming from Smuggler's Cove.

When Penny was asleep, Hetty switched on the wireless and prepared to have a relaxing evening by herself for tomorrow she was again driving up to Morton Main to be with her family. This last week or two the atmosphere between them had lightened. They spoke more naturally together and Penny loved to go, loved to see the pigeons and would sit quietly with her grandda watching for them returning from a race, often her sharp eyes being the first to spot the leader circling round before coming down to the cree.

Frank had acquired a racing whippet too, a small, thin, trembling creature with a gentle nature and big limpid eyes but which could nevertheless run like the wind. And Penny would go with him when he exercised the dog, begging to hold on to the lead and trotting alongside it. 'Steady, Dandy,' she would cry, and the dog would match its pace to the child's.

The nine o'clock news came on and there was a message from the Prime Minister, Mr Chamberlain. Hetty stirred uncomfortably in her chair, reminded of the news reel which had preceded the film that afternoon. Mr Chamberlain was assuring the country that there wasn't going to be a war, but somehow his words rang hollow to her. She thought of the pits back in Durham. After years of working short-time, if they worked at all, they were now going all out. As they must be all over the country. The chronic unemployment in the coal fields had melted away.

Hetty had been a small child during the last war, but had grown up with tales of the horror of it, knew many war widows, attended many Remembrance Day parades as a schoolgirl. The thought that war could come again was horrifying. Then Frank was in the Territorials. Even though he was a skilled miner he would be one of the first to go if there was a war. Though maybe not, she told herself. After all there had been that accident to his back. She fiddled with the knob of the wireless and found a play just beginning. That was better. It was a Noël Coward play, a comedy about the spirit of a first wife who came back to haunt her husband when he married again: *Blithe Spirit*. It soon had her chuckling. The hero sounded something like Richard Hope. Strange the way little things still reminded her of Richard, even after all these years, she thought sadly. Even though she hadn't seen him in such an age.

When the play finished she switched off the wireless and went upstairs, prepared for bed, all thoughts of probable war banished from her mind. She checked on Penny who was sleeping peacefully, the bedclothes flung back and one thumb stuck firmly in her mouth. That was one habit it was time Penny dropped. Gently, Hetty removed the thumb and pulled the clothes closer round her daughter.

She climbed into her own bed and lay there, thinking of Richard, wondering where he was. Surely, if he had been living and working at home, she would have heard something of him in all these years? What a fool she was, hankering after a man who had probably forgotten she existed. She should take Alice's advice and go out more, meet some nice young men.

'How can you find Mr Right if you don't meet any men at all?' Alice would demand. Trouble was, most men Hetty met were either too young or too old. Sometimes she suspected they were more interested in her business than in herself. Trouble was, they just did not measure up to Richard Hope.

295

Chapter 33

Richard was riding his father's stallion, a magnificent animal which to his mind wasn't getting enough exercise. There was only the one groom on the place now and with his father ill, how could it be expected? The horse was mettlesome, eager to go, but Richard kept him to a steady trot. This part of the moor was uneven, the tracks not made up and recent rain had left deep runnels in them.

Richard was thinking over the conversation he had had with his mother at the breakfast table.

'Have you thought of giving up your career and coming home to see to things here, Richard?' she had asked. He had put down his fork and transferred his attention from his bacon and eggs to her.

'What?' he repeated, astonished. Giving up his career had never crossed his mind. And not only that, he was unused to his mother's taking such an interest in things around her. In fact she had not ceased to amaze him from the day he returned from Africa. There she sat, and there was no denying that she looked older than when he had first gone away. Her hair was silver now, her skin still as clear as he remembered it but with a network of fine wrinkles, the jawline softened and not so defined. Yet in some ways she seemed younger. No longer were her eyes clouded; her hand as she picked up her cup no longer trembled so that she had to steady it with the other. It was as if she had come back to normal life and he was well aware what an effort that must have cost her.

'Richard, you look at me as though I am speaking a

foreign language,' she said now. 'You heard what I said perfectly well.'

'Yes. Sorry, Mother. It's just that I haven't thought of giving up my career.' He was doing well in the diplomatic service, was happy, or at least content, his interest in archaeology occupying his spare time. Coming back to England to live permanently was not an attractive prospect to him.

'Well, you should do now,' said Elizabeth. 'Your father is not going to get well and we have to face that fact. The estate needs a firm hand if it is not to slide any further. As it is, were it not for the threat of war we should be thinking of closing the mine for good. The depression hit us hard – I was surprised how hard. Your father kept all his worries from me but since his illness I have discovered that our position is not what it once was.'

Richard pushed aside his bacon and eggs and took a piece of toast from the rack. He spread marmalade on it, then put it down on his plate. Of course he knew that the place wasn't as prosperous as it once was, but then, in this last decade, the old industries of the north had been in deep depression and were only just climbing out of it. But surely there was enough income from the land, rents from the tenant farmers, to keep his parents in comparative comfort? There were not so many servants now although his father needed a full-time nurse, but the house still ran like clockwork.

'I also think it's time you settled down, Richard,' Elizabeth interrupted his line of thought.

This time he didn't answer, just lifted his eyebrows.

'You needn't look like that,' she said. 'I'm serious about this. It's time you thought about getting married, having a family. Has there been no one in all these years?'

No one. Richard thought about Hetty immediately but thrust the image of her out of his mind. There had been girls in Africa. Sisters of his friends, girls who worked in the office. Nothing serious, though, just dates he would take out to dinner, flirt mildly with, take to the theatre in Nairobi. There was one girl, Delia, who'd taught history at a girls' school in Australia and they had become friendly when they met in Egypt. For a time he had thought he could settle down with her but it had come to nothing. After all, they had found, the only thing they really had in common was their interest in ancient civilisations.

'Mother, I know you're lonely, I know you miss Matthew—' he began.

'That's something else I wanted to talk to you about – Hetty Pearson. Your father wouldn't have anything to do with her, but after all she has my grandchild. Her name is Penny, I understand.'

This time Richard was very surprised. 'How on earth do you know that?' he asked.

'I made enquiries,' she said calmly. 'Not personally, of course, but through my solicitor. Evidently they're living in Saltburn-by-the-Sea. Hetty is doing well, I believe.' She looked reflective. 'Hetty was good to me during my . . . my illness. I liked her. A pity she and Matthew – still, that's all behind us now. I personally don't think she was as bad as your father made out. As I say, I knew her well. Oh, you may have thought I was not aware of what was going on at that time but I wasn't altogether off my head.'

'Mother! I never thought for a moment that you were.' Richard got to his feet and went to her, putting an arm around her shoulders and kissing her gently. 'But I can tell you, I'm so happy to see you're recovered so well. Why, you're just as I remember you from when Matthew and I were small boys.'

Elizabeth nodded and clasped his hand for a moment. Tears sprang to her eyes and she brushed them away impatiently. No use crying now for the lost years. She had begun to recover when her old doctor retired and a new man took over the practice. No, it had begun before that. It stemmed from the time when for once she had been fully awake and Havelock, perhaps not realising, had brought her her chequebook to sign. 'Don't bother about the amount,' he had said, 'just sign half a dozen, I'll see to the rest.'

'But what are they for?' Even as she'd asked she had taken the chequebook and pen from him.

'For goodness' sake, Elizabeth,' he had snapped, 'what do you think they are for? Do you think I'm trying to take your money away from you? Robbing you, is that it? They're for the usual household expenses. You know you agreed to pay them until this damn' depression lifts.'

Elizabeth had signed meekly, unable to face his irascibility, fearing he would start talking about her going away for further treatment as he often did. But somehow, for no reason that she could think of, she had begun to distrust him and when the next dose of her medicine was due she had forced herself to do without it, deny herself its comforting oblivion. Though she'd concealed the fact from Havelock. As now she was concealing the trouble there had been between her and his father from Richard. The terrible argument which had resulted in Havelock's falling to the ground, unconscious.

'Never mind now,' she said, patting Richard's hand. 'All that is in the past. We have the future to think of. We—'

She broke off at the sound of a bell ringing, the bell which had once stood by her bedside and which now was used by Havelock's nurse to summon help.

'We're needed upstairs,' she said and rose to her feet.

'Take it easy, Mother, I'll see to it,' said Richard, but she was already at the door and he followed swiftly. Havelock's door was open at the head of the stairs and the nurse was just coming out.

'Please call the doctor, Mr Hope,' she said to Richard. 'I'm afraid your father has had a further attack.' He pushed past her and gazed for a long moment at the figure on the bed. He turned back to his mother and put his arm around her. 'There's no hurry for the doctor, Mother,' he said softly. 'I'm afraid it's too late.'

Hetty was in Guisborough negotiating to buy the boarding house in Diamond Street, the one where she had lodged when she'd first left Hope Hall. Rather she was talking to Mark Sefton, the solicitor she had chosen to handle this deal, for her former landlady was using Hetty's usual Saltburn solicitor.

'There's no need to say who the buyer is, Mrs Pearson,' said Mark. 'Not at first anyway.' He sat back in his chair and smiled at Hetty. She was like a ray of sunshine in his office, he thought. She'd brightened his day with her neat figure dressed in a smart pale green suit with a nipped in waist and pencil slim skirt, a darker green hat pulled down over one eye, a rakish feather curling over the brim. He was only thirty-five himself and struggling to establish the practice, eager to have even a part of Hetty's business for her name and acumen were becoming known in the area.

'I'd prefer it that way,' she said. She thought back to the unhappy days she had spent in that house, the insults which her landlady had thrown at her the day she left. But really, she was not being vindictive in buying the property, it was purely a matter of business. She liked the house, loved its high-ceilinged rooms and tall windows looking out over the sea. And already she had plans formulated in her mind as to how she would have it altered. It would be a hotel especially for young families, with a play room in the basement for rainy days, a baby-minding service staffed with local girls, all of whom she knew personally and all of whom she could trust. She would advertise it during the winter. It would be open in time for the season next year.

'Of course, I would be failing in my duty if I didn't remind you of the possibility of war, Mrs Pearson.' He looked down at her hands, capable hands holding an open blue folder of papers but ringless. She noticed the glance.

'Miss Pearson, actually.'

She didn't always correct people on the point of her unmarried status.

Mark Sefton coughed behind his hand. 'Yes, sorry. What I meant to say, if there is a war, well . . .'

'There won't be a demand for hotels in seaside resorts? But I don't think the war will come so far as Saltburn-by-the-Sea, do you? And it won't last forever either.'

'Saltburn is not so far from Middlesbrough and all its heavy industry.'

'True. But far enough, I think. In any case, I don't think there will be a war. The Prime Minister assured us there wouldn't be, didn't he?'

Mark smiled. 'You may be right but I thought I should warn you.'

'I consider myself warned. Now, if there is anything else?' She closed the folder and began pulling on her gloves.

300

'No, I will be in touch. Unless . . .' He glanced at the clock on the wall. 'You wouldn't care to have lunch with me, would you?'

'Why not? I'd be happy to.' After all, she thought, she had to have lunch somewhere and Mark Sefton was a pleasant enough companion.

They ate in a restaurant near the priory and Hetty was reminded of that other time she had been there and Richard had seen her in the priory grounds with Matthew. She burned at the recollection and quickly put it out of her mind; she was not going to let memories of the past haunt the present.

They had a pleasant meal and Mark Sefton was a good companion, she discovered, attractive and with a sharp wit which kept her entertained. But that was all, she thought, and wondered at herself as she drove her car over the moors on her way back to Saltburn. She was not ready for a relationship. Not that the solicitor had been anything but friendly and polite, no hint of more. But she still raised an invisible barrier between herself and men.

'There's a visitor for you,' said Sylvia as she entered the flat above the restaurant in Ruby Street. 'A man.'

'Oh? Who is it? Didn't you ask his name?'

Hetty took off her hat and placed it on the hall table, running her fingers through her hair. She gave herself a quick glance in the mirror. She was presentable, she decided.

'Hello, Hetty.'

Startled, she looked past her reflection to where another face was suddenly framed in the glass, a face she would have known in any crowd, even though it was so many years since she had seen it.

'Richard!'

He was standing in the doorway which led into her sitting room, smiling and gazing at her with Penny's grey eyes. Hetty's heart lurched and began pounding. She could feel the flush rising in her cheeks.

'I hope you don't mind my coming here, Hetty?'

She found her voice though her throat was dry and she felt like an embarrassed schoolgirl confronted with the object of

301

her first crush. 'Not at all, Richard,' she said. 'How nice to see you. How are you?'

'I'm fine, Hetty,' he said, and stood aside for her to move into the room. She sat in one of the deep armchairs because her legs were strangely weak, then immediately wished she hadn't for she had to look up so far to him. She gestured to a chair opposite and he sat down. That was better, at least he was on her level.

'How are you, Hetty? Though I hardly have to ask, you look well.' He sat back and crossed his long legs and suddenly she saw that he was as nervous as she herself.

'And your mother and father?' It was absurd, she felt, sitting here making polite conversation. She hadn't seen Richard Hope for years, she told herself, she was nothing to him and he was nothing to her, nothing at all. She forced herself to relax, unclench her hands which were in tight fists.

'Well, that's why I'm here,' said Richard. He meant that was why he was in England but she took it to mean that was why he had sought her out, something to do with his parents, not for his own sake at all, and in spite of just reminding herself he meant nothing to her, she felt a pang of disappointment.

'Oh?'

'My father died last month, Hetty.'

'Oh!' Havelock dead? Whatever he had been and however he had treated her she was shaken; he had been such a vital person, somehow it was difficult to imagine him dead. 'I'm sorry. And your mother—'

'Mother is well, considering,' he answered. 'She is much better in herself. In fact she is very well. Sad, of course, but we were expecting it. There was time to get used to the idea. Father had a heart attack a few weeks ago and I came home as soon as I could.'

Came home from where? thought Hetty, with a small part of her mind, and said, 'So you have come to tell me about it?' Why, she thought, why when the family had not come near her since Penny was born? And they must have known where she was, at least Havelock must have.

'Mother wants to see her grandchild, Hetty.'

'No!' She felt like shouting it. 'Penny is my child, mine

302

alone! Your father didn't even acknowledge her. None of you did!'

'I tried to help you,' said Richard. 'I have been in Africa all this time, I haven't been home until now, Hetty. And my mother wasn't in a position to do anything about it until now.'

Africa. And all the time she had thought he was there, at Hope Hall. All the time she had pictured him there, as she had first known him, riding over the moors, working for his father. She stared at him.

'I would like to meet my niece too, Hetty. I know her name is Penny. Don't you think she has a right to know who her father was, who her grandmother is?'

'She has a grandmother. Her grandmother is Maggie Pearson, her grandfather is Thomas Pearson and she has her Uncle Frank.'

'Hetty.' He watched as she rose to her feet in agitation and began pacing around the room.

'I want you to go, Richard. I'm confused, I don't know what to think . . . It's all too sudden,' she said finally, stopping and turning to face him, her arms folded tightly over her breasts. She leaned towards him earnestly.

'Hetty, please, tell me you will consider bringing her to Hope Hall? You must know what it would mean to my mother – her grandchild. She's the only one she knows of at least.'

Hetty looked at the clock. She had heard Sylvia go out to bring Penny from school. In only a few minutes they would be back.

'Go now, Richard,' she said. 'I can't promise you anything, not now, I have to think. Please go.' She almost said: Before Penny comes in, but bit back the words. Panic was rising in her. She wasn't ready for Penny to meet him, she was not.

Richard got to his feet. 'I'll come back. When, though? How long do you think it will take for you to make up your mind?'

'How do I know?' Hetty took hold of his arm and urged him towards the door. 'I have asked you. Please, will you go?'

'Tell me when?' he insisted.

303

'Next week ... yes, next week. In the morning, though.' She couldn't afford to have him meet Penny. 'No, I'll come to you. To Hope Hall.'

Richard was surprised. 'Are you sure? I can fetch you—'

'I can drive myself!'

He stared at her face. At last he was beginning to understand her agitation. 'All right, I'm off. Penny will be in soon, will she? I won't try to see her.' They hurried down the stairs and he opened the front door, turning on the step.

'Saturday then? Is that all right? Come for tea.'

'Yes, I will. All right. Goodbye, Richard.' She heaved a sigh of relief as he got into his car and drove off, only seconds before Sylvia and Penny turned into the street.

Chapter 34

Hetty slept little that night. She rose in the morning, unrefreshed and with a nagging headache, and still had not made up her mind what she was going to do. She sat with Penny and Sylvia, drinking cup after cup of tea and playing with her scrambled eggs, moving them around the plate with her fork.

'Eat your eggs, Mammy,' Penny said in the exact tone Hetty used on her on many a morning. 'Remember the starving children in China.'

In spite of herself, Hetty had trouble holding back a grin.

'Eat your own breakfast, Penny, or you'll be late for school,' said Sylvia, but she cast a concerned glance at Hetty. 'Are you all right, Hetty?' she asked quietly.

She nodded. 'Just a bad night,' she replied.

'I'm finished, Nanny,' Penny interjected. 'May I get down now? I don't like being late for school. We have to stand in the hall for fifteen minutes if we're late.'

'But you haven't had to, you're never late,' said Sylvia.

'No, but that's why,' Penny replied, proving something about the school's disciplinary methods, thought Hetty, she wasn't sure what.

After they had gone, Hetty sat on, pouring yet another cup of tea. She remembered her own mother's comments when she felt her only grandchild had been kept from her. No doubt Elizabeth felt the same. But still, Penny was almost six years old now. If Hetty took her to see Elizabeth she would have to explain, tell her something about her origins at least. And it would have to be the truth as far as the child could understand it.

On the other hand, Hetty's first instinct was to keep away from Richard and his mother; she had had enough unhappiness to last her a lifetime in that quarter. There was Richard too. For a short time Hetty had thought he had sought her out because he wanted to see *her*; for a wild moment she had thought he had realised he loved her. Wishful thinking, that had been! Hetty smiled wryly. She had acted like a silly schoolgirl, blushing, showing her confusion. Oh, but she was confused all right.

There was work to do, she reminded herself. Today she was going to Whitby to inspect the new decorations of the extension she had had built on to the hotel there. It was a sun lounge, light and airy, with huge windows looking over the harbour and the wide sea beyond. A place for visitors to sit on the days when the sea fret swept in from the North Sea, and also a place which caught the sunshine and kept out the north wind in the spring. A place she hoped would extend the season for her. Behind the sun lounge, which opened directly into the reception hall, there was another door leading to new kitchens at the back of the hotel. She had to take Mr Jordan to see them for he had advised the architect on what he considered to be the ideal hotel kitchen.

Mr Jordan was waiting for her as she drew up before Pearson's Marine. Dressed in a smart pin-stripe suit, with his thinning grey hair brushed back from his face, he looked every inch the businessman, though a rather elderly businessman. But he was quite sprightly as he came down the steps and put his briefcase in the back seat before getting into the front beside Hetty.

'Sorry if I'm a bit late,' she said.

'That's all right.' He watched her as she put the car in gear and set off down the steep winding road to the shore and up the other side by Cat Nab, the Iron Age burial ground at the entrance to the ravine where Skelton beck ran down to the beach and spread over the sands in its journey to the sea. Hetty frowned. As always she was reminded of that terrible day when Matthew had the fight

306

with the van driver and she had scrambled up the cliff path to get away from him.

'What's the matter, Hetty?'

She jumped. It was almost as though he had read her thoughts. 'Nothing, I was just thinking of something that happened years and years ago.'

'There's something else. Come on, you can tell me. You've not got in over your head with the deal for the new place? I do have some savings put by, you know, if you need more capital?'

'No, no, nothing to do with the business,' she assured him. 'I didn't get much sleep, that's all.'

'Then you must have had something on your mind. Come on, you can tell me, I might be able to help.'

Hetty glanced at him, his kindly face bent towards her, his shrewd eyes reminding her that she couldn't fool him that there was nothing wrong. Why not put the problem to him? He had some experience of life, and goodness knows she needed a friend to talk to. She was fond of him and there was no doubt that he had grown very fond of her and Penny, they were his family.

They were out on the main road to Whitby now, past the turn off to Staithes and heading towards Lythe. Hetty pulled the car on to the verge, bent her head over the wheel and poured out her troubles. Mr Jordan already knew some of her story. Now he listened quietly as she told him of Elizabeth Hope and how she wanted to get to know Penny. She didn't say too much about Richard, she didn't have to, Mr Jordan could tell what he meant to her when she mentioned his name. Tears were threatening and he handed her the large white handkerchief which he had folded so carefully into the breast pocket of his suit that morning.

So that was why she showed no interest in any of the young men who would have liked to get to know her better. In a way it was a relief to him. For a long time Mr Jordan had thought she was so scarred by her experience with Penny's father that she could never love a man again. He thought of his own dead wife. They had not had a lot of time together and they had not been blessed with children, but they had been supremely happy for a short time and he

307

wouldn't want Hetty to go through life without having known such happiness.

But this Richard Hope, what was he really like? In truth, Hetty had not shown very good judgement in the past, not from what he understood about her at any rate. He looked out of the window at a field of standing corn, only just beginning to show signs of yellow amongst the green. Hetty dried her eyes, feeling silly. She should not have bothered him with her troubles, she reproached herself. It was evident he didn't know what to say.

'I'm sorry I've burdened you with all this,' she said, but Mr Jordan didn't appear to hear; he was too intent on what he himself was going to say.

'This Richard Hope, I'm not sure if I know him. I seem to remember Havelock Hope. Years ago he sometimes came into the restaurant when it was still the George.'

'Oh, Richard's completely different from his father,' Hetty assured him. In spite of herself she couldn't help a warmer tone creeping into her voice. 'He was the only one who was nice to me when I first went to Hope Hall. Of course, he was only a boy himself then and I was just fourteen.'

'Still, he can't have had much about him if he let you go off and have the baby on your own. And where has he been all these years?'

'Oh no, he did come to see me, but it was difficult . . . the circumstances, I was in someone else's house . . .' Her voice trailed off as she thought of Cliff House and its owner. Richard had thought she was taking up with Jeremy Painter. That had hurt.

'You seem to be making excuses for him,' said Mr Jordan.

Hetty forgot about Jeremy as she tried to convince Mr Jordan as well as herself that Richard had done all he could. (Though why did he always think the worst of her?)

'He has been in Africa since Penny was born,' she said.

'Africa? Whereabouts in Africa? Doing what? Surely he got home sometimes?'

Hetty just looked at him, her dark eyes wide in her unhappy face, and he relented. She had said enough to convince him that she was in love with this Richard and he fervently hoped the man was worthy of her.

'Never mind, love,' he said. 'But I don't think it's any good me advising you what to do. You'll have to make up your own mind. I'm behind you whatever you decide, you know that, don't you?'

Hetty nodded and he put his arm around her and gave her a hug.

'Come on, now,' he said. 'Let's get to Whitby and see what's been done to the hotel. I want to be back at the restaurant in good time this evening, I have a party of bigwigs coming out from Middlesbrough and they'll want everything to be of the best. All on company expenses, of course.'

Hetty started the car and pulled out on to the road. For all Mr Jordan had not offered any concrete advice, talking it over with him had helped her make up her mind. She would go to Hope Hall, taking Penny. Saturday would be a good day, for Mr Hutchins had sent word that Charlie was not coming to Saltburn that day. Which was another little worry nagging at the back of her mind. The main one was how she was going to explain to a six year old why she was only just being introduced to yet another grandmother and uncle.

Penny had only once asked why she didn't have a father and that had been when she'd first started Sunday School.

'You did have a daddy,' Hetty had said. 'But he died.'

Penny's face had cleared. 'You mean he's in heaven, Mam?'

'Yes,' Hetty had said, though an image of Matthew consorting with the angels was not one she could readily bring to mind.

'He's my Father in Heaven then, isn't he, Mam?'

The pit Hetty had dug for herself took some getting out of but in the end she succeeded in satisfying Penny.

The news of her once more extended family was easier to give to her daughter than Hetty had anticipated. Penny listened gravely to what her mother had to say and nodded her head, though she had to be assured that it did not mean she would have to give up the relations at Morton Main. And, Hetty thanked her stars, she did not question why she was just being told; she was perhaps too young for that.

* * *

It was with mixed feelings that Hetty drove over the top of the moor to Hope Hall. They were invited for tea. Hetty had telephoned Elizabeth and been surprised at how firm and strong her voice had sounded; she remembered how tremulous it once had been.

'Come about three o'clock,' Elizabeth had said. 'We will have a nice long talk.'

What about? Hetty thought now as she halted and looked both ways at the crossroads with the main road to Whitby. She turned left and drove the few miles to where a small signpost indicated the road to Hope Hall. Before long, the walls of the estate came into view and she followed them round to the main gates. Mr Oliver came out to open them for her, an older Mr Oliver but otherwise unchanged.

'Now then, Hetty,' he said, as though she had been gone days rather than years. But Joan Oliver came out of the cottage and hurried over to greet her with a big smile of welcome.

'Hetty!' she cried. 'I'm so pleased to see you. You look so well, too.'

'You look well yourself, Mrs Oliver,' Hetty replied as she got out of the car and hugged the old woman.

'Aye, we're both tolerable. Now, who's this you have with you?' she asked, smiling at a grave-faced Penny.

'I'm Penny Pearson,' the girl replied for herself. She too had got out of the car and was standing close beside her mother. 'Are you my grandmother?'

'Bless you, love, no. I'm nobody's grandmother, I'm sorry to say,' replied the old woman.

'Come on, Joan, let them get on. I said I'd send them straight up,' urged Bill Oliver impatiently.

'Maybe we'll have time to talk later,' his wife said to Hetty. 'You know, I often wondered how you were doing. I missed you, Hetty.'

She promised to call in if she had time and got back in the car. All she wanted was to get the coming interview over with and be away from this place, the scene of so much unhappiness for her. She had hardly slept the night before for thinking about it. They got back into the car and waved to the Olivers and Hetty went on up the drive to the wide gravelled circle before the main house.

Penny's eyes were wide as she stared at the great house. 'Is this it, Mam?' she whispered. 'Is it an hotel? I didn't know they lived in an hotel.'

'It's not an hotel, Penny. It's just a house, there's nothing to be frightened of. Come on, out you get.'

'It's not like Grandda's house, is it, Mam?'

Hetty thought about the tiny miner's cottage in Morton Main then looked at the imposing frontage of Hope Hall and laughed. Somehow Penny's remark made her feel better though she didn't know why. She felt like going round to the back door, the one which opened directly into the farm yard of the home farm, the way she always used to do when she was in service here. But the imposing front door was opening and it was not a servant but Richard who stood there. As she stared up at him he smiled and ran down the steps to greet them.

'Hello, Hetty, I'm so glad you came,' he said, taking her hand. His grip was firm and cool and she could still feel it when he turned to Penny. The child stood huddled into her mother's skirt but when he bent to her and offered her his hand, she came out and put her tiny one in his.

'This is Penny,' said Hetty, and as if to emphasise that the child was hers alone, 'Penny *Pearson*. Penny, this is Richard Hope.'

'Hello, Penny,' he said. 'I'm your Uncle Richard.'

'Does this house belong to you?' she asked. 'It's a lot bigger than our house and our house is an hotel.'

'Yes, it is,' Richard agreed. 'I'll show you round it later on, if you like. But now we have to go in and meet your grandmother.'

The house was just the same, thought Hetty as she entered the hall. There was the same highly polished wooden floor which she had worked on so often in the early mornings before the family were up. At the rear there was the same narrow passage to one side leading to the green baize-covered door which led to the kitchen. Of course it's the same, she told herself, how could it be different?

Penny hung on to her hand as Richard led them into the

311

drawing room and Hetty squeezed it gently for reassurance. Elizabeth Hope had risen to her feet to welcome them. For all Hetty had been told she was so much improved, it was a shock to see her there, so changed, so *normal*. Her silver hair was dressed in becoming waves from a centre parting, much as the Duchess of Windsor wore hers. There were faint lines on her face but otherwise, Mrs Hope was a beautiful woman, her eyes the same colour as Penny's, the same colour as Richard's. All this Hetty saw in the few seconds it took her to cross the room from the door and hold out her hand to Elizabeth.

'I'm so glad to see you, Hetty,' said her old mistress. 'Thank you so much for coming.' But her eyes were on Penny; she could hardly spare Hetty a glance at first. 'And for bringing my granddaughter to see me,' she added almost in a whisper, and for a moment her voice weakened with emotion and Hetty was reminded of the days Elizabeth was so ill with her 'nerves'.

Penny was quiet. When they sat down on the elegant satin-covered sofas which stood facing each other before the fireplace, sofas which were new since Hetty's day, Penny stood close by her and stared at her grandmother.

'Don't stare so,' Hetty whispered, and Penny blushed and looked away for a moment but her gaze soon returned to Elizabeth. There was an awkwardness about the two women now they were together; neither seemed to know what to say to each other at first and Richard jumped in to try to bridge it.

'Would you like to come with me to see the farm, Penny?' he asked. 'There are horses and pigs and hens. Do you like horses?'

'I don't know,' she answered. 'There are donkeys on the beach at home and sometimes they bring horses there and paddle them through the water. Mr Jordan says the water is good for their feet.'

'The horses are from the riding stable. There's a stable nearby,' Hetty put in.

'Well, there are the cows too, we could go to see them,' said Richard.

'Uncle Frank has whippets,' said Penny. 'He races them

312

and wins a lot of money. And Grandda has pigeons, he's got baby ones too. They have learned to fly now, though.'

'Well, Frank doesn't win a lot of money, Penny,' said Hetty, going red with embarrassment. But Richard and his mother were smiling at the little girl.

'Really?' said Elizabeth. 'How interesting.'

'Have you any dogs?' Penny asked her politely. She seemed to have found her tongue, thought Hetty, rather dreading what she might say next.

'There are sheep dogs in the farm yard,' Richard said. 'And there's a terrier too. Well, are you coming? Or are farm dogs not as good as racing whippets?'

'I don't know. I'll come to see.' Penny released Hetty's hand for the first time and went with Richard to the door where she stopped and looked back at her mother. 'You won't go home without me, will you, Mam?'

'No, of course not,' said Hetty. 'I'll be here when you come back, of course I will.'

'Righto.'

When the door closed behind Richard and Penny there was a small silence. Penny looked across at Elizabeth. She was pleating her skirt with nervous fingers, making tiny folds and letting them go. Doing it again and again.

'I'm pleased to see you so much better, Mrs Hope,' said Hetty.

'Thank you.'

Elizabeth stopped fiddling with her skirt and looked directly at her. 'You know, if it had been up to me I would never have let you go off on your own. I was fond of you, Hetty.'

'I know, Mrs Hope.'

'And when Matthew was killed . . .' She stopped and took a tiny lace handkerchief from her sleeve and dabbed at her eyes. 'I'm sorry, Hetty, I didn't mean to get emotional. I know it must have been a terrible time for you, too.'

'That's all right, Mrs Hope. It's a long time ago.'

'I wanted to bring you back here but Havelock . . . Mr Hope wouldn't hear of it.'

Hetty thought of that time, how Havelock had been – so vindictive, so determined to get rid of her and the baby she

313

was expecting. But she had survived. She had done more than that: she had become a prosperous businesswoman and there was some satisfaction in thinking it was in spite of Havelock Hope. She almost laughed aloud when Elizabeth went on.

'You mustn't think too badly of him, you know. He loved Matthew and only wanted the best for him.' Elizabeth caught the bitter amusement in Hetty's expression and looked away quickly. 'Well . . . as you say, it was a long time ago.'

'Yes.'

'You realise that Penny is my only grandchild. It's unlikely that Richard will marry now.'

'For goodness' sake, he's still a young man. How can you say that?'

'No, I think Richard is not the type to marry.'

Hetty said no more. To her mind, Elizabeth was jumping to conclusions. Or was she warning Hetty off? Did the older woman think she had designs on her son? No, that was ridiculous. Wasn't it?

'I didn't mean to bring this up just yet, not until we had got used to each other again, but now that I've seen my granddaughter . . . she's so pretty, isn't she? And do you know, she looks so much like Matthew and Richard did when they were young.'

'She looks like my side of the family too,' Hetty put in, and she could hear the defensiveness in her own voice. 'She has grey eyes like yours, but she's like me in so many ways.'

'Well, of course.' Elizabeth was silent for a few minutes again and Hetty wondered what it was she was finding so hard to say. She had not long to wait for when the question came it was in a rush and the shock of it was even more sudden.

'Would you consider coming to live here at Hope Hall? After all, Penny ought to be here. She will have a much better chance in life. She will meet all the County people, it's her birthright. She—'

'No! Don't say anymore, it would be a waste of time. I will not consider coming here to live. Never.' Hetty rose to her feet and went over to the window. The blood pumped

314

painfully through her veins, her stomach felt as though she had swallowed a lead weight. She stared out of the window but of course, on this side of the house, she couldn't see Penny or Richard. She wanted to run out of the house and find her daughter, gather her up in her arms and get away from here.

'Well, I know you run a business, Hetty, you have your living to think of. But you wouldn't need to work. You could stay here – I need a companion.'

Hetty couldn't believe she had said that. Did Elizabeth still think of her as a servant?

'No!'

'Well,' Elizabeth persevered, 'if you don't want to give up your business, you might consider letting Penny come to live with me? You know she will have a better life.'

That was enough. Hetty couldn't trust herself to stay in the same room as Elizabeth, she felt like clawing her eyes out. She ran out of the room without another word, straight through the hall and the baize door to the kitchen. Out of the back door and she was in the yard, and there, just by the stables, was Penny, kneeling down and stroking a sheepdog. Richard was leaning against the stable wall but Hetty didn't even look at him.

'Come on, Penny,' she cried, and ran across to her daughter. She picked her up in her arms and ran round the side of the house towards the car for she would not go back through that house, never would she go back inside.

'Hetty! What's the matter?' Richard shouted, and came after her, easily catching up with her as she stumbled along with the child. 'Did Mother say something? She wouldn't mean to offend you, Hetty, really she wouldn't.' He tried to take Penny from her. 'At least let me carry her for you,' he said. 'Or let her walk, she's not a baby anymore. Leave go of her, Hetty. Can't you see you're upsetting her?'

Penny was sobbing now, not knowing what was the matter with her mother. 'Let me down, Mam. Please, Mam,' she cried.

But Hetty shook her head. She didn't stop until she got to the car when she stood Penny down and opened the car door. 'Get in, pet,' she said. 'It's all right, don't cry.'

She ran round to her own side, shrugging off Richard's hand when he tried to hold her. 'Don't touch me!' she shouted and got in the car. The engine failed the first time but then it caught and she was away in a spurt of gravel.

'But why?' she heard Richard shout as she sped away from Hope Hall. The gates were open. Mr Oliver was sitting in a chair outside his front door and began to rise to his feet as she went past, but she was too upset to do more than wave to him. Then she was racing over the moor towards the coast and home.

Chapter 35

Hetty went back to Morton Main the next day, a Sunday, though it was a strain keeping a cheerful face before the family. Fortunately Gran was there for Sunday dinner; the old lady was frail now and, though she wouldn't admit it, needed help with practically everything. 'Blooming arthritis, Hetty,' she grumbled as Frank helped her up from her chair. 'I only used to be bothered with it in the winter time but now it's all the flaming time.'

'Watch your language in front of the bairn,' Maggie whispered fiercely.

'What language? If I wanted to use language, you would know about it,' snapped Gran. There was nothing wrong with her voice or her brain, Hetty thought to herself. But she had heard Gran swear when she got really annoyed and was glad she was restraining herself before Penny.

The little girl was quiet at first. She sat on the sofa in the corner and watched the rest of the family with shadowed eyes. She had slept badly, with frightening dreams, and consequently Hetty had had a bad night too, having to get up often to comfort her daughter.

'What did I do?' Penny had demanded when they got a distance from Hope Hall. 'I was a good girl, wasn't I? Did Grandmother not like me?'

'No, it wasn't your fault, it was mine,' Hetty assured her. 'I had to come away in a hurry. I . . . I forgot I had an appointment.' But Penny was not comforted.

'I hope she's not sickening for something,' said Gran. 'You know, there's diphtheria about.'

'Not here though, surely?' Hetty turned to her mother, a surge of fear rising in her.

'No, not in the rows, nor the village either. But I did hear there was some over West Auckland way.'

Hetty was relieved, that was some distance away. 'Penny didn't sleep much, that's all,' she said. 'I think we'll go home early, I want her to have an early night.'

They set off soon after dinner and well before tea, though Penny grumbled because she hadn't had time to go with Frank when he walked the whippets. But Hetty was keen to be gone. It took all her will-power to keep cheerful as long as she did and she walked on egg shells in case she or Penny let slip anything about their visit to Hope Hall. She wasn't ready to discuss it with her family. In fact she didn't think she would be able to discuss it at all.

The day was overcast and it began to rain during the meal so the weather provided another excuse for her to go early. She was thankful to wave goodbye to them from the car, as Maggie and Thomas stood framed in the doorway.

'There's something bothering the lass, Maggie,' Gran said when she had gone. 'But then, she's always been one for keeping her troubles to herself. I only hope she's not getting mixed up with another man. By, our Hetty has no luck with men.'

'Oh, Mother,' Maggie exclaimed. 'It's probably just business worries, you know what she's like. She's more interested in the business than in men.' She glanced over at Thomas who was standing before the fire in his shirtsleeves and braces, filling his pipe. 'Whoever would have thought of our Hetty in business, eh, Thomas?'

'Aye, she's a clever lass,' he took the pipe out of his mouth to say. 'A lass to be proud of, eh, Maggie?'

In the car, Penny soon fell asleep, slumped in the seat beside Hetty. She looked comfortable enough so Hetty didn't disturb her. But when she arrived back in Saltburn, Penny was still asleep and Hetty had to carry her up the stairs to the flat. Sylvia was back from her visit to her parents and met her at the head of the stairs.

'I'll take her,' she whispered, and Hetty was pleased to hand over her burden. As she took off her hat, Sylvia paused

318

on her way to take Penny to bed. 'You have a visitor,' she said. 'I told him you would not be back until much later but he wanted to wait.'

Hetty immediately thought it must be Richard and braced herself mentally. When she opened the sitting-room door she found she was right.

'You've wasted your time coming here, Richard,' she said without preamble. 'I have no intention of bringing Penny to live with your mother.'

'No, of course not,' he replied, 'I never dreamed you would and Mother was wrong to suggest it. How are you, Hetty? You look tired.'

'So now you're going to tell me that looking after the business *and* looking after my daughter is too much for me, are you?' Hetty's temper was rising though she wasn't sure why.

'Please, I'm not implying anything, I was just stating a fact. You look tired, it's the truth.'

'Well, I'm not surprised. Penny had a bad night and consequently so did I. Now I've just driven forty miles to Morton and back. I have a right to be tired.' She stood before him, confronting him, he thought, and he tried to bring the conversation back to normal.

'Will you sit down? I'm rather tired myself and can't sit until you do, I'm afraid my upbringing won't let me.'

'I suppose you think I wasn't taught any manners, not in a pit village?' Hetty snapped, but she sat nevertheless and he took the seat opposite hers.

'I never thought anything of the sort. You're not being fair in saying that, Hetty.'

'Perhaps I'm confusing you with your brother. I think you're more like he was than I believed.'

Richard sighed. 'I didn't come here for an argument, Hetty.'

'No. Then why did you come?'

'I wanted to explain.'

'There's nothing to explain, it's all perfectly plain. Your mother thinks she's a better person to bring up Penny than I am. And you knew what she wanted when you came here in the first place.'

319

Hetty knew she was probably exaggerating but she couldn't help herself. She sat back in her chair, her hands folded in her lap, her face set and white. She looked very alone, very determined, intent on defending her child, thought Richard. And very beautiful, too. If anything, the years had improved her beauty.

He had been very angry with his mother when he went back into the house after Hetty drove away.

'What did you say to her?' he had demanded.

'I only said it would be better if she came back to live here with Penny, but Hetty refused,' his mother replied. She too looked upset, her bottom lip trembled, but Richard was too angry to feel sorry for her.

'But, Mother, I told you, they live very comfortably in Saltburn, Hetty has a thriving business, why should she want to live here?'

'This is Penny's home, or it should be,' Elizabeth had answered.

'No, it isn't, Mother. Father made sure of that. The child's home is with her mother, wherever she wants to live.'

'I'm an old woman.' Elizabeth's voice shook. 'I want to have my granddaughter near me. You live in Africa, Penny is all I've got—'

'No, Mother, Penny is Hetty's child. I told you, you have no rights over her.' He stopped for a second as a thought struck him.

'You didn't say Penny could come to live here without Hetty, did you?'

Elizabeth didn't have to answer, he could see he had hit the mark by her expression. So now he was with Hetty to try and repair the damage done by his mother.

'Hetty, I'm sorry my mother upset you. You know she would never try to take Penny from you, she likes you.'

Hetty gazed at him. 'It didn't seem like that to me, and what's more I think you only came here to try to get me to give up Penny. You weren't interested in how I was doing, how I had managed since she was born. I always thought you were the only one of the Hopes who had any feeling for people, but I was wrong.' She stopped talking, suddenly realising she had probably revealed some of her own feelings for him, her hurt at his betrayal as she saw it. She stared down at her hands, clenching them until the knuckles gleamed white.

'No, Hetty, that's not how it was at all,' he said softly. 'I came here because I wanted to see you. I wanted to be sure you were all right.' He glanced around the well-furnished room, the deep-pile carpet, the furniture, everything of good quality. 'I needn't have worried, though, need I? You proved yourself well able to take care of yourself and my niece.'

'I did it all on my own!' she flared, choosing to take his words the wrong way. 'It helped that I had a partner, of course—'

'A partner?' Richard was frowning and she could almost read his thoughts.

'Not Jeremy Painter nor any other man! Well, of course, Mr Jordan is a man, but it wasn't like that. He's a family friend, an old man, old enough to be my grandfather. Jeremy Painter was simply my employer for a while, when Matthew was alive. I was never involved with him, I took not a penny from him except my due wages.'

'Please, Hetty, I didn't mean anything. In any case, it's none of my business, is it? How you got started, I mean. The fact is you have done so well—'

A discreet knock interrupted him and Sylvia put her head round the door. 'Sorry to butt in but would you like tea served now, Hetty?'

'Would you care for some tea?' she asked Richard, her voice stiff.

'No, I think I'd better be going,' he replied. 'Thanks all the same.' He got to his feet and Hetty followed suit with relief. Her head was throbbing, no doubt because of the stress of the last couple of days. Sylvia had gone back out, closing the door quietly behind her.

'I will come back,' said Richard. 'Perhaps when you have had time to think over what I've said, you'll realise I'm not so bad as you think.' Hetty watched as he walked to the door where he turned back. 'I have plenty of time,' he went on. 'I have three months' leave and may have more. I could be leaving the service. I will come back. I want us to get to know each other as we haven't had the chance to before.

And I want to get to know Penny.' He hesitated before going back to her. 'Hetty,' he said softly, 'please don't think I'm your enemy. I'm not.' He took her hand and carried it to his lips in a gesture she had only ever seen in films, yet in Richard it seemed anything but theatrical.

'I don't know what to think,' she said.

'Well, I'll go now. I'll telephone one day next week, if I may?' He was no longer stating his intentions but asking her, Hetty realised.

'I'll be busy at the beginning of the week.'

'Saturday then, or perhaps Friday? Thursday?' He smiled at her, his face suddenly boyish, and Hetty could feel herself melting. Hurriedly she snatched back her hand.

'If you like,' she said, and in an attempt to appear indifferent whether he did or not, 'I may not be here, I may have to go to Whitby. No, I mean Guisborough. I have business with Mark Sefton.'

'Mark Sefton?' Richard knew Mark, and frowned. Why was she throwing in the name of a good-looking chap like Mark?

'My solicitor.'

'Oh.'

When Richard had gone, she flopped down in her chair and closed her eyes. She could still feel the touch of his lips on her hand. She rubbed her thumb over the place. She felt her guard slipping. She knew it and a part of her mind told her to be sensible, not to get involved, she wanted no more heartache. Jumping to her feet, she went to the door and called for Sylvia.

'We'll have tea now, if you like,' she told her. 'How do you fancy toasted teacakes? I'm feeling quite hungry.'

'I'll order some from downstairs,' Sylvia replied. She glanced curiously at Hetty, obviously longing to ask about her visitor. Hetty had a look about her, a look Sylvia had never seen before. But instead she said, 'Shall I waken Penny? She's slept a long time, hasn't she?'

'No, leave her, she slept badly last night,' decided Hetty.

It was about six o'clock when the telephone in the entrance hall of the flat rang. Hetty, who had been sitting idly leafing through a magazine and dreaming vague dreams of Richard, jumped to her feet. Because she had been thinking of him she somehow expected it to be Richard.

She picked up the telephone, smiling softly. 'Hello,' she said, 'Hetty Pearson here.'

'Hold the line, please, I have a call for you,' said the operator. Then: 'Please insert your money now, caller.' It must be a kiosk, she thought. Where on earth is Richard? Probably in a pub.

'Hello? Is that Mrs Pearson?' It was Mr Hutchins's voice. Something must be the matter with Charlie was the thought that jumped into her mind.

'Mr Hutchins?'

'Oh, Hetty, I'm ringing to say that Audrey can't come back to work tonight, she's poorly.'

'Poorly?' Hettty was suddenly alert. Audrey had had the day off, she remembered, had gone back to Smuggler's Cove to see her family last night. 'What's the matter with her?'

There was a short silence at the other end then Mr Hutchins spoke again and Hetty could hear the strain in his voice. 'The doctor says it's diphtheria.'

'Diphtheria?' The hall was suddenly dark to Hetty. She swayed and had to clutch the hall table to remain upright.

'Hello? Are you there, Hetty?'

'Yes. Yes, I'm here. Is it bad? I mean—'

'Aye, it's bad, Hetty. Charlie's bad too.'

'Charlie? You mean he has diphtheria as well as Audrey?'

'Audrey's worse than Charlie.'

'Please insert another tuppence if you wish to talk longer,' the operator butted in.

'Just a minute, Hetty.' She heard the sound of the pennies dropping into the box and waited impatiently.

'Are you still there?' she asked.

'I'll have to go now, I can hear the ambulance coming down the road,' he replied, and the line went dead.

Hetty replaced the receiver in the cradle and stood absolutely still, staring at it. Diphtheria. It was here in Cleveland as well as Auckland.

'Is something the matter?'

Hetty looked round. Sylvia was standing in Penny's bedroom doorway. Penny! Hetty rushed across the hall, almost knocking Sylvia over in her haste to get to her daughter. Penny was lying on her back, her mouth open. She was breathing heavily, was she flushed?

'What's wrong?' asked Sylvia from behind her but Hetty hardly heard her. She put her hand on Penny's brow. It was hot, the skin very dry.

'She doesn't look too well, does she?' asked Sylvia. 'I was just coming to tell you. I think she might have a summer cold coming on. I was about to suggest we kept her home from school tomorrow and had the doctor look at her.'

'Mammy?'

Penny opened her eyes and looked up at Hetty. Her eyes were bright and feverish, her cheeks flushed and her voice was hoarse. 'Can I have a drink, Mammy?' she asked. 'My throat's sore.'

'I'll get you one, pet,' said Hetty, and turned to Sylvia as though she had just realised she was there. 'Why didn't you tell me she was so bad?' she cried, and Sylvia looked as though she were about to cry. 'Oh, for goodness' sake, bring her a glass of orange juice, Sylvia.'

'I'm not sure we have any . . .'

'Well, bring some up from the restaurant! Or do you want me to go myself?'

Sylvia rushed off, her air of quiet efficiency deserting her in the face of Hetty's anger. But when she came back, panting slightly from running up the stairs with a full jug of orange juice, Hetty had recognised her own panic and willed herself to stay calmer. Sylvia could be right. Just because Audrey and Charlie had diphtheria it didn't mean Penny had it too. No, it was just a cold, of course it was.

She took the juice from Sylvia and poured out half a glass, then helped Penny to sit up and drink it. But Penny could only take a few sips before she slid back down the bed, exhausted.

'My throat hurts, Mam,' she whispered again.

'All right, love. I tell you what, I'll call Doctor Mac-Pherson. He'll give you something to make it better.'

'Is it morning, Mam? Don't go out, Mammy, please, don't go to work today,' the child said, and Hetty's heart dropped even further. Dear God! she thought wildly. Penny was delirious!

'I'll call the doctor,' said Sylvia, her capable self again. She started for the door.

'Tell him to come at once, will you? Penny has been in contact with—' Hetty's voice dropped to a hoarse whisper ' – diphtheria and she is feverish and has a very sore throat.'

Just because there's diphtheria about doesn't mean that's what Penny is suffering from, Hetty told herself. She sat on the edge of the bed waiting for Dr MacPherson, gazing at Penny who had fallen asleep again. Was she asleep or was she unconscious? Hetty bent closer. How did you tell? She could hear Sylvia in the hall, talking to the doctor. But no, she wasn't talking to the doctor but someone else. Hetty went to the door to hear better.

'But where is he?' Sylvia was saying. 'We need him urgently, we have a child very ill—'

Hetty had snatched the telephone from her. 'This is Hetty Pearson of Pearson's Ruby in Ruby Street. Who is that?' she demanded.

'This is Dr MacPherson's housekeeper. I can take a message for him.'

'A message? We need a doctor now. Where is he?'

'Mrs Pearson, I'm sure nothing is to be gained by panicking. Now calm down—'

'Where is he?' It was practically a shriek.

'It's Sunday, Mrs Pearson. Doctors have to have time off as well as everyone else, you know. As a matter of fact, Dr MacPherson is playing golf. I expect him back any time now, so you see there is no need to panic.'

Golf? He was playing golf? When there was a diphtheria epidemic? Hetty wasted no more time. She put down the telephone and ran down the stairs then back up again to snatch up her car keys. It wouldn't take five minutes to get to the golf course.

'Hetty? Hetty, what's wrong?'

Amazingly, Richard was outside. She didn't take time to wonder what he was doing back again so soon. 'I can't stay, I have to get to the Golf Club,' she said, breathless from her run up and down the stairs. She was having trouble inserting the car key in the lock, her hand trembled so much and she couldn't see properly.

'Hetty, tell me what's wrong? Is it Penny?'

'Yes, it's Penny, I have to bring Doctor MacPherson.' She dropped the key and scrabbled in the gutter for it.

'And he's at the Golf Club?' At her nod he took the keys from her. 'I'll bring him,' he said. 'I'll take your car, mine is at the top of the street. You go back to Penny.'

Hetty looked at him. 'No, I have to go.' She felt that only she could make the doctor see how urgent it was.

'No you don't,' said Richard. He was already opening the car door and climbing into the driver's seat. He even had the seat pushed back and the engine running. 'Go on now, go back to Penny. I'll find MacPherson, you can depend on me.'

He was away before Hetty could protest further, roaring round the corner into Marine Parade.

'Mam, I thought you'd gone away, and you said you wouldn't,' Penny whispered. 'You said you wouldn't.' Her eyes were fever-bright and full of reproach.

'No, pet, I won't, I'm here.' Hetty sat on the bed and took hold of Penny's hot, dry hand. 'I won't leave you.'

Chapter 36

The isolation hospital was an old brick building with four extra wards behind, long, low annexes with tall, metal-framed windows for letting in light and air – only the windows were open just four inches at the bottom and the blinds were down halfway because the sunlight was too strong for the patients' eyes. At least that was what Nurse Rose said when Penny asked her to let the blind up, the one near her bed.

Penny lay in the bed, a black, iron bed not like her own wooden bed at home. She put her hand under her head for she'd no pillow. That was something else Nurse Rose said she couldn't have.

'Lie quietly now, like a good girl,' the nurse had said after she had pushed a stick with cotton wool on it down her throat and almost choked Penny altogether. Taking a swab, Nurse Rose had called it. 'If you're good Matron will let your mother come and see you this afternoon.'

'Two negative swabs and you can go home,' said the boy in the next bed, knowledgeably. He was lying on his side, propped up on one elbow, watching Penny with interest.

'Eric, lie down properly,' Nurse Rose said sharply.

He lay down but when the nurse had gone he resumed his position balancing his head on his hand. 'Your mam will have to look through the window. That's why they've opened it like that, so no germs get out.'

Penny closed her eyes and two fat tears rolled down her cheeks. Mam had promised she wouldn't leave her so why had she let the ambulance bring her to this horrible place?

That horrible ambulance. Even though Mam had said it was coming for her she hadn't believed it for hadn't she always crossed her fingers and touched her collar every time she saw one, and chanted, 'Touch collar, never follow, don't come to my door'? But now it had come for her. Penny was swamped in misery and her throat hurt and her leg was sore where the nurse had stuck a needle in it. She rubbed at the place but the action made her arm ache and she stopped. After a moment she fell asleep.

There was a sudden clatter at the end of the ward and she woke with a start. The smell of food was in the air, it must be dinnertime. She wanted to go to the lavatory, but where was it? She looked desperately around and decided the door at the opposite end to where the nurses were filling plates with mince and carrots and taties must be it. Cautiously she pushed the bedclothes back and slipped her feet out of bed. It was a high bed. She had to jump to reach the floor and thought she was going to fall but she didn't. She couldn't see any slippers so she began to walk in the direction of what she thought must be the lavatory and promptly fell against the foot of the next bed.

'Mind, you'll cop it!' breathed Eric, and he was right, Nurse Rose was running down the ward. She picked Penny up and was cross. Very cross indeed. Penny knew she was going to 'play war' with her as Mam said whenever she'd done something wrong.

'I told you: never get out of bed, Penny Pearson. Never, never never!'

In her shock, Penny wet herself, soaking her nightie first. She tried desperately to stop but somehow she couldn't and water dripped on to the polished floor.

'I just wanted a wee – I wanted a wee! I was looking for the lavvy and now look what you've made me do!' she screamed at the nurse, and began to sob helplessly.

'Dear me, water at both ends,' said a soft voice and there was the one in the dark blue dress. 'Come along, Penny, I'll put you back to bed and Nurse will go and get you a clean nightdress.' Sister it was. Penny thought she was lovely, her voice was so kind and she smiled a lot and didn't look angry at all. She took Penny and laid her in bed and covered her up. 'Lie still now, we'll soon have you clean and dry.'

'I'm sorry, Sister,' said Nurse Rose, sounding scared. When Sister turned to answer her voice had changed altogether, surprising Penny because she seemed like a different lady.

'Nurse Rose, how did it happen that this little girl was allowed out of bed?'

Nurse Rose was stuttering something and Eric had stopped eating his mince and taties and was staring at Sister and all at once Penny missed her mother with such intensity that she thought she would die. She lay in a tight little ball with her eyes shut, not even opening them when Nurse Rose came with Nurse Snowdon and clean sheets and a nightgown. A horrible hospital nightgown. She wasn't even allowed to wear her own nighties any more.

At two o'clock, her bed was turned to face the window along with all the other children's and the window was opened four inches at the bottom and then at last Mam was there, outside the window, and with her was Uncle Richard. Penny was mortified that he should see her with her eyes all red, he would think she was a baby, that she had been crying for her mother. What was he doing there anyway?

'Are you all right, pet?' Mam asked. 'Have you been crying?' Her voice sounded funny but then she had to shout a bit, talking through the window with just that opening at the bottom. Penny had been waiting to tell Mam all about what had happened but she couldn't now, not when *he* was there, how could she? He might be her uncle but she didn't know him really, and every time she thought of the way she had wet herself shame engulfed her. She contented herself with a nod.

'I've brought you a colouring book and some pencils,' said Hetty, holding them up to the window.

'I'm not 'llowed books,' said Penny. 'Sister says I'm not.' Perversely she was pleased to see her mother show her disappointment.

'Sister will keep them until you're well enough to have them,' said Uncle Richard. He was standing close by Mam, too close. 'I brought you a basket of fruit,' he added, holding up a round basket of oranges and bananas and grapes. 'You like fruit, don't you?'

'Yes, thank you. But I don't want to talk now, my throat hurts,' she replied. It did too, it wasn't a lie. Besides, now her mother was there where she could see her, even if she couldn't touch her or give her a cuddle, Penny was tired. All she wanted to do was sleep. And that was what she did, dropping off in an instant like a newborn baby.

They handed the basket of fruit in to the ward office and Hetty and Richard walked out of the hospital to where he had parked his car on the roadside.

'As well as could be expected,' said Hetty, almost to herself. 'Now what on earth does that mean?'

'Come on now, Hetty, it means exactly what it says,' Richard answered, trying to be encouraging. She studied him, to gauge what he really thought. She was confused. She knew that when it came to anything being wrong with Penny she panicked. And she blamed herself because she hadn't realised how ill her daughter had been when they returned from Morton.

It was Richard who had taken charge on Sunday evening, she herself had been as much use as a man off, she thought. Richard had been there for her, from early morning until evening on Monday and Tuesday. He talked to the doctors; helped Mr Jordan when the Board of Health insisted that the restaurant should be fumigated along with the flat and Audrey's room in Pearson's Marine. Hetty was confused because she couldn't understand herself; she felt she couldn't trust her own judgement, not over this. Even after all the years of looking after Penny, and being in charge of the hotel business.

She couldn't eat and slept little, and when she did sleep it was to dream of Cissy, something she hadn't done for many years. She could feel the skin stretched tightly over her cheekbones, feel the ache in her eyes which she always got when she was tired, and knew the weariness must show on her face. Yet she had others to see in the ward, she remembered, Charlie was on the opposite side to Penny.

330

'I must see Charlie,' she said, and turned back to the hospital.

'Of course,' Richard answered, though he wasn't at all sure who Charlie was. He followed her round the outside of the building to another tall window. Mr Hutchins was there, on his own. He greeted Hetty, acknowledged her introduction of Richard before turning back to the window.

'Hello, Charlie,' Hetty said. The boy was lying straight and still under the bedclothes, his glasses reflecting the light from the window and making his eyes owl-like in his white face. But he smiled when he saw Hetty.

'I'm sorry I couldn't come on Saturday,' he said, and Hetty realised that he wasn't as poorly as she had expected; he even had a pillow and his voice was quite strong. In fact, when she glanced at the other small figures in the beds, as far as she could see in her restricted view through the window, he looked comparatively well.

Hetty talked to him for a while, promising to bring him in a chess set, 'If the doctor says it's all right,' and his eyes lit up. The bell for the end of visiting went and she walked down the path to the gate with Mr Hutchins, Richard behind them.

'The doctor says it's only a mild case,' Mr Hutchins volunteered. 'I thank God for it.'

'Yes. Penny too. They shouldn't be in long. But where's Audrey?'

He shook his head and hurried on, walking rapidly up the asphalt path and stopping by the gate. Hetty glanced at Richard and he came forward and took her arm.

'Mr Hutchins?'

'Audrey's not so good,' he said in a gritty sort of voice.

Hetty could think of nothing to say; she just stared mutely at him.

'I haven't told Charlie,' he said and cleared his throat. 'Well, I'll be off to catch the bus.'

'Please, let me give you a lift home,' said Richard. And Mr Hutchins nodded his acceptance.

They dropped him off at his door and Richard drove back to the main road, heading for Saltburn.

'He's a widower, I take it?' asked Richard.

'No, he remarried.' Hetty explained the situation. 'His wife didn't even go with him to the hospital,' she added.

'Some people are frightened of hospitals.'

Hetty sighed. She sat quietly beside him until he parked in front of the restaurant, all dark and deserted now. Mr Jordan planned to re-open it at the end of the week.

'Are you coming in?' She looked anxiously at him. She couldn't bear to go in on her own even though Sylvia was there.

'Of course.'

They sat in her sitting room, close together on the couch. Sylvia had prepared a tray of supper and gone off to her own room after asking after the children.

'More coffee?' Hetty asked him and when he shook his head she sat back on the couch, conscious of his shoulder touching hers, his long legs stretched out in front of him. And even though she was still worrying about Penny, still wondering how she had settled down, whether she was sleeping, was it really true that she was in no real danger, was she lonely, were the nurses comforting her, she was still glad Richard was there, finding his presence so comforting.

'Have you told your parents?' he asked.

She hadn't, not yet. She could have sent a telegram or rung the postmistress and asked her to take a message, but this was not the sort of message she could give in that way. They would immediately think the worst if a telegram came; Hetty remembered them as always bringing bad news when she was a child.

'I can go over there, if you don't want to leave here while Penny is in hospital?'

'Would you?' She made no pretence of demurral and he smiled down at her.

'I'll go now,' he said.

Driving over to Bishop Auckland, he went over the talk he had had with his mother only that morning before he returned to Saltburn and Hetty's side.

'I intend to marry Hetty Pearson if she'll have me after all this family has done to her,' he had said.

'How can you think of such things when Penny is so ill?'

cried Elizabeth. 'Oh, if only Hetty had done as I asked, Penny would not be in hospital now, fighting for her life.'

'Penny is not on the danger list, Mother! Haven't I just rung the hospital to see how she is? The doctors are very hopeful she will recover completely. And don't you ever suggest she should come here to live. Not unless Hetty comes with her.'

Elizabeth looked at him. Richard had never raised his voice to her before. Hetty must mean a lot to him. And perhaps she had been hasty in making such a suggestion. She had liked Hetty when she worked at the hall, remembered her as such a sympathetic girl. If it hadn't been for Matthew . . . and now there was Richard. What was it about the girl that both her sons fell in love with her?

She sighed and gazed out of the window at the moor, the sun lighting the heather in the distance, a curlew rising high, disturbed by a sheep. She imagined its mournful cry as it tried to protect its young. That was all mothers did, tried to protect their young, both she and Hetty.

'If you marry Hetty, she and Penny will be living here then,' she said with satisfaction.

'Don't take it for granted, Mother,' he said shortly. 'Hetty has a successful hotel chain. It may be that I will go to live in Saltburn.' Always supposing she will have me, he thought, doubt rising in him. But he hadn't time to think about it now, he had to go to Hetty.

'Think about it, Mother. Get used to the idea. I love Hetty Pearson and I intend to make her love me.'

Brave words, he thought as he pulled round the corner into Morton Main. What would he do if she wouldn't have him? He couldn't even think of it.

Chapter 37

Audrey was one of those children who did not recover from the epidemic of diphtheria that summer. Hetty and Mr Jordan and all the staff of Pearson's in Saltburn attended the funeral one bright and sunny day. It was held in the Methodist Chapel in Smuggler's Cove where Audrey had been a Sunday School scholar before she moved to Saltburn.

Looking round the chapel from the pew where she sat with Richard, Hetty saw that Mrs Timms was there and Mr and Mrs Watts from Overmans Terrace. Peter was down from Northumberland and stood with his father and step-mother. He looked pale and drawn and his shirt was badly ironed so that the collar stuck up above the back of his blue serge suit. Hetty's heart ached for him. Richard, standing beside her, took her hand and she glanced quickly up at him through tear-beaded lashes and was grateful for the compassion she saw in his face.

Hetty refused an invitation from Mr Hutchins to go back to the house for the funeral tea, though she asked Peter to call and see her before he went back to Northumberland.

'I have to go to the hospital. I'll see Charlie for you, take him something,' she said to the Hutchinses.

Mrs Hutchins sniffed. 'I'm sure he'd rather see you than me.'

I could scratch her eyes out, thought Hetty, though she was careful to keep her face expressionless. Mr Hutchins gazed at her, his eyes full of pain. Hetty wondered if he had regretted marrying again. And would her own life have been different if he had not? Would she have gone with Matthew? Well, what was done was done.

'I'm grateful to you, Hetty,' Mr Hutchins said, 'for all you've done for the children.'

She nodded. 'How are you, Peter?' she asked the boy standing silently by. 'Do you like Northumberland?'

'It's all right,' he mumbled, his eyes on the ground.

'He's got good lodgings, I made sure of that myself,' Mrs Hutchins put in. 'I knew his landlady.'

Hetty hurried away with Richard, glad to go, glad she had Richard to go with her. These last few days she had come to rely on his support. She watched him as he started the car, loving him, revelling in loving him and yet afraid to, she had been hurt so often.

'I'm taking up too much of your time,' she said, turning away from him and staring out of the window at the dusty hedgerows for she couldn't look at him and see the relief she imagined in his eyes. 'I could drive myself to the hospital, you know.'

'I want to go, Hetty.'

'But you must have enough to do with your father's business?'

'Nothing is more important than this, my love.'

I must have misheard, thought Hetty. He didn't say that. How could he say that? He thought she had ruined his brother, caused his death. He thought she had taken money from Jeremy Painter in return for favours granted. How could he call her 'my love'?

They pulled into the entrance of the hospital and all her doubts and fears about Richard were pushed to the back of her mind. Penny was the only person who mattered now. No, there was Charlie too, he needed her. She picked up the parcels she had brought for the children, a picture book for Penny and *The Water Babies* for Charlie. Both children were allowed books now.

'Hang on a minute, Hetty.' Richard laid a hand on her arm. 'I know this isn't really the time, but I must talk to you.'

There was something in his voice which made her not

exactly panic, but her pulse quickened and she didn't want to hear, not now.

'I can't keep Penny waiting,' she said, and hurried out of the car to walk swiftly up the path.

'Hetty—' he began, but she was already going along the side of the building to the window where Penny was. And there were the Pearsons, in a cluster round the window: Mam in her shabby grey coat, a black hat pulled over her hair, Da with his hands stuck in the pockets of his best suit, his grey hair cut in the old-fashioned miner's cut, bending forward as he spoke to his granddaughter. And the way he spoke to her was so reminiscent of the times he had spoken to Hetty and Cissy when they were suffering from some childish complaint that she could hardly bear it.

'You come over and stay with your grandda, pet,' he was saying. 'Just as soon as they let you out of this place. I need some help wi' me pigeons, your Uncle Frank is about as much use as a man off. All he thinks about is his whippets.'

'What's the matter wi' whippets?' Frank demanded, and winked through the window at Penny. 'Dandy's had pups,' he confided. 'You'd better come over anyroad, I'll need someone to watch over them while I'm down the pit. Make sure they don't get out of the shed and on to the road to get run over. I can trust you to do that, can't I?'

Hetty heard Penny laugh happily even before she saw her. The girl was so much more like her old self that her mother breathed a prayer of thanks to God for it.

'Mam! Mam, my swab was clear!' Penny called, and in her excitement she sat up in bed. 'Sister says that if the next one is clear too I can come home. Oh, Mam, isn't it great? Can I go to Morton and see the puppies? Can I have a puppy, Mam, can I?'

The way Hetty was feeling, if Penny had asked for the moon she would have moved heaven and earth to get it for her. 'We'll see,' she said, more out of habit more than anything else. She took out her hankie and dabbed at her eye. 'I think I must have got something in my eye,' she said for Da and Frank looked away, embarrassed at this display of emotion.

'I'll pop round and see Charlie while you're all here,' she

336

said, and walked rapidly away. Richard made to follow her but changed his mind. A last glimpse of his face showed her that he understood she needed to be on her own for a moment or two to compose herself. That was the thing about Richard, she thought, he was sensitive to her feelings.

Charlie was sitting up in bed, reading. He greeted her gravely.

'I didn't expect anyone, Dad said he wouldn't be able to come.' He didn't mention Audrey's funeral and neither did Hetty. And, she recalled, piling misery on misery, he had missed the scholarship exams. But she was going to do something about that. She was already in touch with the Friends' School at Great Ayton and had secured him a provisional place, subject to his passing the entrance exam and his father's signature being on the entrance forms – something she was determined to get. But she wouldn't tell the boy until she was sure.

'I'm allowed home tomorrow,' Charlie volunteered. 'I could have gone today but for . . .' His voice tailed off.

'Oh, Charlie, that's grand! You can come to Saltburn for a while. You and Penny can keep each other company while you get well.'

His face brightened and then he actually smiled. He was looking past her and she turned to see what it was he was looking at.

'Now then, shrimp! What are you doing lying in bed on a day like this?' It was Peter, and right behind him Mr Hutchins. Peter's mood had lightened, his sorrow at his sister's death pushed aside as he talked to his brother.

'Eeh, Peter, I didn't think you'd come,' breathed Charlie. Hetty stepped back from the window, a surge of pleasure running through her, she was so pleased to see them.

'O' course I came, you're me kid brother, aren't you?' Peter demanded. 'Now hurry up and get ready, Matron says we can take you back with us now. Look, there's the nurse come for you.' And there was Nurse Rose to take him to the bathroom where he would have a final bath to make sure he wasn't taking out any germs, and then dress in his own clothes.

'We'll be waiting, Charlie,' Peter called after him.

337

Hetty walked down the path to the end of the block with Mr Hutchins. 'What changed your mind?' she couldn't help asking.

'I thought the lad deserved to get out first chance he had,' the man replied. 'I told Anne I'd come.'

Hetty looked at him. He was not going to criticise his wife to her, of course not, but they both knew how he must have stood up to her. Perhaps now was a good time to tell him of her ideas for Charlie's education. They spent the time waiting for his official discharge discussing future plans for the boy.

Hetty travelled back to Saltburn with Mam and Da and Frank.

'I can make two journeys with the car,' Richard had offered. 'Or we can get a taxi. What do you think?'

'Nowt o' t'sort,' declared Thomas. 'A waste of money a taxi is when there's a perfectly good bus.'

'You go home now,' said Hetty to Richard. 'I'll enjoy travelling on the bus with them, really I will.' So he had gone and it was five o'clock when they all trooped through the front door of Pearson's Ruby.

'By, I'd kill for a cup of tea,' said Maggie as she sank into a comfortable armchair. 'Can I take me shoes off, Hetty, or are you too posh now?' She took them off anyway, without waiting for a reply.

'What about a meal? Did you have anything? I can easily order something from the restaurant,' said Hetty after she had brought her mother a pair of slippers.

'We had fish and chips at Alice's place before we went to the hospital. You can't come to the seaside without having cod and chips, can you, our Hetty?'

She agreed that fish and chips were what made such outings.

'Aye, Hetty, an' you should have told us,' said Frank. 'We shouldn't have had to find out from Alice. If you'd told us years ago it would have saved a heap of bad feeling.'

Thomas nodded his head in agreement.

'Told you what?' asked Hetty.

'About the smugglers and the bag of coins.' Mam gazed

338

at her remorsefully. 'I'm sorry, love. Me mam said I shouldn't be in such a hurry to believe that blooming man. She was right an' all. Condemning me own flesh and blood, I was. But a gentleman he was supposed to be, may he rot—'

'Maggie! Don't speak ill of the dead, now.'

She closed her mouth tightly but her expression spoke volumes.

'We all should have had more faith in you,' said Frank. 'I'm sorry, our Hetty.'

She smiled round at them. 'Well, never mind now,' she said. 'I can't be mad at anyone today anyroad, not when Penny's coming out tomorrow. Now, how about a nice cup of tea?' Dear old Gran, she thought as she went to the door; she had believed in Hetty all the time. On impulse, she slipped into her bedroom and took a box out of the top drawer of her dressing table. She hadn't opened it in years. It was only an old shoe box with something wrapped in tissue paper in it. She took it back into the sitting room.

'I don't know why I didn't show you this before,' she said, carefully unfolding the tissue to reveal what looked like a raggy old piece of washleather. With it was one old coin, a fourpenny piece with what she now knew to be the head of George III on it.

'Why, will you look at that!' commented Thomas. 'You were right, our Hetty, I never would have believed it.'

'Me neither,' Maggie agreed. She gazed at the coin for a minute or two and then looked up at her daughter. 'Well, the fellow that lost that purse has no use for the money now, has he? Strange things happen, eh? And that reminds me, Hetty. That fellow who was with you today . . . Richard Hope, wasn't he? I mind when he came to tell us about Penny being badly. He came before an' all. He was looking for you then, years ago it was. Well, by the looks of you two together, I'd say he'd found you.'

'Mam!'

'Aye, well, I speak only as I find. And I'm sure it's a different kettle of fish altogether from when that brother of his was after—'

'Maggie, watch your mouth,' warned Thomas.

'It's all right, Da,' said Hetty. 'I know Richard is different

339

from Matthew, he's a good man. I would marry him tomorrow if he asked me.'

'He'll ask you,' her mother asserted, nodding her head confidently. But as Hetty made the tea she wasn't so sure. Perhaps he was just being kind? Mebbe just because he was Penny's uncle . . . mebbe he hadn't called her 'my love' that morning. Mebbe she was fooling herself. Hetty rinsed the teapot out with hot water and mashed the tea and poured it out again into the sink and rinsed the teapot, all the while staring dreamily out of the window as darkness came down over the sea and only pinpoints of light could be seen from the ships lining up to go into Tees Port.

'Hetty? Where's that tea then? By, I'm fair clemming for a cup.' Maggie had come in search of her. She clicked her teeth when she saw what Hetty was doing. 'By, our Hetty, you're a proper dreamer, you are. Give that teapot here, I'll make the tea or we'll be lucky to get it before breakfast time.'

Chapter 38

It was a bright Saturday morning when Hetty and Frank went to bring Penny home from the fever hospital. Frank sat beside her as she drove, watching every movement.

'You're not a bad hand at that, our Hetty,' he commented as she pulled to a halt in the hospital grounds. 'I'm thinking of getting a car meself, you know. I'm learning how to drive.'

'Are you, Frank? That's great.' Hetty did not ask if he was sure he could afford it. The pits were working full-time again, she knew that though she refused to think about the reason: the imminence of war.

'Aye, well I've got me overman's ticket,' he said, almost as though she had asked the question. But this particular conversation came to an end in the excitement of having Penny back, being able to touch her at last, feel the child's arms round her neck. By, thought Hetty, this is what I've been missing so much.

'Where's Uncle Richard?' asked Penny as they drove out of the hospital gates and took the road to Saltburn.

Where indeed? Hetty questioned too, though silently. She caught Frank watching her face, looking for her reaction, and carefully kept her eyes on the road. She hadn't seen Richard since the day before and didn't know why. He had been there for her all the time Penny was in hospital. There could be many a reason, she told herself. His mother, his father's business affairs; now he knew she had her family with her perhaps he thought there was no need for him to be there all the time. Perhaps seeing her family had reminded him of her origins, a dark thought indeed. But no, of course not, Richard wasn't like that, he was no snob. Determinedly, Hetty put it out of her mind. Richard would come, of course he would.

The staff of Pearson's Ruby were all at the front door to welcome home Penny. Steve and Mr Jordan and Sylvia and Alice too – she must have shut up the cafe to be there. And more exuberantly, out in the street watching for the car, were Thomas and Maggie and, a surprise for Hetty, Gran too. A frail, more stooped Gran than Hetty remembered but still the same Gran, the smile on her face a ray of sunshine. Penny was carried up to the flat in triumph and laid carefully amidst the cushions on the sofa.

'Now stay there, no getting down without permission,' Hetty admonished, and though Penny protested, she did as she was told. For even though the diphtheria had left her, she was still pale and weak and her dark eyes were shadowed.

'Proper peaky,' was Gran's verdict. 'But never mind, we'll soon build the bairn up. Parrish's Food is the thing, our Hetty.'

They had a bit of a party, with Mr Jordan bringing up tempting morsels from the restaurant for Penny, and Mam muttering, 'Good wholesome food is what the lass wants.' Afterwards, when Penny was carried off to bed for the rest of the day, too tired even to protest, Hetty slipped out and walked along the front on her own. On impulse she followed the cliff path down to the lower esplanade and then on to the sands. There were families on the beach, children digging in the sand and paddling in the water. The sun was warm and for once there was no breeze from the sea. She turned towards Marske. The crowds thinned out as she went until she was on her own on the broad golden sands, with only the sound of the waves on her right and the seagulls swooping and crying in the shallows.

Coming to a cleft in the cliff, with a rock large enough to perch on, she sat down. Just for a few minutes, she told herself. She needed the time to herself to collect her thoughts. She felt restless, slightly out of sorts, and told herself she had no reason to feel like that, not now she had Penny home with her again. She tried to make plans for how she would convince Mr Hutchins that Charlie ought to go to the Friends' School, perhaps could even get a scholarship. He could maybe be a boarder there . . . It was no good, she couldn't think anything through, not today.

Hetty slipped off her shoes and dug her bare toes into the sand, so soft and warm it was, here in this sheltered place. Dreamily she slid down, folding her legs under her, leaning against the rock. She ran her fingers through the sand, back and forth, seeing the light glint on tiny particles as the sun hit them. Suddenly there was a shadow blocking out the sun and there was Richard, standing only a few feet away, saying nothing, just watching her.

'I thought you would be here somewhere,' he said finally.

'Richard!' Hetty scrambled to her feet, brushing the sand from her skirt, pushing her hair back from her face. 'What are you doing here?'

'What else but looking for you?'

He crossed the short space between them and took her in his arms and she stood stiffly for a moment, still unsure. She gazed up at him questioningly. 'Richard?'

'Hetty.' He kissed her gently, a mere brushing of his lips against hers, his arms tightening round her. 'You will marry me, won't you, Hetty?'

She didn't answer for a moment or two, searching his eyes — eyes which no longer reminded her of Matthew's. How could she have ever thought they were the same? Richard's were much warmer than his brother's had been.

'It's not just because of Penny, is it?' She had to ask.

'No. I love you, Hetty. How can I convince you? I think I've always loved you. Dear God, I've been such a fool.' Regret for what might have been washed over Richard. He thought of all the times he had been so close to telling Hetty how much he loved her, all the lost years when they might have been together. If only he had spoken out he could have protected her, looked after her. He buried his face in the nape of her neck and breathed in the essential fragrance of her. 'Oh Hetty,' he murmured. 'I'm sorry, I'm so sorry. Can you forgive me?'

She relaxed. Such a warm feeling swept over her that if it hadn't been for Richard's arms she felt she would fall

343

down. But still . . . she had to be sure. She had to be sure beyond any doubt whatsoever. Richard saw it.

'I don't blame you if you feel you can't trust any Hope ever again,' he said. 'Just say so and I'll go away, I won't bother you any more.'

'Do you mean that?'

'No.'

He didn't, he was well aware that he couldn't go away and leave her, never again. He buried his face in the nape of her neck and she held him, rather than the other way around.

'I could never live in Hope Hall again,' she said.

'That doesn't matter. We'll live where you want to live, it makes no difference to me so long as you're there.'

'And Penny?'

'Yes, and Penny. But only because she's yours and I love her for that.'

Hetty sighed. There were other difficulties to face, she knew that. But . . .

'I'll marry you, Richard,' she said.

They walked back along the sands to the cliff lift which led up to the jewel streets which had been the vision of those Victorian Quakers so long ago. A little shabby and dusty now, on this hot summer's day, but still tall and handsome in their old-fashioned way. The vision went on, thought Hetty dreamily. It had inspired her long ago when she first came here.

Richard held her hand as they walked along Milton Street, past Alice's cafe and the newsagent's. There were children skipping in the alley by the end of Ruby Street, singing:

'Whistle while you work,
Mussolini bought a shirt,
Hitler wore it, Chamberlain tore it,
Whistle while you work.

Richard and Hetty went into Pearson's Ruby Hotel, their arms around each other. Whatever was to come, they would be together.